Blue Skies, Green Hell

A true story about bush flying pioneers
in wild Venezuela—
"I was there"

Marilyn Lazzari-Wing

Copyright © 2012 by Marilyn Lazzari-Wing.

Front cover: AEROVEN's Beechcraft flies by Auyántepui, largest of all tepuis in Venezuela's Gran Sabana.
Photo by Marilyn Lazzari-Wing—1953

Back cover: The author stands in hurricane-force winds at the base of Angels Falls. Tallest waterfalls in the world, it drops 3,212 feet to the jungle floor below. Long before it reaches the talus slope the water becomes a fine mist. It reconstitutes to its liquid form and becomes the Churún River.
Photo by Robert Sonderman—2004

Library of Congress Control Number:		2011914279
ISBN:	Hardcover	978-1-4653-4930-9
	Softcover	978-1-4653-4929-3
	Ebook	978-1-4653-4931-6

All rights reserved. No part of this book may be reproduced or transmitted in any form or by any means, electronic or mechanical, including photocopying, recording, or by any information storage and retrieval system, without permission in writing from the copyright owner.

This book was printed in the United States of America.

To order additional copies of this book, contact:
Xlibris Corporation
1-888-795-4274
www.Xlibris.com
Orders@Xlibris.com
91090

Contents

Dedication		7
Author's Notes		11
Preface		15
Introduction		19
1	"I'm a Bush Pilot. This is What I do."	21
2	"Like in a Hollywood Movie"	33
3	Getting Started	43
4	"Mother, Dad, Meet My Husband, Frank"	52
5	On the Wild Side	62
6	"We're Home"	74
7	"Bear With Me"	87
8	The Art of Piloting	98
9	We Play Hard, Very Hard	109
10	"It's Around Here Someplace"	116
11	"I'm Sick. I've Got to Go Home"	124
12	"I'm Coming Home on Jack's C-46"	132
13	"Not Hardships . . . Just Inconveniences."	135
14	"Home Is Where the Heart Is"	141
15	The Gentleman Rancher	151
16	UFOs—I Believe	156
17	"He's Such a Dreamer"	163
18	Paradise in Green Hell	172
19	"He's Different"	195
20	Ride Vaquero	202
21	"Expect the Unexpected"	216
22	"Welcome—Bienvenido"	226

23	King of the Jungle	241
24	"ASA. It's a Rough Place"	247
25	"I Call Her Eve"	261
26	Search and Rescue Operation	276
27	The Phenomenon of The Catatumbos	299
28	The Meeting	304
29	The Vacation	312
30	The Norseman, Our Cash Cow	316
31	"Oh, Brothers!"	322
32	Gods With Gold Braid	330
33	"There's No More Bolivar"	346
34	"Can We Make A New Dream?"	351
Postscript		359
Epilogue		363
Beyond The Dream		373
Where are they now?		375
Acknowledgments		377
Footnotes		381

Dedication

Blue Skies, Green Hell is
dedicated to my parents,
Arvid and Dot Swaningson,
who gave me the gift of life
and encouraged me to make
an adventure of it.

The following are excerpts from Mother and Dad's letters to me:

You never did like the usual, the routine.
April 3, 1952

I have received many letters from you.
Piled one on another, it looks like a manuscript.
May 22, 1953

Honestly, Marilyn, you must write a book
someday. I've kept every one of your letters,
and they could be used for reference. How
about it? Or maybe you won't start to write
until much later—like Grandma Moses waited
until she was very old to paint. But write you must!!!
May 4, 1954

VENEZUELA

LEGEND
1. CARACAS
2. MAIQUETIA/LA GUAIRA
3. MARACAY
4. CIUDAD BOLIVAR
5. CERRO BOLIVAR/CIUDAD PIAR
6. PUERTO ORDAZ/CIUDAD GUAYANA
7. CANAIMA
8. ASA
9. ANGEL FALLS/AUYANTEPUI
10. CAICARA
11. LAGUNILLAS
12. MARACAIBO
13. SITE - CATATUMBOS
14. SANTA ELENA DE UAIRÉN
15. PARAITEPUÍ

Author's Notes

Blue Skies, Green Hell (BSGH) is a true story about my life in the wilds of Venezuela. All the people are real as are their names. All, that is, but two whose names have been changed, but not their story.

I married one of Venezuela's pioneer bush pilots and that opened doors for me to meet celebrities, scholars, explorers, and provided opportunities for me to fly to unheard-of places in Venezuela's wilderness—the magical Lost World first described by Sir Arthur Conan Doyle in 1912.

Some photographs of this mysterious land that captured drama from a cockpit, and on the last frontier on the Orinoco, were taken by me with my 1951 Brownie Hawkeye camera. Other photos in BSGH were taken by my father, Arvid Swaningson (Swanny), a German photographer I called Eric, and my pilot friends Jesús Indriago and Bob Sonderman. The photos are interesting and validate the events.

Each chapter is preceded by a dated excerpt from a letter I sent to or received from someone in my family. The excerpts introduce the subject of the chapter, the arrival of people to our flying community, or tell anecdotes about my activities. They establish the moving time line for BSGH.

My letters home often included conversations and events described so vividly they made it possible to reconstruct conversations. You'll notice a dearth of profanity. That's because profanity was seldom used. And that's the way it was. For all the *machismo* in the world of bush flying, profanity was not in the vocabulary of our bush pilots.

I was motivated to write BSGH because I deeply care about preserving the history and forgotten lore of courageous pilots and their wives who introduced to the world one of the greatest inventions—the bush pilot. Today, bush pilots flying new, powerful planes as well as aged single-engine Cessnas and antique bi-planes—dinosaurs of the air—still ply the skies over the unforgiving wilderness in Venezuela. They provide the same services to the same places served by AEROVEN, my husband's company, sixty years ago and to places in the Lost World as remote today as they were thousands of years ago.

Angel Falls, Canaima National Park, Venezuela.
Tallest waterfalls in the world cascades 3,212 feet
from the top of Auyántepui to the jungle below.
Photo by Robert Sonderman—2007

Angel Falls forms Rio Churún.
Photo by Jerry Wing-2004

Preface

In few ways, bush flying today is similar to bush flying in bygone years: Bad weather conditions prevail, dangerous terrains challenge the pilots, and aircraft instruments perform the same basic flight functions. But that's where similarities end. Today's aircraft are safer and faster. The engines are better; more powerful and reliable. Instruments—dials and switches—are now in a glass cockpit and have improved backup systems. Available today are long-range radios, up-to-the minute weather reports, radar, GPS locators, electronic moving maps and many more high tech instruments that boggle the mind. I've flown in aircraft with an instrument that shows electricity in clouds. Another lifesaving instrument is a "ground-proximity warning" system that synthesizes information already on airplanes and in a series of urgent messages verbally alerts the pilot as the aircraft flies toward an obstacle—like a mountain. Verbal warnings are repeated. If the aircraft continues to fly closer to the mountain, a loud, insistent voice commands, "Terrain. Pull up! Pull up! Pull up! Pull up!"

Bush flying began after World War I in the Territory of Alaska, northern Canada and the Australian outback. After the war, discharged military pilots didn't want to transition from sitting behind the controls of an airplane to sitting behind a desk; they wanted to fly. In the Northern Hemisphere, some discharged pilots bought surplus WWI aircraft, went to the far north, and began flying medical supplies, food, tools, cargo—all life-sustaining substances—to isolated outposts in regions called bush country. The pilots who flew those planes were simply called bush pilots.

Other discharged flying aces who returned to civilian life with a taste for the wild blue yonder opted to be barnstormers to fly in air shows and circuses that featured aerobatics and wing-walkers. To open the skies to everyone, they offered cheap flights that lasted a few minutes to anyone who'd pay a few bucks. Other WWI birdmen seized opportunities to fly the U. S Mail. The most fearless became test pilots.

Alas, in 1927, federal regulations ended barnstorming, but flyers moved to Hollywood to perform stunts in aviation movies. Stunting was followed by Polar explorations. Wherever there was a risk, you'd find the old time barnstormers.

In the 1930's, commercial airlines began to appear in the US and around the world as passenger interest grew. However, the industry's growth was interrupted by World War II.

Following the Great War, returning veteran pilots, like their counterparts from WWI, wanted to keep on flying. Although commercial airlines were growing and forward-looking airline executives were anxious to recruit the well-trained military pilots, there weren't enough airlines to absorb the number of pilots available. Some veteran pilots went north to the bush country.

In the Southern hemisphere, Venezuela had taken the lead in aviation in 1920 when the government established a School of Aviation in Maracay near Caracas. It graduated well-trained pilots who wanted to fly with Venezuela's developing domestic airlines. But the newly graduated airline prospects from Maracay were in short supply, especially for a country in a hurry to have a presence in the skies—worldwide. That was when the established commercial airlines in Venezuela actively recruited and hired discharged U.S. and Canadian military pilots. But it didn't take long before some of those more adventurous pilots who flew the skies over Venezuela in the twin-engine plane of the day, the DC-3, were lured away from the airlines by tales of gold and diamonds hiding in the rivers in bush country. It was in the remote wilderness south of the Orinoco where bush flying in Venezuela was born.

There are inadequate records introducing the first bush pilot in Venezuela, but the American veteran pilot, Jimmie Angel would surely have been one of them. Born in 1899, Angel hailed from Missouri. He flew for Canada during WWI. After the war, he was a barnstormer, and his specialty was jumping from a plane at night from 5,000 feet waving a pair of flashlights[1]. More a pilot than jumper, he later flew in China, became a test pilot in Chile and flew the bush in Mexico and Panama. He is rumored to have visited Venezuela in the early 1920s. Jimmie was special and you will become acquainted with him as his history-making story is told in one of the chapters. He identified the tallest waterfall in the world and named it Angel Falls. He looked for gold and found fame instead.

While Jimmie Angel may have been the first American bush pilot in Venezuela, he was closely followed by Charlie Baughan. Born in Georgia in 1902, and beyond the age to enlist in the military during WWII, he ferried military aircraft to Europe via Venezuela and Brazil. He fell in love with Venezuela and later settled there. An intrepid adventurer, he established the gold mining town called Icabarú near the Brazilian border and later, in the late forties or early fifties, he discovered the exotic beach resort in the jungle he named Canaima. My first day trip there was in 1952. I stayed for eight days in 1953. It is the subject of Chapter 18. The resort is now part of the Canaima National Park in Venezuela. Founded in 1962 it was enlarged in 1975. For a while, it was the largest national park in the world. It is the size of the state of Maryland. Charlie's exploits and adventures are woven throughout *Blue Skies, Green Hell.*

Readers of *Blue Skies, Green Hell* will meet pioneers in bush flying, like my Venezuelan husband, Frank Lazzzari. He was one of the first bush pilots in Venezuela to establish a multiaircraft flying service. The year was 1951.

A graduate of the Maracay School of Aviation and a captain on TACA AIRLINE, he left the cushy airline job and established a bush flying air service called AEROVEN (AEROACTIVIDADES VENEZOLANAS S.A.). It was the first formidable bush flying air taxi service in Venezuela with a formal roster of pilots flying seven aircraft. Six were single-engine: five Cessnas, and one Noorduyn Norseman. The seventh was a twin-engine Beechcraft. The company's mission was not to look for gold and diamonds but to make available bush flying services to isolated communities; provide medical emergency assistance, haul cargo and general supplies, and create scheduled flights to remote settlements on the Orinoco River. He was highly motivated by the discovery of Iron Mountain south of Ciudad Bolivar and the resultant presence of major steel companies.

The bush pilots' plane of preference? The single-engine Cessna. It was a tough, durable plane that could take the harsh conditions like air fields that were short and usually dirt or grassy swaths cut in jungle and savannah landscapes. Vicious weather prevailed in this vast wilderness and inhospitable jungle—bush country—where mountains were high and some not even on the charts. Radio control towers were non-existent. Flying the bush was risky business.

Bush pilots! Tough men flying tough planes in tough conditions. That's history!

Every detail is the way it happened. And I, the author of *Blue Skies, Green Hell*, was there.

Introduction

Years ago, while looking for something in the garage, my husband, Jerry Wing, happened upon a moldy cardboard box bearing my late mother's handwriting on one side. The words, "Letters and Photographs," were legible.

"What's in here?" Jerry asked as he tapped the box.

"I'm not sure. Probably my report cards from grade school. Maybe pictures of me as a kid sitting in my airplane wearing my leather aviator's helmet," I said mysteriously.

"An airplane?" Jerry questioned.

"Yeah. I loved my airplane. I propelled that white and red stubbed-wing beauty with foot-pedals up and down the sidewalk in front of my home on Long Island." I chuckled nostalgically.

Suddenly moved, I reached up, and motioned for Jerry to give me the box. He lifted it from the shelf and put it on the workbench. "I hope my old college paper on twentieth century aviation is in here. I got an A-minus from Professor Myron Luke at Hofstra. I took it to Venezuela. In his note written on the cover of the paper, Dr. Luke suggested I pursue my interest in aviation. In some ways, I guess I did."

I stared at the box and felt timid about opening it.

My memory flashed back to June 1951 when I graduated from Hofstra College (now a university). On the way home from the graduation ceremony, each of my parents asked me one question. Dad asked if he could see his receipt for four years at Hofstra. He referred to my diploma. Mother asked if I would like a trip to Venezuela to visit my sister, Arline, and her young family. It would be Mother and Dad's graduation gift to me.

"Yes and yes," I screamed with youthful glee. There was only one caveat. I had to promise that while I was away, I'd write letters home—often—several times a week.

That's how I happened to visit Venezuela, and why I wrote long, detailed letters home—about three a week—for more than six years.

I ripped open the box and gasped. It contained seventeen large well-preserved tan envelopes. One by one, I withdrew them from the box and felt compelled to brush them against my face and inhale their musty smell.

Each envelope contained manila files and each file contained letters I'd written from the day I arrived in Venezuela in 1951 until I returned to the United States in 1957. The letters were in date order. The envelopes also contained precious old newspaper articles and other memorabilia that were important to my life in Venezuela. An envelope even contained my college paper about aviation I'd taken to Venezuela after I married Frank. In finding letters, on the back cover of the report, is Frank's hand written note when he hired one of our pilots: "Advise Banta about his salary; Bs2,200 for 65 hours. Banta would like an advance in salary to bring his wife."

I pictured Mother reading the letters and probably rereading each many times. I'd typed my multipage single-spaced letters on tissue-thin airmail paper. They provided detailed descriptions of every lonely moment endured, every sadness that befell me, every happy time and adventure during those wondrous years with my courageous husband in bush country.

I wrote prolifically about the times I'd spent with bush pilots, their wives, famous passengers, roustabout explorers, and determined pioneers. Mother preserved all those letters, newspaper clippings, and some photos—all those memories.

Sitting there with me, Jerry read several of the letters.

"You should write a book. It's practically written." He waved a handful of letters in front of me. "Every letter is a story. Select the best of your stories and you have an exciting book about action adventures—and an accurate historical account of early bush flying in Venezuela."

"Are you kidding?" I asked, but already the idea was taking wing in skies of mind. During those years, Mother had written to me with the same dedication I had written to her and I saved all of her letters. I also saved correspondence to and from my sister. Their letters were filled with comments and questions that prompted me to reply in detail. Gems have been mined from all; irreplaceable treasures that validate history. My brother-in-law, Bill, asked if I'd be using photographs in the book. I assured him I would. He had all Dad's Kodak colored slides and black and white photos. Most were taken in 1953, some were in bad condition, but many could be enhanced and used. Bill gave them to me.

That was the push that took me to a dream I never had, but which became an obsession: To write a book about my life in Venezuela, filled with happiness and joy, tragedy and death. But mostly filled with adventure. For ten years, the manuscript was a work in progress.

Jerry often wonders how many other books in boxes are out there, lost in attics or basements, waiting to be freed from their tethers and take wing. I'm proud to say, here's one that has.

Chapter 1

"I'm a Bush Pilot. This is what I do."

Dear Mother and Dad							May 24, 1955

    Good morning. What a day! Rain and more rain. And when it stops, the heat will descend. Living in the interior of Venezuela for more than three years, I should be used to it all. Yesterday, the temperature reached almost 100 degrees—and the summer is just starting. The rainy season is starting, too.
    I have to take Frank to the airport. He has an early flight.
    More later.

    All my love, Marilyn

    In the large open doorway of the hangar, he stood akimbo, his chest squared to the storm that raged outside. He studied the dark sky and watched lightning pierce through it only seconds before thunder shook the earth. Frank, my husband, had a mercy flight to an unpaved airstrip near the Paraqua River south of us and he waited impatiently for a break in the foul weather. Larger in spirit than his 5-foot-10, 130 pound frame, he was anxious to get going.
    "Are you . . . oh shoot—" I stopped midsentence. My voice had been lost in the thunder.
    A moment later he shouted over the deafening noise of the rain slamming on the tin roof, "What did you say?"
    "Oh . . . nothing." My answer was barely audible.
    Frank saw the look of despair on my face and surmised what the thunder had prevented me from saying; "Do you really have to go?"
    Our eyes met. "I'm a bush pilot, Button. This is what I do."
    "I know," I said softly. In a few months, we'd celebrate our fourth wedding anniversary. I knew about bush flying.
    No one called Frank Lazzari a chicken, just as no one called him a daredevil. I called him the best. President of AEROVEN, an air service with seven aircraft, he had top drawer credentials: formal flight education at the Military School of Aviation in Maracay, a few years as a commercial airline captain, and now three years of rough and dangerous bush flying.

We waited, side by side, in the doorway of the weather-worn building that housed AEROVEN's business office, parts department, tools, and aircraft maintenance area. It was 6:30 a.m. and lightning continued to spike through the sky silhouetting giant storm clouds moving in from the northeast. We both watched our fleet of six single-engine aircraft and our twin-engine Beechcraft rocking in the wind. The Cessnas tugged on their lines tied to rings imbedded in the ramp.

Four Cessna aircraft lined up side by side outside the AEROVEN hangar
Photo by Marilyn

During the night, a ham radio operator contacted the night watchman in the Ciudad Bolivar Airport Radio Control Tower to advise him of an ailing diamond buyer in a mining camp on the Paragua River, south of Ciudad Bolivar. A doctor at the campsite, known more for his taste in whiskey and women than his medical prowess, had made the man comfortable, but the buyer's life-threatening condition needed attention right away. The night watchman notified Frank of the medical emergency. Despite the heads-up, Frank couldn't have planned an early departure even if the weather had been clear. Except at international airports in Venezuela, takeoffs and landings were permitted only between sunup about 6:00 a.m. and sundown about 6:00 p.m. Frank would make every effort to rescue the buyer, of that there was no doubt, but weather would determine when he'd depart. The tower operator called this weather interesting. The AEROVEN pilots called it something else. One thing for sure, there would be no blazing tropical sun this morning. No bright sky, no CAVU—ceiling and visibility unlimited. Just rain.

"It doesn't look good." Frank shook his head, "but if some guy's gut is erupting and his life is hanging by a thread—and he's waiting for me—I've got to do something about it. I'll go as soon as I can." He lit a cigarette. "That guy's out there trying to stay alive, and our big challenge is trying to stay dry."

Even before he'd left the airline, he'd set his sights on a new goal; to establish a bush flying air taxi service with multiple aircraft and bring progress to the country's last frontier. AEROVEN would be the first major bush flying operation in Venezuela's interior. His routes would take him over jungle and mountains in difficult weather with no meteorological reports and radios that had no more than a two-mile range. He would be landing on unpaved and untested air strips cut in unforgiving wilderness.

The rain continued and lightning followed with deafening bursts of thunder. Just then the phone rang. Frank walked into the business office, snapped on the desk lamp and picked up the phone. "AEROVEN," he answered. From the short, one-sided conversation, I knew the Control Tower Operator (CTO) had called.

"Tower?" I asked.

"Yeah. The ham operator called again. The buyer's drifting in and out of consciousness. He's in bad shape. He needs to be airlifted out. Pronto. This airport's shut down. The CTO said we're socked in."

Pensively, he looked out the office window and watched rain streak in front of the outdoor light on a pole that lit the ramp where our planes still rocked.

I took a piece of chalk and wrote "Medical Emergency—Paragua" next to Frank's name on the chalkboard. "Where on the Paragua River?"

He rattled off coordinates. "It's a grass strip. I've been there before." He reached for the mechanic's grease-spotted yellow rain coat and slipped it on over his starched and pressed long-sleeved white shirt and creased trousers. Then he gathered his charts, plotter, clipboard, and a flashlight. Putting on his cap with its protective oil-skin cover, he said, "The rain is easing. I'll pre-flight the plane—as much as I can. Then we'll see what happens."

"Which plane?"

"D," he replied and snapped the key off the hook near the chalk board. "It's a little more comfortable than the others. It's faster, too." FLD was a Cessna 180. It was called a tail-dragger because it had a rear wheel instead of a nose wheel. The Cessna single-engine tail-dragger was the bush pilot's plane of preference: With a tail wheel, the propeller is higher off the ground than a plane with a nose wheel. The higher prop allows it to pass over obstacles in untested grassy fields. It can get in and out of short fields and make tighter turns on the ground; both factors important in short unimproved landing fields in bush country.

Before he left the office, he stopped briefly to look through a pile of papers in the incoming basket on the secretary's desk. "I see a few bills have to be paid. Before you go home, will you look them over?"

He jogged to his aircraft, opened the door, and tossed the clipboard and other things he'd gathered onto the empty seat next to his. He leaned inside and slipped the key into the ignition then did his "walk-around" of the aircraft. He examined the propeller to be sure there were no dings or chips that would interfere with the aircraft's performance. He removed the covers from the intake vents and peered inside to be sure birds had not nested in the vents before they'd been covered. He checked the fuel condition through a quick drain of fuel into a fuel tester. The tanks were full. They were always topped off at night to prevent condensation from forming on the interior walls of the gas tanks. He checked the tires. They looked good. Assured of the plane's exterior, he boarded and retrieved the checklist of normal procedures stowed over the sun visor and referred to it, item by item. He checked switches, circuit breakers, gauges, cockpit controls, and made all the basic cockpit preparations. Then he started the engine, checked the magnetos and made sure the instruments were operable. He let the engine run until the oil pressure was normal and the needle in the oil temperature gauge was in the green for a safe takeoff. Frank's pre-flight inspection, the review of his checklists and his engine run-up were meticulously performed. He considered no short cuts. He considered nothing routine. Everything was by the book.

He activated the lights on the wing tips and the one on the tail and even tested the rotation beacon located under the fuselage of the aircraft. He hardly ever used those lights, but for this morning's flight, he'd take every precaution.

A quintessential pilot, Frank knew he'd likely face poor visibility, low ceiling, winds, gusts, turbulence, and possible disorientation when visual references may be lost. Before we married, he'd told me this wasn't the golden age of aviation when swaggering barnstormers wore jodhpurs, leather helmets, goggles, and white silk scarves that streamed out behind open cockpits. This was bush flying in the nineteen-fifties; a serious business that provided a vital lifeline and emergency service to isolated communities with unattended landing strips. I assured him I could take it and I'd been tested plenty in this—Venezuela's last frontier called Ciudad Bolivar on the Orinoco River.

Ramón, the *gasolinero* (the worker who pumped fuel into the planes), jogged into the hangar. "*Señora, buenos días,*" he called, and then looked at the chalk board. "*Ay. Caramba*" (Good gracious), he sputtered softly and looked over his shoulder through the open door to peer more closely at the rain, once again, slamming the north-east corner of the building.

"Yeah. Caramba," I agreed. The phone rang again. I went to the desk, sat down, and put the receiver to my ear. "Hello."

Blue Skies, Green Hell

The call ended my day off. It was the office secretary telling me she'd be a little late. I'd been working on and off at the office, through a series of secretaries and office managers, since AEROVEN rolled open its hangar door in 1951. I had learned to fly and everything administrative about AEROVEN from the ground up. Frank depended on me. For the first time in my life, someone needed me.

Ramón looked at the chalk board again and inquired about Frank's last minute assignment. I explained the medical emergency. "Is FLD ready to go?"

He signaled two thumbs up and left the office.

Frank called to Ramón and asked him to fill a couple of gasoline cans and stow them in the compartment behind the rear seats. He might need the extra fuel for his return trip.

Gusts of wind pushed sheets of blinding rain across the flat airfield while sharp claps of thunder ripped across the sky. I watched our aircraft still tugging at their tie-down lines.

"What a wind," I said to no one. I made a mental note to check those lines when the rain eased.

Frank turned off the engine and jogged back to the building. He paced inside the hangar and looked at the work area with odd parts assembled on the workbench. He fidgeted and looked at his watch. "Damn. I've lost so much time."

And more time passed.

He looked at his watch again.

"Hey," he said and stood upright with his head cocked. "Do you hear that?"

"What? I don't hear anything."

"That's what I mean. The rain." He poured a half cup of coffee and stared at the sky. "It's easing, and the sky is getting lighter. If I see holes and broken clouds, I'll give it a shot. It's not that far. I should make it down in less than an hour. I'll have a tail wind. It'll be slower when I return. When I make contact with the tower on my return, I'll ask him to contact you, and then find a doctor who can be here. Okay?"

The phone rang again. "Lazzari," he answered. ". . . *Muy bien. Perfecto. Gracias.*" He hung up. "Tower says the buyer's been taken to La Paragua airstrip. That's better. The strip isn't paved, but it holds up under pretty bad weather conditions."

I pressed on. "What was worth the '*perfecto*'?"

"The airport's open again and the ceiling in minutes will be . . . 1,500 feet. That's good. And the rain is expected to end soon." In the distance, thunder continued.

"So I hear."

"At 1,500 feet, I can stay under the clouds. I can see a lot, Button, it's better than flying on instruments." He chuckled wryly. Our light aircraft only had a few basic instruments. You couldn't fly IFR (Instrument Flight Rules)—there were

25

no ground communications. Cessnas had no high tech instruments and radios. "Our instruments aren't like the ones in the DC-3s the big boys fly."

"Eight o'clock," he said. "Maybe the weather isn't so bad. You know how crazy weather reports are. You could pull a report out of a hat and it would be just as valid. He reached out and took my hand. "Button, I've got to go for him. I've got to try. I've flown in every kind of weather we have, and I've made it home every time." He kissed me. "I'll file my flight plan then be on my way. See you later." In CB, the flight plan filed with the Control Tower Operator by every pilot prior to departure included specific data about the aircraft, like its ID and type, and most importantly, things such as destination, route to a destination, estimated time en route, alternate airfields in case of bad weather or emergencies, and other information that would be used for tracking should search and rescue operations be required.

When there were onlookers who liked to hang around the airport to watch airplanes land and take off and to rub shoulders with pilots, we acted as casually as though the kiss and the "Goodbye" were just two items on the aircraft's checklist of normal procedures. When we were alone, our goodbyes were less hurried. I'd come to Venezuela from New York in 1951, and though no longer a stranger in the country, I felt lonely—even a little insecure—when Frank flew out of sight. South of CB all the terrain was unbidden wilderness; savannah, forest, jungle.

He walked briskly from the hangar to his plane. I lowered my head and gazed at pieces of gravel that had been tracked into the maintenance area near the open door. With my right foot, I played with the pebbles, aimlessly pushing them from here to there. I hated the goodbyes.

The day's early light broke the horizon. Ramón removed the tie-down lines. After Frank slipped off the Pitot tube cover, he hopped into the plane and switched on the ignition. The plane came to life with lights and sound as he ran up the engine then throttled down. Once more, he tested the controls and I saw the rudder and elevators move. Then the ailerons and flaps. Slowly, he left the ramp and taxied to the runway.

Confident he'd made the right decision, the engine roared at full throttle. It was a "go."

I watched the small white and red plane start down the runway. It rolled slowly then rapidly gained speed, splashing through puddles along the way. The tail wheel lifted and long before the single-engine Cessna reached the end of the runway it had departed the earth and started its climbing turn to the right and into gray sky.[2] I watched intently while the small plane with wing-tip lights blinking continued to ascend and fly farther away from me. My dry eyes burned from not blinking for that would break my stare and then I'd lose sight of the tiny lights in the sky—my husband and his aircraft. I squinted and concentrated, positive I saw his plane long after it had flown beyond my visual range. And I heard it long after I'd lost sight of it. He had a mercy mission in foul weather. He had to get to the rural airstrip in La Paragua, an arid and flat place. Then he had to turn around and fly home with the ailing buyer.

Frank, a Venezuelan, knew the terrain of his country well. Many of his routine flights were up the Orinoco, with intervening stops on unpaved runways along the way. He did not fly over the river all the way. Instead, he navigated by using his plotter (an odd shaped ruler), compass, and charts.

Recognizable landmarks on the ground—mountains, clearings, rivers and their waterfalls—were reliable checkpoints.

More perilous were flights south over the jungle to towns on the Brazilian border, 312 miles from Ciudad Bolivar. Pilots in single-engine aircraft called that vast, inhospitable region, Green Hell. In this southeast region, other recognizable checkpoints included about 114 tepuís—leviathan flat-top stone mountains with vertical walls that rise thousands of feet out of the jungle.

Four miles or two minutes after pilots departed CB Airport, they were flying beyond the range of the airport Radio Control Tower and all other means of communication. If any rural airstrip had a radio, it had limited range because the number of daily flights—mostly all local light aircraft—were few and more powerful transmitters weren't warranted. There were no tower-controlled airfields in the Green Hell, nor airfields with aircraft service.

On the way to border towns, he'd fly around or over the tepuí, Roraima, elevation about 9,200 feet above mean sea level. He'd cruise over that rock at 12,000 feet, never higher. His plane was not equipped with oxygen. This highest of all *tepuís* was the same mysterious plateau where mythical dinosaurs and pre-historic monsters inspired Sir Arthur Conan Doyle's classic novel *The Lost World*. That wasteland would forever remain remote and forbidding.

Approaching Roraima, highest of all tepuis.
Photo by Marilyn

After I lost sight of Frank's aircraft, I drove my car through puddles across the airport parking lot to the main terminal. Parking as close to the terminal as possible, I ran to its portico, pushed open its green double doors, and walked to the outdoor patio lounge and a vacant table under the roof. I ordered toast and coffee with milk.

I was writing a shopping list on a paper napkin when the CTO stopped at my table. He glanced skyward, "The weather's looking iffy. Another squall or two may come through. If I hear anything, I'll call you. You'll be here?"

I nodded. "Thanks."

"Okay." He left.

I took a moment before returning to the office to watch the airport ramps, taxiways, and, runways come to life. There was joy to be had in the daily sight and sound show, and I'd often reveled in this ritual of organized chaos. Today, because of the foul weather, it felt more like solace as I watched men and aircraft move about before me.

While taxiing, some pilots applied more power than others. Some planes crawled so slowly the engines turned at near idle. Each pilot had his own style of moving his plane from the taxiway to the upwind runway and left his signature in the sound waves in this routine exercise. Pilots either taxied no faster than a walking pace or moved the plane slowly enough to maintain its speed without excessive use of brakes. The CTO choreographed the movements of each plane from one place to another much like a dance director on Broadway planned every step made by performers.

I thrilled to the racket of the airplane engines idling, revving, and taxiing. Different engines had different horsepower so no two planes sounded alike. They all sang different tunes and provided the show's music when they rolled in front of a bedazzling backdrop of morning sky bathed with lavenders, pinks, blues, and a special color I called "sunrise orange" seen only in CB and in the Lost World to the south. Today's distant thunder added drums to the overture, and instead of a bright morning sky, clouds provided a gray backdrop to the planes taxiing to the head of the runway. Planes with dazzling white and red and green lights—some steady, others blinking—and planes whose interior lights appeared to flicker as seated passengers moved back and forth in front of their windows reminded me of the dazzling lights on opening night on Broadway.

I finished my breakfast and drove back to our hangar to wait.

Our earth-bound planes were parked side by side on the ramp outside the hangar; four single-engine Cessnas, one Noorduyn Norseman, and one twin-engine Beechcraft. The Cessnas and Beech shone. Our Norseman didn't shine even when clean. The Norseman's frame, made of both wood and metal, was covered with fabric followed by coats of "dope," a water-proofing and tightening liquid applied to act as a filler to ensure air-tightness. A final coat of white paint and blue trim gave it a finished look.

Blue Skies, Green Hell

I never liked the Norseman. When we bought it in Miami, I walked around inside the plane to have a look-see but I never flew in it. Just never wanted to. With one huge nine-cylinder, 600-hundred-horsepower Pratt and Whitney R-1340 Wasp radial engine, it made the Cessna's 145 horsepower engine look like a toy. Around the airport, people affectionately called it the Cow. The plane's nose art was a crying cow with wings. When it rolled down the runway on takeoff, it sounded like a platoon on motorcycles.

I called Ramón, and together we walked down the line in front of the planes, checked their ropes, tested their knots, and retied several. I checked the time. I'd frittered away almost two hours.

I told Ramón I'd stay around until Frank returned. Also, I might have to call a doctor. Was it only a couple of weeks ago I had to call Dr. Battistini when Tom . . . I erased that thought.

I strolled in front of the line of planes and had just reached FLA parked at the farthest point from the building, when wind and rain surged from nowhere.

"*Señora. Señora,*" Ramón called and opened the plane's passenger door and I hopped in. He told me to wait in the plane until the rain stopped, then he closed the door behind me and ran to the hangar.

At the time, Venezuelan planes had a series of letters painted on the top of one wing, on the bottom of the other, and on the tail assembly.[3] The first two letters identified the country in which it was registered. Our first two letters were YV for Venezuela. The next letter identified the kind of license under which it was registered. Our letter was "C" for commercial. The final three letters on our planes designated the company. All our aircraft carried the letters "FL" for Frank Lazzari, my husband and President of AEROVEN. The last letter revealed the order in which the aircraft had been added to the fleet. Today, Frank flew FLD, our fourth plane.

FLA, in which I sought shelter, was the first in the fleet. It remained a clean plane in beautiful condition despite more than three years of heavy-duty carrying cargo and a variety of passengers. Mud-covered gold and diamond miners wearing tattered work clothes and worn-out *alpargatas* (crocheted sandals) flew in FLA as well as executives from U.S. steel companies dressed in tightly creased tan slacks and crisp white short—sleeve shirts and ties.

Our planes also carried celebrities. Manuel Eudora Sanchez Lenz, Governor of Bolivar State. He only flew with AEROVEN and only with Frank at the controls. Worldwide known celebrities included Walter Montenegro, LIFE magazine writer, and Cornell Capa, award-winning LIFE magazine photographer and founder of the International Center of Photography in New York. Beautiful Jean Liedloff, best-selling author, TV personality, and psychotherapist had flown with us, as had Horacio Cabrera. He was Venezuelan and our very good friend. Horacio had been a Hollywood motion picture sound engineer. He founded the Cattlemen's Association in Bolivar and was a national champion in the treacherous sport called *Toro Coleados*. He was elected Governor of Bolivar State in 1958 and in 1964 elected Senator from the state to the Venezuelan federal government. He became an award-winning author of literary works describing the majesty of the Venezuelan interior. Cabrera's good friend, Clark Gable, a famous motion picture actor between the thirties and the fifties, had twice been a passenger destined for Horacio's cattle ranch, Hato La Vergareña.

I pushed open the window in the door of the down-wind side of the plane and slouched in my seat. I rested my head back.

My eyes fell upon a small crystal cross that hung from a pin and slim thread jammed into the ceiling's fabric above the center of the windshield. It swayed slowly from one side to the other. Although we'd checked the plane's tie-down lines, the aircraft rocked as it strained against the wind.

I flicked the small cross with my index finger. And I prayed.

Who hung the cross? I doubted any of the three full-time pilots would have hung it: Frank; Julio Rojas, his pilot-partner; or Irv Banta, our full-time pilot.

Frank? I could make no judgment about his relationship with God. He was not as faithful to religion as I would have liked. He left all the praying to me. I surely couldn't imagine the other two ever pinning a cross to the felt-covered ceiling.

There was no church in Bolivar where English was spoken. Perhaps some of the American men and their families had devotions at home. Who knows? No one talked about it. I read my Bible.

Other pilots who flew on an "as-needed" basis might have pinned the small crystal cross there. We socialized with most of them, but we knew little about their backgrounds.

Frank used to say some people come to the interior to "get lost." While he suspected some of the pilots who occasionally flew for us fit that category, he never queried them. If they had the credentials to fly and were qualified to fly our aircraft, Frank signed them on. No other questions were asked, least of all their religion.

Courageous airmen all, they flew in and out of our lives but not before making their mark in our memories.

Jimmy Evens was one, so was Bill Murphy and the kid we called Pogo.

Jimmy made a few flights for us, but in 1952, flying for another company, his plane crashed on landing and he died, or in the parlance of pilots, "he bought the farm," trying to get into a small grass strip carved in the jungle by Indians near a mining camp. Frank, Tom Van Hyning (formerly on our full-time roster) and I might have met the same fate at the same grassy air strip if I'd not asserted myself while Frank and Tom argued whether to land. That was a close call.

Bill Murphy, the copilot of the large twin-engine C-46 cargo plane that came from Miami to Ciudad Bolivar every couple of weeks, liked to puddle jump in a Cessna up and down the Orinoco when the C-46 had down time in CB. It was not the Orinoco that swallowed him. Bill could have hung the cross from the ceiling of the plane. He carried rosary beads. God bless him.

And there was the good-looking blonde kid we nicknamed Pogo whose daily exercise was turning the pages of a Pogo comic book while sitting in the comfort of our office, one of the few places in Ciudad Bolivar that boasted an air-conditioner. Occasionally, he flew trips for us. He had his own new plane and when passengers were clean and spiffy businessmen, he'd fly the trip in his plane. He'd fly one of our planes when his run was to the mines where workers' boots were covered with mud from the river bottom. He didn't want that mess in his plane. But Pogo came through when Frank and I needed him most. I knew little about him, but he saved our lives.

To be available to fly for any company that needed a pilot, Tom Van Hyning had quit flying full time for AEROVEN. He wanted to fly free-lance; fly more hours, earn more money. He often flew trips for us. Tom, Shirley and their baby Patty prayed nightly. Oh, Tom. What happened on May 3rd? I blotted it from my mind.

Others who'd flown FLA included Charlie Baughan and Rafael Romero, both living legends still flying the bush in 1955.

The Beechcraft
Photo by Marilyn

Certified to fly any plane we had, I think Charlie Baughan could have flown any plane anybody had in the fifties. Nevertheless, once while taxiing our twin-engine Beechcraft, he damaged the tail assembly. Even though the plane needed major repairs only possible at Maiquetia, the international airport that served Caracas, Frank simply said, "He's getting old." Charlie was 53. The rogue never paid for the repairs.

Rafael Romero most frequently flew the Norseman. A pioneer in bush flying, he was also an outstanding guitarist. He could have played in classical orchestras, the likes of which his famous musician brother, Aldemaro Romero, conducted. Had he made the wrong career choice?

I chuckled as I thought of Jimmie Angel, the most famous of all the pilots whose footsteps had crossed the AEROVEN ramp. Affixing a crystal cross to the inside of a plane would not have suited his persona. An adventurer and maverick, this bush pilot's incredible true story would be told and retold in history. Jimmie had been flying over Auyántepui, the largest of all tepuís, looking for gold and wealth but instead found a waterfall and fame.

I checked the time again. *He's probably on his way home.*

I watched the crystal cross spin slowly in the breeze and closed my eyes.

My memories flashed back almost four years to when I made the flight from New York to Venezuela, and, shortly thereafter, met Frank.

Chapter 2

"Like in a Hollywood Movie"

Dear Mother and Dad	**September 1, 1951**

    I waved goodbye to you long after the plane taxied away from the gate at Idlewild Airport.[4] What a great graduation gift—a trip to Venezuela to stay with Arline [my sister], Bill [her husband], and Victoria [their six-month old baby].

    As we fly along, I'm thinking about how far from home I'll be. I'll miss my friends, activities, my piano and mostly you. I also have to learn a new language. I've been so snug in my comfort zone.

    Moving beyond its safe boundary is a little scary. I've got the willies!

    It's 7:00 a.m. **September 2, 1951**, Sunday.

    Yes, I slept a while. Now we are preparing to land. The flight's been wonderful. Vickie slept almost the whole trip. I'm over the willies and excited—I'm wondering what I will be doing a week from today. I do love you so much and promise to write often. Thank you for this great opportunity.

My love always, Marilyn

My life in the tropics got off to a fast start. During my first week, Bill and an associate came home at the end of their work day to enjoy a drink and, I assumed, make end-of-the-day small talk.

"Marilyn. Meet my friend, Wes. Join us. Have a drink," Bill said.

"Love to. Give me one minute. I just washed my hair." I quickly wrapped a towel around it. "Don't wait for me."

Bill and Wes went to the brass rolling bar in the living room.

I wore a white T-shirt and yellow shorts. *Of all the times for me to look like this.* I fled to the bathroom, combed my hair, pushed it in place, and dabbed on lipstick. What a mess! I returned to the living room where Bill and Wes were sipping drinks.

"What do you want to drink?" Bill asked.

"Thanks—I'll get it in a minute."

"Bill tells me you have experience on the stage," Wes said as he picked up his glass.

"Yes—school plays, college shows. I sang with the college dance band. Heck, I've been on stage since I was a little girl."

"That's what Bill said. In fact, that's why I'm here. I'm in the production side of The Caracas Little Theater Group. We're in rehearsal right now. In October, we'll be opening *George Washington Slept Here*. One part hasn't been cast. Interested?"

"Hey. Great. But how could I learn lines in such a short time?"

"Don't worry about that."

I stood up, walked to the brass cart that held an ice bucket and an assortment of bottles and poured a drink. As I returned to my chair, Wes looked me up and down and said, "You'll do fine." That was the audition.

Twenty-four hours later, I'd joined the cast of GWSH and was in rehearsal. Opening night was Friday, October 5. My life's turn was just like in a Hollywood movie.

My first invitation to a cocktail party, for which the party-loving Venezuelans had gained a level of fame, came about ten days after I arrived. It announced the party would be held on September 22, Saturday, hosted by Olga and Bob Towne. Olga was Bill's sister. "Look," I said to Arline and waved the invitation. "It says the party starts at 6:00 p.m. But it doesn't say when it ends."

"That's the way they do a party here. It ends whenever people leave. Sometimes, it's very late. Olga always has good parties. She called yesterday and told me Bob was inviting some of his single male friends to meet you. Olga thinks maybe you haven't met anyone. She didn't know you're in the Theater Group and you're out at rehearsals every evening. Anyway, she invited Frank Lazzari. He's a pilot, but he may be out of town. He's related someway or other. Bill's family here in Caracas is really big."

Olga and Bob hosted the party in their airy apartment in the high-end suburb of Las Mercedes. It featured good food, drink, and music. After a couple of hours, a few guests began to leave. I thought I'd ask Arline when I should begin to say thank you and goodbye to the hosts when the door of the apartment opened and a late-arriving guest poked his head in. "Am I too late for the party?" he asked.

My eyes opened wide. *Oh. You're just in time!*

With his dancing brown eyes and infectious smile, my heart had skipped a beat before he'd closed the door behind him. He was handsomely dressed in an ivory tweed jacket, white shirt, tie, dark pants, and I noticed tiny gold wings pinned to his lapel. *Ah, the pilot.* I forced myself not to stare at him as he made small talk to everyone in the room. Then, in no hurry, he strolled my way and introduced himself. "I'm Frank Lazzari."

"Hello," I said. "I'm Marilyn . . . Arline Franklin's sister."

"I met Arline and Bill when they were here last year. I heard Bill is working in Caracas now. You're visiting them?"

"Yes. I just graduated from college and my parents thought I would enjoy a visit to Venezuela." I hesitated. "I think they were right." I felt myself blush.

"How long have you been in Caracas?

"About three weeks."

"And what have you seen of our beautiful city?"

"Just driven around a little. I've been to the museums in El Bosque. And the Pantheon."

"How long will you stay?"

"I really don't know." *He asks a lot of questions.*

He ordered two drinks from the strolling waiter who returned promptly with our drinks on a tray. We each took one and then Frank held my elbow and gently led me to a balcony overlooking the city of Caracas and the silhouette of the Avila Mountain, impressive at over a mile high above sea level. He took two cigarettes from the pack in his jacket pocket, gave one to me and lit both. His debonair manner was a sharp contrast to the college boys I'd dated back home—only three weeks ago.

"I would have been here earlier," he said, "but I drove from Ciudad Bolivar yesterday. It's a long trip. I work here in Caracas and in CB as well, so I divide my time." He took a drag on his cigarette and exhaled the smoke as he looked out over the city. The lights in houses and tall buildings and some scattered on the mountainside were just coming on. His gaze returned to me. He looked into my eyes and took my hand in his. "I'll be here a while this time. And I want to show you my beautiful city. Let's start right now. Tonight."

"Tonight?"

"Yes. Will you have dinner with me?" Without waiting for my answer, he said, "and then we'll go dancing."

I thought it was okay to go out with this stranger. I'd already heard a little about the pilot. His brother, Armando—always called "Do"—was married to one of Bill's five sisters. And, after all, he'd been invited to meet me. Arline said he was related—some way.

"Sounds like fun. I'd love to join you."

We left the party in his white Buick Riviera and drove to a small, intimate restaurant. "We can talk better here," he said, leading me to an umbrella table in a courtyard lit by table candles and blazing torches affixed to gold-colored stucco walls. "I want to tell you what I'm doing and I want to learn about you. We're going to spend a lot of time together." He clapped twice and a waiter in white shirt with black tie and black trousers covered by a crisply starched white apron appeared from nowhere. Frank ordered drinks and dinner.

A guitarist approached the table and asked if I had a request. "Because of You," I answered, a popular tune in the States crooned by a young Tony Bennett. The guitarist shook his head apologetically and said he didn't know the song. I asked for a more familiar song, "Star Dust." He nodded, strummed a few chords and sang it in Spanish. I melted.

Throughout dinner, we chatted. "You have a British accent. I like it," I said. "But you're Venezuelan?"

"I was born in Trinidad and educated there. Dad was British. He passed on. My mother is Venezuelan. You'll meet her. She lives in Caracas."

I paused. "Trinidad?"

"A beautiful tropical island and a wonderful place to grow up. I learned to swim. They called me 'Fish.' I play tennis and ride horseback. Do you play tennis?"

"Yes. A little. I swim better."

"Next week, we'll spend a day at the beach. And have dinner there, too." He squeezed my hand. "We'll go to Club Tanaquarena on the Caribbean. It's quite private."

I smiled and shyly looked toward a flaming torch on the wall. *What should I say?*

"Would you like that?"

"Ah—very much." I felt foolish and my palms were damp. Under the table, I subtly wiped my hands on the linen dinner napkin and then wrapped it around my hand.

"I like to hunt. Do you hunt?" He asked.

"Hunt? I've never wanted to. I couldn't kill an animal, but I can handle a gun. I shot on the high school rifle team."

"That's another thing we have in common. I shoot at the *poligano* (shooting range)."

I giggled. Neither witty nor sophisticated words would come.

"Do you like flying?"

"I've loved it since I was a kid and had an airplane."

"You had a plane?"

"A snub-winged beauty, powered by pedals on a sidewalk. I called it Lollypop after a Shirley Temple movie."

He laughed. "I fly, too. Someday you'll fly with me in a real plane. We'll fly high in the blue sky—sky the color of your eyes." He saw the startled look on my face. "Yes. I noticed your blue eyes—the moment we met."

"Oh." Again, I couldn't think of anything to say. I felt so overwhelmed; so inadequate.

Blue Skies, Green Hell

He told me he'd been a captain on TACA Airlines (Transporte Area Campania Anónima). He paused and played with a gold bracelet on his wrist, then added enthusiastically, "I recently left the airline. Now, I'm a bush pilot."

"A what? What's a bush pilot?"

"I'll fly light aircraft—small, single-engine planes. Oh, they're not as small as your Lollypop." Gently he touched my napkin wrapped hand. Gently I removed the napkin from my hand. As though there'd been no interruption, he continued. "I'll be flying in bush country. To remote areas and communities that have little or no connection to the outside world. I'll provide medical service and fly cargo to places in the vast wilderness . . . even to villages in the jungle." He paused and sipped his Scotch and Coke. "And I'll fly tourists and explorers to Angel Falls—and to The Lost World. We'll fly there too. You and I.

"I want to contract with the oil and iron-mining companies operating there—fly personnel, equipment, even do pipeline inspections. Marilyn, I'm in the process of establishing my own air service—bush flying—based in Ciudad Bolivar. The scope is so broad, we'll be flying everyday to a different place on a different mission. There'll be no chance for boredom." He exhaled. "Phew. I'll probably spend a lifetime in the Air Ministry trying to get permits to go into all these places throughout the interior."

"The interior?"

"All major cities in Venezuela are located on the Caribbean coast. Not too far inland the interior begins. The country is not well-developed south of Caracas. The deep interior is just about any place south of the mighty Orinoco River. That's bush country."

"Oh. I have so much to learn."

"I'll teach you," he said. "Ciudad Bolivar is on the south bank of the great river that slices Venezuela in half—east to west. No bridges cross the river, but there is a small ferry. Land south of the river is still somewhat isolated and quite undeveloped. I want to have eight to ten light aircraft and fly up and down the Orinoco to provide air service to villages that have none. But that's enough geography . . ."

"What dreams you have!"

"I'll share them with you." Again, he put his hand on mine.

With the unrestrained enthusiasm of a young visionary, he spoke about the times he'd flown TACA's twin-engine DC-3s to Ciudad Bolivar. "Well-dressed American businessmen filled every seat on every plane. After the plane was airborne, I'd stroll down the aisle of the plane and chat for a few minutes with the passengers.[5] I learned about the mountain of iron that had been discovered southeast of Ciudad Bolivar and the developing business activities in the region. "They all talked about the same thing; iron, iron, iron. It didn't take long before I wanted to get in on the ground floor." He extended his arm and slowly swept it in front of him from left to right and back again. "I see a business

37

that will combine my profession with their needs for rapid transportation from Ciudad Bolivar to the iron mountain at Cerro Bolivar and to Puerto Ordaz on the Orinoco, home base for the iron companies." He smiled. "My dream? AEROVEN AIR SERVICE."

"WOW. I've never heard of such ambitions other than on Hollywood's silver screen."

Then he switched gears and cupped my chin in his hand and stared at me.

"Why do you stare at me?" I said coyly.

"To look at you. Hmm. Yes. Blue as the sky. Your eyes. I'll see them better tomorrow. In the daylight. I'll pick you up at one o'clock. We'll sightsee and have dinner.

"You're a pretty bold fellow," I said softly.

"I think you like it," he whispered.

I felt another blush travel from my neck to my hair line. He's something else.

"Tell me about yourself. Tell me about your dreams."

"Oh." His question pulled me up short. How could I follow his story! I had nothing dramatic to say about myself, but he'd put me on the spot. "I was born in a small coastal village on New York's Long Island. On damp days I could taste the salt air and hear fog horns in the harbor. As much as I like flying, I like sailing, too."

"Ah, yes. I sail. In Trinidad everyone sails. That's another thing we have in common."

"You're way out of my league. I handle a small Sailfish."

"I'll teach you to sail a boat larger than a Sailfish. Now, tell me about your family."

Glad he changed the subject, I spoke of dad who worked in New York City and my mother, my best friend. "I hope you'll be in Caracas during the holidays. They'll be visiting."

"Count on it," he smiled. "Now, what's *this* all about?" He pulled a newspaper clipping from his jacket pocket.

"Oh, no." Feigning embarrassment, I covered my face with my hand.

"Let's see. Dateline . . . Caracas. Newspaper . . . Caracas Journal. The caption says, 'This dazzling blonde is Marilyn . . .' This hooked me. This is why I came to the party."

I cringed as I interrupted. "Please. Don't read more. You embarrass me."

"The photos are nice. Tell me, you're here only a few weeks and you're a celebrity. How did you get the coveted role of Miss Wilcox, the lady who, the newspaper says, walks but does not talk in the next CLTG (Caracas Little Theater Group) production of *George Washington Slept Here?*"

"You're making fun of me."

"What does it mean? 'Walks but does not talk.'"

"I have no speaking lines. I just walk across the stage and up a flight of stairs . . . in a yellow bathing suit and high heels." I giggled as I remembered my audition in Arline and Bill's apartment.

"I want to see the show."

"Please don't make fun of me," I repeated.

"I'd never do that." He gave me a hug. "As a matter of fact, I saw the article and called Olga late last night and asked her if the 'dazzling Marilyn' in the newspaper was the same Marilyn who'd be at her party. She said it was. That's when I made up my mind to come, no matter how tired I was from the long drive. I had to meet you."

"Please don't . . ." I thought he'd had his fun long enough.

Frank saw I felt uncomfortable. "Okay. Forget the article and the show for now, though I'll want to hear all about it. And I'm going to attend, you know. I'll bring my mother. I want her to meet you. Now, tell me more about yourself."

"Well, I studied piano and dancing and I've been singing for almost as long as I can remember." *Damn, I'm dull.* "I like to write. I was on the editorial staffs of yearbooks and newspapers in high school and college. But mostly, I love the stage. Musical productions. Frank, I have no dreams—no idea what career choice I'll make. I'm just not ready to make a decision. I may even go back to school."

I breathed a silent sigh of relief when dinner was served.

After we'd finished and he'd paid the bill, he stood up, took my hand and said, "I'll help you have a dream and make a decision. But now we'll go dancing."

"Great." *Between the music and dancing, I won't have to talk about myself.*

"When did you say you're returning to the states?"

I hesitated and then whispered, "I don't have a return ticket."

"You won't need one," he whispered back.

We left the restaurant and went to a dimly lit late night supper club called Mario's. The walls were covered with dark, smoky mirrors, and we were seated in a cozy black leather booth. The room had the unpleasant aroma of stale cigarette smoke mixed with alcohol and needed to be aired out. But I forgot the stale odor when a band started playing music for dancing, mostly Latin. Only because Frank was a good dancer, was I able to follow. The longer the evening the more sensual the music, and the faster the bongos and drums beat the primitive tempo, the closer we danced. I could hardly breathe, suffocating in the ecstasy of his arms, annoyed with myself for enjoying it so much. We swung our hips to the frenzied rhythm of the music, mostly unfamiliar to me, until my head spun and I felt giddy.

We returned to our table and Frank put his arm around me, pulled me closer to him and said, "Bolivar's reputation is not good. People think it's primitive. But you'll like it."

"I beg your pardon?" I pulled away. "You think I'm going to Bolivar with you?"

He pulled me closer. I did not protest.

"People say it's behind the times. Don't believe them. They don't know. Most haven't been there anyway. You'll decide for yourself."

My eyes widened. "Frank," I said, "I won't go away with you."

He hugged me, "Yes, you will."

Where's this guy coming from?

"I've decided we're going to be married. I just made up my mind. Let's have one more dance and then go. Okay, Button?"

"Button?"

"You're little and cute as a button. That's what I'll call you."

Through balmy midnight air, we drove to a promontory high in the hills on the north slope of the mountains. Gazing over Caracas, glittering in the valley below, he gestured grandly and said, "This is my city. I give it to you." He slowly removed the 18 karat gold ID bracelet from his wrist and gently placed it on mine. The gold wings he'd received when he graduated from the school of aviation in Maracay were affixed to a gold oval disk on the bracelet and his name was engraved on the reverse side. Then he said, "I want you to be my wife. To share my dreams. To be a pioneer with me in Bolivar. To be with me forever. Will you marry me?"

I scarcely caught my breath. This was stuff Hollywood was made of. Though I'd been brought up on Betty Grable movies like *Down Argentina Way* and Ginger Rodgers in *Flying Down to Rio,* I never dreamt of a romance like this. It just didn't happen in real life. Film fantasies never misled me, but like Grable and Rodgers in Hollywood movies, I was being courted in the exotic tropics under a star-filled sky by a handsome *caballero* (gentleman), romantic, and irresistible.

This alluring Venezuelan dazzled me and after a two week courtship, we secretly married in the office of the Prefect in Sabana Grande, a suburb of Caracas, on October 5, 1951. Six of his friends were witnesses.[6]

My wedding day also marked the opening of the show, *George Washington Slept Here,* and following the show we attended a party for the cast and crew. Jim Bonner, Director of the show, caught my eye from across the room. He waved and worked his way briskly through the crowd.

"Hi Jim," I said.

He grabbed my shoulders. "Marilyn. You were something out there. Our next production will be *Born Yesterday*. We'd like you to play the lead role. What do you say?"

It happened just like that. For a brief moment, mixed emotions ripped through my body and thoughts raced through my mind. I wanted to shout with happiness but also cry with disappointment. Being offered the Judy Holiday role on stage in Caracas at the Teatro Nacional was the dream of a lifetime; a golden opportunity if I'd been building my resume or portfolio for Broadway. Had the offer been made a week earlier, I'd have grabbed it.

I was graduated from Hofstra University in New York, May, 1951.

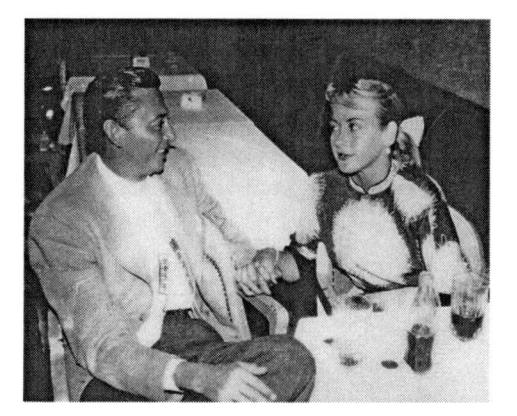

Frank and I enjoy an evening date. I was saying, "I don't like to have my picture taken."

Marilyn and Frank

Frank and I married October 5, 1951.

But not now. There was no option. I alone had determined my destiny. Frank had proposed. I said yes. We married. I selected my future; not school, not journalism, not my name in lights on Broadway, but the wife of Captain Frank Lazzari, a Venezuelan bush pilot. We'd live in a home in Ciudad Bolivar—often referred to as the last outpost on the frontier.

As Bonner turned away, Frank squeezed my hand and I knew I'd made the right choice. Once we told Jim we were married and I'd not be available to play the part, our secret elopement was no secret anymore. The next day, it exploded in the newspapers.

I never thought about my name in lights again.

Chapter 3

Getting Started

Dear Marilyn   **October 21, 1951**

    The news of your marriage came as a terrific shock to us. We were stunned. It took a few days of hard concentration for us to believe it was true. We know you are impulsive and unpredictable, but never thought you would do such a thing as get married without at least telling us of your intentions.

    In reading over your letters, I notice you had been going out a great deal and having a wonderful time, but never dreamed you were falling in love or entertaining the thought of getting married. Had I written to you immediately after we received your letter, this letter to you would have been quite different. Time is a great healer and daddy and I are beginning to get over the shock.

    The problem, if there is a problem, belongs to you and Frank, and we do wish you every happiness. We have a deep hurt in our hearts because you didn't take us into your confidence. You didn't even take your sister into your confidence. We all love you deeply. Arline and Bill felt greatly responsible for you as we had let you visit with them. Had it not been for them, we would not have consented to your leaving the States. This letter is not intended to be a lecture, but . . . . tomorrow, daddy and I will be married twenty nine years, when we say we wish you and Frank the same good luck, the lasting love and the many years of happiness together, you know we are wishing you the very best kind of married life.

    We hope you visit us in New York when you come to Miami on business. Daddy and I will welcome you and Frank to our home. We'll get to know him and realize more fully that we have added another son to our family. It would be wonderful to see you both. It's disquieting not knowing where you are and what you are doing. With our very best wishes and all our love,

Very devotedly, Dad and Mother.

I appreciated Mother's and Dad's comments. I loved my parents so dearly. I asked them to forgive us. In a letter to them I wrote, "I found in Frank everything I hoped for in the world."

During the first few weeks of our marriage, it was all fun and games; long walks at the beach, parties with friends and families, evenings dining in fine restaurants, dancing—lots of dancing—and drives in the mountains surrounding Caracas. We had no real honeymoon, but every day was more romantic than the one before.

Little by little, Frank started to include business calls during our outings. Before long, he was the nine-to-five President of AEROVEN, doing what he had to do to get his air taxi service—with no aircraft—off the ground. Overall, the work was tedious. Usually, it involved the Air Ministry where he logged many hours trying to obtain the AEROVEN license and permits.

"There's so much paperwork, red tape, and time waiting to see people. They say it will take a year before the commercial license is issued. A whole year, Button!"

He also met with representatives from a variety of companies in smoke-filled rooms trying to nail down contracts for his air service. Some of those episodes were little better than putting in time at the ministry. "But I'm learning and getting a lot of experience."

Despite having two partners, all responsibilities fell to Frank. One partner, Amadeo "Shorty" Ramirez, was an engineer who worked in Caracas for Frank's brother, Armando, called Do. He was an investor in AEROVEN and a member of the AEROVEN Board of Directors. Julio Rojas, the other partner, was an engineer and a pilot. He also served on the Board. Both were Ecuadorians and spoke English. Julio, however, still lived in Ecuador with his wife and children. Do was an important advisor to Frank and to the company.

Frank and his partners decided the air service should get off to a fast start with two or three Cessna 170s; a powerful, six-cylinder 145 horsepower engine, low maintenance plane, and spare parts available in Caracas. A strong and durable aircraft, it could withstand the stress of landing on unpaved airstrips which were far more numerous than paved strips in the interior. Frank took the first step when he met with the Cessna representative in Caracas, John Bogart. In the old days, both had been pilots on TACA. Working with John, an American, was one of Frank's most productive activities in Caracas. When I met John, I liked him right off. He suggested Frank look into used aircraft in Florida, and also talk with the Cessna people in Wichita, Kansas. "Explore all options, Frank. Should you decide to buy from me, I'll make you a nice deal." He cocked his head, "If you can't get your aircraft licensed before a year, why do you want to buy planes now?"

The movers and shakers of AEROVEN. Left to right, Frank's brother Armando (Do), Marilyn, Frank, AEROVEN partner "Shorty" Amadeo Ramirez.

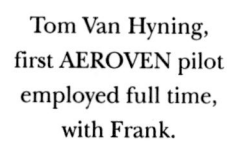

Tom Van Hyning, first AEROVEN pilot employed full time, with Frank.

"Have you heard of LEBCA?"

"Sure, Frank. That's an air service with one plane." He chuckled. "An old C-46 that flies cargo between Miami and Venezuela."

"Right. I don't want to lose time, John, certainly not a year. We've got the money, and we're set to go. It took a while, but I firmed up a deal to license my planes with LEBCA." He explained the agreement; we'll pay LEBCA a flat percentage of the gross income earned from all our aircraft. The arrangement will be dissolved when the AEROVEN license is issued. "The rate is high, but I want to get flying before competition moves into the area."

"Sounds good. Stay in touch. My offer holds."

Occasionally, Frank made a trip to Ciudad Bolivar to further develop the base of operations for his air service. His trips there were spontaneous, generated by his activities in Caracas. I knew this temporary situation—here today and gone tomorrow—would change.

He'd return from a trip to CB exhilarated by his accomplishments, and tell me all the details involved with obtaining space in the only hangar at the CB airport, and nailing down contracts with iron mining and oil companies. He confessed interviews with potential lawyers, accountants, and even office personnel were uplifting.

We planned to move to Ciudad Bolivar when a house became available, but a major problem in Bolivar concerned housing; or the lack of it. There were only a few nice cement-block, stucco-covered houses and they were occupied by employees and families of construction and iron mining companies.

"Nice houses in Bolivar will be available soon," Frank said optimistically. "Iron company personnel live in them now, but soon they'll be moving to Puerto Ordaz. It won't be long before we have a house. You'll like Ciudad Bolivar, Button. Trust me."

One afternoon, quite unexpectedly, Frank returned to Caracas from CB. He burst into Arline's apartment, hugged and kissed me, and blurted out his good news. "Pack your bag, Button," he said, "We're going to the States. To Miami. Going up to buy a plane or two." He put his hands on my shoulders. "Button, so much has happened! Julio arrived in CB and we signed a contract with Orinoco Mining Company (OMC). And then—I can't even believe it—we hired our first pilot, Tom Van Hyning. He's an American from Ohio and flew for the Army Air Force Intelligence in Paraguay during WWII. What a great catch. And his fiancé is also an American. You'll feel like you never left home. By the way, Julio's wife is American, too. Hey, I'll feel like the foreigner!"

"What about Miami?" I asked.

"Yes—We'll drive to Maiquetía tonight. I don't know exactly when we'll leave for the states, but it'll be soon. The plane will be at Maiquetía tomorrow—or the next day."

"What plane?"

"I'm getting ahead of myself." Frank lit a cigarette and explained a representative from LEBCA cabled him in Ciudad Bolivar and said their cargo plane—the C-46—was on its way from Miami to Maracaibo. "As soon as I heard that, I hopped on the LAV (LINEA AEROPOSTAL VENEZOLANA) noon flight, picked up my car in Maiquetía, and here I am. I could hardly wait to tell you. When the C-46 finishes unloading cargo in Maracaibo, it'll fly to Maiquetía. After it unloads cargo there, we'll board it and fly to Miami."

"Whoa—I've got to pack for Miami?"

Hearing all the commotion, Arline made her appearance. "Welcome home, Frank. How's it going?"

"We're going to Miami," I answered. "We're going to buy airplanes."

"And," Frank continued, "after we finish our business in Miami, Button, we're going to New York. I want to meet your folks, and I want them to meet me."

"WOW!" I shouted again.

We three were still chattering excitedly when Bill came home from his office. He'd walked into the middle of mayhem, but after he got the gist of what was going on, he asked, "Whiskey Sours all around?"

Frank raised his glass in a toast. "And here's to going to CB together, Button, as soon as we get back from the states."

"What are you saying?"

"I'm full of good news! I met an American couple in Bolivar. Madelyn and Carlos Freeman. You'll like them a lot. They want you to come with me to Bolivar when we get back from the States. We'll stay at their house until we find a place of our own."

After dinner, Frank and I packed our bags, then kissed Arline, Bill, and Vickie goodbye.

"Would you get a few things for me when you're in Miami . . . or New York?" Arline asked as she handed me a list she'd quickly scribbled. I assured her I would.

Then we made the rounds of Frank's family, said adios, collected their shopping lists, and, at his mother's house, he exchanged his Riviera for his old two-door, black Dodge coupe that had seen better days. We'd park it at Maiquetía.

As we drove the treacherous road over the mountain from Caracas to the Caribbean coast, each of us thought about the trip ahead. Frank would say something about the planes he wanted to buy and I'd say something about the suitability of my wardrobe.

We checked into a hotel in the resort town of Macuto near Maiquetía Airport and the next day, visited Jesús and China Indriago (pronounced hay-soos and cheena), Frank's friends, who lived in a charming cottage near the airport. Jesús was a pilot on LAV. He flew four-engine Lockheed Constellations between Maiquetía and New York. Because China's parents lived in CB, we knew we'd be seeing them often. At last, I had friends in Venezuela.

The next day, Frank received a phone call from someone at the LEBCA office in Caracas. "This is it, Button," he said. "We're on our way! The plane is flying from Maracaibo now. It'll arrive in the afternoon."

We piled our luggage in the car, sped to the airport and waited for hours for the arrival of the C-46. Sitting at a table on a veranda watching planes take off and land, I didn't mind the wait. I looked across the single runway to a small ridge and the Caribbean Sea beyond to the horizon. I squinted my eyes, trying to see the U.S. Of course I couldn't, but that didn't stop me from searching the horizon.

In the late afternoon, the C-46 landed and taxied to an area near the terminal reserved for cargo planes where ground crews waited to unload the cargo and service the aircraft for its return flight to Miami.

Frank drove across the tarmac to the plane, jumped out of the car, and briskly strode toward the man who'd climbed down a ladder attached to the plane's doorway and who seemed to be in charge of everything. Boyish looking, the man was slight of build with black wavy hair. He wore blue jeans, rolled at the cuffs, and a blue and white checked shirt. He looked tired, but his pleasant countenance radiated. As Frank walk toward him, he took a few steps in Frank's direction, smiled and extended his hand. Introductions were exchanged. The man in charge introduced himself as Jack Perez, the pilot and aircraft owner. Then a giant of a man joined the group. Thrusting his large hand forward to shake Frank's, he announced with a pronounced southern drawl, "and I'm Bill Murphy. I fly with Jack. Copilot."

Small talk followed until the big guy asked if anyone would like to eat a side of beef.

With the unloading of cargo and the servicing of the C-46 under way, we four went in Frank's car to a restaurant overlooking the Caribbean for dinner al fresco. For the most part, I listened rather than spoke. I had so much to learn. Jack was a partner in LEBCA. He owned his plane and also paid the owners of the LEBCA license a percentage of his gross income from flights in Venezuela. The men talked—business, business, business.

"Setting up a flying service in CB? Single-engines? That's a heavy assignment. Bush country," Jack commented.

Frank explained his vision for AEROVEN: a bush flying service with emphasis on passenger safety and comfort, a top grade mechanic in charge of maintenance, and an efficient administrative staff. He would seek reliable pilots who would value and honor Frank's standards which ranged from textbook flying to wearing uniforms. Frank and Jack agreed these requirements did not fit the profile of the colorful pilots already flying the bush.

Likeable fellows, all experienced pilots, they'd fly for pay when they needed money, but most of these adventurers were more interested in finding gold and diamonds. They'd fly passengers and cargo when they needed money. Both Frank and Jack knew these footloose and fancy-free legends. Most had flown for TACA. They talked about Sam Fales, Charlie Baughan, Rafael Romero, and Whitey Dahl, although Dahl had died flying near Hudson Bay, Canada. Of course, they talked about Jimmy Angel.

A smile crossed Jack's face and he raised his eyebrows. "Frank, you're going to restrain that herd?"

"Maybe not *them*," and he laughed. Frank agreed he'd have to search long and hard to recruit pilots who would accept his standards, but clearly, AEROVEN AIR SERVICE would be taken seriously.

Jack said he looked forward eagerly for the operation in Ciudad Bolivar to get started. He believed his business out of Ciudad Bolivar would be greatly enhanced once LEBCA had a permanent presence there. He was already flying contracts to haul drums of diesel fuel to Paraitepui near the Brazilian border, and live cattle from Miami to one of the largest ranches south of Ciudad Bolivar, *Hato La Vergareña*, owned by cattleman, Horacio Cabrera.

Jack asked one thing of Frank. "Keep your nose clean. We all have a lot riding on the LEBCA license right now. To survive, we must be in line with rules and regulations. We don't want the Air Ministry to ground us even for a day. I know you understand."

At one point, Jack turned to me and, after some hesitation, asked, "Have you been to Ciudad Bolivar?"

"Not yet," I replied. "I'm looking forward to it." He simply nodded and smiled. "Well, are you ready to fly to Miami?"

"*Vamanós*" (Let's go), Frank replied.

We returned to the airport.

In the tropics, twilight quickly fades to darkness and brightening the black of evening were the colorful airport ground lights that lit the runways and taxiways. Frank explained the blue lights designate taxiways, white lights indicate active runways. Green lights are at the beginning of the runway, and a series of red lights mark the end. "That's enough for your first lesson in airport ground lights."

Silhouetted against the backdrop of color and in the stillness of the quiet early evening, the C-46 looked huge and ominous. I commented about the size of the plane. "Its wing span is 108 feet," Jack said, "and its length . . . about 76 feet. Because there is a rear wheel, the nose is almost 22 feet above the ground.

49

That's taller than a two-story building." To be part of Frank's world, I had to learn about aircraft and understand the language pilots speak.

Built to carry freight and troops in its capacious fuselage, the C-46 had few windows. During World War II, the Curtiss-Wright C-46 Commandos performed as transport planes and made a notable contribution to the success of the supply operation over the Himalayas or "hump," the name given by American airmen who flew the mission. They transported war material to China from India after the Japanese captured Burma and the Burma Road. While some of the C-46's had been operational in Korea between 1950 and 1952, others were sold as surplus.

Jack's plane had been surplus.

To board the C-46, I climbed a ladder to the oversized doorway. Once in the plane, I turned to the left, and a dim overhead light lit my way up the steep incline to the cockpit where there was just room enough for us four. Frank and I occupied an upholstered bench with arm rests behind Jack and Bill. The windows in the cockpit extended almost to the floor, and so high above the ground, trucks' lights were far below.

Bill Murphy had filed the flight plan. Now he sat in the right seat using a small flashlight to illuminate a preprinted checklist held in a clipboard balanced on his right thigh. He began the required preflight check as the oversized door slammed shut. After the checklist had been completed, Jack switched on the two massive 2,000 hp Pratt and Whitney 2800 radial piston engines, first one then the other. The engines kicked over, sent out puffs of smoke, coughed, and then caught on. Jack checked the magnetos, studied the other instruments then pushed the throttles forward. The P&Ws churned. Faster . . . Faster . . . Louder . . . Louder. He held the plane from moving forward by standing on the brake pedals. The C-46 shook violently as Jack revved up the engines. He talked with the tower and Bill continued checking RPMs, oil pressure, fuel, hydraulics, flaps, ailerons, rudder, and elevators. On and on he checked numbers on one dial then another. Jack continued to stand on the brakes.

The Pratt and Whitneys went even Faster . . . Faster . . . Faster . . . Louder . . . Louder . . . Louder. I thought they would explode.

With everything operating properly, Jack eased back on the throttles. Over the lessened roar he said, "There's a lavatory in the rear of the plane. But—ah—ah—be very careful if you go back there. A truck backed into the plane when cargo was being off-loaded at Maracaibo today. There's a big hole." I decided I would not have to use the lavatory until we reached Miami. Frank made the same decision.

Jack eased the throttles forward and worked the brake and rudder pedals to steer the plane. Each pilot has a set of pedals, pressing the top of them works the brakes, while pressing the bottom works the rudder attached to the vertical stabilizer in the tail assembly of the plane. The rudder controls the direction of yaw in the air and the direction of the aircraft on the ground. Jack's feet, moving on the pedals, reminded me of a well-rehearsed tap dancer as he slid his feet from the tops to the bottoms of the pedals as needed to steer the plane. The C-46 rolled, vibrated, and slowly bounced along the taxiway to the head of the runway where it stopped behind yellow stripes on the pavement. He checked his flight controls and ran up the engines one more time. Dark outside, the cockpit was illumined only by the low wattage green and yellow lights cast by the instruments. Phosphorescent, many of the dials glowed.

I'd never before been in the cockpit of a plane preparing for takeoff. I was awed at the activity prior to departure; talk with the tower was almost continuous.

Bill and Jack together pushed the throttles forward smoothly, and the plane rolled down the runway, lumbering and straining to gain speed, bouncing and vibrating and shaking the whole way. The ear-splitting noise level in the plane's unfinished metal interior grew louder as the plane rolled faster. Through the windscreen (windshield), I saw nothing but dark sky until the tail lifted and the nose lowered and I saw the red lights in front of us where the runway ended and the ocean's darkness began. Together both men pulled back on the yokes and the plane lifted, its nose pointed upward. We were airborne and climbing. Finally, at the desired altitude, they adjusted the throttles, pushed and pulled knobs, flipped switches, and cranked handles on the ceiling.

The rattling stopped, and the only sound was the loud, monotonous drone of the perfectly synchronized Pratt and Whitneys. Briefly, through the right side windows, I saw streetlights and hotel lights in the coastal resort of Macuto. House lights twinkled and car headlights cut swaths through blackness. The plane banked steeply to the left, the lights vanished, and everything was dark. We'd completed our turn and now over the Caribbean, we headed north to Miami. I shall never forget my first takeoff from the cockpit in a C-46.

The uneventful flight proceeded according to the manual. Jack gave me a headset and I listened to Frank Sinatra records being played on a radio station somewhere. I dozed, off and on, until the beginning of the plane's descent brought me back to reality. We began to see the bright lights of Miami and Miami Beach. For Frank, it was a dazzling introduction to the U.S.

A smooth landing, Jack greased it on. He cut back on the throttles, danced on the pedals, and the plane slowed to a gentle stop near a hangar, about seven hours after we'd departed Venezuela. Jack shut down the engines, and turned to Frank. "Welcome to the U.S." Then he turned to me smiled and said, "Welcome home."

Chapter 4

"Mother, Dad, Meet My Husband, Frank"

Dear Arline and Bill   **December 14, 1951**

What a whirlwind trip! We visited dealers of used planes. What thieves!

We'll be going to see Mother and Dad in New York when our work here is finished.

I've met interesting people, but none more fun and helpful than Ruth and Mickey [our cousins]. Frank became quite ill, and they insisted we move out of the hotel and into their home in Coral Gables.

We were also running out of cash, so we borrowed money from them. Mother will have a fit when I tell her.

Ruth and Mickey met Jack Perez and Bill Murphy and went out to the airport to see the C-46. Jack invited them to come to Venezuela with him, anytime.

Wouldn't that be neat if they did? Everyone loves Frank.

Love you and will see you soon, Marilyn

Frank contacted Miami dealers in used aircraft and made appointments to see them. So anxious to make a sale, they fussed and fluttered around us as though Frank were Howard Hughes and promised they had just the right plane. Frank saw through their deceit. But me? I had lived a protected life. In only a few weeks, I'd transitioned from college co-ed to young matron and had my awakening—my renaissance! When I married Frank my whole world changed and I began learning about airplanes and the people who fly them. Now I was learning about the people who sell them.

After Frank exhausted the list of contacts he'd brought with him, he went to the "high-tech" source for information in the fifties; ads in newspapers and magazines, yellow pages in telephone books, and newsletters made available by flying clubs.

With the road map spread on my lap and Frank behind the wheel, we drove to airports in Southeast Florida, near and far. We saw every aircraft advertised as a good plane—some just needed a little work.

Frank wanted to be thorough in his research before making the final decision whether to purchase a used plane or a new plane. We took our time and studied every offer so that we felt secure in Frank's ultimate decision to buy a new Cessna 170. Ordered directly from the Cessna factory in Kansas, delivery of the new plane to Florida would be in two weeks.

Though we'd been in Florida two weeks, we'd not enjoyed the lush Florida landscape pictured on post cards, or strolled hand in hand along Miami's white sandy beaches bordered by tall swaying palm trees and high rise hotels. Its colorful night life also remained to be savored.

Now it was time for our second mission—to go home to meet Mother and Dad. Letters from home sounded okay—just okay, but the face to face show-down between us newlyweds and the dear parents we had ignored when making one of the most important decisions of our lives loomed only hours away.

Both of us, feeling anxious about the upcoming encounter, boarded the airliner and said little as the plane took off for New York. Then we heard an announcement on the speaker. "This is the captain speaking." Frank tilted his head. "We have reached our cruising altitude and we'll be reducing our speed. The sound of the engines will change. It'll be much quieter. Here we go." Everyone listened and heard the change. "It's just like when you shift your car. Thanks for flying Eastern and enjoy your visit in New York."

"That's really something," Frank said.

"What?"

"Alerting the passengers to the change in the sound of the engines. We never did that on TACA. It's a nice touch. Without a warning, the change in the sound of the engines might scare the dickens out of someone. We should do that on the Cessnas when we reach cruising altitude and adjust the RPMs."

Frank ordered cocktails to settle our nerves in preparation for the meeting with my parents. The moment of truth fast approached.

"Frank, they'll love you, I know," I said and held his hand.

"I think you're more nervous about this than I," he replied confidently. Suddenly, awe-struck by the sight of New York City as seen through the plane window, the objective to buy an aircraft took second place in the order of importance. "The buildings, the bridges. Look. Just look. The Empire State Building." He eased back his chair and said, "Phew. What a sight."

"You okay?" I asked.

"That was great, Button. Now, the next thing is for you to calm down."

After the plane landed, taxied and stopped near the gate, we gathered our things from the overhead rack and waited for the door to open.

We were first to exit the plane and halted on the platform at the top of the stairs. "There they are," I whispered. I wanted so much to run to my parents but hesitated. My heart raced with anxiety. Frank put one arm around me and waved vigorously with the other. That and his warm smile broke the ice.

We ran down the stairs to open arms and the four of us embraced and kissed.

"Welcome to the family, Frank," Dad said. "So long as you take care of our little girl, we'll love you." Everyone laughed.

"Don't worry about that. She's my little girl, too."

Easy as that.

It was joyful when Frank, Mother and Dad met.
They became good friends.

Eight perfect days with my parents at their home in Garden City on Long Island followed. Right away, they liked Frank and enjoyed entertaining and introducing him at parties hosted for family, friends and neighbors. Everyone found him enchanting and my Aunt Gertie, who'd been known to be a flirt in her younger years, pulled me aside and said, "I can see why you fell for him fast. I would have done the same."

He sang "Vaya Con Dios" and accompanied himself on a borrowed Spanish guitar. But he really captivated his new friends when, using a burgundy taffeta bedspread as a matador's cape, he showed how bullfighters spin and twirl and "cape" the bull. The burgundy bed spread splayed out and the people applauded. After one guest shouted," Ole," the others joined and his performance went into Mother's diary as a highlight of the evening.

A few days before our return to Florida, my parents invited us to spend an evening in the city with them and reserved a suite at the Pennsylvania Hotel across from the famous Pennsylvania Railroad Station. Frank remembered the internationally famous Glenn Miller tune, "Pennsylvania Six Five Thousand," and didn't believe the number was actually the hotel's working phone number until he tried it and the call was answered by the hotel operator.

Blue Skies, Green Hell

Frank relaxes at Mother and Dad's home.

The night before our big evening in the city, Frank delightedly accepted Dad's invitation to go with him the next morning to his office in New York. They traveled the thirty minute trip on the Long Island Rail Road, riding practically through people's back yards in Queens and through the tunnel under the East River to the city. They arrived in Penn Station and walked downtown to Dad's office. For Frank, the whole madcap scene boggled his senses. He'd been to Europe often, but nothing, he said, compared to a day in "the city" as we locals called our home town. Frank found electrifying the sounds of blaring horns and the yelling of taxi drivers in many languages at everyone—at no one. People walked fast and talked fast. By the time he and Dad arrived at Dad's office, Frank had never heard so much noise in all his life. He spent half the day meeting dad's friends and associates who were curious to meet the Latin who'd swept little Marilyn off her feet.

At about one o'clock, Dad received a phone call from Mother telling him we had arrived by car at the hotel. Frank told Dad he'd walk to the hotel and meet us there.

Caught up in the excitement of the city, Frank wanted to be part of the busy and clamorous street scene that had already carried his senses to new heights. Later, he recounted how he strolled along Broadway and followed his nose to the inviting aroma of something being cooked by a street vendor. The bright yellow and blue striped umbrella and chrome cart, a familiar sight to New Yorkers,

55

caught Frank's attention. Although a dinner later in the evening awaited him, he couldn't resist the Sabrett hotdog with sauerkraut and heated roll offered by the vendor who wore an oversized white apron and white overseas cap.

Mother relaxed a while and then did some shopping in New York's upscale department stores while Frank and I toured some of the city's most exciting attractions.

The city basked in the brilliance of its blue and cloudless sky. From the open Observation Deck high atop the Empire State Building, we could see forever in all directions. "That's Long Island, over there," I said and pointed toward the east. Looking south, I said, "See the tall building that looks like a tower with a large clock on it? That's Dad's building—where you were today. And over there. See the Hudson River and Statue of Liberty in the harbor?"

At our feet, world famous buildings radiated energy and streets, choked with traffic, teemed with excitement. The tooting of the ubiquitous horns from automobiles, trucks and buses provided the background music.

Mother arrived back at the hotel first and we closely followed, Dad was last but in time to order wine for the first of many toasts for good luck and much love that prevailed all evening.

We changed our clothes and went to the Cafe Rouge in the Hotel Pennsylvania for an evening of dinner and dancing. Frank and I danced to a familiar Latin tune and after we returned to the table, Mother nudged me and whispered, "All the girls here never took their eyes off Frank. He attracts a lot of attention."

"I know all about it. I felt the same way when I first saw him." I giggled as I recalled our meeting at Olga's cocktail party. Was that only two months ago?

A couple of days later, we kissed Mother and Dad goodbye at the airport. Torn by the separation I thought my heart would break. Too many goodbyes.

"Well, honey, when are you two coming back?" Dad asked.

"Please, Dad, we haven't even left yet." He hugged me one more time.

"Take care of our little girl," he again instructed Frank.

Our visit ended too quickly, but we had to return to Florida and then to Venezuela, so far away. A river of goodbye tears at the airport washed away all uncertainty any of us might have had. As much as my parents loved Frank, he felt the same toward them.

The Cessna arrived in Miami a day or two after we did. Disassembled and loaded on board a cargo plane, it was ready to go. After another day, Jack called and said we'd be leaving that night. We'd not had the time to walk hand-in-hand on Miami Beach.

We arrived at the airport by taxi as twilight gave way to darkness, and the reflection of Miami's gaudy lights bounced off the clouds. The C-46 seemed black and colossal against the luminous backdrop. In profile, the plane reminded me of a dinosaur.

Blue Skies, Green Hell

Frank and Marilyn enjoy the evening with Mother and Dad in New York City at The Pennsylvania Hotel.

Crates of fresh vegetables stacked high waited to be loaded into the plane. I wondered how anyone could see by the light from the dim bulbs in the interior. Just when I thought another box would never fit in the fuselage, a truck loaded with crates of cabbages and boxes with little holes in their sides backed up to the over-sized door. Cargo handlers on the truck handed the boxes to other men in the plane who stacked and secured them in place.

I circled the plane with Frank. He stopped to look at the tail wheel. "Does that tire need air?" I asked.

"That tire, Button, tells me this ship is overloaded."

The C-46 had a full load of cargo and a full load of fuel. That's heavy.

Jack, a copilot named Ray, and Frank, all in raised voices, discussed the apparent overload of the plane. Jack surprised me by being somewhat cavalier. "This is routine, Frank. After we burn off some fuel, it'll be okay." I remembered Jack cautioning Frank about keeping his nose clean and not straying from rules and regulations.

At last, Jack gestured for us to get aboard the over-loaded plane and prepare for our flight over the Caribbean to Venezuela. The flight plan included a stop at Aruba where some of the cargo would be unloaded. Another pilot, deadheading to Aruba with Jack and Ray, occupied the padded bench with armrests in the cockpit behind them.

Inside the plane, I saw an old mattress with soiled ticking squeezed into a space between the bare structural framework on the left side of the fuselage and the boxes piled to the ceiling that filled the rest of the fuselage. The mattress was tucked under the plane's one window forward of the large door. That's where we'd sleep, kneel or sit cross-legged Indian style for the duration of the flight.

Jack boarded the plane last. He tugged at the over-sized door and it slammed closed. "We won't have trouble taking off," he told Frank as he squeezed by him. "I've requested the longest runway." He stepped over me. "Anyway," he said, "you know it's as much about the center of gravity (CG). The weight and balance." He continued into the cockpit and closed the door.

"What'd he mean?" I quizzed.

"There's a center of gravity in every plane. That's the point where the entire weight of the plane is said to be concentrated. Usually where the wings intersect the fuselage. It's all about weight and balance and aircraft stability." He explained that if more weight is behind the CG, the plane would be tail heavy and have difficulty taking off. "You wouldn't want a plane to be nose heavy either." He grimaced. "We could throw cargo out the door if we can't gain altitude," he joked.

One dim light on the ceiling remained lit casting weird shadows on the walls and boxes with small holes in the sides. Then we heard the peeping of thousands of baby chicks coming from the boxes.

One at a time, the large radial P&W engines whined, coughed, and caught on. The puffs of smoke from the engines, visible in the dark sky lit only by airport ground and hangar lights, vanished in the night air. With both men pushing throttles forward, the engines' RPMs increased, the thunderous noise grew louder and in my mind's eye I pictured the cockpit; Ray reading aloud the checklist, Jack standing on the brake pedals while he talked on the radio with the tower, the green light from the instruments creating an aura in the otherwise darkened cockpit.

Finally, all systems ready, they eased back the throttles, released the brakes and the plane crept forward slowly, made a slight turn to enter the taxiway. I imagined Jack pressing his feet on the rudder pedals, and brake pedals as needed, to steer the heavy plane as we taxied and taxied and taxied.

Though I'd only flown with Jack once before, I'd learned so much about airplanes in Miami I felt like an old timer in this business. I sat hunched in a cross-legged position nonchalantly looking out the window and waiting for the big "GO."

The colorful blue ground lights along the taxiway passed under the wings and airport building lights faded behind us. On and on we rolled.

The plane vibrated and rattled just as it had when we taxied to the runway in Maiquetía, only this time I felt the vibrations on the window with my hand, and sitting in the fuselage, I heard the strident noise of the naked, structural steel quite loudly even though the cargo absorbed some of it. Long minutes

Blue Skies, Green Hell

passed before I felt the brakes slow the plane and finally only one brake as it turned the plane 90 degrees. The engines were run up one more time, then eased, then I pictured the C-46 centered on the white line in the middle of the runway, throttles pushed forward, and it was like all hell broke loose as the bucket, as they affectionately called this old plane, shattered the stillness of the evening sky.

All Florida must have heard the C-46 start to roll down the longest runway at the Miami International Airport. Louder . . . Louder . . . The plane labored under its load, straining to gain speed, struggling to lift its tail, and lumbering at what seemed a perilously slow speed. Though I couldn't see them, I imagined the red lights at the end of the runway looming closer and closer. I held my breath. Maybe Jack and Ray did, too, as they pulled back on the yokes. The plane lifted and shuddered. Airborne. The engines urged this clumsy, noisy monster onward and upward.

I watched the city lights disappear below us and then it was dark. We were over the ocean. Just past midnight.

Slowly. Ever so slowly, we gained altitude. Then, as though magically released by earth's gravitational pull, the plane pointed skyward and we began to soar. The overloaded bucket once again won its challenge in the sky. Quietness prevailed as Jack and Ray synchronized the engines into a humdrum drone.

Peep, peep, peep. The cacophony at takeoff had masked the gentle peeping sound of the baby chicks.

Frank stood up and went forward. He returned with two cups of coffee. "Quite a takeoff," he said. "Jack knows his plane, all right."

"I'll say," I replied. "We didn't even have to throw out the cargo."

He handed the cups to me and sat down cross-legged. "You know, this was an expensive venture. Hotels, food, car rentals—wasted days driving around looking at planes that just wouldn't work for us. Add the cost of shipping the new plane! All things considered—it would be more prudent if we just bought our Cessnas from John Bogart in Caracas. He'll cut us a good deal—and he always has a new plane for sale—readily available." He sipped his coffee. "But I did meet your mom and dad and that was worth every cent. They're great people."

Sunlight streaming through the window awakened us. Cumulus billowy clouds, like tall, puffy columns of white cotton candy filled the sky and the plane threaded its way between them, banking gently to the right and then to the left. The motion was smooth and fluid. The plane seemed to be gliding, waltzing. We were far from all mankind's wonders, but close to God's.

The plane began its descent. It continued to dip its wings first to one side then the other and, at last, I saw the turquoise Caribbean and the flat, windswept island of Aruba. The plane landed and after rolling a short distance it stopped and the engines shut down. I put my fingers in my ears and shook my head. I'd not realized the prolonged noise would cause slight temporary deafness.

The large door swung up and out and a blast of hot air rushed into the plane. Flying all night at about 10,000 feet, the temperature inside the plane had been comfortable. The temperature at Aruba was scorching.

"Have a good ride?" Jack asked as we departed the plane.

"Ethereal, Jack. Especially the last hour." I said.

"I like that, too." He put his hands together, palm side down and made the motions a child would make when showing how a plane turns and banks. "We just picked our way through the clouds and had a good ride."

We walked to the mustard colored terminal. It felt good to stretch my legs and everything seemed right with the world. The pilot who had been deadheading stayed behind to supervise the unloading of the cargo. I looked forward to a good breakfast.

There being no other aircraft arriving at Aruba at that hour, the restaurant was not open for breakfast. I told Frank that coffee would be fine. The flight to Maracaibo, our next stop, would be short and we could get breakfast there. Frank gave the waitress our order.

Jack and Ray, frequent clients at the restaurant, simply asked for, "The usual."

The waitress appeared carrying a tray with four cups of coffee and two shots of brandy. Frank and I drank our coffee plain, while Jack and Ray poured the shots into their coffee cups. We paid our respective bills and returned to the plane.

A large number of boxes containing the peeping baby chicks had already been stacked on an open truck and now being off-loaded were crates of lettuce and cabbage that had been stored in the back of the plane and out of my sight during the flight. Considerable cargo remained.

The pilot who had flown with Jack and Ray to Aruba remained on the island, so Frank and I shared the padded bench up front. I felt uneasy about Jack and Ray each having consumed a brandy "Can you fly this plane?" I whispered to Frank.

"Don't worry. They're okay. It's a short flight. We'll be in Maracaibo real soon."

After we landed, Frank suggested we get a scheduled commercial plane to take us back to Maiquetía instead of waiting a few hours for the unloading process to finish. *Great idea.* "Thank you, Jack. We'll see you soon."

We purchased tickets for the flight back to Maiquetía. The plane was a Martin 202 which we boarded by climbing a stairway that dropped down from the inside of the rear of the ship. "Flying coffin," Frank mumbled. "That's what they call this plane."

Blue Skies, Green Hell

How many times, I wondered, can I pray for a safe flight? In the years to come, I'd often pray for a safe flight and most of the time I wouldn't be in the plane.

Within a few days of our return to Caracas, Frank departed for Ciudad Bolivar and I stayed with Arline, Bill, and Victoria. I knew he'd be back soon to oversee the unloading and reassembling of the Cessna after it arrived in Maiquetía.

Ten days later, I could hardly believe my ears when I heard the front door of the apartment open and Frank call me. "Button. Button. Are you home?"

With him was the pilot he'd hired before we went to Miami. Frank introduced me to Tom Van Hyning. Bearing a strong resemblance to the movie star Charlton Heston, he was wearing a cowboy hat at a rakish angle, a wide Indian belt with a large silver buckle and high heeled cowboy boots. He'd fly the new plane back to Bolivar while Frank and I made the return trip in Frank's car loaded with stuff we had brought from the States.

After introductions were made, Tom tipped his hat with his hand in a polite salute and departed for Maiquetía in a taxi he had waiting at the curb. He'd supervise the crew assigned to reassemble the new Cessna and, after Frank tested the plane, Tom would fly it to CB.

"I told Julio you and I thought we should buy our Cessnas from Bogart. It would be financially prudent. He agreed." Frank laughed. "It took us weeks and *mucho dinero* (much money) to not buy a plane in Florida, but order one from Wichita . . . then we paid to ship it here and have it reassembled! It made no sense! I cabled John two days ago. He said he has a spanking new plane for us. We just have to license it. I'll get that done in a few days then Tom will come back and fly the second plane back to CB. We're really in business now, Button. Oh, yes! The Freeman's can't wait for you to come down."

"*Bolivar son. Para los qué salgan*" ("Bolivar, here we are . . . for those who want to leave"). It sounded like a serious challenge.

Chapter 5

On the Wild Side

Dear Mother and Dad   **March 4, 1952**

    This is it! At last! It's almost 10:00 p.m. and I have only a minute to jot a note to you before we leave for CB.
    Yes—we're on our way. As you know, we've been planning to leave Caracas for weeks. I don't know how many times I've written that we're leaving tomorrow, and we didn't leave. It's been tough keeping the bags packed and laundry clean while being ready to leave on a moment's notice.
    I'm so glad I was here to celebrate Vickie's first birthday.
    Looks like we'll make it this time. I'll write next from CB. I love you and I'm so homesick . . . Leaving here and Arline and Vic and Bill is so tough. I'm really on my own now.

Love you all. Marilyn

    I thought the challenge would be living in Ciudad Bolivar. Not getting there. But I learned the trip of about four-hundred miles southeast from Caracas to Soledad on the north side of the Orinoco and Ciudad Bolivar on the opposite shore was not for sissies. I felt a little intimidated by stories I'd been told about marauders or roadway pirates who preyed on lone cars and their drivers who sped through the long black of night to the mighty Orinoco. Rumor had it that notorious highwaymen, well-experienced in the fine art of ripping off motorists, made off with their money, jewelry, car, or whatever they wanted. Frank said the drive from Caracas would take about twelve hours, barring trouble, and most of it driven at night.
    In 1951, despite the Orinoco's length, between 1,300 and 2,000 twisting miles from the headwaters to the Atlantic, no bridge spanned the mighty river that slices through Venezuela and divides the country in half, north and south. All vehicles—trucks, buses, cars—crossed the river between Soledad and Ciudad Bolivar aboard one old ferry that was said to be a converted WWII landing craft. The boat made round-trips during daylight, usually between 6 a.m. and 6 p.m. We departed Caracas near 10 p.m. and, ideally, would arrive at Soledad at 10:00

a.m. the next morning after the early morning traffic crunch at the old ferry had ended.

Upon leaving Caracas, we'd drive south, first over narrow and curvy two lane mountain roads with neither guardrails nor streetlights and then long stretches of unlit straight roads in flatlands called *llanos* (plains). I looked at the trip as being one more piece in the puzzle we'd created when we married. I could count the hours now until we'd begin our lives together in Ciudad Bolivar.

By 9:00 p.m., we had finished loading the car and had enjoyed a light dinner. Then it was naptime. Too excited to sleep, I could only rest a little. While planning the trip, I'd been advised we would not be traveling in the white Buick Riviera, but would be using Frank's old Dodge.

"Once we get through Caracas and over the mountain in the south, there's one road to Bolivar," he said. "It's flat with long stretches of dirt ribbed like a washboard and strewn with rocks. Some the size of your fist. They really beat up a car—on top and underneath. It's not a comfortable trip." Then he added, "Be sure to wear old clothes."

At ten o'clock we were ready to leave. I kissed Arline and Bill goodbye. We all cried.

"Look at it this way, Marilyn," said Bill, referring to my departure to the last outpost, "You'll be a pioneer. Isn't your favorite poem, 'The Explorer'?" He retrieved a Kipling anthology from a book shelf and opened it where a book mark had been placed. "Here," he said, "from your book. 'Something hidden. Go and find it. Go and look behind the ranges—Something lost behind the ranges. Lost and waiting for you. Go.' How prophetic! You'll have an adventurous life. You'll like that."

"Yes. I will. I'll see behind the ranges and find the last frontier—the last outpost," I winked then replied. "And I will like that. I like being a pioneer already."

Similar to the treacherous road that serpentines over the Andes north of Caracas between the city and the sea, the two lane road south of Caracas zigzags up one side of the mountain and down the other. Frank said that in the darkness of the long night the broken white line painted down the middle of the two-lane blacktop road had the same effect as an opiate inducing sleep. I imagined the drive would be lonesome and plenty scary.

Signs of life disappeared shortly after we left the crowded suburbs of Caracas and drove up the mountain. In silence, broken only by sounds of wind rushing by the moving car, we approached an alpine-looking town called Los Teques. At 4,200 feet elevation, cool crisp air blew through tall evergreens.

At each town's entrance and exit along the way, a heavy chain hung suspended across the main road and a National Guardsman signaled us to stop. He'd check our *cedulas* (papers and photo identifications) and enter our names in a logbook before he lowered the chain and allowed us to pass. The routine was repeated all the way to Bolivar.

"Why do they do that?"

"I've heard a few reasons," Frank said and explained that travelers can be warned about road conditions ahead like wash-outs and landslides. Reminding me about the myth of the evil-spirited highwaymen, he said that since everyone's name is in a log book a highway marauder would be quickly identified and apprehended.

"Sounds good," I said.

"Sure, it's a security checkpoint." He looked thoughtful. "Anyway, it's probably a hold-over from an old law still on the books." He plucked a cigarette and a shiny aluminum Zippo lighter from his shirt pocket. He spun the lighter's wheel and a torch flared brightly. He took a draw. "Years ago, travelers were required to go to the police station to get a permit just to leave town. They had to advise authorities of their destination. Each traveler reported to the police station in every town to get clearance on to the next town. In this wilderness where towns are few and far between, it's a safety feature."

Thunder rolled softly in the distance and a light rain began to fall. We paid no attention. "Nowadays," he continued, "some people complain about the law."

"But the law makes sense," I said. "In fact, I like that safety feature. We're out here in the wilds. Alone."

"Damn right," he agreed. "You want the authorities to know you're here. Hell, what if we had serious trouble? We'd need help."

"Are we in the interior now?" I asked.

"Yeah. Sort of." A light rain started to fall. "There are no guards and chains in the deep interior." He chuckled. "No paved roads, either."

The narrow road, cut from the side of the mountain, left an unguarded drop-off to a black abyss on the left while the passenger side of the car hugged a ditch where the road and the mountainside met. Stretches of the road were unpaved although construction equipment here and there indicated road improvement in progress.

The light rain intensified with each mile we completed.

"Is this the dry season?" I asked Frank.

"It is, but sometimes a squall comes up—especially here in the mountains—and as fast as it comes up it goes away. The rainy season usually begins in April," he said cautiously. "This rain shouldn't last."

It wasn't long before I felt the car being slammed by rain. Thunder rolled around us as jagged bolts of lightning slashed through the night sky—dangerous, powerful, and unpredictable.

"This is a squall?" I asked over the rain beating on the car.

Blue Skies, Green Hell

As we exited from a small town, Frank commented, "Look at that, the guard has left the chain lying on the ground. With the rain and all, I guess he doesn't want to come out of his shack to check our papers."

Although Frank had eyes like an eagle, he could not see through the gusts of rain. Driving slowly, he opened his door a few inches, jutted his head out and looked between the open door and car's body—just enough space—to see the road ahead.

Suddenly, he stopped the car. "I can't see a damn thing," he said. "I've got to get out, find out what this is. I've never seen anything like this."

Taking the flashlight with him, he stepped from the car and sloshed in mud as far as the front fender and stopped. After shining the flashlight from left to right, straight ahead, down and then up the mountainside on our right he returned to the dry interior of the car.

"Button. This is bad." He wiped the rain from his face with his handkerchief. "You won't believe it. The front wheels are only a few feet from a complete wash out. The road isn't there. It's been swept away, down the mountainside—into black emptiness. Had I gone a little further, we'd have crashed into a ravine." He exhaled and stared straight ahead watching rain streak past the headlamps. "No one would have found us. We almost got it that time. We have to turn around and go back. Look out your side window. Can you see mud starting to slide from the mountainside?"

"Oh, God. Yes. Rocks, too."

"We've got to move fast to get out of here."

He put the car in reverse and slowly started to back the car up the two-lane road we'd just descended. Even though he leaned out the partially open door, he couldn't see the road behind. A river of mud oozed swiftly downward. He stopped the car, closed the door and cranked the handle to close the window.

"New cars have back-up lights. This antique doesn't, and I can't see out the rear view mirror or out the door, Button. You've got to help. I'll get out and walk next to the car. You drive. Back up very slowly. I'll give you directions."

"Frank, I don't know how to drive this car. It has a manual shift." I raised my voice to be heard over the sounds of the storm echoing through the mountain valley. "I can't do it." He knew I'd always driven a car with automatic transmission.

Frank retrieved his tan raincoat from the back seat. As he struggled into it he said, "You can. You know how to drive the car. Anyway, there's no option. You've got to do it."

"What do you mean, 'I've got to?' I don't know how. You taught me how to drive this old car up and down your driveway . . ."

"And you did very well," he interrupted. "You went forward and backward."

"But I never put it in second or third."

"You won't use second or third now."

65

"So you want me to back up and turn the car on a narrow mountain road that's going up hill behind us."

"You can do it. Only a short distance—a hundred—at the most a hundred and fifty feet. It's a gradual grade—almost none at all. Then we'll be at a turn-around," he insisted.

"I can't."

"You have to do it," he said getting out of the car. "Put one foot on the brake, the other on the clutch, and shift. Remember? And let's get going before a land . . ." His voice trailed off—lost in the sound of the storm. He plodded to the front fender, looked around and sloshed back.

"I'm . . . I'm terrified," I said. My pulse quickened as I moved into the driver's seat. He didn't hear me through the closed window. Grabbing a small handle on the side of the seat and near the floor, I pulled the seat as far forward as possible. I stuffed my folded jacket behind me.

He shouted, "Open the window." I cranked the handle. "Can you drive with the door open a little . . . looking backward?"

"I've done it in a car I didn't have to shift."

Disregarding my statement he said, "Okay, I'll give you directions. And I'll stay right by you. If I drive, you'll have to get out and give me directions. Would you prefer that?"

I wrestled with myself; *I can . . . I can't . . . I must . . . Oh, God.* "Okay, I'll drive." I swallowed although my cotton-coated mouth had no saliva to swallow. My heart beat rapidly. My pulse even throbbed in my fingertips. I tried to remember how easy it had been moving his car in the driveway.

"Okay. Just go slowly. Very slowly. And listen to me. Do as I tell you and we'll make it out of here. Remember, do exactly as I say. It's slippery."

Over the sound of thunder I listened to him call out directions. "Put in the clutch. Shift to reverse . . . let out the clutch . . . easy. Accelerate. Brake. Brake . . . Whoa . . . Slow down."

With the help of God, I safely backed the car up the mud-covered road until we reached a place where the road had been widened to allow cars to turn around. "Now, you'll turn the car around. Clutch and shift into first. Ease forward—slowly—turn your wheels to the left—Stop. Stop. Clutch. Shift to reverse. Now, turn your wheels to the right. Clutch—shift—ease backward . . ." Grinding gears got his attention. "When you shift, Button, use the clutch . . ." He raised his voice even louder. "Use the clutch!"

"Okay. Okay." The car chattered and bucked and stalled. *Damn it.*

I started the engine and turned the car little by little. Back and forth. Back and forth. My arms ached from yanking the steering wheel from left to right and shifting the old car. At last, I had turned it around. Forgetting how to put the car in neutral to let it idle, I just turned off the ignition and the engine stopped. I put on the parking brake with the car facing north and uphill. Greatly relieved,

I slid to the passenger's seat. This episode preceded the days of power steering and brakes, and had been a very real struggle for me.

The rain never let up as we backtracked, weaving our way around fallen trees, rocks and through mud to the guardhouse outside the town we'd passed through earlier. Frank stopped the car. Again, he saw no guard on duty and the security chain lay covered in a sea of flowing mud. I trembled. Cold and scared, I didn't want to be alone, so I followed Frank into the guardhouse where we found the guard asleep in his chair. Startled when Frank awakened him, the guard jumped out of his chair and saluted Frank before he realized Frank was no official.

"Señor. Señor," he stammered.

Frank spoke sternly about the washout and our near fatal accident. The trembling guard put his hands together in prayer, closed his eyes and Frank heard him begin to say something about God having watched over us. "*Diós te bendiga*" (God bless you). *Lo siento* (I'm sorry). *Culpa mía* (My fault)." Frightened and shivering, the guard reacted more from fear than from cold.

Frank spoke in Spanish. "Now, go pull up that chain. And stay awake. Do you have a phone?"

"*No funciona*" (Doesn't work).

"When your chief makes his rounds, be sure to tell him about the washout," Frank said firmly, and shook his head in disgust at the terrified guard.

"Poor soul," Frank said as we returned to the car. "He thinks I'll report him to the authorities. I should, you know." He wiped his face with his wet handkerchief. "But I can't. He's terrified as it is." He started the car, put it in gear. "Now we backtrack. I know a cutoff that'll take us back a ways where we can pick up a road to San Juan De Los Morros. We'll be okay."

"I thought we were near San Juan."

"We were . . ."

"Thank God for saving our lives," I said.

"It was a close call."

As we journeyed on, occasionally Frank shook his head. "It just wasn't our time," he'd say and finally, "You were okay back there, Button." We stopped briefly and he removed his raincoat.

"Coffee?" I asked as I reached in the back seat for the thermos.

"Good idea."

Still recovering from our near miss with death, I poured a cup of coffee with unsteady hands and gave it to him. I poured another for myself.

"I knew you could do it," Frank said.

"I was scared, Frank."

We drove away from the rain into fair weather to where the bone-dry land hadn't seen rain in months and on the road you could see a sharp line between the wet and dry surface.

"See? That was just a squall back there," he said chuckling. "Nothing to it."

"I know. It's not the rainy season." I opened my window and deeply breathed the fresh air. "Oh, that's nice." I studied the map. "Where are we?" I asked.

"I don't know exactly where we are. But we're moving and it's not raining. San Juan de Los Moros is about sixty miles from Caracas and we've been traveling four hours." He lit up a cigarette. "This trip is full of surprises." He blew smoke up to the ceiling. "Oh, hell, it could have been worse. We're alive."

In the dark of night, we drove the undulating mountain road with steep slopes and luxuriant tropical growth to the flat plains south of San Juan de los Moros; the Gateway to the Llanos. Population 6,000, San Juan laid claim to being the largest city between Caracas and Ciudad Bolivar.

We had passed through a few small towns and there were not many more between San Juan and the Orinoco River. Most of the interior towns through which we had driven were less than a mile long and perhaps only a few blocks left and right of the main road. Each boasted the standard small town layout that included a Plaza Bolivar, Catholic Church and a hotel with a restaurant of questionable quality. I felt pity for the people who lived in the houses and worked in *bodegas* (stores) all made of clay with roofs of corrugated metal held in place by large rocks.

At night the towns were asleep and very still—aside from the dogs that barked as they hurried to destinations only they knew. Streetlights along the road within the towns provided a soft rosy glow, a welcome break from the long spells of inky darkness in the wilderness between towns. The distances from one town to the next seemed endless. We rolled on for hours.

Daylight and signs of life come early to the llanos south of San Juan, and as the glow of early sunrise tinted the landscape, I saw people stepping out the front doorways of their houses, stretching, yawning and beginning to go about their daily routines. The wide dirt strip between the road and mud structures became a walkway and playground for naked little boys, plainly dressed bare-footed little girls, barking dogs, groups of women carrying laundry in baskets on their heads to nearby watering places, and men sitting around rickety tables drinking coffee. Latin music, even at this early hour, blared from jukeboxes in the bodegas.

"Is this town anything like Ciudad Bolivar?" I asked, cautiously.

"No, it's not like this." Frank answered.

Without warning, we left the smooth asphalt behind and rumbled on to a roadbed of gravel and rocks. Suffocating dirt swirled high over the dry, hard surface, ridged and ribbed like a washboard that crushed my spine for the next hundred miles.

Driving through the storm on the unlit mountain road, Frank's full concentration had been required and we'd barely spoken. Now, because of the racket from the road, we wouldn't have heard each other had we spoken. Except for the bounding rocks flying every which way crashing on and under the car, we rode in silence. The heat was stifling, so we rode with the car windows open and ate dirt, breathed dirt, and coughed dirt. The same fine reddish dirt that thickly covered the car's windshield and headlights, stuck between my teeth and tasted bitter. Inside my head, I heard the grinding of the grit in my teeth. I wanted to spit.

Frank stopped the car, got out and wiped off the windshield and headlights with newspaper. From the glove compartment, he took out two clean white handkerchiefs. After we swished water around in our mouths and spit it out, we drank some to refresh ourselves, then we tied the handkerchiefs around our faces below our eyes. Frank started the car, and we resumed our drive.

"We look like bandits."

"It'll help," he said with muffled voice.

The llanos. This region of tall grasslands, endless and flat, is where ranchers make a living off their land and their cattle. It is the cultural heart of the country. People living here have a quiet and simple lifestyle enjoying local fiestas, lively music, and a dance called *el joropo*. They are a people with few material needs, but are highly resourceful and will survive whatever ordeal or disaster confronts them.

I looked at the map to see how far we had traveled but couldn't figure it out because of our backtracking. It looked as if we'd traveled only a fourth of the total distance to Bolivar when we reached a town called El Sombrero. With Frank showing signs of tiring and the car needing gas, we pulled into a one-pump gas station. A crudely painted sign hung on the door knob. "*Cerrado*" (closed). Frank said, "This is a good place to stop. We'll rest in the car. After the station opens, we'll fill up and be on our way." With the car parked under a mango tree, we slept.

At 8:00 a.m., we filled the gas tank, cleaned the windshield and used the unisex restroom with a hole in the floor for a toilet. Cold water trickled from a rusted faucet. Good thing I had tissues in my pocketbook.

Before getting back in the car, I carefully opened a brown paper bag that had been stashed in the back seat behind a spare tire, and took out two turkey sandwiches, compliments of my sister. We ogled the sandwiches and my mouth watered. Then I bit into one. "I know why they call this a sandwich. It's made of sand." I tasted the sand and heard the grinding of grit between my teeth. "The damn dirt got in the sandwiches—even with all the wrappings. Ugh!" I gave up. I filled my mouth with water from the thermos, swished it around and spat it out on the ground by the car. "The dirt in my mouth is awful." Despite the mouth wash, I still heard the sound of sand grinding between my teeth. I wiped little grains of sand from my tongue with a paper napkin.

We drove at a moderate rate of speed over the road made of red dirt and fist-size rocks as dust, again, swirled around us. Frank squinted to see through the dirt-covered windshield; we couldn't keep it clean. If we slowed, the dust cloud caught up to us, and long before we could see a car coming toward us, we saw its huge red cloud. When we passed each other the rocks flew high and wide and careened down banging on the hood, windshield, and roof. Because the dust in the air was blinding, it was not unheard of for cars to be sideswiped.

Rocks kicked up under the car could smash parts of the undercarriage and exhaust system. No car traveling the road escaped damage. Frank maintained a steady speed to prevent the car from skidding. The road was slippery in places where piles of gravel had been dumped on the roadbed to fill potholes and as yet had not been spread by the moving vehicles. To be sure, driving between Caracas and Bolivar was demanding and put you and your car in harm's way. I understood why Frank did not make the trip in his Riviera.

As we continued southward, we encountered few vehicles and the towns were smaller and separated by great distances. The vast country seemed endless.

Morning in the llanos meant the beginning of the day's intense heat. Frequently, we dampened our handkerchiefs with water from the thermoses stowed in the car and wiped our faces and back of our necks, but there was no remedy for the sweltering heat and suffocating dirt.

Then as suddenly as the flying rocks had started, they stopped and dust subsided. Once again we were on a two lane road paved with asphalt. Feeling exhausted and filthy I wondered what lay ahead. Occasionally, we came to short sections of the road that had been covered with freshly spread hot tar as slick to drive on as icy roads on a freezing day in New England.

Frank sensed my anxiety over the primitive towns through which we'd driven. "I can't promise the heat will be less in Bolivar. You'll get used to it. But I can promise you Bolivar is nothing like the places we've been seeing. You'll do fine," he assured me. "You'll make the adjustment, if you want to. That's all it takes."

With the air free of red dirt I looked ahead and saw flat terrain in all directions. Although visible for a prolonged period of time, we seemed to make no progress toward the horizon. An eerie illusion. Occasionally, we'd drive over two planks of wood that substituted for a bridge that spanned a deep gully made by flash floods in the seasonal rain.

We were riding through world-famous Venezuelan oil fields surrounded by rigs that looked like giant antenna-towers and pump jacks—called nodding donkeys—whose arm-like mechanisms rocked rhythmically up and down. Flames belched from the tops of hundreds of derricks burning off the gas.

From time to time, we'd pass an intersection, unguarded and unmarked except for one or two crosses near a pedestal upon which rested the remains of a wrecked auto; a reminder of what speed can do when caution becomes an after-thought. The side roads at the junctions were utility roads used by oil camp workers.

A long stretch of the drive from Caracas to Ciudad Bolivar was on a road bed of rocks.

This ferry at Ciudad Bolivar, the only means to cross the entire length of the Orinoco River, was said to have been a modified American WWII landing craft.

Madelyn and Carlos Freeman. My dearest friends during all my years in Venezuela. I still miss them.

Between El Tigre, heart of the oil country, and Soledad at the river, the road was straight as an arrow for almost one hundred miles except for one slight jog of maybe 40 degrees. The ride was tedious. Even though it lightly smelled of oil, the sun shone through clear air.

We were about an hour away from Soledad when we had a blowout. "I expected this," Frank said, getting out of the car to change the tire. "No trip would be complete without one." While he changed the tire, I stood by and watched, amazed at how calmly he took the setback. He worked and I sweated. It was hot. Very hot.

"What do you think the temperature is?" I asked.

"Fahrenheit? Oh, in the nineties." He stood up. "We measure temperatures in centigrades." He gathered his tools and old tire and threw them in the back seat. "It's early in the day and we're in March. It'll get lots hotter later on." He walked around to the driver's side and stopped short of opening the door. "Maybe you'd like to drive a while?"

"Not really, unless you're tired."

"I'm okay."

We arrived at Soledad in the afternoon. We'd traveled the distance between Caracas and the river in fifteen hours. "Not bad. Sometimes I make the ride in less time," Frank laughed, "but not often."

As we neared the car ferry we stopped at another checkpoint. This time we had to get out of the car, walk through a box of a chemical-laced mixture that looked like mud, while National Guardsmen sprayed our tires with a liquid chemical. The procedure disinfected our shoes and tires in an effort to prevent the spread of *Afstosa* (Hoof and Mouth Disease) to the rich cattle land south of the river.

We parked the car on the old converted WWII landing craft, and as it pulled away from the ramp, we walked to the rusted chain that crossed its stern. My eyes focused on the long flat black-top road over which we'd traveled. Scenes of the trip played in my mind's eye; the driving lesson during the storm on the mountain road, the guardsman who'd neglected to tend the chain at the entrance to a small town, the twisting turning road down the mountain with steep slopes and luxuriant tropical growth to San Juan de Los Morros, the flat llanos, the dirt road with rocks raining down on us, the endless drive through the oil fields. And the heat. We'd made it. It had been a good trip. *I'm a pioneer.*

"Looking back?" Frank said.

"No. No," I shook my head. "Not looking back. Just remembering the ride and the towns, Frank." I replayed the trip for him as I talked about the established small towns laid out in an orderly fashion each with its church, village square—always called Plaza Bolivar—and bodegas; rooted and well-grounded places. They had laws, regulations and history. They were settled.

"Land on the north side is the tame side of the river," he said.

I took his hand and we walked toward the bow. In the middle of the river I caught sight of an enormous rock with carved markings to show the rise and fall of the river's depth.

The swift current pushed the ferry's side as though challenging it to stay its course. Partially submerged tree trunks and branches having floated freely for hundreds of miles from upstream, perhaps all the way from the headwaters in the Amazona Region and Stone-Age Indian country, now smacked the sides of the antique ferry daring it to complete its journey to the opposite bank. Whirlpools spinning deep in the dark tea-colored water invited the boat to come inside, yet there was little disturbance, no more than a ripple as the ferry chugged onward.

I pointed to the far bank and then put my hand above my eyes to shade them from the sun's reflection on the water. "Over there and beyond. That's not settled. That's our land."

"That's the wild side, Button. Are you ready for it?"

"Yes. As long as you're with me."

We stood close together, both facing forward. Silent. His arms wrapped around my shoulders. The river breeze blew my hair back. We watched the river bank and exit ramp draw close and closer. Comfortable and secure in his arms, I wondered about tomorrow; for me, for us. I tilted my head back and looked up at his face; so confident. From that moment I had only Frank to rely on. In that, I felt secure.

On the far side of the Orinoco River I saw Ciudad Bolivar sprawling on a rocky promontory. I saw a large yellow and white cathedral glistening in the dazzling sunlight atop an outcrop. I saw pastel-painted houses with white trim and ornate wooden balconies. I envisioned interior courtyards and fountains reflecting the cloudless sky and midday brightness. We'd crossed the Orinoco into another world, an unknown and mysterious world.

The sky was blue. "Ciudad Bolivar, Button. We're home."

Chapter 6

"We're Home"

Dear Arline and Bill   **March 10, 1952**

So, Ciudad Bolivar is an awful place! Whoever said that was wrong. It's not bad at all. The heat is bad—like New York in the summer. I can get used to it. The section of town near the airport is lovely.

The main road from town to the airport is called Avenida Táchira. It looks like Florida. It's lined with trees. Many houses on the avenida have fences in the front along the sidewalk. The fence is really a series of metal fence posts four feet apart with rows of wire strung from one post to the next, separated by about 10 inches. Flowers attach themselves to the wire and grow. At the fence top the flowers drape and delicately cascade.

The *abastos* (grocery stores) sell canned and frozen foods. So far, I like it here . . . a lot. And the Freemans are wonderful. We love being with them. Life is good.

Much love and miss you, Marilyn

Home. Home. I said it to myself over and over. Frank had said, "We're home." How strange it sounded. In all our planning, I'd never thought of Ciudad Bolivar as my home. No. Garden City was home. Long Island was home. New York was home. The USA was home. Everything north of the Caribbean was home. Ciudad Bolivar, my home?

Frank drove the car off the ferry, up a steep ramp of dark gray slime-covered cobblestones. At street level, he continued on a narrow road with sidewalks barely wide enough for a person to walk then stopped at a blind corner. "This is the old colonial part of town. Dates back to 1764," he said as he shifted the car and started to climb the steep road ahead.

Buildings, constructed almost to the corners, made it impossible for drivers approaching an intersection to see oncoming side street traffic.

Blue Skies, Green Hell

We made left turns and right turns and drove up and down steep hills and passed houses and stores made of a compound, all attached one to another, all painted in pastels and neon bright colors. Some displayed colorful medallions painted on white walls. All were attractive and picturesque. It was quiet yet exciting.

We passed *Los Correos* (Post Office), *talabatería* (leather shop), *zapatería* (shoe repair shop), *librería* (bookstore), *panadería* (bread shop) and the Western Union.

Black ornamental iron grillwork adorned all the windows on the outside while wooden shutters on the inside provided privacy from curious passers-by. The narrow streets and old buildings reminded me of scenes in the Tyrone Power movie, "Blood and Sand," set in old Spain. I even thought I heard clacking castanets, the seductive strumming of Spanish guitars, and the stomping of high-heeled flamenco dancers dressed in long ruffled skirts, black mantillas, and hiding their faces behind lace fans.

A sharp descent took us past a movie house to a small triangular-shaped park with trees and flowers and grass and a small open-air roadside stand with a hand-painted sign in front that said *El Triangulito* (The Triangle) and advertised *arepas* (corn biscuits) and chocolate toddy for sale.

"You'll love it there. I go often. One of my favorite places," Frank said.

"Okay," I replied softly. From its appearance, I doubted I'd like the place, but decided to defer judgment. Bill's final words to me when we left Caracas rang in my head. He'd said I'd be a pioneer living in a frontier town. He'd even sounded envious. Frank had said I'd make it—and make it I would.

Leaving the hilly area of the city behind, we drove on a road straight as a ruler called Avenida Táchira. I looked in awe at a street that resembled those in Florida, beautifully landscaped with lacy palm trees and brightly colored flowers still sparkling with early morning dew. Avenida Táchira ended at the airport. Large houses on the avenue appeared to be old and elegant Spanish Colonials. Attached to the outside of each window was ornate black iron grillwork similar to the famous ironwork made in Seville, Spain. Other houses, however, displayed highly polished hand-turned bars made of mahogany. As we neared the avenue's terminus, a few of the houses looked new—and beautiful.

We also passed a two story school building painted mustard yellow with white trim that had the words, *Nuestra Señora de los Nieves* emblazoned across the frieze. "Our Lady of the Snows," I translated. "They've got to be kidding."

"Our Lady is the Patron Saint of the city," Frank explained.

A traffic circle with an obelisk marked the end of Avenida Tachira and the entrance to the airport grounds. As soon as we entered, I saw the control tower prominently perched atop the terminal.

"Well, what do you think so far, Button?"

"I'm awed. It's all so beautiful." I paused and took a big breath. "And it doesn't look like what I thought a frontier town would look like. Flowers, trees, lovely houses. Even the terminal building is attractive—so tropical." I took off my dust-covered sunglasses and wiped them on a cloth I found on the floor of the car. "Frank, what surprises me most is, well, this is it. This is my home. Ciudad Bolivar is my home. All the time we talked about coming to Bolivar, I never thought about it as home." I sighed and rested my head on the back of the seat. "Now it's hit me."

"And you feel . . . ?"

"I'm okay." I smiled and nodded. "I'm very okay. I know I'll like it. I like it already."

"I have to let the airport folks know we've arrived—and to see if Tom or Julio's here . . . or anyone else I know. Then we'll go to the Freemans." He pulled the car into the circle drive in front of the terminal and stopped under the shade of a large mango tree. "Tom might be in the office. He'd love to see you again. Want to come in?" Frank continued.

"Oh, I couldn't go in and meet anyone looking like this. I'm filthy," I said shaking my head no. "I'll wait here."

"Tomorrow morning, then. I want you to meet all the people here." He leaned over and kissed me. "We'll have a good time in Bolivar."

"Wait. I have a question. Sometimes you say CB. Other times it's Bolivar. And once in a while you say Ciudad Bolivar. What's what? What should I say?"

"Whichever you want. I guess it's best to say CB when you're with English speaking people. But everyone understands . . . whichever." He hopped out of the car. "I won't be a minute," he said and disappeared into the airport terminal building.

Vines with spiky leaves climbed white stucco walls of the quaint airport terminal, and red bougainvilleas, still bathed in dew, reflected the early sunlight. Light breezes that had blown from the west quit and the motionless palm fronds on the trees looked artificial. Birds broke the silence as they sang their morning songs.

The heat made me feel sticky and uncomfortable and sweat began to roll into my eyes and down the back of my neck. Despite the heat, I rejoiced being in Ciudad Bolivar at last and especially on this glorious day that had followed our exhausting trip. I looked up into the cloudless blue sky and thought it looked the same as the blue skies over Mother and Dad's house.

With some of the bounce missing from his step, Frank returned to the car. "Tom's not here," he said.

"He's flying?" I asked.

"No. Tom's just not here." He hesitated then said, "I don't understand. I looked at some files and it seems like the plane hasn't been making very much money." He pensively stared out the driver's window across the parking lot to the east at an aged wood hangar, grayed by the weather and topped by an equally aged large water tower. "I want to base our operation there. In that building. We can rent it, but we've got to make money first." He started the car's engine. "For now, we'll keep the planes in the big hangar over there." He nodded to the lone hangar west of the terminal and drove to it via the tarmac that passed in front of the terminal, an area usually reserved for airplanes discharging passengers. "No planes are due in now," Frank said in answer to the perplexed look on my face. "There's not much air traffic at CB."

We saw the white and red plane parked in front on the hangar's open doors and I nearly had a fit. Painted on the left side of the plane near its nose in fancy red script, I saw, "Shirley B," the name of Tom's fiancé.

"Did you know about this?" I tried to control my jealousy.

"I did not." He wiped his forehead with his handkerchief. "I'll take care of it." He walked to the plane. "At least, it's not nose art. Tom was a military pilot, you know."

We left the airport and drove a few blocks to an unpaved side street left off of Avenida Táchira. "The Freemans live down here," he said.

A cloud of red dust filled the air in and behind our car. "I thought we left the dirt roads behind us hours ago," I said. The dirt stuck in my throat and I coughed.

Most of the houses, made of mud compound or cement blocks, had corrugated metal roofs held in place by rocks on top. The houses were painted in the same colors as those we'd seen in the old part of the city. Palm trees, tropical plants and flowers growing in cans of all sizes dotted grassless yards and lent a winsome touch to the bucolic neighborhood.

"Downtown roads are paved. But outside the city, most roads are dirt," Frank commented.

Driving a couple of blocks to the Freemans' home, Frank dodged dogs running this way and that, chickens sauntering back and forth across the road and a pig waddling down the middle of the road in front of the car as though it had been chosen to lead the way. The only time I'd been close to farm animals was when I sang, "Old MacDonald Had a Farm." I'd never imagined a place where farm animals vied with cars for the right of way.

"This is Ciudad Bolivar, Button. Not really a city. It's pretty, but at the same time a rural place in limbo. Time has passed it by." He stopped the car. "Here we are."

Large fruit trees in the hard dirt front yard protected the Freemans' small cinder-block house from the rays of the sun. A bodega with a wooden shack attached to it stood within a few feet of one side of the house. We parked on the road in front of the house and walked across the front yard to the screen door. Small gray-brown chameleons scampered out of our way and ran up the walls of the house. I halted in the middle of a step. "You'll get used to them," Frank said. "They're harmless. As you walk, stomp your feet. They'll run away. They're in the houses, too."

Frank called through a screened door, "Hello . . . Carlos . . . Madelyn. Anybody home?" In the quietness, I heard birds singing in the trees.

"Coming," answered a female voice speaking English with an American accent and in seconds I saw a smiling petite Madelyn Freeman; blonde hair, snappy brown eyes, perhaps a tad older than I, and a couple of pounds lighter. "Come in." She smiled and graciously held the screen door open for us. "I've been waiting for you."

We exchanged polite niceties, and then Madelyn brought cold drinks on a tray and invited us to sit at the unfinished wooden table surrounded by six handmade chairs, also unpainted, with pieces of cowhide, still with hair, nailed in place for seats. I observed several ashtrays on the table. Beautiful woven Indian baskets had been artfully placed on the wall. Shiny red deck paint covered the cement floor. Two wooden boxes, painted red, had shelves and held books and knick-knacks.

As the cold drink passed over my parched tongue, I felt renewed. We lit cigarettes and a conversation started that would last, with interruptions, for almost seven years. I liked Madelyn. And I liked Ciudad Bolivar better with each passing minute.

I commented on the beauty of the baskets hanging on the wall.

"They're gifts from the *Camaracota* Indians south of Auyántepui in the Gran Sabana. We stayed with them for a while."

"Stayed with them?" I questioned.

"They're primitive but friendly. I learned a lot from them."

During the six months I'd spent in Caracas, I'd longed for friends near my age. Now, in the most unlikely of all places, a frontier town in the Venezuelan interior on the wild side of the Orinoco, I'd met Madelyn Freeman, warm, friendly and American.

Madelyn showed us our room. Just off the living room, it had a blue floral print curtain hanging on a pole across the top of the doorway. Two cots with mattresses and steel springs looked inviting as my bones ached from the long drive. A small lamp placed on a box between the cots provided electric light. Several boxes with shelves were for our clothes and other boxes contained clean towels. The boxes had all been painted in bright colors and the box-tables were draped with colorful fabric. A few hooks on the wall held hangers for our use. Two windows, one faced the front of the house the other faced the side, had matching floral print curtains hanging over them for privacy and to darken the room for daytime siestas.

"You'll probably want to shower and rest a while. The bathroom is down the hall." She gestured toward the rear of the house. "Carlos is out. He'll be back a little later. He's been so anxious for you to arrive. Me, too."

There were no hot water heaters in Bolivar, but a large outdoor water tank on the roof of each house, baking all day in the torrid sun, provided ample warm water. On extremely hot days, water ran from the indoor faucets for several minutes before fresh cool water poured through the pipes.

After a shower and siesta I joined Madelyn in the living room. I wore a light cotton shirtwaist dress. Madelyn wore blue jeans and a white blouse neatly pressed.

Frank joined us and spoke about the plane's lack of income-producing flights. His concern showed heavily on his face. "Got to find out what's up," he said and left for the airport.

The Freemans' maid, who also worked as nanny, brought a blonde haired, blue eyed two-year old into the living room. Smelling sweetly of baby powder, this beautiful, delicate child was covered from head to toe with prickly heat rash.

"This is our daughter, Lilly. She's always like this," Madelyn said despondently, "until we go to Caracas, then the rash disappears. This heat is no good for her. Carlos and I got used to it—you will, too. But not Lilly. Carlos thinks it would be better for her to stay in New York with his mother. But I can't even think about not having her with us. But maybe he's right."

"Hey, what kept you so long? We've been waiting for days," Carlos said as he burst through the squeaking screen door allowing it to slam behind him. He smiled and his squinty blue eyes twinkled. He threw his big tan cowboy hat on a chair, then removed a gun belt with a pistol in its holster and tossed it on top of a red box. I stared at it, a little shocked at seeing the gun. No one I knew on Long Island carried a gun. *I guess it's okay. Frank carries one.*

"I've been waiting for days, too," I replied. His brown hair, prematurely sparse and receding, emphasized his pleasant face and warm smile. "First, one thing then another. I'm glad we're finally here."

"The same thing happens when we go to Caracas. Delays. Always delays. Never know when we'll return 'til five minutes before we leave." He pulled a chair out from the table and sat down. "Tom and Julio have talked about you and we couldn't wait for you to get here. They thought you and Madelyn would hit it off just fine."

"And we have," declared Madelyn, smiling.

"Thanks," I said. "I didn't know what Ciudad Bolivar would be like. Didn't know what to expect. I'm so happy you invited us. Tom and Julio sort of broke the ice for me." I chuckled. "They've been going back and forth between Caracas and Bolivar for a couple of months."

"Where's Frankie?"

"At the airport. He'll be back soon."

Excusing himself, Carlos said we'd talk more later, but first he had to shower. He'd just made a long drive on dirt roads from the home of a diamond miner who lived a few miles outside town. He carried one of the cowhide chairs with him and disappeared behind a navy blue curtain covering the doorway to their bedroom. As he swished the curtain to one side, I caught a glimpse of a beautiful cherry wood double bed and dresser, vestiges of civilization left behind in Caracas and the States.

"When it's terribly hot, like today, Carlos sits on a chair under the shower and reads. He wears a wide-brim cowboy hat to keep the water from getting his book too wet."

Madelyn didn't mind that I giggled. She didn't laugh when she nodded and said, "Oh yes, he's eccentric."

"I think he's got a great idea," I said.

"You'd think we'd get used to the sun and the heat and I guess we do. But we never stop talking about it."

"Are there other Americans here?" I queried.

"We're it," she didn't laugh or smile. She said it in her already familiar matter-of-fact way and gestured with her left hand—fingers together like a paddle. "Until recently there were others, but they've mostly all moved to Puerto Ordaz. There's nothing much there yet. Just iron business and construction and a few houses. But here? CB? Like I said—we're it."

Madelyn came from landed gentry in Snow Hill, Maryland. She graduated from Katherine Gibbs, a fine secretarial school in New York City. Her mother lived in Snow Hill. Carlos' parents were divorced. His father, a Venezuelan, was an eminent engineer and lived in a posh area of Caracas called "Country Club." His mother lived in New York City. Carlos grew up in both locations but attended school in the United States. He was a graduate of the Merchant Marine Academy in Kings Point on Long Island. Following his service as a sea captain, he became a diamond buyer in Venezuela. Carlos and Madelyn met at a horse show in Madison Square Garden in New York in which she participated. It was love at first sight. They married and went to the Venezuelan jungle for their honeymoon and his work.

The long, hot summer had just started and Madelyn said that she didn't wear panties when it's hot. "You get rid of what you can. Wear a dress or a skirt and blouse. That's it. You know, in Venezuela, ladies can't wear shorts or sundresses or anything that might help us be comfortable. But as far as I know, no one has yet said we have to wear underwear."

Whoa. Even though I'd been shocked by her statement, I nodded agreement.

"They haven't caught up with the times," she concluded.

I excused myself and went to my room. Timidly, I started to unbutton my dress, but as I opened the first button, I bashfully glanced toward the window to be sure no one was peeking in. I pulled the dress over my head and placed it on the cot. My bra stuck to my sweaty body. I pushed the bra straps off my shoulders

Blue Skies, Green Hell

and opened both hooks. *Can I really do this?* Phew. It felt so good to pull off the dreadful, sweaty garment. I flung it on the cot. *What a relief.* As I slipped the dress back on, I felt myself blush at my new found freedom—and comfort.

Having finished his shower, Carlos came back to the living room and joined us. "I'll have coffee," he said to Madelyn. "After Frank gets here, I'll switch to scotch. We all will." Madelyn hurried to the kitchen and quickly returned with a cup of black coffee. A fresh pot of coffee was always on the Freeman's stove. Carlos lit a cigarette and started talking about his work that involved buying diamonds which eventually wound up in Harry Winston's in New York.

The afternoon flew by. We talked about many things, from diamond mining to the rigors of the car trip between Bolivar and Caracas. It seemed like we'd known each other for years. Before I realized it, Frank came home.

"Hey, Junior," Frank said reaching out to shake Carlos' hand as he swung open the screen door. Carlos was named for his father, thus the nickname, Junior.

"Frankie. What took you so long? They need you here." He lightly smacked Frank on the back. "Planes don't fly without you."

"You got that right," Frank replied, and as Carlos made scotch drinks for us, Frank told how the plane had not been working, except for flying the contracts. There'd been only a few deposits made to the company's account. He said he'd talked to the airport manager who'd told him that Tom flew up the river often and offered the record to Frank for his review. "Can't get it out of my mind. Tom's paid for 65 hours between ignition on and ignition off—whether he has cash paying passengers, cargo or flying empty. He says he's been flying, but people in the river towns are just not ready to fly in small planes. The plane's hardly earning anything on that river run. Our contract with OMC (Orinoco Mining Company) keeps us afloat."

I set the dinner table and watched Madelyn perform culinary magic on a stove with three kerosene burners.

During dinner, Frank agonized over the lack of business. "It's odd." His brows furrowed. "I arrived a few hours ago and I've already lined up work for two planes for the next few days. Julio should arrive tomorrow with our second new plane. Just in time. If I had another plane, I'd have booked it, too."

"Hey, Frankie, you can use my plane," said Carlos, trying to lighten Frank's burden. Carlos, also a pilot, flew a Cessna on pontoons, not wheels, and said he had about 400 hours flying time. His plane was tied up in the city at a dock on the Orinoco. He flew to diamond mines and landed on rivers. "I'll check you out. It flies differently than planes on wheels. Weight of the floats changes the balance."

Still tired from the long, arduous car trip, we said an early good night, went to our room, and sat on the edges of the cots facing each other. Frank, speaking just above a whisper, said he'd given Tom instructions to fly contract work first, then the route up and down the river and anything else that might come along. "I know I'm only talking about a couple of weeks. But I just don't understand. We want to keep Tom busy. Julio's in Caracas now, picking up the new plane from Bogart. He hasn't flown much, but he has plenty of administrative work to do and contacts to work on." He lit a cigarette, watched the smoke hang heavy in the still air and wiped perspiration from his forehead with the back of his hand. "What do you think?" he asked.

I shrugged my shoulders. "About Tom? I have no idea."

"I hope I'm wrong, but Tom could have been flying passengers and cargo, collecting the money but not depositing it." He eased himself back on the cot and folded one arm under his head. "I want to trust Tom. I like him a lot. He's a fine pilot. Great experience. Been flying since he was 14. I don't know."

"Well, why not ask him? See what he says?"

He snuffed out his cigarette. "I guess we'd better get some sleep. What a day. Happy we're here together?" He didn't wait for my answer. He stripped down to his jockey shorts, folded his shirt and trousers, and put them on a box. He sat on the edge of the cot, leaned across the narrow isle between them, kissed me, stretched out on his cot. "We'll go to the airport together tomorrow. Goodnight, Button." He turned out the lamp and fell asleep before I had a chance to tell him I loved him.

I undressed, put on my cotton shorty pajamas, and went to sleep very quickly.

After breakfast, at about eight o'clock the next morning, we told Madelyn and Carlos we'd be at the airport, and invited them to join us at the patio lounge for the cocktail hour. "I want Button to see the office and meet the people at the airport. Get to know them. I've got a short flight this afternoon. I think Julio will fly back from Caracas today. He's flying the new plane from Bogart. See you later."

Frank and I drove the three minute route to the airport, parked the car and entered the front of the terminal building. "Going to speak to Tom?" I inquired.

"Yes. First thing," Frank answered, pulling himself up tall. "I see Tom's jeep. He's here. He has an early flight."

I followed Frank to the doorway of a small office. He went in and I leaned on the door frame. "Hi, Tom," I said. He was seated at the desk with his feet in soft Oxford shoes propped on the desk's pull-out shelf.

"Hey, Marilyn. Welcome." He didn't stand.

I cast my eyes furtively around the small and dismal office. "Thanks, Tom."

"How do you like the heat? We're only a few hundred miles from the equator and practically at sea level." He seemed friendly.

"I'm okay, though it makes me feel tired. Madelyn says that will pass."

Blue Skies, Green Hell

The small talk didn't distract me from noticing the walls in the office yellowed by age and cigarette smoke, smeared with dirty hand prints and marked by old Scotch tape that had probably been used by a former tenant to hang pictures. An out-of-date calendar hung on the wall behind the desk. The furniture included an old wooden desk stained by splotches of blue ink from ink bottles that must have spilled over. Cigarette burns edged the desk as if the carpenter who'd made it had planned them in his design. A two-drawer metal file cabinet with rust around the bottom and two metal chairs needed paint. Coffee rings on top of the cabinet cried for soap and water, at the very least. A black telephone placed at an angle near one of the corners on the desk next to an old Underwood typewriter, a pad and the stub of a pencil completed the office equipment. A bare light bulb attached to the end of an electric cord hung from the ceiling where sheets of cracked paint peeled and water stains shouted the roof's leaking. One dirty window overlooked the parking lot where a few cars baked in the early morning sun.

Frank flipped through files in the old cabinet. "Plane's been out almost every day but not making money." He closed the drawer.

Hearing the start of a difficult conversation and having more than satisfied my curiosity about the office, I said, "See you later." The electricity between them sizzled and I quickly exited.

Tom's back was to the door so I stayed within ear shot and from time to time peeked in the room. I easily rationalized my eavesdropping—Frank wouldn't have to tell me the story later.

Frank walked to the dirty window and put his Ray-Bans into the glasses case attached to his belt. Leaning one arm on the window sill, he turned slowly and faced Tom. Then, as if to delay the conversation, he pulled a cigarette and lighter from his shirt, fumbled with his lighter, finally lit up. He exhaled a long string of smoke. I felt his pain in having to talk about this matter with Tom. He sincerely liked Tom.

"I'm troubled, Tom. Why do you think we aren't making any money?"

"I guess everyone's been waiting for you, Frank. You're the big honcho around here. You're *El Señor Presidente*. I'm just a jockey." Tom, strikingly handsome, somehow looked sinister and smug. Or was it my imagination? "Frank, I flew plenty of hours and miles—from one airfield to another up and down the Orinoco. The *llaneros* (plainsmen) are not ready to hop into a plane. Not ready to trust us bush pilots in small single-engine planes. They think pilots are Gods with gold braid. That's what they see in the movies——pilots flying big planes and wearing fancy uniforms with gold on their sleeves and caps. I told you. They're afraid to fly in small planes. They'll get used to it in time. I flew plenty of hours, Frank, in an empty plane. Hopefully business will pick up."

At that moment, I saw a well-dressed businessman walking toward the office and correctly presumed it was Tom's passenger. As I strolled away from the doorway, I glanced over my shoulder for one last peek and saw Frank, hands on his hips, staring out the window. It had been a short conversation and had ended abruptly. From my point of view, nothing had been settled and I couldn't conceive of Frank bringing up the subject again.

Seeing his passenger enter the office, Tom lowered his feet, stood up slowly, took his time adjusting his large cowboy hat to its rakish angle and greeted his passenger with a cheery smile. "I'll file the flight plan, and then we'll be off," he said, saluting casually with two fingers and strutting toward the tower stairway.

Frank left the office and caught up to me. I told him I'd eavesdropped on his conversation.

"Button, I can only keep my eyes and ears open. I can't bring it up again." We'd arrived at the airport patio lounge. He scanned the horizon slowly then said, "Maybe what he says is right. Maybe he should be above suspicion." He put on his sunglasses. "I'll take the trip up river. Tomorrow. See what it's like." He took my elbow and guided me to a table.

As we finished our second cup of coffee, we watched Julio land the new plane and taxi to the tarmac in front of the patio lounge.

"FLB," said Frank proudly.

We walked out to greet Julio, spent a few minutes exchanging small talk and a few more looking over the new plane. Like a new car, it had a special smell.

"I've got a flight," Frank said to Julio. "Just down to Cerro Bolivar and back." He waved an envelope addressed to the chief of the camp.

They watched FLA with Tom at the controls taxi past the patio lounge. Tom gave us a one thumb up sign to acknowledge he'd seen us. His plane rolled slowly down the taxiway to the runway and we watched it lift off. "We've got a hell of a lot to talk about," Frank said.

"I have to get coffee and a sandwich. I didn't eat when I fueled up at Barcelona," Julio said. We sat at one of the many weather-beaten metal Cosco tables on the patio. After he called his order of a ham and cheese on toast and coffee to a passing waiter, he asked, "Do I still have my room at the Normandy?"

"Yes. Tom's there, too."

"Good. Good." Julio and Tom had developed a close friendship. Julio ate rapidly and after he dabbed his moustache with a small paper napkin, he stood up. "What are we waiting for, partner? Let's go."

Frank filed his flight plan, and then the two walked away from the patio and headed to the plane. Looking forward to my first long flight in a small airplane, I swung along with them. Frank stopped suddenly, turned to me and said, "Hey Button. Will you stay at the office? Take messages. Answer the phone. You know—I'll be back in an hour or so. And watch for the Freemans. If we're delayed, they may get here before we get back."

"I have a question, Frank."

Julio walked on as Frank turned to me.

Entrance to the Ciudad Bolivar Airport—1951.

Ciudad Bolivar airport terminal with DC-3, the plane of the day, at the lone gate.

Frank and I stand by YV-C-FLA, AEROVEN's first plane.

"I don't speak Spanish perfectly. I'll be nervous—especially on the phone."

"You'll do fine, Button." He smiled.

"Just one question?"

"Sure." He put his hand on my shoulder.

"Sometimes I don't know when to use the word 'lo' or 'le.' Is there a rule?"

He thought a brief moment. "There's no rule. Say whichever you want. The person you're talking to will know what you mean. You'll do fine."

Frank caught up to Julio and they walked to the plane with arms swinging vigorously while I, disappointed, and more than a little nervous, walked slowly back to the table where we had been sitting. I watched them board FLB, start the engine and roll away. A few minutes later, I saw the little plane zip down the runway and take off.

A few people, mostly waiters, luggage handlers and airport workers, loitered around talking and smoking.

I got the willies. *I hope the Freeman's come soon.*

Chapter 7

"Bear With Me"

Dear Mother and Dad   **April 20, 1952**

It's so darned hot. I sweat and can't eat. I don't feel well. Dr. Battistini, a German doctor here, says it's not amoeba but he doesn't know what's wrong. Frank's partner, Shorty Ramirez, says, "Everybody gets sick when the seasons change."

Devotedly, Marilyn

Frank and I were alone in the bleak and sparsely furnished AEROVEN office in the airport terminal building waiting for Julio and Tom to return from their flights. Frank walked to the window that overlooked the parking lot and beyond to the old wooden hangar.

"Business has picked up a lot and I've arranged to rent the hangar over there." He gestured to the old hangar at the end of the parking lot. "We'll move in when the renovation's finished. That won't be too long." He paused. "Ah . . . ah . . . Button, until we can hire someone, will you work for the company? We'll lose business if no one is in the office to answer the phone, book flights, and take messages." He recited things that had to be done regularly. He needed someone to dispatch planes, place orders for spare parts, monitor the weight of the cargo being flown, keep records like engine logs and flying time on the aircraft's frame, watch over the gas supply. The list went on and on. He concluded, "I need someone I can trust. I need you."

"Wow." I wondered if I could do the job. "I want to help, but I don't know much about this business."

"You can do it. You've been helping out in the office for a month—since we got here. You know a lot already. I'll help you get started. Maybe after Martha arrives, you two can share the work—until we can hire a secretary or, better yet, an office manager."

I sighed. "I knew it would happen. I just knew it. Since the day after we arrived here, when I came to the airport, and you and Julio flew off to someplace and left me alone to watch the office. I just knew it." I sighed again. "The job's temporary? Only when you're flying or can't be here?" Seeking reassurance, I reminded him we'd been in Bolivar over a month and we were still living with the Freemans. "Actually, Frank, I like working in the office. It's fun. But we've got to find a house."

While he waited to hear more from me, he tested the lock on the old window.

"Okay," I continued, "I'll work, but only if you can arrange to rent two houses near each other. Maybe even side by side." Morrison-Knudsen, an American construction company operating in Ciudad Bolivar, had leased several small but nicely planned and well-built houses from a local builder. They'd housed their employees, but had recently begun moving them to M-K housing at the Port. Frank knew the right people in M-K and I hoped he'd be able to arrange to rent two that became available.

"It's a deal. You do the office and I'll take care of getting—two houses?" He stopped talking.

"Yes. Side by side"

He looked quizzically at me and asked, "Freemans want to live next to us?"

"Madelyn and I have talked about it. Yes. We four get along swell, and you guys are away so much, Madelyn and I wouldn't be alone. We've seen two houses side by side near the head of the runway. They're empty."

"I've seen those houses. I'll see what I can work out."

And so the office moved from the depressing closet-sized room in the quaint terminal to a renovated old gray wooden hangar next to the parking lot and I went to work. When Frank and Julio were both flying, I did whatever I could to help with the administration and paperwork. Frank set up systems, wrote instructions, made suggestions, and in the evenings he'd answer my questions. Before long I knew my way around his air service business.

One section in the hangar was walled off and—voila—we had an office with carpet on the floor, two clean windows that let the sunshine in, and a window air conditioner installed through the wall. Another part of the interior of the hangar was walled-off and had a door made of cyclone fence with a lock for safe storage of parts, tools, and equipment. A large, colorful sign bearing the company's name, AEROVEN, was painted on the outside wall of the hangar that faced the main terminal's parking lot. Very impressive!

Every day I learned more about the aviation business; I learned how to test the fuel for contaminants and which tools to hand Frank when he worked on the engines. Before the guys took off on their trips, I'd place a box of tissues in the cockpit, open the plane's windows and prepare a thermos of coffee if one had been requested. The company couldn't pay me, but I went with Frank on trips up and down the Orinoco to primitive towns and Indian settlements and into the Green Hell to diamond and gold mines. Best of all, I learned to fly. Now, that's compensation!

Blue Skies, Green Hell

Fulfilling his end of the deal, Frank secured the two houses near the head of the runway. Made of stucco-covered cinder block with front porches, they were only a year old. One was white and the other yellow. Ciudad Bolivar had very little air traffic—a couple of DC-3s departed in the morning, one landed and departed at noon, and two landed in the late afternoon. Other than those few big planes, a few small ones like our Cessnas made up most of the runway activity. The noise wouldn't bother us. Carlos and Madelyn were as excited as we. I wrote to Mother and Dad and predicted everyday would be a party after we were in our houses.

At last, after more than seven months of being married and living with friends and family, Frank and I had our own place where we'd just close the front door, lock out the world and say "go away" to all intruders. Alone. Just the two of us for the first time.

I called it my palace, this little flat-roofed white stucco box with a carport, surrounded by yellow-colored bleached-out dirt, wimpy weeds and no trees. Not protected by guards dressed in waistcoats of black and gold velvet, black tights and purple hats with red feathers or by tall stone turrets or a moat designed to keep out invading armies; this palace was protected by an errant cow, a donkey, and a fence with upright posts and heavy duty barbed wire strung between.

No fine white horses with plumes on their headgear pranced on a regal parade ground to herald our arrival. Instead, cattle wandered down the middle of the road on which we lived, Calle Negro, and up to our front door.

Frank drove us to our houses; Madelyn, the maid, baby Lilly, and me. We'd been cleaning for days and now we planned to put the finishing touches on them before the big moving day. He left us, waved goodbye, and drove back to the airport.

We'd taken a break when first I heard, then saw Jack Perez's C-46 glide overhead. Whooping with joy, knowing it carried my furniture from Caracas, Madelyn and I chased the plane's shadow as it flowed gracefully across the bleached dirt between the two houses toward the landing strip behind our back yards. We watched it land, heard the TEEK TEEK as tires touched the paved runway and saw tiny puffs of smoke blossom behind each tire.

After Frank moved out of his mother's house and to Ciudad Bolivar, his mother sold her house and moved to a small apartment. Now, the plane carried all the furniture she gave us—her dining and living room furniture as well as pots and pans. It also brought lamps and other accessories given to us by Frank's brothers and sisters. Everything had seen years of service, but we treasured it all and gratefully accepted the family's gifts.

From the day she arrived in Venezuela, Arline was homesick, so she and Bill, preparing to return to the States, gave us tables, a washing machine, window blinds, dishes, linens, and throw rugs. These were aboard the C-46.

"It's all in the timing," I said enthusiastically to Madelyn as I watched the C-46 roll to a stop at the far end of the runway, turn and taxi toward our hangar. "It's all coming together. The window screens and other things Frank ordered for the house will be delivered any day. And now the furniture is here."

Still watching the C-46 taxi, Madelyn interrupted my moment of bliss. "Timing," she said. "Look over there." She nodded to a small truck parked at the curb in front of the houses and drew my attention to several men dressed in light gray work clothes and baseball caps. Slung over each one's shoulder was a silver colored metal container about three feet long with a six inch steel wheel on the top and a rubber hose with nozzle attached to it. They began to walk toward my front door. The metal containers strapped on their backs bore the letters DDT painted in red.

One of the men told Madelyn they'd return to spray the interior of our houses in the morning. They returned to their truck, shuffled some papers and trotted across the street to the light green house that bore the name *"Malva."* Houses in Venezuela were not numbered. Instead they had names. Neither Madelyn's nor my house had names or numbers and were referred to only by color. Mine was white. Madelyn's was yellow.

To control malaria, the government sprays the interior of all the houses in Bolivar with DDT about twice a year. "The treatment is good," Madelyn offered. "It even kills cockroaches—for a while. Down here, they grow pretty big. After the workers leave, we'll have to clean counter tops, kitchen drawers—places like that." She suggested I call Frank and ask him to hold the furniture in the hanger until the house had been sprayed.

I crossed the street to the house called Malva and asked the maid if I could please use the phone, explaining I was the new neighbor and my phone had not yet been installed.

At the office, Frank picked up the phone after the first ring and sounded disappointed when I told him about the DDT. "It's just one more thing," he mumbled and then hurriedly added, "I'll be right over."

Within minutes, he pulled his car into the carport on the right side of our house. "Think Madelyn has a cup of coffee?" he said as he approached our freshly scrubbed porch with white double front doors.

"I'm sure she does. The coffeepot goes where she goes." I went to her house and returned with two cups of coffee. Her maid followed with two cowhide chairs and set them on the covered cement porch near our front door. Frank motioned for me to sit down.

"Button," he lit a cigarette, sat down and his sigh was long and loud. He cleared his throat. He struggled getting started and after a few "mm's" and "aah's" he took a deep breath and lowered his eyes.

I interrupted. "You have to go to Caracas."

"How did you know?"

Blue Skies, Green Hell

I couldn't answer. Instead, I fought back tears.

This wasn't his first trip back to Caracas for business with the ministry since we'd arrived in CB. When the ministry called, Frank hurried. "Everything hit the fan today. The Air Ministry grounded our planes. Carlos' plane may even be involved."

"What do they want now?" I grumbled.

"I'll find out when I get there."

Crushed by the news, I saw my Cinderella-like visions of locking the world out of our palace fading from vivid gold to dismal gray and finally vaporizing completely, leaving in its place a white stucco box filled with cardboard boxes, and a front porch surrounded by dirt and weeds.

While staring into the cloudless sky he murmured, "I wonder if we'll ever get our business off the ground."

"I wonder if we'll ever get our marriage off the ground," I replied despondently.

He crossed his legs and played with the crease in his tan pants, then, putting his coffee cup on the cement floor next to the chair and standing up, he said, "It's not what we planned, I know. But it's got to be this way for a while." He spoke barely above a whisper. "Bear with me. Remember, Button, these separations are as hard on me as they are on you."

We stood up. He gripped my shoulders and pulled me close. "I'm going with Jack to Maiquetía—now. He came down just to drop off some cargo and our furniture. It's a fast round trip. I'll go to Maiquetía with him, and then up to Caracas and straighten out this mess. You've been a trooper, now you've got to help me again, Button. Please." Each statement was spoken just a little softer than the one before. I could hardly hear him when he said, "We'll get through this together." Abruptly, he changed the subject. "Ah . . . ah . . . I wish I had more time to talk. But Jack has to leave. You know, after he flies to Maiquetía, fills his tanks, he'll be off to Miami. He's got a long haul ahead of him. I can't hold him up." He paused. "So much has happened today and I have so little time. It's like I'm on a Ferris wheel that just keeps going around and I can't get off the damn thing." He took his handkerchief from his back pocket and mopped his face. "There's more. But where do I begin?" He paused again. "Tom's not flying for us anymore. I'll have trouble with Julio, I know. He and Tom are thick as thieves. They're at the airport now, laughing like nothing's happened. We'll talk more when I get back."

"What happened?" Shocked, I disregarded his lack of time and instead had to satisfy my own need for details. "Julio knows?"

"Yes. He's said nothing. Nothing yet." Quickly, he told me Tom occasionally had complained about not flying as much as he wanted to and that other air services wanted to talk business with him. Frank pursed his lips and exhaled. "I told him, 'Feel free to cancel your contract with us anytime.' Tom replied, 'Right now is as good as any.'"

"Wow. Two planes, a third in the plans, only two pilots and you'll be in Caracas."

He interrupted me. "Tom said he'll fly for us, any time—but without a contract. That's a plus for us. No contract means no base pay and no benefits like insurance. It won't be too bad. This morning, I hired another pilot. Name's Irv Banta. He's working for OMC at Cerro Bolivar. You'll like him. He's American, a really pleasant guy. He was an Army pilot and flew B-24s in Germany. You know, great training and experience. Oh, his wife, Magda, is a German girl. She speaks English, so you'll have another friend. After he gets a house, she'll come over. She's still in Germany."

He kissed me hurriedly. "I've really got to go. I've also got to get Irv's ticket."

"You're saying he's replacing Tom but he hasn't got a pilot's license?"

"Yeah. He hasn't flown much since he left the military. I'll arrange for his license. He'll be okay. We need him. The Beechcraft we'll be getting from Jack has two engines. In the service, Irv had a multi-engine rating. He'll do fine for us." As he took a cigarette out of his pocket he asked that I do whatever I could to help the new man. "God, I'm glad you're here." He cupped my chin in his hand and raised my head. My eyes remained downcast. "Look at me, Button." I looked up and our eyes met. "I'm depending on you."

I went from Cinderella and her knight in a shiny white and red airplane to Humpty Dumpty. I'd be put back together again when Frank returned. "This is like old times," I said. "Only now I'm in Bolivar and you'll be in Caracas."

"I have a surprise for you. Remember the gas stove we looked at that was too expensive and we couldn't afford?"

I nodded.

"I bought it for you. I told them to deliver it whenever you want. Just let them know. And the window screen people will be here in two days."

"Oh, God," I uttered weakly, "Thank you." Although he was running himself ragged, trying to get business, signing contracts, flying, managing most of the administration of the company, dealing with the Air Ministry, and shouldering a variety of problems that ignite without warning, Frank had not forgotten me.

"I love you, Frank. I'll do all I can. Count on me."

"I've got to run. Got to get my stuff from Freeman's house." His kiss was a quick one. As he trotted to the car, he called over his shoulder, "Julio will bring the car to you." He opened the car door, "Oh, yes—sleep at Freeman's 'til they move over here. Don't stay here alone. And tell Madelyn, I'll look up Carlos. I'll bring him up to date on the move and about the planes being grounded. I think he's staying with his father."

Then Frank was gone.

Madelyn saw him drive away and carrying two cups of coffee in her hands she crossed the short distance between the houses. "Coffee?"

"Thanks."

What's up?" she asked.

"Not our planes."

I told Madelyn what had happened and the string of things I'd been asked to do. I added that Julio would bring Frank's car to me. "At least we'll be able to get around." I sipped the coffee. "I guess I'm being selfish." Madelyn didn't comment. "I know. He's busting his chops, Madelyn, and I'm sulking." Again, Madelyn made no comment.

We looked around as we heard Madelyn's maid approaching.

"*Señora Madling.*" It was Madelyn's maid calling. Carrying Lilly in her arms, her alpargatas scuffing the dirt between the two houses as she walked to us, she announced, "*No hay electricidad. No hay agua, tampoco*" (There is no electricity. There's no water, either).

Madelyn and I sat down and lit cigarettes, drank coffee, and watched the sun begin to set.

With Tom following in his old burgundy colored jeep that emitted smoke every time he shifted gears, Julio drove Frank's car into the carport and gave me the keys. "You want the car now?"

"That's fine. Thanks"

"Tough luck, Marilyn. But since the planes are grounded, I'll be at the office, so you don't have to come over." Julio looked around and commented that I probably could use the time at home anyway. "Let me know when you want the furniture."

I nodded. "Thanks," I said as Julio hopped in Tom's jeep and they drove away leaving a trail of smoke behind. They looked and acted like teenage boys out for a good time. They didn't have a care in the world. They didn't have to go to Caracas and deal with government people; didn't have to coordinate everything involved in moving into a house. And they didn't seem to be worried about the planes not flying and not making money. Julio didn't seem concerned that Martha and their kids had not yet joined them, and Tom hadn't yet made weddings plans. Carefree—that's what they were. "Go away," I griped softly as they drove out of sight.

At the same time I heard the C-46's engines kick over and I turned in time to see the plane roll to the end of the taxi strip at the head of the runway.

Standing at the fence at the back of the houses, Madelyn and I watched the C-46 stop and turn. The engines revved to top speed, and the prop-wash from the engines blew flat the tall golden weeds in the field and kicked up swirling clouds of dirt and stones that stung our faces. We covered our eyes and turned our heads away from the biting grit until we heard Jack power down and we no longer felt the abrasive sting on the backs of our necks. The plane idled for a few minutes.

Torturing myself, longing to be with them, I heard the Pratt and Whitneys rev up again and watched the powerful plane roll forward, slowly at first, then pick up speed as it ripped through the heavy, humid air. Faster and faster it rolled down the runway. The ground shook beneath my feet. The tail lifted and the bucket was airborne. Wheels up, it banked to the left and flew out of sight taking all that I loved with it.

I wanted to turn back the clock to days of romantic music when our love was new. Whatever happened to Betty Grable and Don Ameche? It had been a long time since we last went dancing and I didn't hear romantic music anymore. The words from a song, composed by Mark Gordon and Harry Warren featured in the 1940 movie, "Down Argentine Way" raced through my head; "Where there are rumbas and tangos to tickle your spine, moonlight and music and orchids and wine, you'll want to stay . . . ." Had we lived out our glory days of passion and fantasy in romantic Venezuela?

Se acabó la fiesta. (The party's over)

Almost two months had passed since we'd chugged across the powerful Orinoco aboard the old ferry, and I'd felt secure in his arms. I knew it would be a cinch for me to adjust to the wild and untamed outpost in the wilderness. Being afraid never entered my mind—even when Frank was away on business and, except for Madelyn, I was alone in a foreign land. I was, however, resentful—especially when I saw Julio and Tom tooling back to my house in the old burgundy jeep.

Julio jumped out carrying a large box Jack and Bill had brought to me from Miami. "Jack and Bill sent their apologies for not having time to visit with you. But they were in a hurry."

Every time they came to Bolivar, Jack and Bill brought something for me. They surprised me with things I couldn't get in my frontier town—Wonder white bread, Hershey's chocolate syrup, and Campbell's tomato soup. Often, they'd bring something special like a chocolate layer cake from a bakery in Miami. Sometimes Jack had a package from Mother containing clothes and shoes or whatever I'd asked for.

"Thanks for bringing the box to me."

This time, the large box also contained a small one with dog biscuits. I smiled through tears that filled my eyes as I read a note scrawled on the side of the box of biscuits. "It says, 'Love to Tailspin and Loop from Stubby.' Stubby's my dog back home."

Two puppies were recent additions to our household. Frank had surprised me when he rescued two wild puppies he found wandering at the airport and brought them to the Freemans. The two needed a home and Frank knew our move to our house was imminent and invited the pups to share our house with us. Both were fawn colored, only a few weeks old and hard to tell apart. We named them Tailspin and Loop. "We'll watch them grow and teach them all kinds of things. It'll be good training for when we have a baby," Frank had said as he cuddled the pups.

Blue Skies, Green Hell

I'd made no answer. He'd spoken often about having a baby. While I wanted a baby as much as he, there would be no baby until we had more stability in the household; fewer separations and more permanency. I saw Madelyn with Lilly and knew the difficulties they had. The dogs were good company and all that I needed for now.

"Let's pack it in and go home," Madelyn said. We locked our houses and within minutes she and the maid with baby Lilly in her arms wearily climbed in my car and we drove back to Madelyn's house.

Several days later, we rented an old truck and a driver who moved all the possessions we had at Madelyn's to our new houses and then moved my furniture from the hangar to my house. The window screens were installed and the gas stove delivered.

Without Carlos and Frank around to do things like put up shelves and hang curtain rods we did those things for ourselves. We had no power tools, but I bought a star drill and a hammer. My first of many tools. To hang curtain rods, we had to install brackets, but first we had to sink anchors into the walls made of cement blocks. Over and over we'd take turns tap-tap-tapping and turning the star drill. We needed the patience of Job as we "drilled" holes for every bracket in our houses.

Madelyn and I figured our way out of situations like the broken water pump and living without water for days, multi-day power outages, intermittent telephone service or no service at all. We dealt with other problems that cropped up without warning such as leaky windows when it rained and sudden auto repairs. Madelyn had a sewing machine and we made curtains from fabric our mothers sent to us via Jack and we built furniture out of boxes. With written instructions and a diagram from my dad, we learned to rewire broken lamps. We shopped together. We talked about "back home" together and laughed together. We took care of each other when we didn't feel well.

I became aware of how uniquely Madelyn handled the same problems I had. She accepted and justified her husband's long absences when he traveled to Caracas, to the mines in the deep interior, or to the States. She did it without a fuss and he was away almost as much as Frank. She gave him her full support and cooperation and always went about her daily activities calmly and confidently. I marveled and envied how well she handled the separations.

When I became bedridden with tonsillitis and a raging fever, Madelyn gave me daily injections of antibiotics prescribed by Dr. Battistini, the only doctor in town who spoke English. Madelyn fed my dogs and cleaned their corral. She took care of Loop who came in heat and had to be separated from Tail Spin. She did the food shopping and picked up my medicine from the pharmacy. She stayed overnight with me at my house. She prepared and brought food to me.

Our sign on the side of the hangar faced the parking lot and attracted attention.

I learned to fly. What a thrill!

Our White Palace.

Blue Skies, Green Hell

Never could I have survived without Madelyn. She was a very strong, loving person.

Her strength and courage set examples for me, and being with her every day, my own youthful weaknesses and selfish behavior were replaced by a new maturity. I gained greater respect and admiration for the enormity of Frank's responsibilities. I understood the need for his absences and his need for my cooperation.

I found joy and contentment in this, my home on the frontier.

Madelyn showed me the way. I loved her as I loved my sister. I can't imagine what life would have been without her.

I managed the house and kept up with office activities. Frank counted on me and had full confidence in me. I didn't let him down. Belief in each other and a commitment to love each other held us together. I'd needed this time without Frank. I'd needed this time to grow up.

Thank you, Madelyn Moore Freeman from Snow Hill, Maryland.

Chapter 8

The Art of Piloting

Dear Mother and Dad	May 15, 1952

    Well, there was no good movie last night, so we went to a fair. I didn't go on any ride. I'm not feeling well enough. My doctor still doesn't know what's wrong with me. Anyway, I won't go on the rides with Frank. The ones he likes best are airplanes that hang from wires. Frank insists on flying them upside down. I don't know how he does it. He says he uses his weight. I ask what weight? But it's really funny. When he's in the darn thing, a crowd actually gathers to see what he's going to make the airplane do.

    He wins prizes. Tonight he won a stuffed panda! A few in the crowd follow him from one ride to another.

    He says he likes flying real planes, but they're not as fun as flying planes on wires.

My love always. Marilyn

    My house on the frontier was comfortable and pretty and at last, I felt happy and in control of my life. Business improved steadily, and except for the days when I didn't feel well, we had good times. So good, in fact, one day I felt up to confronting the challenge of driving our car on the steep hills in the city.

    Despite its prominence as being the only "city" between the Orinoco and the Brazilian border and between the headwaters of the Orinoco in the west and its junction at the Atlantic, no traffic lights swung at intersections in Ciudad Bolivar. The city, never having lost its colonial charm, continued to be Venezuela's last frontier. Although shopping was limited and the hospital antiquated, the city attracted people who lived in distant villages up and down the Orinoco and south of it. They came to Bolivar for the best of whatever it was they needed and could not get in their rural and primitive settlements. Thus, the automobile and truck traffic within the city shared the narrow, steep roads with braying donkeys pulling rickety wooden carts piled high with boxes made of wood slats and wire that contained cackling chickens destined for the market.

With my shopping list in my pocketbook and car keys in my hand, I felt up to the challenge of driving Frank's old Dodge coupe to the city to shop in stores on steep hills. Not knowing how to shift gears on the hills, I'd been parking the car on a street in the outskirts of the city and walking up and down the hills between the stores, the Post Office and where I had parked the car.

As I backed out of my dirt driveway, I waved to my good friend and neighbor, Malvina Rosales. She lived in the house called Malva across the street. Prominent not only in Ciudad Bolivar, but in all of Bolivar State, Malvina always dressed in black and wore white gloves. She stood taller than most women and carried her extra weight with self-assurance and confidence. She had white hair and wore horn-rimmed glasses. I told her of my plans to go to the city and drive the hills, though I'd never done that before. "*Me voy allá, también. Me voy contigo*" (I'm going there, also. I'll go with you), she said. "*Te enseñaré cómo manejar en las Colinas*" (I'll teach you how to drive on the hills), she added.

Off we went. As we neared the city she said we'd go up and down the small hills before driving on the steep ones. As we rolled along, she told me how to use the brake and accelerator with one foot—my right toe on the brake and my right heel on the accelerator. My left foot worked the clutch. It seemed complicated, but she said I'd get used to the foot work. I thought of Jack Perez as he danced on the pedals when he maneuvered the C-46 on the taxiway.

Ready to try a steep hill, she suggested we go to the Post Office. Oh Lord, I thought, that means we have to stop and park on a hill that is one of the steepest in the city. All parking in the city was parallel to the curb. My heart beat rapidly.

Following her instructions to go slow, go fast, put in the clutch, shift, release the clutch, use the brake, I arrived safely at the Post Office. The only vacant spot was in front of it, and painted on the road in huge white letters it said, "*No Parque*" (No Parking).

"*No te preocupe*" (Don't worry), she told me and gestured for me to park in the place clearly marked, "*No Parque.*" I easily pulled into the large space. Getting out of the car, she warmly greeted the policeman whose duty it was to enforce the "*No Parque*" rule. "*Hola. Hola*" (Hello) she called to him as she stood waving and smiling and telling him I was her new neighbor and she was teaching me to drive.

I waved and called, "*Buenos Días, Señor.*" He smiled broadly and gold in his front tooth glinted in the sunlight.

Next challenge in the journey was to drive down a steep hill that ended at the river. With sweaty palms, a dry mouth and a fervent wish that I had worn a life vest, I did just as Malvina instructed and we went down the hill fully under control. I turned onto the *Paseo Del Orinoco*, a beautiful tree-lined street, one lane each direction separated by a wide island of trees, reflecting pools, and gardens. It bordered the Orinoco and claimed title to the most crowded and busiest street in the city if not, I thought at the time, the whole world. Malvina said she'd go into the hardware store on the Paseo with me. "*Mira allá*" (Look there), she said pointing to a small parking place in front of Humberto's hardware store. I told her it was too small, so I'd have to back into it—parallel park. Cars, lined up behind me, started to blast their horns and, in true Venezuelan fashion, impatient drivers banged on the outside of their car doors with the palms of their hands.

"*No te preocupe*" (Don't worry), she said gesturing dismissively with her white gloved hand. She jumped out of the car, ran around it to the middle of the Paseo, and standing with her feet apart, holding her hand in the air like a policeman, she stopped the single-lane traffic and told drivers waiting in the cars to give me time to park as she was teaching me to drive and this was the first time I'd tried backing into a parking place.

My face became hot and reddened and I wished I was any place but in the middle of the Paseo, with Malvina Rosales holding back all the traffic while I backed into the parking space. I was mortified.

Once I was parked, she waved the waiting cars on and greeted most drivers by first names. I didn't want to look at anyone, but knew I had to. I put my head out the car window and thanked everyone who drove by. "*Gracias. Gracias*," I sang out, smiling, although I would have preferred death to this embarrassing situation. Malvina remained in the road until the last car had driven past. Complete and overwhelming delight lit her face, and so pleased with her success and uncompromised victory, she flung open the door on my side of the car and held it wide open so I could get out and, again, traffic could not pass. Finally she said to me, "*Vámonos a comprar*" (Let's go shop).

On the way home, I thanked her profusely for teaching me the fine art of driving and parking on hills. She said I drove well enough to get my Venezuelan driver's license. At her request, I gave her my New York State driver's license and a couple of days later she brought my Venezuelan license to me.

"Looks like we got home just in time," I said in Spanish, casting my eyes at the dark ominous clouds moving rapidly toward Bolivar. "We'll be in for some heavy rain." I heard the first rumble of thunder.

As she got out of the car at her house, she asked me if Frank was flying. "Yes. He returned from Caracas yesterday. It was a short trip. He had to locate a spare part and bring it back. But he left this morning to fly to Puerto Ordaz. That's where this bad weather's coming from." She turned, looked up in the sky and seemed surprised by the encroaching clouds. Whereas weather was a bush pilot's on-going concern, it had never been one of hers. "It's moving our way," I said.

She commented about Frank's numerous absences. I nodded and said, "When he flies locally, up and down the river, or work generated by the contracts, the flights are usually one day. Few overnight trips are scheduled, but sometimes he overnights when he has bad weather." I shrugged my shoulders. "He's away much longer when he goes to Caracas. But I understand—that's for business, too."

I wished Malvina a pleasant evening, drove across the street and into my driveway. The sky blackened, the rains came in fiercely and the wind howled. My English speaking maid from the West Indies, Guillermina Alexander, brought the dogs in the house and closed the windows. "The weather is bad," she said. "Is Mr. Frank coming home today?"

"I think so. But if he learns about this storm, maybe he'll be out 'til tomorrow."

With the windows closed, the air in the house was stifling, even though the oscillating fan whirred on high speed. I sat at the dining room table sipping the iced tea Guillermina had prepared for me and looking out the window at the rain pelting the side of Madelyn's house next door.

"I'm going to rest a while," I told her. Loop and Tail Spin followed me to the bedroom, jumped on the bed ahead of me, but dove right off and scurried under it when they heard deafening thunder rumble across the black sky. "Poor things," I said to no one as I stretched out on the bed.

Damn heat, I thought, and opened a few buttons on my blouse. Sometimes the heat caused an itchy rash on my skin. Most of the time, I just sweated and felt sick and exhausted. Drinking ice water and lying in bed helped, but only as a temporary fix. There seemed to be no permanent cure for the rash. It came and went without warning. As for my stomach, I felt squeamish much of the time and everyone said, "It's the amoeba" or "It's the change in season," and summarized the whole mess, saying, "Everybody has it," though "it" could not be defined.

I found the best remedy to be a cold shower. Routinely, I showered twice during the day and once before going to bed. When it was too hot to sleep, I'd shower again during the night and while still dripping, I'd run from the shower to the bed and collapse, getting relief as the breeze from the fan blew across my wet body. The relief lasted only as long as it took for both the sheet and me to dry. Frank did the same. Sometimes I wondered how he had enough stamina to fly an all day trip after a sleepless night when the unbearable heat kept him awake.

Then I heard Frank's plane over head. He didn't "buzz," but it had to be him. At the time, I believed him to be the only pilot flying.

I buttoned my blouse as I ran toward the window at the rear of the house.

The heavy wind blew sheets of rain against the house, and windows on the east side leaked. After Guillermina and I put cloths and towels on the terrazzo

101

floor under the windows to absorb the water, we listened to the wind howl and the rain lash the house.

"I'm so afraid," she said. "Can he see the ground?"

"Oh, probably a glimpse. He sees something or he wouldn't be coming in." I looked up at nothing and listened sharply. "But I think he's going around again."

Her black eyes grew huge. "Madam. His plane is so small." She turned her back to me as she used a corner of her apron to dab away a tear from her eye. "And the wind is so strong."

"He got this far, Guillermina. He's a rock."

I could not shake off her simple words: "His plane is so small and the wind is so strong."

Quite suddenly, the rain moderated and the sky lightened as the clouds began to break up. We stood by the rear window looking beyond the wire fence and grassy field to the head of the runway. He'd land southwest to northeast, and we'd see him land. Loop ran from under the bed, jumping and barking, to the window where Guillermina and I stood. Tail Spin remained shivering under the bed.

Looking up and scanning the sky, I saw a break appear in the low gray clouds and I glimpsed Frank's white and red plane fly over. He rocked the wings.

"Madam. What does it mean?"

"He just said 'hello' and asked me to meet him at the airport."

Loop knew Frank was about to land. Every time he came home from a trip, she ran wild jumping and barking. She behaved like that only when he took off or landed. Planes could take off and land all day and she'd sleep through the noise. But when Frank sat behind the controls of the single-engine Cessna, she knew it and never wrongly identified his plane. This time, forgetting about the storm, she raced to the rear window and repeatedly jumped up and down, whined and barked. It was an uncanny phenomenon for which no one had an explanation. Guillermina picked her up and held her quivering body. While Loop feared the storm, her fear was overridden by her love for Frank. The only thing she knew was that Frank would be home soon.

I watched Frank ease down and land. As he entered the taxiway off the runway, I smiled, petted Loop and told her I'd bring her daddy home soon. "We'll be back for dinner."

I called to Guillermina, "I'll be right back." I grabbed my car keys and rushed out the front door.

Frank and I arrived at the hangar at the same time. I parked the car near the hangar door and ran inside the old building.

He jumped out of the plane, ran across the parking lot and followed me in. "It was hell up there." He used his handkerchief to wipe the rain water from his face. "That plane bounced. The seat belt damn near cut me in half. And this weather's not over."

The sky brightened, but that lasted only long enough for us to tie down the plane by putting a line through rings under each wing and securing them to rings imbedded in the ground. The tail was similarly secured.

Frank did his paperwork in the office while I made a cup of coffee for him. "That was a hell of a storm." He put his pen on the desk. "You get a strange feeling up there in weather like this. You want to go with your intuition, but you can't. You sit there and take whatever the Gods throw at you while you keep your wings level, and you concentrate on the plane's airspeed, altitude, artificial horizon, vertical airspeed indicator, and the compass. You watch all your instruments and you believe in them."

With full fury and violence, the wind returned, blowing the rain horizontally through the black sky. Just then, we heard another light plane fly over. Frank looked up from his work. "Oh, God. It's Tom or Julio. Both are flying today and, I think, are due back about now." He looked up at the chalk board. "Julio is coming in from Caracas. He may not make it. Tom took a trip for us to La Vergareña. After that, I don't know where he was going." He picked up the phone and tried to call the Airport Manager in the main terminal. With his finger, he tapped the phone's cradle, click, click, click, click. No answer. The phone was dead. "Get in the car," he said.

We sped from our hangar to the terminal across the parking lot through deep pools of water causing it to fan out on both sides of the car. He parked near the terminal entrance, and we rushed into the building. The airport manager was not in.

"Ever been up to the tower?" he asked.

"No."

"I'm going there now. Want to go?"

"You bet."

"Now, Button, we'll go up two flights of stairs inside the building. Then we have to go up the outdoor stairs to the tower. The wind will be strong. You can stay here if you want."

"I'll go with you." In all my life, I'd never seen a harder rain, a blacker sky. Undulating waves of rain swept across the airfield's barren acres.

"Come on."

I followed him to the stairway, and up two flights to a door marked "Exit." He pushed the door with all his strength and it barely moved against the strong wind holding it back. "Give me a hand here." Together we pushed the door. Gripped by the wind, it swung back and slammed against the outer wall of the building.

"Oh my God," I said. Frank didn't hear me. I saw the outdoor long flight of stairs. The steps without risers were made of iron. More like a ladder with handrails than a stairway, it was very wet and slippery. The stairs took us to the control tower three stories above ground level.

"You okay?" he called over the wind and rain.

"Yes." I nodded vigorously.

Frank went up first and I followed on his heels. I could see between the steps, to the terminal's roof and the ground below. The tug of the wind pulled my body away from the steps and I feared I'd slide between the wet steps and Frank would never hear me fall to my death. My hair slipped out of the silk scarf that held my ponytail, and my long hair lay plastered on my face and over my eyes.

A plane flew low overhead. I involuntarily ducked.

The tower door opened from the inside and we rushed in. "I tried to call," Frank said to the tower operator.

"We're having communications trouble," answered the operator.

"Is that Tom?" Frank asked the tower operator.

"I think so. Whoever it is, we can't reach him. But he's been around the area almost forty minutes." Loud static and crackling came from the tower radio. Then we heard bits and pieces of Tom's voice as he attempted to make a connection. The tower operator gripped the radio transmitter. "This is Ciudad Bolivar. Come in, please."

No reply.

"Wind's at seventy-five miles an hour," Frank said, looking at the indicator.

"And it looks like this storm might hold together a while," the tower operator added.

"I hope he has reserve fuel." Frank explained to me that the plane should carry sufficient fuel to reach its destination, and, when possible, an hour's worth in reserve for just such emergencies. But without weather forecasts in the interior, pilots had to use their own judgment about reserve fuel based solely on visual observation or reports from other pilots.

We listened to the rain, the static, the sound of Tom's plane, and his voice crackling through the radio. Over and over, the tower operator talked rapidly into the transmitter calling him. He made no connection. Beads of perspiration covered Frank's forehead. Again and again, he mopped his face and the back of his neck with his handkerchief. I wondered if Tom could see anything. The black boiling clouds churned all around.

The sky started to brighten even though the rain continued, but the storm had all the signs of moderating. We dashed back down the slippery outdoor steps, down the indoor stairs and into the car. We sped across the parking lot to the hangar. Just as we'd begun to fear that Tom had probably exhausted his fuel, he broke through the low overcast and safely touched down at the head of the runway, giving himself plenty of distance to roll to a slow speed without braking too hard. He taxied his plane close to the hangar, jumped out of the plane and jogged inside.

"What a ride," he said. "At times, the plane seemed to stand still." He looked at Frank. "You just get in?"

"Yeah. Had the same thing."

"I was flying on fumes the last few minutes. My tanks are dry."

"Five minutes ago, TCO told us you'd been over CB almost forty minutes."

"My greatest fear was running out of fuel."

Tom swished water from off his clipboard. He said he'd refueled so the tank was full, but there was no way he could have accurately judged the extent of the storm or the extra flying time it required.

Together, we three rolled Tom's plane to the tie-down rings and secured the aircraft.

All paper work completed, Frank and I invited Tom back to the house for dinner and were about ready to leave when Julio, racing the clock, roared overhead, and touched down on the Ciudad Bolivar runway. It was just six o'clock.

"What a day this has been. I didn't think he'd make it back tonight," Frank said as he watched Julio taxi to the hangar. "Think you could have made it back, Button?" The tension had eased.

"From Caracas? Of course," I said. "I could fly that trip anytime, but I'm not quite ready to fly in this weather. Give me another lesson and a little practice time, then watch me."

Julio's tale of the storm was less hair-raising. As he flew over the llanos, he saw black sky ahead with heavy clouds and rain. He knew the weather conditions were bad and he wouldn't be able to get around the storm. He could, however, avoid it by landing on the road and waiting it out.

The three had talked many times about their feelings when a black wall of storm clouds is ahead and there's no way to get around it and no place to land. You hit that black wall, they'd say, and you feel your body tug against the seat belt. Buffeted by high winds and severe turbulence, your plane lurches and bounces; it drops in downdrafts and defies gravity in violent updrafts. Bad weather can play tricks with your mind—and your inner ear. Your equilibrium can't keep up with the rapid and erratic movements of the plane, and you learn to disregard your vertigo and surrender your soul to the plane. You fly that machine every inch of the way.

Circling the airport meant being slapped by the winds on all sides as you turn your plane from one heading to another. It slows you down when you head into it. That's when you feel as though you're standing still. When you go crosswise to the wind it pushes you sideways and you drift. That drift affects your navigation. With the wind at your tail, it blasts you from behind. You fight it, but you don't lose your concentration. That's how professionals fly and live to talk about it.

They talked with steady, calm voices, even laughed a little while I listened. *Macho men. What does it take to scare them?*

Tom and Julio came back to the house with us. Our palace had already become the watering hole for our bush pilot friends, and for pilots who flew the DC-3s, as well. They'd drop in to visit their *compadre* (buddy), Frank, and for a drink or a bed and shower if the hotels in town were full or out of water or electricity was down.

I hurried to the front door and on to the kitchen to alert Guillermina there would be two guests for dinner. She enjoyed our visitors, especially when they were pilots. A serious person who seldom smiled, she was mesmerized by their stories, and often eavesdropped to hear their stories of derring-do and adventure. She was one of those local people who thought, as Tom often said, pilots were "Gods with gold braid."

While Frank and I dried off and changed clothes, Tom and Julio poured their drinks. They mostly talked about flying in bad weather. All had a host of stories, but none more frightful then the one they'd just experienced.

We chatted about Tom's upcoming marriage to his fiancée, Shirley Barger, while we enjoyed a fine dinner of steak and all the trimmings. Shirley was scheduled to arrive in Maiquetía from Washington, D.C., in a few days. Tom said he still had to make arrangements for the wedding. Frank and I told him the papers we'd needed for our civil wedding when we were married by the Prefect in Sabana Grande, a suburb of Caracas, and the papers we needed when we were married in The American Church by Pastor Beck two months later. When he said he didn't have clothes for the occasion, Julio said he'd lend him a suit, shirt, and tie, and Frank loaned him underwear, shoes, socks and a white handkerchief.

"I think you'd better take some time off and get up to Caracas. Arrange a little honeymoon before you get back. There are nice hotels at the beach. Unless you have other work, we won't need you for a while," Frank said.

"Thanks. Hey, you guys are swell." We toasted his health and happiness. Tom joined us with a Coke. Tom never drank anything stronger than soda.

Following the impromptu stag party, we drove Tom and Julio to their hotel in the woods called Le Normandie. The sky, clear of all storm clouds, was filled with early evening stars.

Two ladies staying at the hotel while their husbands looked for suitable housing in Puerto Ordaz, were seated in their usual wicker rockers on the hotel's front porch. The stillness of the night bore no resemblance to the terror that had struck the area only a few hours earlier.

"Hello," they called out and waved. "Here come the pilots and the lady." That's what they called us. We seemed always to be together and most evenings we stopped at the hotel for a final round of drinks and more talk. "Were you flying today?" they asked.

Paseo del Orinoco. Main Street in Ciudad Bolivar. Orinoco River is on left. Stores are on right.

Ciudad Bolivar Airport. Notice the outdoor stairway to the Control Tower.

"All three of them," I answered, "although Julio set down on the road north of the river and waited out the storm." I leaned toward them and said softly, "Bad today. They say it was as rough as it gets. They say they'll be sore tomorrow from the rough ride."

While the men ordered the drinks, one of the ladies asked me, "And what do you do when hubby is out flying?"

"Well, today, while Frank was exercising the art of piloting a plane in a severe storm, I exercised my own art of piloting the car over the steep hills in the city. Probably not as difficult, but I didn't do badly for the first time. Maybe I'll solo tomorrow."

They told us they'd learned their husbands had secured housing and they'd be leaving the hotel in a couple of days. "You've all done so much to brighten our days here. We've looked forward every evening to your visit. You're special. The pilots and the lady. Always joking and telling good stories. You have fun all the time. We'll miss that."

Frank and I stood up and started making our way to the car. As I passed them I whispered, "It's not fun all the time. Today wasn't fun." I winked.

We'd started to pull away in our car when Tom called, "Thanks. Hey, that was a swell stag party."

"Can't wait to meet the bride," I sang out. "Good luck."

As Frank and I drove home through the woods on the winding muddy road, he asked me what I did all day.

"Oh, I drove into town and did shopping."

"Did I hear you say you're driving on the hills now?"

"Yes. Malvina went with me . . ."

"She's a great lady," he said before I finished my sentence. "Nice you two get along so well." He pulled into our driveway. "I'm tired. It's been a helluva day."

Chapter 9

We Play Hard, Very Hard

Dear Mother and Dad   **June 10, 1952**

Let me tell you about a place we found last week, a new place to go dancing. We're no strangers to a dance floor, but this one is funny. The floor is covered with linoleum. The overhead lights are fluorescent—ghastly bluish. Tables are metal Cosco tables like people use in their kitchens. The music is live—Latin—which I like and can dance pretty good so long as I'm with Frank.

When the live music stops, American records are played. We have a good time. You know how we love to dance. We go with Madelyn and Carlos. Of course, they're as crazy as we are. Shirley, Tom's wife arrived. She's very nice. Sometimes we play canasta with Tom and her. It's a quiet evening and a nice way of passing time the night before the guys have morning flights.

More later. Got to run. Frank just called and we're going flying. He has to check his mags, whatever that means.

What a life. Love you. Marilyn

With the passage of time, driving on the steep streets was a snap and the strange way of living with the man I loved—here today and who-knows-where tomorrow—no longer seemed strange at all. I'd grown up and triumphed over tough times and difficult conditions to survive in Bolivar. We called the conditions inconveniences. That made it lots easier to live with.

Sometimes, Shirley and Tom joined us for movies or cards. We enjoyed being with them.

Despite Tom's serious nature, once in a while, we engaged in activities that were a little reckless, even dangerous.

Like the Sunday afternoon Frank thought he could liberate some good spare parts and instruments from a light aircraft that had crashed in a small clearing about an hour by plane south of CB airport. Tom had just returned from a short flight and joined Frank and me at the patio lounge. Frank had a scotch, Tom and I drank cokes.

Frank began talking to Tom about Jimmy Evens who'd lost his life in the crash. Frank had recently flown over the crash site and noticed the plane had been moved off the strip leaving enough distance, he thought, for a light aircraft to land. The abandoned plane and its instruments and parts, available just for the taking, seemed to be in good condition and worthy of an observation flight.

"Hey, Tom. Want to go flying? Look over the area?"

"Sure, I don't think Shirley has anything planned for us this afternoon. We may go to the movies tonight. Let's go." I had nothing to do, so I went along for the ride. Tom's sober condition was normal and Frank's one drink wouldn't impair him.

We hustled to our hangar, went through the routine of preparing the plane for departure. I tested the fuel, Tom filed the flight plan, Frank loaded some tools, made his pre-flight inspection and we were off.

I didn't know Jimmy very well. Even though he'd flown a trip or two for us, I knew him only as young man, pleasant, likable with the kind of face you don't remember. He'd been to the house a few times for dinner, but just about every pilot who landed at Ciudad Bolivar had done that.

While we flew south, Frank told Tom about Jimmy Evens, an experienced bush pilot who should have known better than to try to land on an airstrip on a gentle upward slope in the forest, cut too short and too narrow by natives with machetes. A line of trees at one end and a ridge sprawled at the opposite were natural obstructions and rendered the short field difficult if not dangerous for landing and taking off.

Nearby miners had arranged for natives to clear the strip so Jimmy could bring in supplies. A disaster was waiting to happen; the natives had left a tree stump in the strip.

Jimmy's plane left Ciudad Bolivar, rumored to be overloaded with supplies, flew over the savannah and rainforest to the clearing. The strip stretched out below, and Frank believed that surely Jimmy must have noted that it had been cut very narrow. But the tree stump in the middle may have been the one feature he didn't notice. He attempted the landing and lost the challenge. The plane's wing could have easily passed over the stump had it had wiggle room. But after touching down, Jimmy didn't have room to steer around it and the slim tree stump speared up through the bottom of the fuselage smashing the plane and Jimmy, too.

A freak accident, Frank figured Jimmy landed too long. Perhaps he'd not side-slipped the plane for a short landing.[7] Jimmy should have set his wheels down at the beginning of the strip instead of half way. When he realized what he'd done he may have tried to abort the landing, but was too low and too slow and that's when the deadly spear pierced the plane making it Jimmy's last landing.

Natives found the wreck and buried Jimmy's lifeless body under a nearby tree. For some unknown reason, the plane had been rolled off the strip.

No other plane attempted a landing until FLA soared over the treetops.

"We'll make a couple of passes," Frank said and Tom agreed. They flew low over the field and carefully observed the strip mumbling "yes" and then "no." After three passes over the grim site, Tom concluded the width of the field was okay. "We can land all right and even get by that stump. But, we need a longer field for takeoff. There's no room to get out."

Frank objected. "I'm not sure about that. Let's take another pass," he added, pushing the throttle forward to give the engine more power as he pulled back on the yoke to fly up and around again.

"I don't think we can," said Tom.

"I think we can," Frank retorted sharply.

They bickered back and forth and their voices grew louder and the tone belligerent. Finally, Tom folded his arms and looked out the right side window. "Damn it. It's your plane. You fly it," he shouted at Frank. "Do what you want. But we won't make it. We'll wind up with Jimmy—under the trees."

Then Frank took his hands off the yoke and throttle, folded his arms across his chest. "You're so damn smart, you fly it," he said and looked out the left side window.

Now the little plane had no one flying it. "Damn it! Somebody fly it or I'll come forward and fly it myself!" My hollow threat ruffled no one. I pulled myself out of the back corner of the rear seat, grabbed the back of Tom's seat in front of me and pulled myself forward so I could lean between them and shout over the sound of the engine. "I don't want to land here. I want to go home."

Frank continued to look out his window. "It's two against one. The plane's yours, Tom." I collapsed back in my seat as Tom took the controls. "The plane is mine," he muttered. I'd not been afraid as the two stubborn men behaved like sulking children, but their reckless behavior angered me. Frank's eyes never strayed from his side window as Tom turned the plane, gained altitude and put it on a northerly heading back to Bolivar. Frank rested his head on the seat back and went to sleep.

We'd flown forty-five minutes when Bolivar came in sight and Tom got tower clearance to land. He gently set it down then taxied to our hangar.

I liked the way Tom flew a plane and thanked the good Lord that we'd gotten over the differences we'd had with Tom when we'd first arrived in CB. Frank's lack of success developing a regularly scheduled air route up and down the river supported Tom's insistence that local folks in river towns were not ready to accept flight, especially in small planes. We all let bygones-be-bygones.

111

"Thanks, pal," Frank said as Tom shut down the engine. "You were right." Affectionately, he lightly tapped Tom's shoulder. He looked back at me. "That was someone else in this plane, Button. It won't happen again. *Yo te promiso*" (I promise you).

I never heard a word about the flight we took to Jimmy Evens' crash site or the easy loot available. And Frank's promise was good as gold. He never again flew after he'd had even one drink.

When no flights were scheduled for Frank the next day, our evening entertainment frequently began with cocktails at the airport lounge or at one of our houses. We dined, danced, played tennis and swam at a new "country club." Plain and not a rival for any country club any of us had ever seen, it became our refuge and provided a delightful change from the patio lounge.

We joined Tom and Shirley for quiet evenings at the movies or playing Canasta, but our most frequent fun-loving companions were the Freemans. I reveled in the joyous occasions with them. They were loose and such fun. They were our dearest friends.

Most often, we four played Monopoly with the instructions and game board written in Portuguese, and Scrabble in Spanish and English at the same time. We ached from laughing because Carlos and Frank made up Spanish words and rewrote rules. When Madelyn and I caught them cheating, a near riot ensued, all in the name of fun. We drank a Venezuelan drink called Ponche Créma; it tasted like eggnog. As we'd predicted long ago, every night was like a party. When Carlos and Frank were away, they worked hard, and when they came home, they played hard.

We could always count on the Freemans to join in spontaneous and sometimes calamitous activities; good times were unrestrained. With the Freemans, social activities picked up and we sallied a tad more impulsively.

Perhaps playing hard compensated for long, lonesome times when we didn't play at all.

A casual dinner of toasted cheese sandwiches and chocolate toddys at the Triangulito was often followed by a movie that flickered and jiggled across an old patched screen in the open air theater in down town Ciudad Bolivar. A small roof covered only the last few rows of metal folding chairs set on a cement floor. Our newly acquired cushions for the hard chairs made a big difference in our comfort. However, when it rained, chaos ruled as chairs occupied by patrons in the front rows were dragged on the cement floor to someplace under the overhang. The clanging, scraping chairs and rain beating on the metal roof competed with the soundtrack of the movie. The chairs and rain usually won.

A big night at the movies also included a stage show. The movie would play for twenty minutes, stop, and a live vaudeville-type act would perform for twenty minutes. Then the movie would resume. With only a few people in the audience, we four loudly encouraged the stage performers by applauding vigorously and whistling approval. I'm sure both audience and performers were happy when the movie resumed.

Frank, Madelyn Freeman, Carlos Freeman, and I.
Together, we had the best of times.

Dining at the Triangulito one evening, just before movie time, we heard guitar music coming from a block away. Out of the darkness, wearing white *liqui-liquis* (a white linen suit worn by Venezuelan men on Sundays and special occasions) and black *peleguamas* (a cowboy-type hat made of black velour) several men came strolling our way. A woman with them wore a bright red skirt and white blouse with ruffles. She, too, wore a black peleguama. All were playing guitars and singing Venezuelan *joropos*, typical music of the llanos. They stopped at the Triangulito to entertain a small group when Frank borrowed one of the guitars and joined the merry group of revelers. He played well, had a nice voice, an engaging smile and his brown eyes flashed around the crowd that had gathered to enjoy the street entertainment. When he played and sang the popular "*Alma Llanera*" (Song of the Plains), the crowd applauded. Then they cheered when the woman put down her guitar, attached maracas to her alpargatas and danced to the rhythm Frank played. The crowd grew larger and gathered closer, encouraging Frank to do just one more, "*Uno más*" (one more). He thanked them, returned the guitar to the group and we went on to the movies.

Another place to dine was at The Black Horse Café, a combination restaurant, lounge and gift shop located across the street from our palace and set back from the road several hundred feet under large and very old trees. Owned and operated by two Germans, the barroom was paneled in light colored knotty pine and quaint artifacts from Bavaria had been artfully hung on the walls.

A large mirror behind the bar reflected the room, which looked more like a saloon from out of the American old west than a German Beer Stube which may have been the owners' intent.

At The Black Horse Café, we dined on Bolivar's most delicious hamburgers, and, if Frank had no plans to fly the next day, we'd stay and dance and imbibe late into the night. The Café remained open as long as we were there. I usually wound up in the café's gift shop. I made several unique purchases and today, a Bavarian plate I purchased there hangs in my kitchen.

A jukebox loaded with American records played good music for listening and dancing. My favorite records featured Eddie Fisher; I played his recordings of "With these Hands," and "Anytime," over and over.

No one else stopped at the Café while we four were there, and there might have been a good reason for that.

Occasionally, we'd start to dance on the small hardwood floor between the bar and the one round table with four overstuffed brown leather chairs in a corner. Carlos would suggest we dance on the bar. When the German bartenders saw us step on the barstools then on to the bar top where we'd dance, they'd duck and crouch on the floor in back of the mahogany bar or escape to a small storage room near the bar. They'd remain there in anticipation of what they feared might happen. Dancing was okay, but when Carlos whipped out his pistol from its holster and fired a round or two into the ceiling, they wanted to be under cover. Carlos was not the first to pump bullets into the ceiling. The evidence of those who'd come before was within full view. However, Carlos may have whipped out his pistol with a little more panache than those who took credit for being the first.

Carlos' closing act was also memorable. I can still hear him shout, "The moon is full tonight. Let's go make love in the savannah." That's when we hooted and hollered, jumped off the bar and jogged to Carlos' car. Oh, how frenzied were the pleasures of our romantic youth.

"Put the bill on the tab," Frank called over his shoulder to the bartenders who, having lived through yet another shoot-out at The Black Horse Café, rose from the floor, peeped over the bar rail, finally stood upright, and returned to their positions behind the bar. They watched us speed off into the dark night toward the unpopulated pasture a few miles south of Bolivar.

Carlos parked on the side of the unlit and unpaved two lane road. We jumped out of the car, scrambled across a small ditch that ran parallel to the road, and then we'd all squeeze between the middle strands of wires. The Freemans went left and we went right.

Made uneven by clumps of weeds and grass pounded for years by roaming cattle, the ground under my bare feet felt hard and prickly as I ran behind Frank to a spot under an old Acacia tree, both of us scattered our clothes along the way in the warm, sultry night air. Frank carried an old red blanket loaned to him by Carlos who said he'd liberated it from the merchant vessel on which he'd been a captain a long time ago. Holding the blanket in both hands, Frank flailed it just as a *matador* (bullfighter) works his cape when he's getting ready to make the kill. While Frank studied flying at the school of aviation in Maracay, he visited nearby *tientas* (ranches where bulls are raised and young ones are "caped" by would be matadors). There he learned the art of being a *torero*. The young bulls were never hurt and luckily neither was Frank.

Having planted both feet firmly in the course grass, he said, "*Ah-ha toro.*" Then standing erect with his blanket held by both hands out to one side and still with his feet together and his back arched he slowly twirled with the graceful ballet movements of a matador while letting the blanket splay out and float down to cover the ground.

"Ole" I responded. Out of breath from having jogged from the car in the heavy night air, we collapsed on the blanket. And under the cover of moon and dazzling stars, we were one and we were together, devouring each other's passions and dispelling our loneliness.

Chapter 10

"It's Around Here Someplace"

Dear Mother and Dad   **September 9, 1952**

    Did I tell you I flew with Jack and Bill in the C-46 to Paraitepui near the Brazilian border? Jack said Paraitepui is so far south that the landing pattern takes us over Brazil.
    Frank says no one actually knows where the border is because the area's never been surveyed. It's in the jungle.
    Julio's wife, Martha, and family arrived from Ecuador.
    She's tall and pretty. She's lots older than the rest of us—in her mid-30's. Her young children are well-behaved.
    We invited her to come along on the trip in the C-46, but she said she had to unpack bags and boxes. The kids are too young to be of much help.

Love you so much. Marilyn

    I was seated behind Jack Perez and Bill Murphy in the cockpit of the C-46 when I first saw Auyántepui and Angel Falls. Only a handful of people in the civilized world had heard about Angel Falls. Fewer had seen it.
    Jack and Bill landed in CB the night before—just before 6:00 p.m. With both of the acceptable hotels full, they joined us for dinner at our palace and slept over. During breakfast the next morning, they invited Frank and me to tag along to Paraitepui. Frank had other business planned, but I went along for the ride of a lifetime. We flew one hour and forty-five minutes over the Gran Sabana, a formidable and wondrously strange landscape.
    We flew through fierce storms that battered the 56,000 pound (gross weight when loaded) C-46 all over the sky. Our cargo? Fifty-five-gallon drums of diesel fuel, all well tied down. After the turbulence moderated, I caught glimpses of the terrain below that appeared to fit the description of a great savannah. The further south we flew, the more foliated the land became and dense rainforests changed to solid jungle. Rivers snaked through it, and turbulent rapids became gushing cataracts.

Blue Skies, Green Hell

Then I saw my first tepuí soaring up from the jungle floor like a fortress almost a mile high with vertical walls of sandstone rising above the jungle-covered talus slopes. During the rainy season, the tepuís are usually clear of cloud cover only in the early morning. Later, they are shrouded by mist and fog, and clouds swirl within their canyons. By afternoon, heavy rains obscure them. That's when pilots really watch their altimeter and don't fly below 12,000 feet. We landed at Paraitepui, a flat strip on the top of a high but softly rounded ridge-top referred to by those who live there as *un altiplano* (high plain). We set down on the strip. I held my breath as the plane rolled fast toward scrawny, bare trees and shrubs, while Jack stood on the brakes until the plane stopped just feet from the straggly brush near the edge of a drop-off.

"Someday I'm going to go right through the trees and roll off that damn strip and into the abyss on the other side," Jack said and mopped his brow with the back of his hand.

"And I won't have time to get out the beads," Bill drawled, making reference to rosary beads he allegedly carried but no one had seen.

It was quiet, cold, and eerie. A light rain began to fall again. Indigenous people from the Pemón tribe, living in this Godforsaken part of the world, use blankets at night because it's cold and damp.

Jack suggested I wait in the small shack at the edge of the field and get a cup of coffee. "If you're cold," he said, reading my mind, "I'll get a blanket from the plane." Then he cast his eyes skyward. "Doesn't look like this weather will break. We may have a rough ride back." The windsock blew straight out as though it had been starched.

Nothing existed on Paraitepui except the airstrip, the few scruffy bushes, and a couple of weathered shacks. Inside one, an old gent served coffee. The sky darkened and the sound of rushing wind broke the quietness of this desolate place that, during creation, God had probably decided not to finish.

Sheltered in the shack and comfortably wrapped in the army blanket, I sipped coffee until Jack appeared at the door. He beckoned me to join him.

I crossed the lonely, windy field and arrived at the plane just as the last of the empty drums we'd transport back to CB were loaded and tied down.

Not sure whether I trembled from fear of the anticipated rough flight home or because I felt cold, I climbed the ladder to the huge cargo door. From inside the plane I turned and took one last look through the doorway at Paraitepui. "What a forsaken place," I uttered.

Then I heard Jack say, "Okay, let's go." He slammed the large door shut. He walked ahead of me up the steep incline to the cockpit and squeezed into his seat. I sat on the bench behind Jack and Bill and buckled up as one engine then the other turned over. Spellbound by the barrenness of Paraitepui, I paid no attention to the pilots' exercise of checking things. All I wanted to do was leave Paraitepui and the bad weather. In my head I heard Jack saying, "We may have a rough ride back." *Well, let's get on with it.* I felt uneasy surrounded by the ominous dark sky. The plane roared and shuddered as we rolled, faster, faster. I hung on to the back of Bill's seat and saw the few scruffy trees near the end of the strip at the edge of the high ground fast approaching. They put back pressure on the yokes, and our wheels were barely off the ground, when we flew over the brush and passed beyond the rim of the high ground. I heard Bill say, "Gear up." Then my stomach reached up to my throat as the nose dipped and the plane's speed increased as we descended toward the ground below. I closed my eyes. I heard the power increase and felt like I had pulled a few G's when we changed direction and ascended sharply. I wanted to scream "Noooo," but even a moan wouldn't come out of my dry throat. Every fiber of my body tensed. I held my breath and felt limp as fear exploded within me.

"Did you like that?" asked Jack after we were safely airborne and climbing.

I sat back in my seat and heaved a sigh. "Bill, do you have a prayer book?"

"That would take the fun out of it," Jack replied. "You weren't scared, were you?"

"You bet I was." I laughed nervously, and then nodding said, "Okay. Now I get it. You set me up for that when we landed and you said someday you'd roll off that damn strip and into an abyss."

"Would I do that?"

"Yes. You're nuts," I concluded.

Searching for a cigarette in my bag, I reminded him of the time Frank and I flew with him from Bolivar to Maiquetía when he cut the left engine, feathered the prop then shouted in alarm, "Oh, look at the left engine. The prop's not turning." He hadn't gotten me that time as, a few seconds earlier, I'd heard him loudly whisper to Frank and Bill that he would shut down the engine and feather the prop to scare me.

"Actually, the Paraitepui airstrip is about 4,600 feet above mean sea level, and depending on conditions and the weight we have aboard, sometimes we have to take off like that. We descend to pick up speed and regain lift. Then we can safely ascend to our desired altitude. It's a common maneuver."

After my stomach settled and my hand steadied enough for me to hold a match to my cigarette, I asked Jack why I'd seen no sign of life back there. "What's the diesel fuel for? Who uses it?"

"It's for a diamond mine. I can never stay long enough to see the mine," he said. He explained that mining diamonds is a very big operation in that part of Sir Arthur Conan Doyle's Lost World. "Weather permitting, next time you come with us, we'll look around."

"The weather, so far, hasn't been as bad as I expected, Jack."

"No." He abruptly changed subjects. "But look ahead at twelve o'clock (dead ahead). See that island above the clouds—it's the top of Auyántepui. That's why it's so hard to see Angel Falls after the early morning. The falls cascade from the top of Auyántepui into a canyon. Devil's Canyon."

Blue Skies, Green Hell

"I've heard about it."

"Maybe we'll get a chance to see it today."

As we cruised toward the mysterious-looking tepuí, Jack told me about the American bush pilot, Jimmie Angel, who came upon the waterfalls by accident and thought it was probably the highest in the world. In 1949, only three years before I landed in CB, his claim was validated and he attached his name to the falls, Angel Falls. Until then, only the Indians knew about the falls. They'd called it, Churún Merú.

Stories about Jimmie Angel are sometimes absurd. I believe the story Frank told me. He and Jimmy were friends.

The saga of Jimmie Angel's claim to fame started with him sitting in a bar in Panama in February 1930. It is rumored his pockets were filled with money he earned flying rich gamblers and crooked politicians to secret places. While perched on his usual bar stool, Jimmie was approached by a scruffy-looking old man. "I hear you'll fly anywhere for a price."

Jimmie thought the old man sounded like an American and decided to hear what he had to say. "Sure, I'll fly any place if the price is right. What's this about gold?"

Some said the stranger looked as though he'd had his last bath the day he was born and they said he smelled like it, too. With sparse gray hair, wrinkled face, and one eye closed when he talked, he told Jimmie about a river of gold where he'd been and wanted to return. All he needed was a plane and a pilot. Jimmie opened his eyes wide when he heard the word gold. The saucy old man jammed one hand in his pocket and said, "How do you like this?" He withdrew a handful of gold nuggets. "There's plenty for you, if you're interested."

Jimmie was interested. "Where's this river of gold?"

"In Venezuela," the old man answered in a whisper with one eye still closed. Leaning closer to Jimmy he said in a soft voice, "You get us to Ciudad Bolivar, okay? I'll show you the rest of the way. It's in the *Gran Sabana*."

"The what? The *Gran Sabana*? Where's that?" asked Jimmie.

"In southeast Venezuela. I've been traipsing around that part of the world for a long time." He described a wilderness of grasslands and terrifying jungle that hugs the talus slopes of the foreboding tepuís, colossal tabletop mountains with treacherous canyons and vertical walls. "The tepuís reach a mile high—straight up—out of the jungle. Too high to believe. Strange country you see only in your dreams—or nightmares." The old man leaned closer to Jimmy and slowly whispered, "But most of the time it's just called the Green Hell. It's between the Orinoco and Brazil."

Angel continued to listen to the old man who said he'd been at the base of a tepuí with vertical walls where a massive waterfall had formed a basin. He scooped up stones from the basin and found his first gold nugget. Assuming the nuggets had fallen with the waterfall, the old man figured the point of the gold's origin must be on top of the mountain. It took days for him to climb the vertical wall, but sure enough, on top of the mesa he saw a river flowing to the waterfall and gold covered the river bed. He took as much gold as he could carry and then he made his way down the mesa and out of the jungle by walking, crawling, and floating on logs in rivers. "I swear. I know the way," the old man concluded.

It was Jimmie's kind of gamble.

A month later, Jimmie and the old man headed south to Ciudad Bolivar equipped with miners' shovels, cans of food and ten empty five-gallon gasoline cans. At the Ciudad Bolivar airport, the plane was refueled, empty gas cans were filled. The two flew out and headed south. Adios civilization. *Hola oro* (Hello gold).

Flying over the Gran Sabana, the old man expressed bewilderment at the number of behemoth mesas that rose like citadels from the jungle floor. The tepuís were numerous and all looked alike.

Suddenly, from a wall inside a canyon of a tepuí whose walls rose thousands of feet to the top of the sky, they saw a waterfall cascading down its vertical wall.

"This is it. I'm sure this is it," the old man shouted, his faced pressed on the glass window next to him. "Gold. It's there. It's ours for the taking, Jimmy."

Jimmie made a short landing on the tepuí's flat surface. His four-seat plane rolled over a surface of sharp pointed rocks until it stopped. Both men jumped out of the plane, ran to the icy cold river, flopped in it and grabbed handfuls of the precious nuggets. Feverishly digging with their hands and trowels in the river bottom for an hour, they retrieved seventy-five pounds of gold—at the time, worth $20,000. On the market in 2010, that amount of gold would have been worth approximately $1.5 million dollars.

The tracks made by Jimmie's plane as it landed and rolled over grasses, plants and small vegetation indicated serious problems. Jimmie walked the distance from where the plane had landed to the edge of the tepuí and judged it insufficient for any kind of takeoff roll. Couple that with sharp edged rocks that could tear up the tires and Jimmie had great cause for concern.

According to the story, at the far edge of the tepuí, Jimmie peered at the hostile jungle below; he said he could see a mile down, and returned to the plane. Both men got in and buckled up. The engine kicked over and Jimmie let the plane roll slowly to the edge of the cliff and off the tepuí. As it dove toward the talus slope below, the plane picked up speed. Jimmie pulled back on the yoke and pushed in the throttle to raise the nose of the plane and ascend. He'd used the canyon to pick up flying speed. He maintained his wings level and quickly made a few adjustments—carb heat and flaps—as the plane thumbed its nose at gravity's grip and raced skyward, up and out of the canyon.

"Hell," Jimmie said to friends when he told his story, "I just let gravity do its work."

Angel proclaimed he never again found the river of gold he and the old gent had located. But from time to time, Jimmy was seen at the CB airport, allegedly on his way the Gran Sabana. Jimmie Angel landed in the history books, not for a record gold strike, but for having identified the tallest waterfall in the world—cascading in a canyon in Auyántepui. Waterfalls of extraordinary dimensions are not uncommon within tepuis and falling from their vertical outer walls, but Angel Falls beats them all.

Jack flew the C-46 toward Auyántepui until we were enveloped first by wispy clouds and then heavy ones that obscured our vision.

"I think it's around here," he said.

"What's around here?"

"Angel Falls. I want you to see the falls." He pulled back on the throttles to slow the plane's speed and began circling as he descended through the clouds.

Entrapped in a gray world, I couldn't see a thing. "You don't really have to show me this today, Jack. I can come with Frank, you know. Or maybe the next time you're here."

He acted as though he'd not heard me.

"It's around here. Someplace," he repeated. The plane seemed unusually quiet and I thought I could hear the rushing wind outside. I pulled the old Army blanket tightly around me and continued to shiver—or tremble.

I tapped Bill on the shoulder. He'd been sitting up straight and leaning forward in his seat, his right elbow rested on the arm of the seat and his chin nestled in his hand. His left hand lightly held the yoke. He glanced at the tachometer and occasionally adjusted the throttles. His eyes pierced the clouds ahead. "Bill, I don't need to see it today." I paused then barely whispered so only he could hear me, "Bill. What are we going to do?"

Straining his eyes as he looked through the windscreen at white nothingness, Bill half turned his head and the words came slowly and softly through his exhaled breath, "We make with the beads." (Free translation—pray with our rosary beads).

"There it is," Jack yelled. Still circling with the plane moderately banked, he'd let down in Devil's Canyon near Angel Falls. The clouds dissipated and I looked up and saw the sky. We were in the canyon and below the level of the mesa's summit. I stared at a high cliff of sandstone. Then I saw a plume of water bursting out of crevasses and subterranean streams a little below the mesa's rim. I saw great volumes of water falling and tumbling. Below the midway point of Angel falls, the water vaporized into mist that swirled at hurricane force until it reconstituted into a waterfall eventually forming the Churún River.

I screamed and shouted, "Wow," or something like that. Then I unbuckled my seat belt and stepped from one side of the cockpit to the other to peer out the side windows and to see up and down. I saw it from every angle. I punched the air with my fist and shouted again. "WOW!"

Jack dipped the wing of the plane so I could see a full-length view of the falls, the river that flows from the falls, and the rapids that dance over the rocks down the river bed. Jack made a steep turn to the left away from the waterfall he'd already flown too close to. He circled down and then up again and I watched the foaming water swirl like a drill into a smooth, rounded canyon carved over millions of years. The canyon wall shone. At the base of the falls the wet shale is even unfit for jungle plant life as gale-force winds whip around and water splashes fiercely.

"Oh, my God," I breathed.

Jack pulled back on the yoke, eased out of the bank, pushed the throttles forward and the great plane gracefully flew away from the falls and out of Devil's Canyon.

"How about that, Marilyn! Glad you came today?"

"Oh. I'll never see anything like it. What a remarkable sight!" The fear and uneasiness of circling in the clouds had already been erased from my memory at the sight of the world's tallest waterfall. As we flew by Angel Falls, it seemed like a fine spray blew on the windscreen and wings of the plane. Although it probably was a light rain, I like to think it had come from the falls. An ethereal moment in time. We were silent.

I'll never know whether Jack flew by instruments, of which there were few by today's standards, or the seat of his pants, which is, indeed, how old-timers often flew their planes when they judged the yaw of their plane and the degree of the plane's bank by the feel of their bodies shifting in their seats. But during the drama of the descent through the clouds into the canyon and the sudden vision of the overwhelming torrent of water racing more than 3,000 feet downward, I lived a moment that gave me a lifetime of memories.

After we left the canyon and gained altitude, I tried to catch my breath and wait for my heartbeat to return to normal. I'd seen the incomparable Angel Falls.

"Let's go home," Jack said.

* * *

I saw Angels Falls many times during the years that followed. While I experienced the ride of a lifetime with Jack, every flight to Angel Falls thrills me.

On December 8, 1956, Jimmie Angel was killed on landing in Panama. He was 57 years old. His ashes were scattered over Angel Falls in 1960.

Curtiss-Wright
C-46 Commando;
affectionately called,
"The Bucket."
Photo by Marilyn

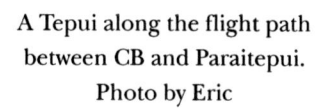

A Tepui along the flight path
between CB and Paraitepui.
Photo by Eric

Three shacks at the airfield
at Paraiteipui
Photo by Marilyn—1952

Chapter 11

"I'm Sick. I've Got to Go Home"

Dear Mother and Dad   October 4, 1952

    We're in Caracas—both here to see doctors. You know I haven't felt well for a long time. Tests made in Bolivar ruled out amoebic dysentery. I'll get another opinion. Frank will see his doctor about his ear problems. When he flies high altitudes, his ears bleed and ache. I'll let you know when I know more.

    Irv's wife, Magda arrived. I've been so sick, I haven't had time to get to know her. She's a year younger than I and very pretty. I know we'll get along.

    Oops, I'm out of paper.

Devotedly, Marilyn

    After I told Frank I'd never felt worse in my life he insisted I go to Caracas with him and have a physical checkup. I'd had the same symptoms for months and they'd been debilitating; painful abdominal cramps, diarrhea, attacks of nausea, loss of appetite and weight. Doctor Battistini in Ciudad Bolivar prescribed several kinds of drugs, but none worked. He concluded amoeba was not the cause and suggested I see a doctor in Caracas for more tests and another medical opinion. Frank also planned to see his doctor because of his continuing ear trouble.

    As I packed my clothes for Caracas, random thoughts raced through my head.

    No question about it, Frank needed to see his doctor, but I also believed Frank wanted to see his mother. She put him on a guilt trip when she thought too much time had elapsed between his trips to Caracas. She'd cable him in Bolivar and say she was getting old, he was too far away, she needed him to take care of some of her business. Whatever she thought would work to get him back, that's what she wrote.

    In one of her letters she wrote that her house had been broken into and she wanted Frank to come to Caracas and stay with her while the locks on the doors were changed.

Blue Skies, Green Hell

"Why you?" I asked. "She has two other sons and four daughters, all well-to-do, all married, all living in Caracas."

"I know." He sighed. "I know." He said no more about the incident. Nor did I. He did not go to oversee the changing of the locks.

She made it difficult for him. Frank would always be her little boy. Her youngest and most pampered offspring had been the benefactor of her generosity. She paid his tuition and expenses at the school of aviation in Maracay, and later financed his partnership in the air service even though she didn't like the idea of him flying. Frank felt indebted to her.

His mother made it hard for me, too, giving advice on everything from home decoration to animal care. She told me to take care of her Frankie. "You must look after him and serve him. He's the lord of the manor—the king of his castle," she'd say.

When it got too much for me, Frank would say, "She's an old lady who wants to help and doesn't realize she's interfering. Take her advice when you want—disregard the rest and do what you want." It still wasn't easy.

As in the past, we stayed with her and had no privacy. Early every morning when she thought I was still sleeping she'd shuffle into our bedroom with a cup of demitasse rattling in her shaky hands and awaken Frank by cooing his name in a dulcet whisper. "*Frankicito.*" Then she'd sit on the edge of his bed and serve him his "*cafecito.*" She whispered in Spanish. I didn't know what they talked furtively about. I put up with it. Frank knew it was difficult for me and apologized for her behavior. He said he couldn't do anything about it. He was caught in the middle.

I also knew Frank's doctor would order him to quit smoking—again. However, the order would bring conflicting advice from his mother. We'd gone through this before. After other visits to the doctor when he'd been told he needed bed rest and to stop smoking, she always took pity on him.

She'd whine in her high pitched voice, "Poor Frankie needs his cigarettes." While I'd take his cigarettes away from him, she'd offer him one of hers every time she passed his room.

Although I told her cigarettes were bad for the health of the lord of the manor and king of the castle, she'd squeak in baby talk, "Frankie needs his little smokes." Before I met Frank he'd had a pneumothorax (collapsed lung) that healed itself after bed rest. He was ordered never to smoke again.

"You'll kill him," I told her. "Is that what you want to do?"

"Poor Frankie. My darling son." Her standard answer.

I wrote home, "She drives me nuts." I wanted so much to like Frank's mother, but she wouldn't let it happen.

Mother wrote back she was glad I still had spunk.

I did not look forward to the Caracas trip. However, for my own well-being, this time I had no choice. I closed the lid of my over-packed suitcase and sat on it so it would close and lock.

Frank neatly packed his things in a suitcase half the size of mine, in half the time, and snapped the locks closed with no trouble.

We drove across the street to the airport, parked the car near our hangar and boarded the noontime flight to Maiquetía. It arrived on time. We flagged a taxi at the airport and headed over the mountain to Caracas and his mother's apartment.

All a twitter when we arrived, she paled when she learned we were both sick. "It's okay, Mami," soothed Frank, his voice soft and syrupy, as he put his arms around her. For a moment, I felt sorry for his mother; so tiny, so frail, she melted in the warmth and security of his arms. I knew that feeling. "Don't worry about us. We'll do for ourselves and don't even think about missing your poker games or mah jongg."

The next morning, we borrowed a car from Frank's brother and drove to Frank's doctor's office located in the Centro Medico building in the suburb of San Bernardino. Frank saw the doctor first. After numerous tests, the doctor prescribed ear drops and some antibiotics. Additionally, he ordered bed rest for a few days and then he emphatically ordered no smoking. "And no flying," the doctor declared sternly. "Not for a month, at least."

Frank nodded and I hoped he would pay attention to the doctor's orders. He needed rest, and being grounded, I delighted thinking about the time we'd have together.

Frank retreated to the waiting room and the doctor began his examination of me. At the conclusion he told me to get dressed and go to his office.

In his office, I looked around and wondered why doctors' offices, whether in the States or Venezuela, all look alike. His oversized desk had a lamp on it with a tinted shade to soften the glare of the light. Two burgundy-colored leather chairs with brass buttons on the arms were placed at angles in front of the desk. A bookcase full of books, family pictures and knick knacks completed the room. Lots of knick knacks—a little golf club paper weight and a tennis racquet pen holder. He sat behind his grandiose leather-topped desk, looked at me and gestured to a chair.

"Sit down, Señora." Then he told me preliminary results showed advanced colitis that might be causing problems with my appendix. He said if we quiet the colon, perhaps the chronic appendicitis would subside. "There is no cure for colitis."

He said his nurse would give me shots of penicillin and streptomycin and then added, quite matter-of-factly, "What you must do is change the way you live." He told me to change the things I do and the way I do them and explained that colitis is brought on by tension and emotional stress. "Just walk away from

Blue Skies, Green Hell

whatever it is that causes tension and stress in your life." That's what he said. "Just walk away." So I did. I left him twiddling the stethoscope that hung around his neck. "Reductions in your emotional stress are imperative . . . ." His voice faded.

He caught up to me at his nurse's station, and while she gave me an injection, he wrote a prescription for a sedative. "Señora. Take the medicine and put ice packs on your appendix for five days. You need bed rest. If this doesn't help, then you'll probably need surgery." His voice faded as I again walked away—this time to the waiting room and Frank.

"I've got to change my life," I said, and told Frank about the shots and waved the paper with the prescription. "More medicine. Every doctor I've seen has a different prescription for me. Maybe someday I'll get the right one."

We walked to the car. "That's what he said, Frank." I mimicked the doctor's stoic recitation about the emotional stress and the colitis. "Frank, I may have to have an appendectomy."

We drove in silence through Caracas and up into the hills. "And me?" Frank finally spoke. "It's the same old story. Bed rest. No flying for a month."

"And smoking?'

He sighed, lowered his voice and replied, "And no smoking."

Near 5:30 p.m., we stopped at a restaurant—a charming old Spanish colonial house with a broad porch and an interior courtyard where a gentle breeze played with the leaves that dangled from tall trees. Interior walls of the small rooms located off the courtyard were of mahogany, the extra wide floor boards, warped by time, were uneven under our feet and creaked when we walked on them. The tables, each set for four guests, had small candles, a white linen table cloth, and napkins. Crystal water goblets on the tables and the crystal chandelier hanging from a mahogany beam in the center of the room reflected the candlelight. Except for soft Venezuelan music in the background the empty restaurant was silent. In Venezuela, main dinners are usually served at noon. A light evening meal is served as late as ten o'clock. Thus, we were the only diners.

A dark haired hostess, a little too haughty, led us to a table. We looked at the menu until a waiter came to the table. He took our order for two scotches. "I don't feel much like eating, Frank."

"That's what you say when we're in Bolivar. You say you don't eat there because it's too hot. It's not hot here. Please eat something." The waiter brought our drinks and Frank ordered filet mignon for both of us.

We held hands across the table. I spoke first. "I love my life in Bolivar and my friends there. But mostly, I love you. If I could change one thing—I'd have you home more often." I sighed. "I don't mean fly less. I mean I wish you didn't have to come to Caracas so often."

"Button. I'm the only one who can get things done at the ministry. Julio and Shorty are foreigners. That makes a difference. You know that. And you can always come with me to Caracas. Instead of staying at my mothers, we could stay at a hotel or Shorty's apartment when he's working in the field."

I nodded. "Don't pay any attention to what I just said. I've been handling things in Bolivar very well. I have good friends, Madelyn and Shirley, and now Martha's there. And Magda, too. I'm lucky." I stopped talking, lit a cigarette and stubbed it out. "I feel so damn sick and that jerky doctor says I have to change my life." I repeated, "I love my life in Bolivar."

We sipped our drinks and Frank leaned back in his chair. He put one hand in his trouser pocket while he rolled a stirrer on the linen table cloth with the other. "I want to be with you too, and we will have fun—again—like we used to. We can't always be sick. Things will be better when we have our own license. There'll be fewer trips to Caracas, fewer separations." He tapped a cigarette on the back of his hand and lit it. "And don't tell me I shouldn't smoke. This isn't the time for that."

"I want to get back to good times, too." In my mind's eye I saw Frank playing guitar and singing. I saw the Black Horse Café. I saw the moon over the savannah.

He sipped his scotch. "And maybe then we can start thinking about having a family. Maybe a baby would bring stability—more togetherness. We both want that."

My stomach flip-flopped. I was dumbfounded. *How crazy to bring up the subject of a baby.* Of course, I wanted a baby, but if it wasn't the time for him to quit smoking, it certainly wasn't the time for us to think about a baby. "We can talk about it after I'm feeling better," I replied indifferently.

As we talked, I became aware of a strange itching sensation first in my hands and then my knees. I tenderly rubbed my right knee, then my left. Hot to the touch, I looked at my knees and bellowed, "Oh my God, look at my knees. Look, Frank. My knees are swollen and they're hot. My hands, too!"

Frank told the hostess to cancel our dinners.

We quickly drove back to the doctor's office in Centro Medico. Fortunately, the doctor had evening hours. Frank joined me in the examining room.

The doctor looked at my hands and knees then packaged his diagnosis and remedy in a few tight sentences. "I don't think it's anything. Maybe it's an allergy to soap or perfume. Let's wait a few days. Perhaps it'll go away."

"This is nothing?" I asked Frank as I pointed to my swollen knees. "What a jerk," I said in a stage whisper. I didn't give a damn whether he heard me or not. Frank helped me off the table and we left his office.

For the next five days I stayed in bed with ice packs on my appendix. My swollen condition worsened and the symptoms of colitis remained much the same. Daily, Frank reported my status to the doctor.

Blue Skies, Green Hell

Frank, also in need of rest, found quiet time difficult. "I'll take care of myself in a few days," he said.

Our attention shifted from colitis to the swelling. We phoned the doctor a few times and he continued to have no idea what was wrong. I suggested vigorously I might be allergic to the shot he'd given me. He denied with equal vigor that medication had caused an allergic reaction. He told me to wait a little longer.

Over the next couple of days, my knees remained like footballs and my hands looked like balloons about to burst. In addition, great welts covered my body and I could barely see through my swollen eyelids. My throat began to swell. Nauseated when I tried to stand up, I stayed in bed and got up only with help; I couldn't raise my head off the pillow without feeling dizzy and light-headed.

Frank's mother and her friends were playing their usual serious game of poker at a card table in the living room and Frank was sitting with me when the phone on a table in the hall outside our bedroom rang. I heard him talking to Jack Perez in Bolivar. They chatted for quite a while, taking advantage of the unusually good connection between Caracas and CB.

After he hung up the phone and came back in the room, he said, "Jack'll be here tomorrow. The next day he'll fly back to Miami. You're going back with him."

"Thanks be to God. I want to go. This doctor doesn't know anything. All he says is, 'Wait. Wait. Wait.' I'll die if I stay here waiting."

Frank sat on the edge of my bed and studied his folded hands. "Button, I can't go with you." He lowered his head. "Julio needs me."

"Julio needs you? I need you." I barely got the words out. I closed my eyes and the room spun. I had no strength to speak. *I can't imagine why I'm emotionally stressed.*

"While I'm here, he's running the business. I worry about him messing up the books," Frank declared. "And he and Irv can't do everything. Maybe Magda and Martha can pitch in at the office. Magda's been here a month now. She could type letters. If Tom can fly for us, then I can go to New York. I'll join you."

"You're talking in circles, Frank." I put the back of my hand to my mouth. "I'm scared. And now I have to fly home—alone." I reached for his hand.

"It's so much to ask of you, Button. But Jack and Bill will be with you."

I turned my head away in despair. "They'll be with me as far as Miami."

"They'll take care of you. Trust them. Jack said to tell you he won't joke around. We'll see the doctor tomorrow morning and tell him you're going to the States and he's got to give you something so you can make the trip. A sedative—or something." He leaned toward me and kissed my sweaty forehead. "You've got to go. I agree—it's the only way you'll get well."

129

I had no appointment to see the doctor but Frank called ahead to say we were coming. One look at me and the receptionist rushed us into an examining room. The doctor hastened to my side and Frank started to tell him what to do. That was followed by the doctor telling Frank to wait in the outer office. In stern voices each spoke a few unkind words in Spanish and Frank huffed out.

"I'm sick." I barely mumbled to the doctor who looked bewildered. "Please help me."

I recalled Carlos telling me about his allergic reaction to a shot of penicillin after he'd been injured in the jungle. My symptoms resembled those Carlos had described. Madelyn gave him an intravenous injection of calcium and he recovered quickly. "Please give me calcium in my vein." I wasn't even sure what I was asking for, but I told Carlos' story to the doctor.

"Calcium will do you no good. It will do nothing," the doctor said, brushing off my suggestion. He left the office and returned with three other doctors who stood over me as I reclined on the examining table. One by one, each examined me, poked me here and there and listened to my heart and lungs. They spoke so fast and excitedly in Spanish, I couldn't understand them.

The three hurried out of the office and I was alone with the doctor who knew nothing and apparently had learned nothing from his associates. "What did they say?" He didn't answer me. I guessed my condition confounded the four. "Please. Give me a shot of calcium," I pleaded one more time. "I am going to the States tomorrow. You don't know what to do, so why not give me calcium? It can't hurt me." I paused. "Do you have a better idea?"

He grumbled and grunted and shuffled around his office, flipped pages in a big book on a window sill. He stared out the window and finally started to prepare a needle. "It won't do any good," he said and then added he needed to warm the solution. He disappeared. When he returned he told me I would feel a wave of heat come over my body. Then he stuck me in a vein. For once he was right. I began to feel warm all over. Exhausted, I enjoyed the warmth, and felt pleased that at last something was being done for me—even though I knew not what—nor if it would help.[8]

He withdrew the needle from my arm then said, "I will not give you authorization to leave the country or enter yours." He also refused to give me a sedative.

"I don't need papers." He looked astonished. I did not tell him I'd fly home on a cargo plane as crew and thus needed no special papers to leave the country nor enter mine.

When the doctor called the next day to inquire about my condition, Frank told him the rash and swelling were subsiding and I was able to eat. Sarcastically, Frank urged the doctor to look into calcium as an effective antidote for an allergy to medication or an allergy caused by a patient taking too many medications. He added that he might want to pay attention to his patients.

Blue Skies, Green Hell

Then Jack called. He was in Maiquetía and planning to fly to Miami the next day.

The next morning, still slightly weak, though feeling much better, we had breakfast with Frank's mother and then drove over the mountain to Maiquetía where we met Jack and Bill. They said they'd fly a course that would take them over the islands where they could set down in case I needed emergency medical help.

"It's time she saw her own doctor. First it was colitis then her appendix, now—whatever it is she has. I worry about her, Frank. We'll get her home, even if we fly all the way to New York."

"I'll phone every night I'm in Caracas," Frank said. "When I go back to Bolivar, I'll send cables. Just get well."

"I'm scared, Frank, and I don't want to fly alone all the way to New York. I don't feel good about this whole trip. I wish you'd be with me."

"I love you, Button."

"I love you. And you—please take care of yourself. No smoking? We both have to get well."

Then I was in the C-46 taxiing to the runway, taking off, heading north, and going home.

Chapter 12

"I'm Coming Home on Jack's C-46"

October 14, 1952, early a.m.
Frank sent a Western Union
Telegram to Mother and Dad.

MARILYN COMING HOME TODAY ON
JACKS C46 STOP SHE WILL CALL
YOU FROM MIAMI STOP
LOVE FRANK

Time passed quickly. As usual, Jack gave me a headset and I listened to American music over the radio. I still had a slight rash, but mostly I was tired. I put my head back, closed my eyes and dozed.

And then the left engine coughed and the plane lurched. I awakened with a start, and in less time than it takes to tell, the engine died. Jack bolted upright in his chair. "I've got the plane," he said loudly and grabbed the yoke while his eyes rapidly scanned the instrument panel in front of him. He looked up at the ceiling, grabbed a handle over his head and turned it. He clicked other switches. He looked back to his instrument panel and studied each as pointers and numbers swiftly moved from one setting to another. Again, his eyes flashed from over head and back to the panel. Bill Murphy, co-pilot, who'd also fallen asleep, awakened, grabbed his clipboard, attached it to his thigh, and began to make notes.

Then the right engine missed. It missed again and died and then there was no sound of engines, just the air rushing by the large cargo plane. I don't know whether the plane shook or I did as the plane's nose dipped. Bill called on the radio. "Mayday. Mayday. Anybody." He spoke into the microphone. I couldn't hear any more of what he said over the sound of the wind.

I was scared, paralyzed with fear. Frozen in my seat, I began to sweat and my knees trembled. I didn't know what was going on, but the ride became rough and chills tap-danced up my spine as the old plane bumped and the radio continued to crackle. Jack said calmly, "Raft's on the bulkhead next to you, Marilyn. Don't do anything unless I tell you." On past flights, I'd seen the emergency door to my right and the raft folded in an army-green net bag and—out of boredom—I'd read the instructions. I'd read them over and over.

Now, I shivered and read the instructions again. I knew them by heart. I feared the raft might be heavy and I hoped I had the strength I'd need . . . if . . . .

The plane's descent was at a fairly steep rate, My body tugged against the seat belt. With both engines dead, I'd expected the plane to fall like a rock, but it didn't. Instead, it had sufficient air going over the wings to keep the plane aloft. It glided and bounced. It was extremely quiet, except for the sound of air whooshing by us. I didn't know what each instrument was for, but I knew about the altimeter and watched the pointers in it spin as we dropped from 10,000 feet to 8,000 to 6,000 to 4,000. I stopped watching the pointers and instead looked out the window. We were going down and the sea was coming up to meet us. WHOOSH. *Come on, Jack. Get this damn thing going.* I exhaled through pursed lips. I couldn't control my trembling, my knees quivered and my thighs felt weak. Mostly, I felt sick in my stomach, not because of an allergic reaction or colitis, but because I was afraid, sick afraid. The Caribbean looked close. I wondered if the water would be cold. WHOOSH. Jack and Bill worked. I didn't know what they were doing. As for me, my heart palpitated and I could hardly breathe.

And then as quickly as the left engine had died, it started. It didn't cough, didn't squeal. It just started smoothly. Then the right engine did the same. We were low. Very low. I saw white caps on the water when Jack and Bill pulled back on their yokes, pushed the throttles forward, performed a few other miracles and our descent changed to level flight. We picked up speed, ascended, and I heard the comforting sound of two healthy Pratt and Whitneys running smoothly in synch with each other.

Lots of things had raced through my mind as the plane fell, and the real passage of time is confused. I don't know. Maybe it was five minutes; it only seemed like a lifetime.

"Jack?" I whispered. "What happened?"

"Well," he spoke haltingly. "Ah . . . ah . . . we fell asleep. Bill and I. The gas tanks went dry. I switched tanks. Took care of that." He paused and sort of shrugged his shoulders. "But the carburetors iced up, too."

His voice was tranquil—almost cavalier. I could hardly believe his calm demeanor after such a terrifying experience.

"You both fell asleep?"

"Yeah."

"I dozed off, too. If I'd seen both of you sleeping, I'd have awakened you—but . . ."

"When the plane's on autopilot, it's easy to drop off—and the fuel tanks have to be switched manually."

I wasn't angry, just frightened, and felt this might be my last ride on the C-46. Even if I wanted to fly on it again, I was certain Frank's last word would be a firm, "No."

"You're not going to set down on an island and, ah, look things over? Find out about the ice in the carburetors?" I asked.

Jack said that wouldn't be necessary and explained that he knew immediately that the problem had been caused by an empty gas tank, and when he turned the gas valve to switch tanks, it took time for the fuel to start to flow and reach the engines—and for them to start. He said he had time because we'd been flying at 10,000 feet and the empty C-46's sink rate at best glide speed was probably about 2,000 feet per minute. "We had time to work everything out."

"But Bill called 'Mayday.'"

"Routine. SOP. You know."

"And your iced carburetors?" I asked. "Over the warm Caribbean?"

"It doesn't much concern air temperature. It's a function of both decreasing air pressure and vaporization of fuel in the carburetor's venturi. We'll be okay now."

I'd received more information than I understood and made a mental note to ask Frank about the venturi. Then I looked at Bill quizzically. He gently patted my knee and silently mouthed the words, "I'm sorry." Bill, always kind and sensitive.

The crisis over, Jack and Bill flew along as though nothing had happened. I, however, knew something scary as hell happened and sleep, even rest, eluded me for the balance of the flight. I concentrated on the sound of the engines for the next few hours. Properly functioning and synchronized, they droned steadily; no longer sounding monotonous but instead reassuring. Darkness took over daylight. I felt uneasy and jumpy until I saw the coastline of Florida brightly lit on the horizon in front of us. Leaning forward and resting my elbows on my knees, I cradled my head in my hands and said another prayer of thanksgiving.

Jack landed the plane at the International Airport in Miami and taxied to a building where he stopped and shut down the engines. We exited the plane and went in the building and on through Customs and Immigration. I had only one hatbox, but the customs people seldom checked crew members' luggage anyway.

"Take care and feel better soon. We'll see you when you go back," said Jack quite routinely. I nodded, not believing for a minute he'd ever see me in that plane without Frank. "Bill, take Marilyn to Eastern Terminal?"

"Sure thing."

"Bill, after the cargo is loaded, we'll head back . . ."

"To Venezuela?" I asked and my voice rang with shock and disbelief.

"Yeah. Got one more trip. We'll overnight there and head back tomorrow."

"Goodnight, Jack. Thanks for the ride." Within a few minutes, Bill and I were at Eastern Airlines Terminal getting my ticket.

Standby. I had plenty of time to wait. It was late and flights were few and full.

Chapter 13

"Not Hardships . . . Just Inconveniences."

Phone call to Mother and Dad   **October 15, 1952.**

"Hi Mom. I arrived in Miami a little while ago . . .
I came up with Jack and Bill . . . I'll call when I know my flight number and ETA in New York. Love You. 'Bye."

I saw a water fountain, walked to it and looked at it in wonderment. Imagine, pure water, from a water fountain in a public building. What a luxury. I'm home!

"Let's get something to eat." Bill took my arm and led me to a coffee shop in the Eastern Airlines Terminal. "I'll stay with you a while. Then I'll go back to the plane."

"No sleep?" I asked.

"After I call my wife, I'll probably doze a little before we takeoff. Takes time to load the plane."

"I remember," I said. "What about the plane? Is it okay?"

"Sure. It's okay. It's really in great shape despite its age and the wear it gets." He gestured to an empty booth and led me to it. "It's well maintained. That plane's a real workhorse."

I slid into the booth quite easily. With a little difficulty, Bill, a tall man, slid in the seat opposite me.

A waitress with frizzy red hair, wearing a starched pink uniform with white collar and cuffs came to the table. "What'll it be, Honey?" she asked, her pen poised over a small pad.

I looked at the young lady and my mouth uncontrollably dropped open. I said nothing.

"English sound good?" Bill asked.

"You read my mind. I hadn't realized I missed it."

"Are you feeling well enough for coffee and a grilled cheese sandwich?" His sapphire blue eyes complimented his tousled blonde hair. He wore tight blue jeans, a fitted blue shirt and a wide leather belt—and I wondered where he carried his Rosary Beads, the ones he often joked about using in emergencies.

135

Bill, attractive and in control of a quietly laid-back demeanor, had a deep soft voice and slow southern manner of speech that enhanced his appeal.

"I'm feeling good. A little tired. Coffee and a sandwich sounds super," I answered.

"Want anything in your coffee?" the red-headed waitress asked as she chewed her gum.

"A little milk, please," I answered.

After the waitress had taken the orders, I said, "Frank would really love it if you'd come down and fly with us a while. We have plenty of work. Our planes stay busy, especially in the dry season. And we'll be getting Jack's twin-engine Beechcraft soon." I knew Bill liked to fly the Beech. It was everybody's favorite. A sweet airplane.

"I'd like to come down for a while, but my wife won't exchange her Miami lifestyle for your hardships in Bolivar."

"Bring her down for a visit. Stay with us. She'll see how good it is."

"Not even for a visit," he insisted. "She won't come. And . . ." he played with his wedding ring, "we have two children." I nodded slowly. I understood the problem. The Rojas children had recently arrived in CB and already Julio was looking into boarding schools in Barbados for them to attend. Bill leaned across the table and pressed my small hands between his, so large and so strong. "I'd like to fly with Frank, but I just can't."

Bill commented on how I'd been pleasantly surprised by the sound of hearing English spoken in the coffee shop. "And I watched you drink water from a public water fountain. Did you worry about parasites?"

"Sure. For half a second." I sighed. "I know what you're driving at. You have it pretty easy here. But I bet I have more fun."

"And you don't mind soaking your fruits and vegetables in water with halazone tablets or dousing them in boiling water to peel them?[9] And it's fun when you run out of halazone and you throw a few drops of Clorox in the water you soak your fresh fruits and vegetables in?"

I brushed my hair back from my face with my hand. "All that you say is true, but if I'm having a good time with Frank—and friends—that's what matters."

It wasn't the first time Bill kidded me about hardships of life in Bolivar. But, I'd follow up his fun by accusing him of being soft.

"Hardships are things that are difficult to endure," he'd say.

I'd counter, "We don't have hardships. We have inconveniences."

"You're a good sport and you laugh at things others would cry over. Was it a few weeks ago you said you had to have a new leg put on your dining room server because it had been eaten by termites?"

I giggled. "It turned out to be more than one leg. They ate the legs on my dressing table, too."

"You just made a long flight because of your health. And you have another trip tomorrow."

"Right again, Bill. We do lack medical facilities in Bolivar. But they're getting better all the time, and, hey, when I go home to see a doctor, I see my family, too. It's a vacation."

"And another thing," he continued, "When your dogs are sick, you fly them to their vet in Caracas. Why? Because in CB the vets don't handle small animal business. They take care of large animals." He sipped his coffee then said, "What about those power outages?"

"Hey, Bill—enough, okay?"

We drank our coffee and ate our sandwiches in silence, the quietness broken only by the sound of my spoon clinking the inside of my coffee cup "When all is said and done, I love it in Bolivar."

"You know. I'm only teasing you."

"We may have a few bugs and things. But in Bolivar, I've never seen a snake. You probably have more snakes in Florida than there are in Bolivar."

"You've got me there."

Then I remembered a day I visited Madelyn, when suddenly out of the corner of my eye, I saw baby Lilly creeping on her hands and knees across the room; she moved at top speed and babbled excitedly. When I saw the attraction, a black fuzzy five-inch long centipede with two huge stingers in the front, I swept her up in my arms just as she'd reached out to grasp the deadly insect. I screamed and Madelyn, who'd been in the kitchen, came running. She saw the insect and grabbed the Flit gun—a manually operated pump sprayer filled with deadly insecticide called Flit—and doused the centipede. I watched it writhe in its death throes until finished off by Madelyn's broom. Seconds later, she swept the dead insect out of the living room and into the dirt outside. She'd killed one of the most deadly bugs. Madelyn said I saved Lilly's life.

I learned that day to pour household poison down bathroom and kitchen drains, and shake out my shoes before I put them on to be sure no scorpion had crawled in. I checked between the sheets before going to bed just to be sure no creepy crawly waited to share the bed with me.

We had window screens made. No one in the interior used screens. They said they cut out the breeze. In Bolivar, one might ask, "What breeze?"

We nailed strips of rubber along the bottom of exterior doors to prevent snakes from crawling under. We'd learned that trick when, on our honeymoon, we visited Frank's friends, Jesús and China, in Maiquetía.

I couldn't get fly paper or fly swatters in Bolivar—and we had giant-sized flies. So, Dad made a giant size fly swatter which Bill brought to me. Bill must have forgotten that or I'm sure I would have heard about it.

There were times I had no writing paper and with none available in stores, I'd use the inside of envelopes which I'd first steam open. Mother frequently sent tissue-thin airmail paper to me.

Telephone service to Caracas was spotty at best. Most often I couldn't get through at all. But what could I expect, when even local telephone service was unreliable.

Frank and I sacrificed in order to pay for a gas stove. Most appliances were fueled by kerosene. And there were few appliances. No dishwashers, no clothes driers. Clothes washers didn't have a spin cycle. Instead, you fed your wet clothes from the wash tub to and between wringers on top of the machine that squeezed out the water. I hung our laundry outdoors on rope lines except in the rainy season when I didn't do much laundry. The sun and the heat rotted the clothesline rope and it was hell when the rope broke and wet sheets fell in red dirt.

There were no dress shops in town and no shoe stores. It was a good thing shampoo and nail polish were available in the drugstore because Bolivar had no hair dressers and no manicurists.

When the frames on my sunglasses broke, it took six months to replace them.

I battled mold and mildew every day. It grew in the closets, on the shoes, luggage, pocketbooks. One weekend, Mrs. Perez Jimenez, the first lady of Venezuela, came to Ciudad Bolivar and the social whirl didn't stop for two days. Frank and I were invited to all the festivities. The first event was a private formal reception and dance at the Governor's house. I had planned to wear a special formal I'd brought from New York, strapless and red. A few days before the Governor's Ball, I opened the trunk in which I'd carefully packed my red gown between layers of tissue paper and found the gown damp, covered with mildew, mold, and dead spiders. Frank sent our regrets to his friend, the Governor. I tossed out the dress.

The next night, I borrowed a gown from Magda to wear to the ball at the Gran Hotel in the city.

Even with two grocery stores, I could not get tomato soup, chocolate syrup, white bread, tuna fish and other staples that line the shelves of kitchen cabinets in the States. I'd drive two hundred miles roundtrip to friends living in the oil company camps on the north side of the Orinoco where I'd shop in their commissaries. There we purchased pork, chicken and other delicacies. If a plane and Julio or Frank were available, we'd fly to the commissaries to shop. That was classy shopping and no hardship.

"And friends? Bill," I continued, "I have good friends and that means a lot. I love Madelyn like a sister, and because Frank has coincidentally recruited pilots whose wives are Americans, we have a full social life. We have good times with great people."

Blue Skies, Green Hell

Bill said I practically ran a boarding house for guests because the hotels and restaurants were inadequate. "And every pilot in town thinks your palace is their home."

I assured him both Frank and I loved entertaining. "And," I emphasized, "it's pretty nice having a live-in maid who cooks, serves table and cleans up after meals, and day workers for house cleaning and ironing. A live-in house boy does floors and windows."

"Even with domestic help, she wouldn't come down."

"I'm sorry, Bill. I'm sorry for you." I fidgeted with my paper napkin and then put it under the coffee cup to prevent spilled coffee from dripping. "Bill, there are plenty of trade-offs. A great one is a life on the frontier filled with adventures. I've seen Angel Falls more than once. Few people—other than natives—have seen it. And it's still being written up in National Geographic and Life as a new wonder of the world." I looked at my watch. "And peanut butter and chocolate cakes from a bakery in Miami are flown to me by a couple of swell guys in a C-46."

"You haven't talked about the times Frank is overdue—when you expect him home by six and after the sun sets you're left alone looking into an empty sky—and you ask yourself where is he—is he safe?"

"I knew he was a pilot when I married him. And it is a very real concern. But I loved him from the start and accepted the risk."

"You don't play—what if?"

"Does your wife? She has the same fears—and she lives in Florida. Overdue? That hardship's not limited to Ciudad Bolivar—the last frontier—or the Lost World."

Bill knew I dreaded the thought that one day my life of adventure would probably end. Frank had said often that as the business grew, it would be prudent for him to be in Caracas—full time—to take care of that end of the business. "I'll enjoy every minute I live in CB. I don't want to think about leaving. I can't imagine a life off the frontier—with no adventures, no flights to Angel Falls, no parties with the most interesting people I've ever known. I love Ciudad Bolivar. I'd prefer never to leave."

Bill had a long night ahead and I worried about that. I didn't want to see him go. But I couldn't be selfish and expect him to stay with me any longer. I'd be okay until my plane departed. "I wouldn't be upset if you went back to the plane, caught some shut-eye." I added that I thought flying a round trip between Miami and Venezuela—about sixteen hours—was not only a hardship, I called it dangerous. "I wouldn't want my husband flying those hours. Frank flies about one hundred hours a month—with a good night's sleep at home almost every night."

He finished his coffee and stood up. "Sure you're okay, now? I can stay, you know."

139

I nodded. "I am, Bill."

"You're tough, but not as tough as you think," and chucked me under my chin. "Get well, Marilyn. We'll see you when you're ready to go back."

I smiled and nodded. "Take care of yourself, Bill." We looked at each other a second longer than usual. He gave me an *abrazo* (hug). Then he turned and I watched him leave the coffee shop, walk down the long corridor, push open a glass door and disappear into the darkness.

I never saw Bill Murphy again. Sometime during the first days of January 1953, while flying a light aircraft over the Florida Everglades, Bill and his aircraft disappeared. By January 31, no one had heard from him or seen his aircraft despite exhaustive search efforts. The search and rescue was called off. I agonized over his death; a dreadful loss.

My friend, Bill Murphy. Gone. Death. Now that's a hardship.

Chapter 14

"Home Is Where the Heart Is"

Dearest Frank   **Early a.m. October 15, 1952**

    I'm in the Miami airport, ready to fly north. My trip here with Jack will be told and retold many times. Wait 'til you hear it the first time! Oops . . . I'm being paged. I'm on standby. More later.

Love you. Marilyn

    I had a "standby" reservation on each of three planes—one after another—but not lucky enough to get a seat on any. Alas. At 2:00 a.m., the voice of the lone ticket agent echoed in the cavernous terminal, "Mrs. Lazzari. Please come to the ticket counter." *What more can happen?* "Sorry, Mrs. Lazzari. Our last plane to New York has been cancelled. You're on the first plane out—8:00 tomorrow morning."
    I made one last call to my parents. Throughout the long night I'd phoned Mother and Dad as the status of my flight changed. They had as little sleep as I.
    I carried my hat box containing clean clothes, exited the terminal, and flagged a taxi.
    "Ride lady?"
    "Please," I said, opening the car door and dropping into the back seat.
    "Where to?" He asked.
    "See that sign—TraveLodge Motel? That'll be fine if it's open."
    "That's just the other side of the parking lot. I don't want to steal your money, lady. But it'll cost a few bucks just to go across the parking lot. There's a minimum, you know."
    "That's okay. Just drive me there, please"
    I checked into a tiny room, and without washing my face, taking off my clothes, or removing the bedspread, I fell exhausted on the bed. Despite a blinking pink neon sign outside the window that illuminated the room intermittently, I slept for a few hours. After receiving my wake-up call, I splashed cold water on my face, looked in the mirror, and noticed the red swelling had all but disappeared. I looked normal and I felt alive.

Outside the hotel I hailed a taxi and returned to Eastern where I found my "standby" seat had been upgraded to First Class.

"I hope I can sit on the left side," I said to a reservation clerk.

"I'll see what I can do."

From the window on the left I'd see Manhattan, the Statue of Liberty, the skyscrapers. Always thrilling. Though still tired, my heart quickened even as I thought about returning to my New York family. I hadn't suffered too much from homesickness during the year I'd been away. True. I'd kept active in my home in Bolivar, at the airport, and in my social life. I had little time to be dragged down by homesickness. Now, however, I became anxious to see New York and my family. I felt more "homesick" the closer I came to my former home on Long Island. The question of where is "home" had begun to trouble me the day I arrived in Bolivar. At last, I had it figured out. I would call Bolivar my home and New York is my former home where my family resides.

Following takeoff, the stewardesses[10] served breakfast with the weakest coffee I'd drunk in a year. Venezuelan coffee is strong and robust.

Still exhausted from having been ill in Caracas, frightened half to death on the C-46, and not having slept long enough in the TraveLodge, the oversized seat in First Class gently cradled my weary body. Just on the edge of sleep, the stewardess tucked a soft blanket around me. The large plane cruised quietly and smoothly and lulled me to sleep.

As we approached New York she awakened me. "We'll be landing soon. I know you'll want to see New York City. Everybody does. Even those who live here," she whispered as if in awe of the sight herself.

"Yes. Thank you."

The man sitting next to me had a round face, thinning hair, wore a brown plaid sports jacket, medium-brown trousers, brown loafers. He wasn't from New York. Seldom had I seen a man from New York dressed in either brown or plaid, or wearing loafers—certainly not in The City, as we locals called New York. He fidgeted this way and that trying to peak out the window. I thought about switching seats with him, but I didn't. Selfishly, I wanted to see my city as much as he did. Compromising my silent controversy, I said, "I'll scrunch over here closer to the window so you can see better." I raised the arm rest that separated our seats.

New York, a city between two rivers on an island of bedrock 305 square miles, grows only skyward. Spires from skyscrapers reach up so high they're sometimes in the clouds. I felt energized by this city where every description started with the best, the biggest, the most, the highest, the smallest, the noisiest, the first, the busiest or the greatest; New York—the city of superlatives. A reporter once wrote that New York was the economic engine that drove the world.

"Can you see the Statue of Liberty?" I asked the man in the brown plaid jacket and brown trousers. He strained and I knew he couldn't make out anything. I excitedly called his attention to the city's marvels and then I turned

Blue Skies, Green Hell

my head and looked at him. The poor soul's face wore a vacant, glazed stare that suggested he was either in la-la land from medication, or overpowered by the sight of The City.

As for me, I felt an electrical charge just thinking about the dramas that play out daily in New York and how much a part of it I had been; the fine restaurants, the first-rate shops, brightly lit Broadway, the best theaters and the unequaled Fifth Avenue Library. I'd spent many hours at the Library researching papers when I attended college. I'd eased my way around the rooms with hundreds of stacks of books in the magnificent mausoleum-like building; a thrilling experience for a young student. Outside the main entrance, statues of two gigantic cement lions named Patience and Fortitude guard the Library and welcome visitors. They were named by Mayor Fiorello LaGuardia who decreed patience and fortitude were the qualities New Yorkers needed to get through the Great Depression of 1929.

Growing up in a country setting on Long Island, and living a twenty-five minute train ride from the city, was a blessing. I had it all. I realized, however, to out-of-towners arriving in New York, America's doorstep, the towering city of steel and glass may be overwhelming.

As we banked steeply, my seat-mate closed his eyes. He looked uneasy and I hoped New York wouldn't gobble him up. I also hoped he had packed a dark gray suit and black shoes.

The plane landed and taxied and taxied and taxied. At last, it turned and stopped. I heard the bell ding that signals passengers it's safe to unbuckle and line-up to deplane. I jumped out of my seat, grabbed my hat box and pocketbook and squeezed in front of the still-seated man clad in brown. I hurried the few steps to the open main cabin door. I saw my parents first in line at the terminal door, eager to run to the plane when advised it was safe to do so. I thanked the stewardess and while the ground crew locked the stairway in place, I spoke to the Captain, who leaned casually against the cockpit's door frame, "My husband's a pilot. He switched from flying these big birds to flying the Venezuelan bush in single-engine Cessnas. Some difference!"

He laughed and said, "Ah. A bush pilot. A lot of my buddies have gone down there to fly. I'd like to go for a while, but I've got a family."

That again. "Great flight, Captain. Thanks." After the stairway was secured, I ran down the steps to my parents as they hurried from the terminal building to greet me.

After big hugs, Dad threw a bright red fall coat around my shoulders. We all laughed. "I forgot your weather is chilly," I said. "I don't have any cold-weather clothes, anyway."

"We'll get you fixed up, Honey," Dad said and put his arms around me. Just under six feet tall, he was a nice looking man with a strong presence. "It's great to have you home."

Then Mother put her arms around me. "Oh," she said, "You look so tired."

"Wait 'til I tell you why." We embraced and I recognized her favorite cologne, Bond Street by Yardley. "You smell so good."

"Do you have luggage?" Dad asked.

"No. Just this. My hatbox."

Dad grabbed my hatbox and we headed to the parking lot. We all talked at the same time, so no one heard each other's joyous conversation. We laughed and giggled and suddenly Mommy and Daddy's impetuous daughter became their little girl again. What fun we'd have—after my surgery. Oh, how I loved my family.

During the drive home, Mother told me she'd made an appointment with Dr. Montgomery, a surgeon, for the next morning.

At the house, we enjoyed a quiet day together. I unpacked my things, played with Stubby, the family's old Boston Terrier, and Frank called. We all went to bed early in preparation for meeting the doctor at 8:30 a.m. the next day.

It took only a few minutes before Dr. Montgomery announced he agreed with my Venezuelan doctor's diagnosis about the colitis and appendicitis and added that continual aggravation of the colon had inflamed the appendix. While he called the condition chronic, neither an emergency nor serious, he said it could become acute. "We'll take it out tomorrow. You don't want to risk emergency surgery sometime in the future."

Then he parroted the Venezuelan doctor's advice. "The operation won't rid you of colitis. For that, change your lifestyle; get rid of what's causing your emotional stress."

I checked in at the hospital that same evening. After Mother and Dad made sure I was comfortable, they said goodnight, good luck and told me they loved me. How comforting to have them nearby.

The surgery went well and when I awakened I saw a vase containing two dozen long stem red roses and a cable from Frank. I cried.

Mother and Dad visited everyday and I wondered how I could ever have managed this episode without their help and most of all, their care and love.

After five days in the hospital, I went back to my parents' home to recuperate and be the star at parties hosted by them.

My new life created a lot of interest and curiosity. Everyone wanted to hear about life on the frontier. I'd been away only thirteen months but had a decade's worth of adventures to tell. All seemed so bizarre to them: learning to fly a small airplane, traveling in a small airplane to food shop in one of the stores at an oil company's camp a hundred miles away, seeing the world's tallest waterfall in a jungle, having a live-in maid who also cooks. I talked nonchalantly about inconveniences of living in a frontier town but did not focus on them. I had to tell them about my experiences with the medical community, but I added my case might have been unusual.

Several friends with whom I'd visited New York museums and theaters throughout high school and college years asked about the differences in cultures between Venezuela and the U.S. "In Caracas, everything is available," I said, and described Caracas as a modern city with museums, cathedrals, concert halls, theaters, libraries, fine restaurants, nightclubs; everything you want. "There are lots of fine stores. Oh, yes. Everyone siestas after lunch, which is the main meal of the day, and in the evening, they eat a light meal—very late—even after ten o'clock."

"But you don't live there. What's it like where you live?" someone inquired.

"Oh, that's a different story," I chuckled.

I found it difficult to describe the culture south of the Orinoco. Greatly influenced by beautiful, uncomplicated and proud indigenous people, their music, art, hand-woven crafts, and their beaded necklaces, baskets and hammocks adorned a culture that bore no resemblance to one my friends would be able to imagine or comprehend. "As different as it is, I can't imagine living any other place or doing anything other than what I do with my husband and my friends."

In my mind's eye, I saw the lady who danced the joropo with maracas attached to her alpargatas, the live stage shows at the movies in the rain, our escapades in the Black Horse Café, the moonlight trips to the savannah.

"Would you like to come back home?" someone asked.

"Bolivar is my home." I heard myself defending Venezuela and my life there. I felt a strong yearning for CB, my dogs, my friends, our many visitors, and most of all, my husband. "I love it there. Everything about it."

My friends talked about fashions, furniture and first words from their babies. To me their lives seemed routine and unalterably dull and monotonous. I had matured and learned a different lifestyle that included flying airplanes and seeing dramatic landscapes every day. Now I felt strange among my old friends. We had nothing in common. We had grown far apart. We had nothing to talk about and I wondered if their placidity reflected contentment or boredom. What I had always assumed would be permanent relationships had blown away, like puffs of smoke, and had become nothing more than transient friendships. It was a difficult awakening and it troubled me for years. It still does. Over the years, I've left a trail of wonderful friends. *Is this common?*

My dear Father enjoyed entertaining, but never missed an opportunity to tell everyone he couldn't understand why Frank had not joined me. I wearied from hearing his repetition. I understood Frank's need to be in Bolivar and the more Dad talked about it, the more I wanted to go home to Ciudad Bolivar—to Frank.

Mother was never as vociferous as Dad in her desire for me to visit although her letters made it abundantly clear they both missed me greatly. I suspected she'd have preferred in her letters not to ask when I would be coming north, but she followed Dad's prompt.

As my time to depart the U.S. and return to Venezuela approached, Mother and Dad arranged several gala evenings in New York. One included attending a Broadway musical, "Wish You Were Here," starring Florence Henderson. I wondered if that hit show had been selected for a special reason.

When the overture started and the curtain opened, the brilliance and dazzle of the show reached across the footlights and swept me up in a mood dominated by joyful singing and frenzied dancing. For a moment, just a wee moment, I wished I could be on the stage singing and dancing and basking in bright spotlights aimed at the stage from high in the theater behind the audience and colored footlights at the edge.

But quite involuntarily, I put my finger tips over my mouth, and shaking my head, uttered softly, "No. No." I briefly closed my eyes.

"What is it, dear?" Mother whispered.

"No." I repeated. My voice choked. "Oh, Mother. I don't want to be on the stage. I wouldn't swap my life in CB even if all the spotlights on Broadway shined on me."

Broadway. The magical world of make-believe, the dream of every little girl who tap-danced at her daddy's lodge talent show or belted out a song from the Wizard of Oz in a school production, was no longer the dream I wanted.

Now the theater reeked of fluff and foolish fantasy.

When the curtain closed and the cast took several bows and the audience jumped to its feet and cheered, I knew the role that had been written for me didn't include glitz and glamour. It didn't include Broadway or my name in lights. My starring role without an opening night was that of a bush pilot's wife—a young adventurer living the exciting life that others lived vicariously through books and movies and theater.

The show ended and sounded the finale to my childhood dreams.

We'd been at their home about an hour when Frank called. "How are you feeling?"

"I'm so glad you called." I whispered that I wanted to come home and thought the doctor's discharge would be very soon.

"I can't wait to see you." He told me, Captain Manuel Mendoza, his friend and Chief Pilot of LAV International Division, the government's highly respected airline, had a flight to New York next week. "I want you to fly back with him. If it's okay with your doctor, come back next week." He'd heard, of course, about my experience in the C-46, and lacking the usual lilt in his voice, he asserted I'd never fly on the C-46 again. I had no arguments about that. "Manuel will call you when he arrives."

"I'll be ready."

Blue Skies, Green Hell

Capt. Mendoza called on schedule. "We'll leave day after tomorrow. I have your ticket," he said. "But you'll ride up front with me. We'll have a good flight. Frank misses you."

Early on the day of my departure, Dad took to the airport my new pieces of luggage filled with things I'd purchased, and he handled all the paperwork involved with checking in. Thus, we avoided crowds and the hassle at the airport in the evening. The plane would leave at 11:00 p.m.

About 9:00 p.m., we left the house. The door closed and locked behind me. I began to ache with homesickness for my family. How could I hurt the dearest people in the world? How could I be so thankless? Insensitive? I didn't know what I wanted. Confusion and doubt ruled my heart and mind.

Dad slowly backed the car out of the long driveway, giving me plenty of time to look once more at the house and to remember where I'd spent a lifetime and had gathered so many beautiful and endearing memories.

Saying goodbye to my family was more sad and tearful than when I first went to Venezuela. At that time, I'd planned only to vacation with my sister and return within a year or so. But to the surprise of some, and chagrin of others, I married and everything in the world changed abruptly, for all of us. Now, one way or another, there were broken hearts at each end of the trip. Mother's. Dad's. Frank's. Mine.

The words of farewell rang again; we'd become champs at saying goodbye. And as we hugged each other at the airport I realized homesickness and saying goodbye to those I loved was a hardship Bill Murphy and I hadn't even considered. Mother and I shed more than a few tears. Dad, a stalwart, would have cried had he not been proud and self-disciplined. Mother told me repeatedly my room would always be there for me. "Ciudad Bolivar is so far away." Sadly she said, "We can't even talk by phone unless you are in Caracas."

"We'll always be here for you, honey," Dad added.

"I have a husband who needs me, who loves me, and a home and dogs and a life I've chosen. And I love them all." I hesitated. "And I love you. But do you know how difficult you make it for me? How I struggle with this guilt?"

Dad changed the subject. "Just let us know if you need anything. We'll get it for you and send it with Jack." I knew as soon as I was on the plane Mother would collapse in the safe haven of Dad's strong and comforting arms. He loved her so much. Theirs was a beautiful love. A perfect love.

I had left them abruptly, but even after a year, we'd not stopped missing each other. How awful, to be caught in the middle of this. To be pulled apart by each side and wanting to be with each side. Just when I thought I was so good at growing up, I became a little girl again.

Shortly before 11:00 p.m. sixty impatient passengers, destined for a seven or eight hour flight through the night, over miles of open water from New York to Venezuela, crowded at the terminal door expecting it to open at any second.

Once open and the signal given to board, the people would push and shove and run a race to the portable stairway to board the Connie—nickname for the Lockheed Constellation—shining in the glow of the airport lights. Seats were not reserved. It was every man for himself and everyone wanted to be first to board, first to select the best seat, as if it made a difference. That's the way it was when you boarded a plane fifty years before the new millennium.

I kissed Mother and Dad goodbye and headed toward the plane. The overstuffed round hat box was not as heavy as my heart. The scent of Mother's heady perfume stayed with me and I overcame the urge to cancel the trip and stay with my parents a little longer—or forever. I did love them so much. I hoped they knew it. My footsteps faltered as my knees weakened. I stopped once during the walk to the plane, turned and waved. I took a deep breath, but it did nothing to quell an emotional rush that seized every fiber of my body. I struggled to the mobile stairway, weighted down more by guilt than by what I carried. Half-way up the unsteady stairs I wanted to turn and see them one more time, but I feared I'd lose my balance so continued to the small platform at the entrance to the Constellation's main cabin. Then I turned again and waved and blew a kiss. I couldn't see anything through my tears. I knew they were watching; Mother crying and Dad fighting back tears. I looked toward the bright lights of New York City and wondered if New York on the Hudson had ever been like my frontier town, Ciudad Bolivar on the Orinoco.

Before heading to their home, Mother and Dad would remain at the airport and watch the plane depart and fly out of sight. They'd wait a long time before returning to their empty home to go to bed and try to sleep. They'd awaken on and off all through the night, envisioning the white plane with stripes the colors of the Venezuelan national flag along the fuselage flying me farther and farther away over the dark ocean and they'd wonder why this had happened to them. And they'd lie close to each other, hold each other and cry some more. They'd pray for my safety. And my return to New York.

I entered the Constellation through the main cabin door. Captain Mendoza, a small man who looked out of proportion to the large aircraft he flew, leaned on the doorway to the cockpit and smiled broadly. "*Señora Marilyn.*" He nodded his head. "*Estás listo a regresar a casa*" (Are you ready to return to your home?)

"Yes. To my home in Ciudad Bolivar," I said softly and smiled.

I selected a seat on the right side of the cabin not too far back, stowed my hat box in the rack overhead, sat down and leaned back. For a moment, I closed my eyes and rubbed my forehead.

"Señora. Are you feeling all right?" the stewardess asked.

"Yes. Thank you." I opened my pocketbook to retrieve a tissue and saw a picture of Frank I'd had on the night table next to my bed. "I'm ready to go . . . to go home."

Blue Skies, Green Hell

The Constellation's four engines turned over one by one. First they whined and their mellow roar followed as Mendoza ran them up. The plane vibrated gently. Easing the throttles back, the Constellation slowly taxied, turned, and stopped. Then the powerful engines roared as the plane rolled fast, then faster and we were airborne. The white plane pointed skyward then south over the ocean.

I'd come to New York during the daylight. Now, leaving at night, I saw a different city—one with lights on bridges sparkling like crystal necklaces. Skyscrapers lit brightly as night housekeeping and maintenance crews readied the buildings for the next day. Neon lights of all colors dazzled the cityscape and New York became the world's jewel box.

After we reached our cruising altitude, Capt. Mendoza strolled through the main cabin nodding and talking to passengers on both sides of the aisle. Finally, he stopped at my seat. "We'll have a fast trip tonight. I'll catch the winds aloft and make good time. I do that, you know. Come up front. I'll show you around."

I thanked him and said I'd be there in a little while. First, I had to recover from the emotional upset of one more goodbye. He rested his right hand on the back of my seat and his left on the arm rest. "So tonight you leave one jungle for another, Marilyn." He smiled.

"Yes, from the cement jungle in the North to the Green Hell in the South?" I laughed and reflectively said, "And Captain, I love both and I'm comfortable in both."

"Few can say that, Marilyn." He stood up. "*Tienes mucha suerte* (You're very lucky.) You are loved and wanted at both ends of your trip. Come up front. We can talk more about these jungles." He took a few steps then turned around. "Both challenge the traveler."

In a few words, Mendoza said so much. He turned sadness into joy. I knew I'd be able to deal better with goodbyes. I'd remember his helpful thoughts for years and his interesting concept; both challenge the traveler. At that moment, my mind raced back in time to the man in the brown plaid jacket and brown trousers. I hoped he enjoyed my city. I hoped he survived.

I visited with the Captain in the cockpit for only a short while, commenting about how the Connie flight deck seemed quite unlike the Captain's seat and instrument panel in the Cessna. I thanked him for our earlier conversation.

As the Connie neared the Venezuelan coastline, my spirits soared. Frank would be there to greet me with a tight embrace, a tender touch, a smile, a kiss.

We landed and taxied a short distance and I waited for the door to open and the stairs to be rolled into place. From the window, I saw Frank waving to Capt. Mendoza in the cockpit and making a "thumbs up" gesture. Frank had been permitted to pass through the official check-points and meet me at the bottom of the mobile stairs.

I exited the plane, ran down the stairs and into his arms.

"Oh, God, I'm glad you're back. I've worried about you."

"I've been surrounded by people, but was lonesome. I missed you every minute. And I worried about you, too."

"I've been in Caracas for a couple of days." He took my hand. "I'm ready to go back now. My work here never stops. But I won't talk about work. There'll be plenty of time for that when we drive back to CB."

"We're not going to stay in Caracas?"

"No. No, Button. We have a room at a hotel on the beach. We can rest here today, swim a little, have dinner and then start our drive home about midnight. Oh, it's good to have you back." He hugged me.

My cheeks flushed with excitement. No one could make me feel the way he did.

Going through customs was a cinch despite all the new things I had loaded into my hatbox and new pieces of luggage. "You'll like the hotel on the beach."

The white stucco hotel with its sea green trim glistened in the sunrise. Our room with double doors opened onto a balcony overlooking the Caribbean. Mist carried on the ocean breeze refreshed my face made dry by the long overnight flight. I inhaled the aroma of sea air, and tasted the dry salt on my lips.

A soft breeze tenderly played with the sheer curtains and I heard the ocean waves rhythmically slap at the sandy beach.

"Tired?" he asked hesitantly. Then, without waiting for an answer, he pulled me on to the bed. "Can we, ah . . . make love?"

"What do you think," I answered seductively. As I kicked off my black patent leather high heels, Frank started to open the buttons of my fashionable steel-blue dress.

Chapter 15

The Gentleman Rancher

Dear Mother and Dad   December 12, 1952

I heard a lot about Horacio Cabrera during our drive back to CB. He's been a client for quite a while. He's a well-known and influential rancher. Frank likes him a lot. Horacio owns an *hacienda* (a ranch) near Ciudad Bolivar and an *hato* (huge cattle ranch) located an hour by plane to the south. He charters our planes to travel between his two places.

Horacio is a National Champion in the sport called Toros Coleados. It's a dangerous sport that involves bulls and horses.

Frank has ridden horses most of his life. Now he's training for Coleados.

Horacio invited us to spend a day with him at his Hato La Vergareña. We'll fly down early tomorrow, spend the day on a cattle drive. Then we'll hunt a tiger. Down here jaguars are called tigers. The animal's been getting Horacio's cattle. Seems like we have planned a very full day. Sometimes I have to pinch myself to realize this is my life.

Love you and miss you. Marilyn

Suntanned, smiling, he rode tall in the saddle atop a proud white stallion on the green savannahs of Venezuela. He lived a full life and made a fiesta of it. That he would become an award winning author of the highest order in Venezuelan literary works—often called Venezuela's greatest writer in literature—and then would be propelled into national recognition never crossed my mind. Nor would I have predicted that his immense popularity among his countrymen would result in his election to the office of Governor of the State of Bolivar in 1958 at the age of forty-eight and in 1964 he would be elected to represent the State of Bolivar in the Senate of the federal government. He was a luminary in Venezuela.

I knew him as a champion coleador. I knew him as a frequent passenger on board our planes. I knew Horacio Cabrera de Sifontes as a cattleman; a gentleman rancher. I knew him as a good friend.

After Horacio Cabrera extended the invitation for Frank and me to spend the day riding in a cattle drive on his ranch on the Paragua River, Hato La Vergareña, I foundered as I looked for the right words to express my embarrassment: I did not know how to ride a horse. Everybody in his world rode.

The words flowed haltingly from my lips. Horacio smiled and said, "*No te preocupé*" (Don't worry). Then in English, "My wife will give you a lesson and she'll have a gentle horse for you." Horacio confidently controlled the world around him, and with the same quiet demeanor with which he'd orchestrated the transportation in the C-46 of select cattle from Miami to the hato, he'd arrange for me to learn to ride. While he maneuvered his world to his satisfaction, he maintained his gentlemanly charm. "Come early," he said smiling. "Then you'll have time to learn to ride and we can start the cattle drive before the heat. We round up the cattle the day before and move them out the next day."

Later when Frank and I were alone and making our list of things to take for the outing at the hato, I quizzed Frank. "A lesson? Frank, he said just one lesson to ride a horse?"

"If that's what Horacio said, that's what he meant. He'll probably fix you up with a mannerly, calm horse. Anyway, you can do it." Frank's confidence in me came as no surprise. Horacio's did.

The day before the safari, we shopped for ammunition for Frank's pistol and rifle and my shotgun. Frank bought me a black velour hat that matched his and hiking boots which he said would be suitable for riding horseback. Our major purchases included new thermos bottles. At the last minute, we also purchased a package of crackers to take along in case we got hungry. Frank said we'd leave the airport at 6:00 a.m.

Delayed by an early morning low ceiling, we took off later than planned. I flew the plane most of the way, but as we approached the hato's main house and airstrip, Frank took the controls. The airstrip at the hato frequently had a crosswind; the landing is made more difficult as the wind blows across the airstrip rather than parallel to it. Frank would perform this tricky transition of the plane from the air to the ground with the steady hands of a professional aviator.

Of course, cattle, ranch hands and Horacio had already moved out but one who had remained behind gave us our bearings by nodding his head once with lips pursed in the direction toward which we should fly. The gesture was Venezuelan sign language. The ranch hands had a roaring fire burning and a long stick running through the carcass of a whole pig, all of which leaned on a support over the fire pit. This Venezuelan barbecue was called a *ternera*. They said they were cooking the pig for lunch. Occasionally, while we talked, one of the men rotated the stick. The tantalizing aroma of roast pig filled the air and suddenly the crackers I'd brought along for sustenance had no appeal.

Blue Skies, Green Hell

We took off and after flying several minutes, we spotted Horacio and the cattle drive in progress. Not wanting to frighten the herd but to attract attention, we flew a little slower but not too low. Taking off his large white hat and waving it in circles over his head to acknowledge us, Horacio then pointed the hat in the direction of the house. Frank rocked the wings to signal he understood.

The hato covers several thousand square miles and Frank wanted me to see the beauty of this part of the region called Guayana. We flew to one of its boundaries on the Paragua River. "Look there, out your window. This forest is filled with magnificent pine trees." Horacio had spoken casually that someday he might consider going into the lumber business.

I savored the beauty of the fertile savannah land with thick grass and clear, sparkling water in meandering streams and tributaries. The sun, the grasses and the water all provide food, water and shade for cattle the year round.

"This land is a cattleman's dream," Frank said. "About an hour by plane from Bolivar, it's remote and blessed with beauty and quietness."

The hato served as a bellwether for Venezuela's cattle industry, and by introducing a scientific breeding program, Horacio had brought a new dimension to ranching.

After flightseeing, we landed again near the house and waited for our friend to arrive.

"*Hola*," Horacio called from atop his white stallion. "We left early to move out the cattle." As he dismounted, he said he regretted I would not have a chance to ride a horse.

I didn't share his regret. Not one bit. Silently, I thanked God for the bad weather in CB.

Walking past the fire pit and the roasting pig, Horacio told the ranch hand in charge of the ternera that we'd leave to hunt the tiger. "We'll be back no later than two o'clock." He called over his shoulder to Frank, "I'll round up the hounds. We'll go on foot." He blew a horn and the barking dogs came from all directions, running, prancing, and jumping as they circled him. I thought I saw some smiling.

Armed with our guns, and led by a pack of happy dogs and a few ranch hands, we started the hunt. We trod through dense undergrowth shaded by large trees; some trees so tall that leaves reaching for the sun grew only on the treetops. We slipped on moist undergrowth between barren trees with low-hanging leafless branches. Tree roots crept along the ground and made walking difficult.

Every so often, we stopped and listened.

"What are we listening for?" I asked Frank.

"Sounds," he whispered. "With so many twigs on the ground, a large animal in the forest may give away his position by stepping on them. But we must listen sharply."

Except for the barking dogs, it was very quiet in the woods where a damp pungent smell of mold hung in the still air and small butterflies danced in narrow shafts of sunlight. "I don't hear anything except the dogs," I whispered back.

My gun in its case began to feel heavy. "Do you see any signs of a jaguar?"

"No. Nothing. Not even spoor."

We walked a little farther, then turned to head back. "The day will not be lost, Marilyn. Look up there. In the tree." Horacio nodded with pursed lips to doves sitting on branches high above us. "You have the first shot."

As I took my shotgun from the case, loaded a shell, and prepared to shoot, Frank whispered, "The wind is light. You'll have just one chance."

"I know," I replied softly.

"You can do it."

I sighted, held my breath and squeezed the trigger. As one dove fell to the ground, Horacio shouted "*Qué bueno*" (Very good).

I exhaled, my hands trembled. I did not tell him that I could only hit a stationary target. He'd made me nervous and I felt lucky to have hit one dove—even with my shotgun.

We headed back to the house where we hungry hunters devoured the succulent roast pig. The dove was roasted, but I had none of it. A ranch hand retrieved several coconuts from a sack and whacked them open with a machete. He gave me the first and Horacio poured in rum. I swished the mixture with a straw and sipped the pleasing beverage.

Our host waved his arm and a ranch hand magically appeared in a jeep. The driver hopped out and Horacio beckoned us to get in the jeep with him. "Frank, you sit in the back seat. You've been here before. This time, I want you, Marilyn, to sit in the front and see one of my favorite places. It's not far." We drove slowly and he talked. "As a young boy, fourteen years old and foolish, I became involved in politics—no big involvement—but big enough for it to put me in jail for four years. I opposed [the dictator] Juan Vicente Gomez in a small, insignificant way. That's all." He stopped and let the jeep idle. "All the time I suffered in jail, I thought only about this—my beautiful country. My beautiful savannah. My forests. My rivers. They weren't mine then, but I knew one day they would be." He drove on in silence, and then again stopped the jeep. This time he cut the engine. We parked at the top of a small ridge. "I thought of this," and he spread his arms in front of him and opened them wide to embrace all that he saw. He spoke softly as he described the next years in Columbia where he sought expression through his writings and began to publish his literary works about his beloved land, the savannahs in Venezuela. "I love to write and I love my country. I combine both my loves. And I look to the future to do more to protect this great land whose soul sings to me. This is my Venezuela."

Filmmakers took an interest in Horacio's literary work and encouraged him to go to California and join the production crew of a Venezuelan film called

Blue Skies, Green Hell

Joropo. At her request, he wrote the script for Venezuela's most famous actress, Doña Barbara. She also insisted on the best production crew for her film, and Horacio, already a well-known and respected writer and sound engineer, was selected for a key position. The call from her instructing him to assist in directing the film came as no surprise. "All the time," he said, "despite the excitement of Hollywood, my heart," he tapped his right hand over his heart, "remained here—on the savannah." Then he smiled. "Has Frank told you one of my friends is Clark Gable? He visits here at the hato once in a while. We hunt and fish."

I understood when Horacio said he felt homesick and compelled to return to Venezuela and to this incredibly beautiful scene in front of us.

"What do you think, Marilyn? Can a city girl like you enjoy this wilderness?"

"I love the energy that comes from the city, Horacio. Here I feel serene and free. You've been to our cities. You know what I'm talking about."

In silence, we drove back to the house. "I'm building five houses just over there. They'll be for Rosa and me and the ranch hands. And there'll be one for you and Frank the next time you visit. I want you to know my country and love it as I do."

Frank thanked Horacio and said we should be leaving.

"Aren't you going to practice toro coleados?" I asked.

Frank tapped his belly. "Not after that lunch. *Qué sabroso*" (How delicious)!

"Frank's been practicing. He's told you?" inquired Horacio.

"A little, but I want to see for myself."

"He's a fine rider. He's fearless. That's what it takes. You'll probably see him at the next Coleados. For now, you'd better get going. Darkness comes quickly."

As we walked to the plane, I saw a small light brown deer with white spots and a perky tail. Horacio told me she was wild, but from time to time, appears at the hato. She came running out of the trees and looked like Bambi. As we walked to the plane, Bambi walked with us and stood nearby while we said our goodbyes and Frank did his pre-flight. She continued to watch even as we started the engine and began to taxi. Then she abruptly turned and fled back into the forest.

We took off and waved to those who watched us leave.

I'd never forget that glorious day with Horacio Cabrera, a man of great strength and stature and so filled with pride for his land and his country. I felt humbled in his presence.

Horacio Cabrera, born in 1910, died in 1995. Governor of Bolivar State, Senator in the federal government, and an acclaimed writer of Venezuelan lore, he had fulfilled both his dream to protect his glorious country and to preserve in writing his beloved Venezuela.

Chapter 16

UFOs—I Believe

Dear Mother and Dad   **May 20, 1953**

The trip to Caracas was a last minute thing and I had no time to write to you. Frank could only be gone a few days as he had to be back here for a meeting. I went because I needed a haircut.

We returned from Caracas a few days ago.

Frank's sister, Bully [Lucilla Hatch], came with us. She'll visit a few days.

What I'm going to tell you about our trip home is the truth! I know you'll believe me. As you know, when we drive all night, we're well rested and drink only water. So what I'll tell you was not an illusion caused by wine or lack of sleep.

It was about 4:00 a.m. in the morning.

Frank was driving and I was in the seat next to him. Lo and behold, we saw a flying saucer . . . .

My love always, Marilyn

According to "Project Blue Book," the U.S. Government reports of Unidentified Flying Objects, sightings over the United States were down in 1953 compared to those reported in 1952. Sightings, however, were up in Europe, and according to the unofficial reports made by natives in Venezuela's interior, sightings increased significantly. Venezuelan folk lore has it, during the fifties, the Gran Sabana had the most sightings of UFOs anywhere on this planet. Those mysterious sightings are still talked about by old timers in hushed tones.

No moon at all, only a few stars brightened the dark sky as we began our long drive from Caracas to Ciudad Bolivar.

Well talked out, the three of us, Frank, his sister Bully, and I, rode the black-top road in silence. Moving along about fifty-five miles per hour, it was cool and we rode with our car windows cracked open about an inch. The sweet scent of springtime grasses helped us stay awake. Sometimes I put my head back and closed my eyes for a brief moment, but I felt it my responsibility to chat with

Blue Skies, Green Hell

Frank from time-to-time if only to prevent him from falling asleep at the wheel. The tires rolling quietly on the pavement and the broken white lines painted on the black pavement were sleep-inducing.

Thoughts meander like an old river and conversations have a way of being meaningless or mundane when you're cruising along a dark road in the middle of nowhere—in the middle of the night.

I shattered the peacefulness. "Frank," I said in a hushed voice that bristled with disbelief and wonderment. "Frank. Look. Twelve o'clock . . . up a little." I paused to catch my breath. "Slow down," My pulse raced. He slowed, his eyes focused straight ahead and then up a little.

All he said was, "Phew."

Bully bolted upright, leaned forward with her arms folded across the top of my seat and whispered very softly, "What's up?" She had flashing black eyes and her hair was pulled tight back and fashioned into a knot.

Frank turned off the headlights, stopped the car, and turned off the engine. We cranked down the windows. "Bully. Look straight ahead. Then follow an imaginary line straight up. Not too high."

She gasped. She'd seen it.

We all watched the brightly lit object in the sky ahead of us come closer and lower. A cone-shape brilliant ray of light shone from beneath it.

"Frankie," she whispered. "What is it? Is it . . . ?"

He murmured, "I don't know. I'm not sure." Within minutes, our eyes adjusted to the darkness. Straining to hear something other than the soft sounds of crickets and wildlife rustling through the brush, we focused our eyes and ears on the bright light. It grew brighter and seemed to draw nearer and lower. As it moved, it slowly started to rock.

"Let's get out," Frank said quietly, opening his car door. We tiptoed forward, sat on the fenders, and breathlessly, watched the brightly lit object.

It looked like a concave disk with a large bulge under it from which emitted the light ray. Spellbound, I held my breath. Then the disk started to move higher and higher and I feared it would disappear, but it remained visible for several minutes. We slid off the fenders, stood next to the car and waited for something more to happen. I shivered and my eyes smarted as I watched the object in the black sky. I couldn't believe I was actually looking at a flying saucer.

We exchanged startled glances. I gripped Frank's hand. Uncertainty rang in my voice when I asked if we were seeing a UFO.

We ruled out aircraft. In Venezuela, none flew at night, other than large passenger planes at very high altitudes on long international flights. Moreover, we heard no sound of aircraft engines.

We ruled out reflection from street lights, as there are no streetlights in the llanos. There is only barren, lonesome wilderness.

This is a copy of the sketch of the flying saucer I made in the letter
I sent to my parents after we had seen the flying saucer.
It reminded me of a street light.

I felt insignificant in its presence, not from fear but with reverence. The sight took respect and curiosity to a new dimension. Then the UFO disappeared behind a cloud.

Minutes later, the brightly glowing disk-shaped object burst down through the cloud. Inverted, this time its bright ray of light beamed upward into the cloud above it. It remained motionless. So did we. Then it rose and disappeared in the cloud. Fascinated by what we had just witnessed, we stood in silence a few more minutes.

Frank had eyes like eagles; he saw everything and missed nothing. "I believe we've seen a flying saucer." He rubbed his eyes with finger tips. Because of the darkness, he could see nothing to help him judge relative distance, size of the disk, its altitude or its speed. With some reticence, he finally said he thought it hovered lower than one thousand feet. Maybe eight hundred.

Were we concerned that the object might land and aliens inside might exit and bring harm to us? Or whisk us away? I didn't know how the others felt, but I wanted it to land. I had no other thought and no fear.

On the road again, we didn't say much but our eyes continually scanned the sky. Edgy and hopeful, we yearned to see the craft one more time.

"Is that it?" someone would ask excitedly. No. It was gone.

I could hardly catch my breath. "I feel certain we were watched. They were interested in us. Why else would it have gone away and then returned."

"Bully," I said, "It never fails. Something always happens during the drive from Caracas."

"But nothing like this," Frank added softly.

The rest of the trip rolled by quietly. Finally, we watched dawn break on the horizon. We'd arrived at Soledad, across the Orinoco from CB.

Crossing the river by ferry and seeing Ciudad Bolivar on the promontory shimmer in the morning sunshine overwhelmed me, as it did every time I made the crossing. I couldn't suppress my excitement. "It's beautiful, isn't it Bully? I just love it here."

Frank drove the scenic route to our house pointing out to his sophisticated sister the important sights as we went along. "That's Western Union and that's the movie theater. Here's the Post Office and there's our favorite place to eat, El Triangulito."

Bully raised her eye brows. "Favorite?"

"You'll see," he said.

Before heading home, we stopped at the airport and met Julio. "Hey, good thing you came along," he said and invited us to a party at his house that evening.

Any reason for the party?" one of us asked.

"It's a housewarming party. We had to move," Julio replied. "We didn't mean to make noise, but the landlady yelled at Martha and the kids for slamming the gate and sliding furniture across the floor. They're just little kids. We couldn't stay there any longer. We're in a new house up the street from where the Freemans used to live."

"We'll be there. Thanks. We'll be over after a shower and nap," Frank said and we headed home.

Given a quick tour of our little palace, Bully learned the location of the important rooms; the kitchen, the bath and her bedroom. Then each of us showered and stretched out on our beds for much needed sleep to be ready for the party at Martha and Julio's.

As I hopped out of the car in front of Julio's house, I gasped. "Wow! What a house!" Martha met us at the door. "Congratulations, Martha. Your house is gorgeous."

"Thanks. Let me show you around. You'll love it. We were lucky to get it. The rent is lots more than we should be paying on what Julio earns. I don't know how we can afford it. But he told me not to worry and to go ahead and sign the lease." She whispered. "He also told me to buy some new furniture, and a fridge. I got the fridge. Come see it."

I opened my eyes wide when I saw the eight foot fridge. Another "Wow!" raced from my lips.

Even before our first drink, Frank led me to the area in the living room set aside for dancing and pulled me into his arms. We whirled and twirled and moved our hips and feet as we danced to the arousing Latin music. Then he danced with Bully whose Latin steps were provocative and sensual. They moved their hips and their bodies swayed rhythmically, and if she'd not been his older sister, I'd have been upset. But since she'd taught him to dance, I merely joined in with the others who applauded their every turn.

After our first drinks were poured, we breathlessly told our story of the mysterious light over the llanos. We waited for questions or expressions of disbelief.

Carlos stifled a pretend yawn. "Yeah. I've seen some."

"Me, too," added Julio.

"Oh, yes," said Martha. "We saw one over Canaima when we stayed over one night last week."

One by one, guests told their stories about flying saucers. They'd been seen everywhere. I'd thought we'd bounce into the party and dazzle everyone with our unusual experience. When Tom and Shirley said they'd never seen a flying saucer, I felt much less the outsider. Everyone agreed there was every good reason to believe they exist.

A month later, Tom and Shirley surprised us with an early morning visit.

"Anybody up?" Tom called as he passed the bedroom window?

"Be right there," Frank answered as he donned his robe and opened the front door. "Come on in. Sit down." He beckoned, "Guillermina. Coffee, please?"

"Couldn't wait to get here." Tom sipped his coffee. "Frank, a flying saucer flew over Avenida Tachira last night. I swear. This is the truth."

I quickly zipped up my robe, joined the group and listened to their story about a very strange light that lit up Avenida Tachira. "A very bright light," Tom said.

"It moved slowly," added Shirley. "First I saw a beam of light, not too high, shine over the road. It moved toward the airport."

"Actually, it woke us up—shining so brightly," Tom said very softly, "It had to be a flying saucer."

"Maybe they're in the area," I interjected. "Gives you a funny feeling." I poured more coffee. "When we saw ours, I knew we were being watched. I'd have given anything for it to land." I nodded to make my point. "Actually, I believe we were privileged. We'd been selected to be observed."

"Someone's civilization is light-years ahead of ours," Tom mused.

"Do you believe in extrasensory perception? Telepathy?" I asked everyone.

Tom struck his thoughtful pose; head tilted upward, eyes tightly closed. "It's a possibility," he replied.

"I believe." I recounted my extrasensory perception experiences with my roommate, Mary DeMott, at Green Mountain College in Vermont in 1948. "We'd read about ESP and played around with it wondering if we could read each others' minds. It started out as a joke, but we were pretty good reading simple thoughts we each had. We spoke with Psychology Professor Richard Trumbull who gave us tests that had been developed at Duke University."

"And?" asked Frank impatiently.

"Our scores indicated we had some ability to communicate telepathically. Prof Trumbull asked us not to play around anymore. We didn't. But the point is telepathy's been studied for years."

"What's this leading to?" Frank spoke, again, impatiently.

"I get it," Tom said vigorously." Do you think we can communicate with those—uh—those aliens in the saucer by ESP?"

I nodded. "Why not try?"

"Yes," he replied and his eyes opened wide as he anticipated the next suggestion.

We made a plan for the four of us to meet every evening at six-thirty, hold hands and concentrate on meeting "them" at a specific time and date. For the site, we agreed we'd need an uninhabited area in the savannah south of Ciudad Bolivar with plenty of room to land our small plane and, hopefully, ample room for a saucer.

"I know a place. I think it's perfect," added Frank, now in tune with Tom and me. "I'll check it out next time I fly that route."

"I'm ready," Shirley said.

If for any reason we all couldn't be together for our nightly meetings, those of us who were in Bolivar would meet and perform the ritual. The person(s) not with us would stop and concentrate on the rendezvous wherever he was. We gave ourselves a month to concentrate on communicating with the aliens and hoped our messages requesting them to meet us would be transmitted and received.

A month later, the four of us, plus baby Patty Van Hyning, assembled at the airport, boarded one of our Cessnas and flew southward to the lonesome savannah country. We landed safely in the grassy savannah and got out of the plane. The sun shone brilliantly and clouds floated slowly high above us. Little black and yellow moriche birds flirted with leaves in the trees and fluttered from one branch to another.

Frank identified compass points, pointed each of us in a direction and asked us to walk a couple of hundred feet. "That tree beyond the little red bush is about the distance I think we should each go," he said. "All agree? Good. We'll be within sight of each other, but not too close."

"And when we get there, we'll concentrate and watch the sky," Tom added.

I walked to my designated place and sat on the grass, concentrated and waited and waited hoping with all my heart I'd look up and see the disk hovering above me. The savannah was eerily quiet. I knew they'd come.

But after an hour, I returned to the plane; dispirited. No contact had been made.

Marilyn Lazzari-Wing

Tom, Shirley, baby Patty Van Hyning and I leave the AEROVEN aircraft and head out to our assigned locations where we waited for a UFO to land.
Photo by Frank

"I think we were presumptuous," Tom said, thoughtfully. "To their way of thinking we may be lowly earthlings—cretons—beneath them in a lower station of intellect—not worthy of their immediate response."

A couple of nights later, we four dined at the Triangulito and then went to the movies at our open-air theater. We were watching *Knights of the Round Table* when my eyes were drawn away from Robert Taylor on the screen to the dazzling diamond-like stars in the dark, cloudless sky above. Then I saw it. Something shining brighter than any star. "Look up. Look up," I said in hushed tones to the other three. "To the right."

Their gasps signaled they, too, saw the flying saucer. Overwhelmed by the sight, we watched as it moved slowly in our direction. It was not as low as the saucer Frank and I had seen in the llanos, but it hovered for a long minute in the sky over the open-air theater. We clearly saw its shape; a concave arc with a bright light coming from beneath its structure. Then it disappeared in a cloud.

"Was that their answer to us?" Tom asked as we left the movie.

That happened almost 60 years ago. I've never seen another flying saucer, but every clear night, wherever I am in this world, I still cast my eyes upward with hopes of making contact. I believe!

Chapter 17

"He's Such a Dreamer"

Dear Mother and Dad   **July 7, 1953**

Here's a funny story! The night before last, Julio and Frank had a meeting at the office then went to the Normandy Hotel to pay Capt. Levy's bill. He's a helicopter pilot. He'd been down a few days to demonstrate the helicopter. Levy gave me a great ride. Anyway, they met Hank Vanderputty from OMC and had a few drinks. Frank came home, showered and we went with Madelyn to get a sandwich and toddy—then to the movies. (Carlos is away.) So yesterday while I worked, Martha burst into the office:

"Well, what story did he give you last night?"

"Story? They went to the hotel and met Hank Vanderputty."

"The hotel doesn't stay open until 2:00 a.m.," Martha said.

. . . Martha thought Julio and Frank had been together until late. Well, all day, Frank has been pretending to polish his imaginary halo. I miss you.

Love always, Marilyn

The cable Carlos sent Madelyn from Caracas instructed her to prepare for a cocktail party at their house. He was coming home on the afternoon LAV flight with big-time American investors. Feverishly, Madelyn and I worked to get her house ready for Carlos and his entourage, and my maid worked with Madelyn's in the preparation of the hors d'oeuvres. Carlos, such a dreamer.

Madelyn, putting finishing touches to her tablecloth with an iron, stood the iron on its heel and said, "I'll be right back. There's a cow on my front porch." She went out. "Shoo—shoo," she said, gently prodding the cow off the porch with her hand on its rump. A final "Shoo" did it. She returned to her ironing. Madelyn, so pragmatic.

Frank's trip to Caracas had been extended, so I'd planned to go to the Freemans' party unescorted. However, about noontime, I received a cable from

Frank announcing his homecoming on AVENSA's afternoon plane. "I have good news," the cable read.

Dressed in alpargatas, faded blue jeans and a red and white checked blouse, I went to the airport and waited at the gate in the fence that separated the airport lounge from the tarmac. The LAV plane had already landed. I watched the AVENSA DC-3 land, taxi, turn, park in front of the gate, and shut down its engines. The door opened and the ground crew pushed portable stairs to the plane's doorway. As passengers alighted, my heart pounded like a schoolgirl's waiting for her date to show, fearful that something might have happened and he wouldn't be there. *God, let him be there.* I saw the stewardess come to the door and say something to one of the agents on the ground. She was preparing to leave the plane. *Where's Frank?* This wouldn't be the first time he missed his plane.

When I saw Captain Mitchell, the AVENSA pilot, start down the steps, my heart sank. *No, not again.* I closed my eyes for a second and when I opened them I saw Frank coming down behind Mitchell. *Thank God.*

He waved goodbye to his pilot friend, then picked up his luggage from where it had been dropped on the tarmac from the DC-3's rear cargo door. He sprinted to the iron gate where I was standing and hugged me. "Button, God it's good to be home. I have so much to tell you. You won't believe it." Walking to the car, his light blue suit jacket blew open in the soft late afternoon breeze and his tie whipped over his shoulder—he never used a tie pin or tack. I liked that wind-blown look.

"I can't wait to hear."

I started the car and we left the airport parking lot. "Maybe it isn't something you'll hear," he teased.

"Not something I'll hear?"

"How about see and hold?" He kissed me. "Really want to know what I have?" He continued to tease me.

As we approached the house, a taxi was leaving Freemans. I drove into our driveway.

"Hey, what's going on at the Freemans?" Frank asked.

"Carlos and his associates just come in on LAV. They're having a cocktail party and we're invited." I opened the front door of our house. "Can you show me your surprise?"

"No. No. Not if we have to go to a party next door. You'll want to savor what I have."

"Not fair. I'll be in suspense the rest of the evening. Please tell me what it is I'll see and hold."

"I can't do that. That would ruin it. Want to guess?"

"Come on, Frank. You're silly."

"Okay. What will you give me for a hint?"

"I think we're running out of time and I still have to shower."

"Later, you won't think I'm silly. Okay. Get ready for the party. You'll be sorry."

He went to the dining room and started to arrange pages from a yellow legal-size pad in orderly piles on the dining room table. The large oscillating fan on a pedestal stirred the air and some papers flew to the floor.

While he sorted through his things, I went to the bedroom and selected the dress I'd wear to the party. I wondered about his surprise. What was it that I could see and hold?

As I stepped into the shower, I heard Frank on the phone with Julio. Damn, I didn't have time to eavesdrop.

The Freeman party would be fancy, so after I showered, fixed my hair, and put on lipstick, I slipped on a new dress that was off-the-shoulder and had a full skirt that swirled out when I turned. With large red roses and green leaves on a field of white and tied neatly at the waist with a green cummerbund, it was a dress June Allyson might have worn in scenes with Alan Ladd in *The McConnell Story*, a favorite film of mine about pilots and flying. My white sandal high-heels completed the outfit.

"Which big shots are we meeting tonight?" queried Frank, as we walked next door.

"I think they may be investors working with Carlos on the development of a residential country club."

"A residential country club?" His brow furrowed. "Here in Bolivar?"

"We'll learn more tonight, I'm sure."

When we arrived at the party, Carlos greeted us at the door then quickly kidded me about showing off my new dress, "to those less fortunate." Everyone laughed.

With the green wicker furniture I had loaned her, Madelyn's living room resembled an outdoor garden. She had placed colorful wild flowers and flaming candles around the room and affixed branches with leaves and delicate lavender blossoms across the tops and down the sides of the windows. What a difference candles and flowers made.

"Madelyn," I whispered. "The room looks beautiful."

Carlos' associates were businessmen, one from New York and one from Washington, D.C. They were quite formally attired in dark suits, starched white shirts and conservative ties. With the ambient temperature hovering close to 100 degrees Fahrenheit, they quickly shed their jackets and ties and rolled their shirt cuffs up one turn.

They arrived sheathed in mystery. My game was to learn who they were, where they were from, what business they were in and what they planned to work out with Carlos. This game had no rules, programs, or scorecards.

"Hey, Frankie," Carlos said pompously, "I'd like to charter one of your planes tomorrow to show my associates around the area. Maybe go to Angel Falls. Is the Beechcraft available?"

"Sorry, Junior," Frank replied. "I just spoke with Julio. All our planes are reserved tomorrow. The next day, too."

The associate Carlos introduced as Harry hailed from New York, and we talked like we were at a college reunion. Living in a foreign country, there's nothing quite as comfortable as meeting someone from "back home." While Frank and the other businessman loitered at the makeshift bar Madelyn had arranged on a card table, Harry and I stood at the front window overlooking the porch the cow had trod only a few hours earlier.

We made small talk. First, he said the small pieces of luggage on the porch were theirs and he guessed Carlos would drive them to the hotel later. Then he admired my dress, and went on to ask a couple of innocuous questions. I had a few questions of my own; I wanted to hear about his business interests.

That he introduced the subject of flying and the aviation business in Bolivar was natural enough. Frank's occupation as a Venezuelan bush pilot and his American wife often served as icebreakers in conversations. "How did you two meet?" and "How does a girl from New York like living on the last frontier?" were the most common questions asked. However, Harry's fascination was more with Frank's air service than knowing how Frank and I met. His interest alerted my curiosity and I wondered why he asked how many planes we flew, how did we get most of our business, did we handle cargo, were our planes leased or purchased, where did our pilots come from, did we fly C-46s? To most of his questions, I replied, "I really don't know much about the business." He was too inquisitive for my money. I doubted this man planned on building a country club.

When I saw Frank alone at the bar, I excused myself and drifted toward him. I handed him my empty glass. "Can you do something about this?"

"I see you're making a big hit with your *paisano*." (countryman).

"Something weird's going on here, Frank. That gentleman, Harry, asks only about our air service. I sense I have to be cautious with him—not give him much info. He hasn't said anything about a country club. Maybe I've got these men confused with others Carlos said might be coming down. I'll try to learn more."

Frank laughed and shook his head. He said I had a knack for getting down to "brass tacks" and learning much more than he could.

Frank gave me a drink and I sashayed back to my new friend.

"You were talking about C-46s?" I asked before he could speak.

"Yes. Carlos couldn't seem to locate any for sale when he was in Miami."

"I'm surprised," I said, wondering why Carlos wanted to locate C-46s.

"You know about C-46's?"

Then I really put my foot in my mouth. "C-46s are in Miami. They're old and need work. But they are there."

That seemed to startle my new friend. "Hmm. That's odd."

Blue Skies, Green Hell

I wanted to ask why Carlos was looking for C-46s. That's when I realized I'd already said too much. "Well, maybe there are no more." My reply was totally stupid.

"Carlos," Harry continued, "made an exhaustive study and predicts measurable growth in the air cargo business in Bolivar." I lost my breath when he said, "The principal owner of the LEBCA license will sell it. Do you know him?"

I wondered how to answer that simple question. Of course, I knew the owner. "I—ah—yes." It was a simple answer.

"Carlos is quite an operator. He's putting together a deal for Ben and me to buy the LEBCA license. Carlos will be our man in Venezuela." he said. "Seems like Carlos has good contacts."

When Frank started the business, he agreed to pay a percentage of our gross profits to use the LEBCA license until the ministry issued Frank the AEROVEN license. Our planes had been flying under the LEBCA license since November 1951. It was a fair deal and the Bolivar flying community knew about the arrangement. Carlos knew about it.

I wondered if Frank knew the LEBCA license was now for sale. I began to sweat. The magnitude of Carlos' betrayal suddenly dawned. I guessed he intended to corner the air freight market by arranging for his associates to purchase the license under which we operated—our very life's blood. As top man in Venezuela, Carlos would be in a position of considerable power over his good friend, Frank. Instead of inviting Frank into a business partnership, he'd gone outside the community and brought in strangers to bankroll his venture. I had only two things to do pronto: settle down and exit gracefully. I smiled and said, "I'm all out of cigarettes. I'll find Frank. He'll have one. Anyway, I don't want to monopolize all your time."

"Well, I've so enjoyed my time with you. You're a delightful lady," he said.

I'm sure I am! I smiled as I nodded politely and backed away.

Again, I caught up with Frank at the bar. "We have to leave. Now. I talked too much and want to get out of here. I heard terrible news." I looked around and spotted Madelyn.

"You're leaving so early?" Madelyn asked as she replaced an empty dish of snacks with a full one.

"I'm so sorry. Frank's bushed and he has a big day tomorrow. Two flights." We hugged. "We enjoyed everything. Thank you so much."

"I'll see you tomorrow."

Frank and I walked across the dirt between the houses and went in ours. As I closed the door behind us, I collapsed back on it. "Phew. You'd better sit down."

Frank looked puzzled. "What's the terrible news?"

167

We sat on the sofa. "Harry told me the LEBCA license will be sold to him and the other gentleman at the party and that Carlos had put the deal together." I brushed my hair back with my hand. "He said Carlos predicts great expansion for C-46s in Bolivar and, get this, Carlos will be their man in charge in Venezuela."

I sat with my elbows on my knees, head between my hands.

Frank took my hand. "Come with me." He led me to the dining room where his papers were spread over the table and on the floor. I watched him flip through several stacks then finally withdraw an impressive looking document. "Here's my surprise. My good news. You've made me keep this to myself all evening." He gave me the paper. "Now you can see and you can hold my surprise."

I only read a few of the words when I squealed with glee, twirled around and threw my arms around his shoulders. "Frank you've got it. You've got it!" I yelled. My hands held the document that certified the license for AEROVEN had been issued.

"We can fly all over Venezuela. It's a great license."

"You've got the license." I could hardly believe it.

"Now what were you saying about LEBCA being for sale?" He joshed. "Who cares? We are now AEROVEN. We just have to paint the AEROVEN name and the ID letters on the planes and adios LEBCA."

"YV-C-FLA..." I said.

"Yes and B and C and all the rest to come—the sky's the limit. Button, back in April, I learned our license would be issued soon. Well, it took longer than I expected. But I've known about Carlos and his moves since last May. That's when he started to try to work a deal. I knew it wouldn't go through. Everyone in the ministry knew it wouldn't. I didn't say anything to you."

"Why not?"

"I didn't want your relationship with the Freemans to be affected. You've needed them and they've been good to us, especially to you when I've been away. Madelyn's your friend. I figured it would sort itself out someday. We've said it before, 'Carlos is such a dreamer.' That's all it was."

He sat down in a dining room chair. "I even knew Carlos couldn't find C-46s for sale, and I couldn't figure that one out until I remembered our first trip to Miami to buy a plane. Remember that, Button? We had no contacts and wasted a lot of time. Carlos has no contacts in the aviation industry—neither in Florida nor in Venezuela."

"I'm speechless. You knew everything," I said.

He laughed softly and nodded his head. "Pretty much. My contacts in the ministry—and in aviation in Caracas—are solid. They're long-standing."

Frank poured two drinks and we returned to the sofa in the living room. We sat down side-by-side. He explained Carlos had probably noticed the growth of aviation—passengers and cargo—in Bolivar and saw a lucrative business opportunity. Rather than start from scratch in developing an air service, the quickest way to the money was to buy a commercial aviation license. At the suggestion of Carlos' well-connected father, probably the Americans came down to look over the deal that Carlos tried to orchestrate. The men we met had their eyes on an air service and not on a country club.

"Carlos doesn't know I've been onto his scheme." He walked to the front window. "But I don't understand why he didn't talk with me about getting into the business. Maybe we could have worked something out. Anyway, the threat of a takeover is over. Hell, there never was one."

"Why would Carlos do such a thing?" I asked. "We're friends."

"As it says in the good book; the love of money is the root of all evil. To Carlos it looked like easy money. I guess Junior had better find another get-rich-quick scheme and it won't be in the airline business." He sipped his drink. "Maybe we'll get this framed," he said as he walked to the bedroom and carefully put the letter on his dresser. "God, it was a long time coming."

Early the next morning, as was customary when Carlos wanted to speak with Frank, he'd walk between the houses, pass our bedroom window on the way to our front door, and call in, "You guys awake?"

"Come on in, Junior. The door's not locked," Frank answered as he stretched. He put on a terry cloth bathrobe and slippers and went to the door.

Dressed in a white tee shirt and blue and white cord slacks, Carlos held a lit cigarette in one hand and a cup of coffee in the other. His hands trembled as they often did. I suspected too much caffeine.

"Hey, Junior." Frank said. "Nice party."

"Good morning, Carlos," I said as I followed Frank to the living room.

Carlos walked to the sofa, and before he sat down, he blurted out, "I think you know, Frankie, my associates are going to buy the LEBCA license." He took a drag on his cigarette and exhaled smoke high in the air. "That guy in Caracas is out and, well, I'm in. I'll be the new Director of LEBCA in Venezuela." He looked pleased with himself. "And I'll be your boss." He sat down.

Frank put his hands in his robe pockets, stood close to Carlos and looked down at him. He enunciated slowly, "You'll never be my boss, Junior." Then he strode slowly to the small table, removed the coffee pot from the electric heater, refilled Carlos' cup, than refilled his own. Carlos, stunned and silent, waited for Frank to continue.

"No one will be. No one will ever be my boss." Frank went to his dresser in the bedroom and retrieved the letter. "Look at this, Junior," he said reentering the living room. He gave the document to Carlos whose eyes opened wide as he read the document. "AEROACTIVIDADES VENEZOLANA S.A.," Frank said proudly, "That's AEROVEN. Do you see where it says President Frank Lazzari? And the first two letters of identification for all our aircraft in the fleet will be FL. My initials, Carlos. My license. LEBCA's out and AEROVEN is in."

Carlos stumbled over words that wouldn't fly and finally stammered, "Congratulations."

"And I talked with LEBCA officials just before I came home. They said firmly the company's not been sold. Case closed. I suggest you and your associates forget about LEBCA and concentrate on some other business, Junior. Perhaps a country club."

An uneasy Carlos finally said, "No hard feelings?" He stuck out his hand. Frank shook it, but didn't reply quickly. Finally, he simply said, "No. No hard feelings."

"See you later," Carlos said and left.

"Well," Frank smiled, "He came in here full of himself. He's a little deflated now."

"I feel as though I've lost a friend," I said. "I feel like someone died. When he said he'd be your boss, he looked so self-satisfied."

"He's embarrassed now."

"And I don't know how I feel about Madelyn now. She surely knew all about this big deal."

"Hold that thought for a minute, Button." He looked out the front window, stared into the blue sky, and turned slowly to face me. "I'm perplexed. He swaggered in here and announced he'd be my boss." Frank wrinkled his brow. "Button, he thought he'd be in charge of LEBCA *and*, apparently, its aircraft. Even if his associates bought the LEBCA license, our planes would not go with the deal. LEBCA doesn't own our aircraft. Even if we didn't have the AEROVEN license and he did buy LEBCA, we'd refuse to sell our aircraft—if the offer was made—and our contract to lease the LEBCA license would be over. Our aircraft would never be his to manage. He's known the AEROVEN license was about to be issued and my business with LEBCA would be dissolved. Hell, everyone in CB and Caracas knew that. It's been no secret since we arrived in fifty-one. Does Harry and what's-his-name think the planes come with the purchase of the license? Frankly, I'm missing something here. Maybe I haven't got the full story. And frankly, I don't give a damn."

"Maybe they didn't think your license would be issued so soon."

"I just don't know. I like Carlos. He's a nice guy. But he's way off balance here."

He sat next to me on the sofa, tore a sheet from his tablet of white lined paper and folded it into a glider. He threw it and watched it soar up and glide to the floor. "That's Carlos' career in aviation."

"You've got a handle on your situation. But I haven't. I'm hurt. Madelyn was my best friend. I don't know what to do."

"Want my advice?" Frank asked.

I nodded. "Yes."

"Let it go. It's not important. Madelyn is still your friend. That's what's important. She's a lovely, sincere person. Carlos? We know he's a dreamer."

Blue Skies, Green Hell

"I've needed her since we arrived over a year ago."

"Button, maybe she needs you as much as you need her. And I promise, Button, I won't let this episode make a difference between Carlos and me. You and I will always owe them for having welcomed us into their home when we had no place to go. And we've had great times with them. We've both enjoyed their company." He chuckled and put his head back and rested it on the cushion. He squeezed my hand. "Some of our best times have been with Madelyn and Carlos."

Frank was always fair dealing with people. His eyes drifted to our bedroom and to the window in our room that faced the Freemans' house. "Maybe his associates don't even know LEBCA is *not* for sale. We have nothing to regret. Nothing to have hard feelings over. He didn't hurt us in any way."

He walked to the kitchen. "Guillermina. If there's more coffee, would you please bring it and some juice and toast to the living room. We can't very well eat in the dining room until I pick up my papers."

We loved our palace with fenced corral for our dogs,
Tail Spin and Loop, but the house was too small.

He returned to the living room. "I've been thinking about this house, Button. It's hot. We've talked about buying air conditioners for the windows and planting trees—but we'd be investing in a house we don't own." He sipped his coffee and then told me he'd really been thinking about moving to a nicer, bigger house, one with more rooms, a bigger kitchen. "One that has large trees for shade and a bigger fenced yard for the dogs. A patio so we can have parties at home. Everyone comes here and they have a good time—but sometimes it's pretty crowded. A larger house would be better. I've had my eye on a house just now being built. It's nearer the airport than this one. It's a house with many angles and lots of windows. It will catch breezes and never be hot. Want to go see it?"

Chapter 18

Paradise in Green Hell

Dear Mother and Dad   August 22, 1953

As usual, I'm busy today and hardly have time to write.

Tomorrow, I'm going on vacation to Canaima. Not for just a day . . . a real vacation this time. Four days.

When I couldn't find anyone to go with me, I had almost given up hope of going. Frank had said I could go to Canaima (Yes . . . he's still in Caracas) on one condition; I go with someone. Well, I'm going with China and her husband, Jesús, one of Frank's best friends! We spent time with them when we were on our honeymoon in Maiquetía waiting for the C-46. Anyway, tomorrow at eight a.m. I'll fly over the savannah and jungle to Canaima and I'm bursting with joy. So, until I get back from the beach with the singing sand, Canaima,

All my love always, Marilyn

I'd been sitting at the Ciudad Bolivar airport patio lounge having a Coke and chatting with Charlie Baughan, our dear friend and a legend in bush piloting. In WWI, Charlie flew with the Canadian Air force. After the war, he flew in Central America and in the Middle East. Too old to fly in the air force in WWII, he ferried airplanes from the U.S. to Europe via South America and across the ocean to Africa. During those years, he saw Venezuela and after WWII he found his way back and was recruited by TACA. A few years later, Frank graduated from the school in Maracay and was recruited by TACA where he met Charlie.

A little too independent and restless to be an airline pilot, Charlie transitioned to the bush and helped settle a town called Icabarú on the Brazilian border. However, his most famous discovery was an exotic beach in the jungle. He named it Canaima, after the evil god that is believed by some to live on Auyántepui. Charlie had a reputation for exaggerating, but I believed his stories had truth woven through them. After all, Canaima is paradise and Angel Falls are breathtaking as Charlie always told his friends and business associates. At age fifty-one, Charlie had 27,000 flying hours.

Blue Skies, Green Hell

He had a big voice made gentle by his Georgian accent and kind manner of speech. In pictures I'd seen of him taken when he wore the grayish-blue TACA uniform, he cut a snappy figure. A big man, he overpowered the single-engine Piper he occasionally shoehorned himself into.

He lightly blew on the cup of coffee he cradled in both hands. "My love affair with Canaima started in the late forties. I was just a boy at the time." He chuckled and ran his fingers through his full head of steel gray hair. He set his cup on the table and patted his gray mustache with a paper napkin. "I was flying a twin Cessna and had one passenger aboard traveling north from Icabarú to Ciudad Bolivar. I said to my passenger, 'The weather's clear. Let's swing by Angel Falls.'" He described how he circled the falls and then exited through Devil's Canyon. He'd flown a short distance over the Carrao River when a heavy mist rising from the river splashed on his windshield. He circled the area he'd just flown over. "Glorious," described Charlie. He'd flown over seven golden waterfalls cascading into a lagoon surrounded by a pink beach. "Honey, right away I was smitten by its primal beauty. My heart raced when I saw a grassy clearing just behind the beach and the deep fringe of jungle. I was tempted to land until I remembered I had a passenger. Whoops! I high-tailed it back to CB."

He bade his passenger a nice evening. "Then I made a few purchases of canned food, matches, coffee, flashlight, and a couple of tarpaulins—things like that. I filled some gas cans and stowed them behind the front seat of a Piper I borrowed for my personal excursion." He needed the gas to refuel his plane for the return to Ciudad Bolivar. "Early the next morning I took off for paradise."

He decreased his altitude as he approached the grassy area behind the beach until he flew just high enough to make sure there were no obstructions on the field, then he flew up and around and safely landed.

He walked the short distance to the beach, stooped down and ran the pink sand through his fingers. No, he thought. This is not sand! He collected a sample in an old envelope he had in a pocket.

At dusk he made a fire from sun-dried driftwood. After dining on a can of beans and a cup of coffee heated over the fire, he dug a large hole and lined it with a tarp, stretched out his weary body in the hole, covered himself with the sides of the tarp, and then pulled the warm sand over the tarp.

"At first, I shivered and felt cold, but after a while, the warm sand soothed this old body and, Honey, I basked in the glory of my beach in my jungle. And my sunset. Oh, the magic of that sunset and my star-filled sky. I didn't sleep a wink." Instead, he made plans to develop an exotic resort in the jungle at this bend in the river. Charlie made a claim on the land in the vast wilderness—and it became his.

"You know the rest," he said. "I met Alejandro 'the hermit.' He'd been roaming around the Gran Sabana for years looking for gold and diamonds. He worked with me and a few of the indigenous Pemón folk. We built the camp, little by little." He lit a cigar and took a few puffs. "When Canaima had a few thatched shelters, we were ready to receive nice folks who wanted to see paradise. I started to invite friends." He sipped his coffee. "I met Rudy Truffino in Caracas and he flew down with me to look for gold and diamonds. Well, I introduced him to paradise, and he never left. He's the General Manager of my camp."

"Marilyn," he said, "I want you to come to Canaima. See it now. Oh, I know you've been there on day trips ever since you and Frank arrived in CB last year. Now that I have shelters, I want you to stay a few days. Get to know it. In time, I'll share my paradise with the world, but I want you to enjoy the Canaima experience now." He puffed on his cigar. Then he drawled, "It'll be developed someday, known around the world. I'll be called—King of the Jungle. His arms stretched out in front of him and moved in giant arcs as he described his vision. Canaima will be an exotic resort with rich-colored flowers, white and lavender orchids and colorful, noisy jungle birds. Monkeys will swing in the trees. You'll be able to say, 'I saw it when . . .'"

"Actually, Charlie, I'm planning to visit there as soon as I can—like now," I replied. "Frank's in Caracas. He'll probably be there for two weeks." I sipped my Coke. "He said I could go to Canaima if someone went with me. None of my friends can make it," I sighed. "But I'm not giving up hope."

"Something will turn up." He casually puffed on his cigar. "How is Frank?" he asked.

"Good, Charlie. He's working on a deal with Texaco Oil." I stood up. "I have to go to the office. Want to come over and see who's there?"

Charlie and I walked across the asphalt parking lot. Softened by the noontime heat, I hoped the hot tar wouldn't stick to the soles of our shoes and then make a mess on the floor of our hangar or the carpet on the office floor. The building was old, but we kept it neat and clean.

"Hola," I said to Elena, the company secretary. "Where's Julio?"

"He's on a trip." She looked at the clock on the wall. "He'll be back soon." She gathered pencils in need of sharpening.

"And where's everyone else?" I asked. "On a hot day like this, this place is usually full of people."

Elena simply shrugged.

The air-conditioned office drew people like an oasis in a desert. It was a convenient stop for anyone who wanted to drop in, cool off and "hangar talk" (talk about flying) with whichever pilot at the airport chose to relax in the cool office. "Sorry, Charlie, there's no one to talk to."

Just as he prepared to leave, a car drove up and stopped in front of the hangar. I recognized its occupants right away. "Hello." I ran to the car and enthusiastically greeted our good friends from Maiquetía. "China. Jesús. It's great to see you. It's been a long time."

I'd met these nice people at their cottage in Maiquetía shortly after Frank and I married. Having learned to speak English at the same time he learned to fly in Texas, Jesús spoke English with a Texas accent and could fool anyone into believing he called the Lone Star State home. China, however, understood some English, but didn't speak it, so we conversed in Spanish.

Jesús, a pilot for LAV who flew the Lockheed Constellations to New York, greeted Charlie. It seemed like everyone in aviation in Venezuela knew Charlie; Jesús also knew just about everyone in Venezuela's flying community. Although only twenty four years old, Jesús had already logged 6,500 hours in the air.

"Welcome. It's great to see you," I said.

"Is Frank around? Jesús asked.

"No. He's in Caracas. Are you here visiting China's folks?" I asked.

"Yeah. A few days vacation."

I held my breath and then blurted out, "You'll be here on vacation for a few more days?"

He nodded. "Our baby is with us. His grandparents like him to spend time with them."

"Ah—Ah—Do you have other vacation plans?'

"No. Just hoping to spend some time with you and Frank."

"No plans," I mused. "How about joining me for a few days in Paradise—at Canaima?"

Jesús and China looked at each other and simultaneously said, "Sí. Qué bueno (Yes. How good)." Jesús asked, "Charlie, do you have room for three guests at Canaima?"

"My dear friends," Charlie drawled, "If every thatched shelter was filled, I myself would build one for you." He adjusted his large straw hat. "You three are among my favorite people," he playfully snookered. "When can you come?"

Their visit was God-sent. I knew it would please Frank that Jesús and China would be my companions in the isolated and remote camp in the jungle. We chatted and finally agreed we could all be ready in a day or two.

I looked at the chalk board in the office that showed the planes, pilots and dates they were reserved. "Charlie," I said. "Is it ok for us to come day after tomorrow? Looks like we have a Cessna available for a few days. We could stay three or four days. Is that okay for everyone?"

"There's one guest now, but there's still room for everyone. And while you're there, I'll come down and we'll spend some time together. I usually visit Canaima at least once a week."

"Jesús? We've got a Cessna available. Do you mind flying on your vacation?"

"*Vamanós.*" (Let's go).

"Then it's settled."

In the office, we planned our exotic vacation to Canaima and the Lost World. With Charlie's help, we compiled our shopping lists. He told us he'd recently installed a generator and had a fridge so we could bring meat and other things that required refrigeration. We'd shop tomorrow and leave the following day.

Just then, Julio landed. A few minutes later he was in the office. All the pieces to my vacation puzzle came together. I introduced him to China and Jesús and told Julio about our plans for a Canaima odyssey. "It looks like we have a Cessna available. Jesús said he'd fly it."

Julio's quick reply surprised me. "How would you like to go in the Beechcraft? I'll take my family for a day's outing. They need a break, too." All the family comprised his wife, Martha, three children and Martha's mother, who I called Mrs. M. She was visiting from the States. Including two seats in the cockpit, the twin-engine plane carried nine people. We just fit.

The Rojas' planned to spend the day and enjoy a beach picnic in the jungle. China, Jesús and I would remain about four days. For our return, Julio said he had a trip scheduled with a couple of tourists who wanted to visit Canaima for a few days. He'd be returning to CB empty. We could return with him at that time. What luck!

The next day, China and I shopped for provisions; food, drinks, soap that floated, toilet paper, tubes of citronella, citronella candles and hammocks. For my personal use, I packed two towels, a flash light, two bathing suits, two shorts, two shirts, some unmentionables, and a few packs of cigarettes. I wore jeans, a cotton shirt and my alpargatas. I also took a few seventy-eight RPM records. Charlie said he had a record player that worked fine when the generator was operating.

Martha called and said she'd bring the picnic; cake, the makings for sandwiches, salads, and a thermos filled with something cold to drink. Within a few hours, we'd arranged a royal outing. We left for Canaima at eight a.m. on Sunday, August 23, 1953.

Taking off at that early hour all but guaranteed clear skies. We flew south over a varied landscape; lush savannah, a carpet of jungle, gigantic tepuís, rapids, and rivers.

Fifty-seven minutes after our departure, we buzzed the Canaima campsite at the edge of the lagoon to announce our arrival and landed in the grassy airstrip carved out of the heavy foliage. We all carried the provisions to the beach, a short walk through overgrown yellow weeds, scratchy underbrush, and up and down a sandy hill. Ah, Paradise.

Picture seven powerful gold-colored waterfalls casting clouds of white mist high in the air and cascading into a roiling sapphire lagoon surrounded by shimmering pink beach and verdant rainforest; tall swaying Moriche palm trees surrounding the lagoon and three even growing out of the water; vibrant red and blue Macaws flitting among tropical foliage; small green parrots chirping as they played with berries; howling monkeys swinging from tree to tree. Picture Canaima.

Blue Skies, Green Hell

As we walked, we slid our feet on the dry beach, now identified as pulverized quartz, and it sounded like violin strings being plucked.

Each time I visited Canaima, I stopped on the path leading from the grassy air strip to the pink beach to absorb the picture as though I'd never seen it before. An artist would carry a full palette of colors to capture the magic of Canaima.

Rudy Truffino greeted us. Later, he'd be known as "Jungle Rudy." He came to Canaima from his native Netherlands via Ciudad Trujillo in Santo Domingo. After he met Charlie in Caracas, he visited Canaima—and never left. He called home a tent not far up the hill near a smaller tent where two camp workers lived.

Then we met a photographer on assignment from Germany to photo tepuís and the jungle for a magazine published in his homeland. I don't think I learned his name, but I called him Eric.

Finally, we met Vilma and Alejandro. Vilma, a sturdy good-looking blonde from Germany, often visited the deep jungle's best-known resident, and ultimately, Vilma and Alejandro were married. When I met him, he was called Alejandro the Hermit. Much later, when rivers and cliffs and campsites and overviews were named for him, people dropped the word "hermit" and called him by his proper name Alejandro Laime (pronounced "lie-may"). Just to say you met—even better—were well-acquainted with Alejandro, brought instant respect to the person who made the claim. Vilma and Alejandro were in Canaima to guide Eric on photographic expeditions.

The two lived at a bend in the Carrao River called Mayupa less than two hours away by *curiara* (dugout) with an outboard motor. Built on a promontory, their Indian-style house made of bamboo and palm leaves had no windows but open doorways which they covered at night with small tree branches held together by vines. Alejandro came to Venezuela in 1940 and, except for occasional trips to Ciudad Bolivar or Caracas for provisions, he never left his jungle paradise. Charlie said Alejandro lived off the land and found enough gold, diamonds and other gems to pay for his meager needs.

After Charlie began flying tourists to Canaima, Alejandro, for a modest fee, guided small groups of wannabe adventurers around the burgeoning campsite and the seven waterfalls. For the valiant traveler who wanted more demanding expeditions, he'd take them on the Carrao River to the Churún River; to a place he called "Laime's Overlook" to see Angel Falls close up.

The overlook is a large flat rock a short distance from the base of the towering waterfall. Although extremely difficult to reach, it remains one of the best places from which photos of the tallest waterfall in the world may be taken.

Of the few Caucasian men I knew who had given up modern conveniences to live in the bush, Alejandro was the most intriguing and intellectual. Jungle Rudy was not far behind him. Both were somewhat mysterious.[11]

The camp at Canaima consisted of a couple of thatched shelters. Each had one wall secured to the thatched roof by poles lashed to corners and secured to stakes in the ground.

The roof had a green tarp thrown over it and was secured to the shelter's frame. A large dark green tent was the guests' dining room and housed a fridge, a hand-hewn picnic style table, and benches. Several Adirondack chairs were on the beach.

Rudy led us to our shelter. He scowled when he saw our soft wool *chinchorros* (knitted hammocks) and rolled his eyes. Wryly, he said, "You'll need a sturdier hammock, one that will keep out the cool, damp air along with bugs and other things you'll not want to encounter during the night." He disappeared and returned in minutes carrying three "McArthur" hammocks. Seeing my look of bewilderment, he rolled his eyes again and said, "I will help all of you hang the hammocks."

Made of army green canvas and mosquito netting with vertical and horizontal zippers, they were designed to protect the sleeper. He handed each of us a wool blanket. "Spread this in the bottom of the hammock so you can wrap in it. It will keep you warm and help keep out the dampness from below." As he left the shelter, he pointed to a nail in the pole. "This is where you hang your knapsacks."

Our accommodations were simple; one shelter and three hammocks that were comfortable and almost rainproof. The bathtub was the lagoon, and the toilet was behind the camp and up a hill anyplace in the jungle. It wasn't first-class, but it was perfect for rustic Canaima.

While we'd been learning the do's and don'ts of the campsite and readying our hammocks, almost everyone had changed into swimsuits and waded into the clear, cool water of the lagoon. Martha forewent the swim to set up lunch. Her mother didn't swim either, saying she didn't want to get her hair wet.

China, Jesús and I, along with Julio and the kids, enjoyed splashing in the lagoon. Two swans paddled around us.

"Hey, everybody," Martha called, "Lunch is ready. Come and get it."

We waded out of the water and dashed to the table in the dining tent now set up with paper plates, sandwiches, and salads.

We were enjoying Martha's lunch when Julio interrupted our repast in Paradise. "Hey, folks. I'm sorry. I don't want to ruin a nice lunch and great day, but it looks like bad weather is coming from the north. Rain. When you finish your cake, we should begin to pack up and leave. We might have to fly around the storm. The trip back may take longer." Whenever Julio spoke, whether at a serious meeting or a social gathering, he usually spoke softly and in apologetic or servile tones.

Everyone helped pack up things the Rojas family would take back with them. We raced the bad weather to the airstrip and helped load the Beechcraft.

Jesús, China and I stood at the side of the grassy clearing and waved goodbye to Julio and his family. Through a haze of disturbed locusts, we watched the Beechcraft takeoff, soar over the line of trees at the end of the strip, bank, and fly northward out of sight. Our only connection with civilization disappeared into threatening skies.

Alejandro and Vilma said they'd return the next day to escort Eric on a journey by boat to the seven waterfalls, hike up the rocky terrain behind the falls and on to the Carrao River. We accepted their invitation to go along. Then they said goodbye and departed on their two hour boat ride to their home.

In our paradise, time was of no importance; we had no plans, no goals, no limitations. We had nowhere to go, no money, and nothing to buy. We'd crossed into the "Lost World."

After our robust dinner of charcoaled steak and baked potatoes, we walked along the beach for a little exercise. However, the storm Julio had seen coming toward us rolled into Canaima and we jogged back to camp. I went to my side of the shelter, crawled into my hammock, wrapped in the blanket, and pulled closed the zippers. That's when the worst part of the wicked weather swooped in.

The howling rainstorm brought gusting winds to our primitive shelter. The tied-down tarp flapped against its roof of palm fronds. Palm trees bent and blew against each other making swishy sounds as rain beat a rapid tattoo on the tarp that lay over the thatched roof. Occasionally, rolling thunder echoed in the lagoon competing for attention with the roar of the falls while the storm raged through this timeless place.

The weather was clear the next morning. Fronds and coconuts strewn about the beach were already being swept up by the two camp workers.

Alejandro and Vilma did not show up that morning, but Rudy loaded up the aluminum boat, hopped in first, then China, Jesús and I boarded. Next came Eric, laden with an impressive black leather bag filled with high-tech camera equipment. Rudy pulled the cord on the outboard motor several times and finally it started. He pushed off and headed the boat toward the foot of one of the seven great falls.

The nearer we came to the falls, the more deafening they sounded. Roiling waters rocked and pitched the boat. Between the spray and the turbulent lagoon, we got our first soaking and whooped with joy. Eric did not whoop. Instead, he nervously hovered over his camera bag.

Rudy drove the boat to one side of the waterfalls' base where he hopped out and tied the boat to a tree. He flung his knapsack over his shoulder and took the lead, striding on an 18-inch wide strip of sand at the river's edge. "Come along, everybody," he called out. Less inclined to be dexterous, Eric secured his camera bag over one shoulder and cautiously followed Rudy. Then I jumped out of the aluminum boat followed by China and Jesús. We followed Rudy and

Eric. Suddenly, they made a sharp right turn at a large boulder and disappeared from view. When I made the turn to the right at the boulder, I was confronted by a steep rock-filled rill with water still running down it from the previous night's storm. The top of the rill wasn't in sight. It looked old and probably had begun to form a million years ago when river water flowing high atop the waterfalls had carried rocks of all sizes and other debris down the runoff as the water returned to the river below the falls. Rudy and Eric had made good time and were well ahead of me on the steep and craggy incline. I could barely see them for the scrub brush, sharp-edged rocks—some covered with slimy moss—and thin trees that barely survived the harsh clime.

"Marilyn," I heard Rudy call. "Do you need help?"

After a few steps on this tortuous climb I knew the alpargatas I wore were not appropriate footwear. I also knew the climb was far more serious than any I'd ever made and felt uneasy without a staff or rope or even a sturdy tree to grab for support. Worse, I'd never before sunk into bog up to my shins. With each step, my feet squished into soft, spongy ground and the arduous ascent required my greatest effort and concentration: It tested my courage. With only skimpy branches from scrub brush to hold on to and branches from skinny trees to pull myself up from one level to the next, I called out confidently, "I'm okay."

I peaked over my shoulder and saw Jesús and China behind me doing far better than I. They had each other—and they wore sturdy shoes!

Exhausted, I reached the top of the falls and beheld a most splendid site; cascading water that cast a mist high into the air, and vast, lush savannah beyond. I don't know how high I climbed, but Rudy said it was about 150 feet.

Traveling Indian-style, one person in front of the other, we trekked through thick brush and tall weeds to the river's edge where Rudy, using his knife, cut down grass to make a small clearing. It proved to be an ideal spot for the lunch he had carried in his knapsack from our camp.

While Rudy set up the sterno stove and unpacked a large jar of soup, a couple of pots, sandwiches, crackers and coffee, Eric photographed vistas from the top of the falls and took shots of us as we ate. A quiet fellow who stayed mostly to himself, he spoke only in German and only to Rudy. When Jesús spoke to him in English, Eric struggled as if he didn't quite understand. Belying a shy demeanor, Eric later sent each of us a set of beautiful photographs he'd taken of Canaima, the tepuís, and of our expeditions through the jungle and on the rivers.[12]

Rudy said he believed China and I were the first women ever to climb to the top of the largest waterfall that cascades into the Canaima lagoon. I regret not having carved my initials and the year on a tree! Following lunch, we packed up the remains of the lunch, and descended the rill to the boat at the water's edge; the descent required much less courage than the ascent.

Along the way I asked, "Any snakes around here, Rudy?"

"Not many here, Marilyn. Maybe tomorrow. More tomorrow." His voice trailed off.

Rudy needed some persuasion to speak our language. He was a good-looking man, seldom smiled, but his attentive ways exuded confidence. Wearing a tan shirt with short sleeves rolled up one turn and standing tall and erect with his blonde hair falling casually over one eye, he looked like a hero on the cover of a romance novel.

He usually avoided talking about his past and only casually mentioned he'd traveled to Central America from his native Netherlands after World War II. I asked why he'd made the long journey, but our conversation ended abruptly when he said the weather looked bad and suggested we hurry back to camp.

Alejandro and Vilma arrived by curiara in time to join us for dinner. They stayed overnight at Canaima to facilitate an early start the next morning on a photographic expedition up the Carrao River beyond Hacha Falls. They planned to reach a location opposite Auyántepui.

They said with proper river conditions and time on our side, we might make it to a location from where we would see Angel Falls.

Because we'd travel in the aluminum boat with outboard, the success of our trip depended on an early start, good weather and river conditions. To skirt rapids and treacherous river currents, we'd portage the boat on dangerous jungle trails.

"I'll awaken all of you in time for breakfast," Rudy said. "Wear slacks and boots." He raised his eyebrows and looked disapprovingly at my mud-caked alpargatas.

I shook my head and shrugged my shoulders. "This is all I have with me."

"And wear your bathing suit under your clothes. Bring a towel. You might have a chance to swim." Lighting a cigarette he said, "I will not be with you tomorrow, but I will prepare lunch for you to take along. I'll be here when you return." He left.

I was awakened by the sounds of birds and people stirring around the camp. I slipped into my bathing suit, shirt and jeans and then stuffed a towel in my knapsack. The gray morning didn't bode well.

"Snakes?" I asked Alejandro as we boarded the aluminum boat.

"Possibly yes. Poisonous and mean." He spoke softly. Before we shoved off we got a crash course in Herpetology. Warning us first about the anacondas that grow to thirty-six feet in length, he urged us to be watchful of low branches dangling over the water. He offered details that made goose bumps pop on my arms. "That's where they wait—ready to fall on a victim passing under the branch. They wrap around their prey and then constrict it—a lethal squeeze." He gritted his teeth and his face grimaced as he described how the anaconda strangles its captured victim. "They're on land, but are not as effective as in the water." He said we also might see other snakes like bush masters, called *cuaima* in Venezuela, and the loathsome and venomous serpent fer-de-lance, called *tercio pelo*. "Rattlesnakes and boas may be around, too. Remember, while you enjoy all the scenic beauty of this Lost World, keep eyes open. Look up and down."

"How about bugs?" I asked.

"Yes. Tarantulas, scorpions, poisonous lizards. They're all here. Be alert. If you think you see something, let us know. Above all, be calm." He paused. "It's mastery of fear that counts." I nodded. "Your Mark Twain said that." Then he announced, "If everyone's ready, we'll leave now." He strode away.

"Okay, let's go," called out Jesús.

The outboard engine purred smoothly as we crossed the lagoon. We beached the boat, anchored it to a tree and unloaded its contents prior to portaging around rapids. China and I hefted our share. We carried net bags filled with provisions. Young and strong, we believed we'd be a great assistance to the band of explorers until we saw Alejandro lift the outboard off the boat, carry it up the embankment and put it on Vilma's shoulder. Leading the way, she set a rapid pace.

"We'd better not say we feel tired, even if we are," said China softly in Spanish as we watched Vilma and the outboard disappear up the overgrown trail.

The men unhitched the boat from the tree, carried the boat up the embankment and then on to the narrow trail. Alejandro told us to follow Vilma and said they'd bring up the rear.

Indian-style, we trekked on the slick path to the river. The hair bristled on the back of my neck when I thought of what might lie overhead or under the brush. My alpargatas were wet and I slipped on the leaf-covered path and wet foliage. I found a long, sturdy branch and used it as a walking staff to steady myself.

Here and there, the jungle permitted shafts of sunlight to filter through its growth. Shadows played on leaves, and ground-covering vines and roots seemed to writhe and wriggle. It was dusky but far from silent as the air filled with the screeching and howling of monkeys, the whistling and screaming of macaws.

Before long, we descended a rocky embankment, put our boat in the water, loaded the gear, took our places and carefully navigated the Carrao River. The water was dark, almost black from tannin caused by decaying vegetation. So thick was the jungle, we could barely discern the shoreline. Hanging vines, thicker than my arm and attached high in the trees were being moved and jerked about by unseen sources hidden in the leaves. Monkeys? Macaws? Critters? Monsters? Tarzan? Maybe Canaima, the evil one who lives on Auyántepui?

It was almost one o'clock when we unloaded the boat and its contents, and tied it to a tree at the water's edge. On the opposite side of the river, in awesome silence, we saw Auyántepui—the incredible massive block of sandstone, soaring high into the clouds with countless waterfalls of extraordinary dimensions, its talus slope below cloaked in dense vegetation. The fortress-like flat-top mountain was eerie but magnificently beautiful. Years later, this location would be called Isla Orquidea (Orchid Island).

Vilma set up the sterno and "kitchen" while Alejandro went off with Eric to take photos. China, Jesús and I helped unpack the lunch and even before the two returned, we'd started to enjoy the results of the absent Rudy's culinary artistry.

Noting the sun had disappeared behind clouds, Jesús looked up. "Bad weather is moving in," he warned.

After Eric and party returned, Jesús suggested we eat and be ready to leave quickly.

"Rain. It happens every day about this time," Alejandro said as he packed up. "We will not be able to continue on to see Angel Falls, but at least we may not have to portage the boat on the way back. Changes in the weather affect river conditions." He sipped from his thermos. "Of course, we might get rained on before we get all the way back to camp. Did everyone take pictures?"

On the return trip to Canaima we turned into a small river, hardly larger than a swollen stream, where we saw *baba* (small crocodiles), morocoy (turtles) and an abundance of jungle birds. Occasionally, we bent low in the boat in order to pass under hanging branches. With only narrow slits of gray daylight peeking through the trees, and quietness shattered by the sporadic cawing of wild birds and the clang-clang of the Conoco birds, the river took on the aura of a dark and haunted Lost World.

For the balance of the journey back to camp, we zipped over rapids around which we had carried the boat earlier. Despite a fine rain, we made good time traveling on the river. Back at Canaima, we shed our shirts and jeans and jumped in the lagoon to cool off and rid ourselves of sweat and the dirt we'd attracted during the day. After the swim, we toweled off and put on dry clothes. The clanging of the dinner bell echoed throughout the camp, calling us and the workers.

As we ate, the soft rain changed to a violent downpour. It beat so fiercely against the canvas tarp covering the dining tent it made it difficult to hear dinner conversation. The torrential storm boomed around us and lightning streaked through the black sky. Twice during the mayhem, lightning struck the antenna on Baughan's shortwave radio.

It would have been a terrifying evening even if Alejandro had not started to tell stories about the evil one called Canaima who roams the area and lives on Auyántepui.

"Some say he's a myth, but my Pemón friends swear he's real and say they have seen heel prints in the mud on the talus slopes." As he tore off a piece of the freshly made bread and smeared it with canned butter, he whispered, "They say he walks upright and is vicious and murderous." Between stories, I went to the doorway and watched lightning skip across the dark sky, lighting the region just long enough to see black storm clouds that surrounded the camp.

"Do you think Canaima's real?" I asked Alejandro.

"Oh, yes." Alejandro's eyes grew big and reflected the candlelight. "He lives. Marilyn, he's not an imaginary God or spirit," Alejandro insisted. "Canaima is a living Indian who is very *macho* (manly) and *muy vivo* (very alive). He lives alone on Auyántepui and roams the Gran Sabana." Alejandro lighted a kerosene lamp and shadows danced on the walls of the dining tent. "I hear tell he controls the Indian population through fear." His eyes were haunting in the light of the lantern as he lowered his voice to just above a whisper, just loudly enough to hear above the storm if we leaned across the picnic-style table and huddled close to him.

"One time," Alejandro said, "I heard Canaima went to an Indian settlement and called to one of the Indians. He ordered him to come out of his house. Frightened for his life, but obedient and respectful, the Indian came out of his round house." He paused.

"And what happened?" I asked in a hushed voice.

Alejandro put his hands together and with emotion welling in his throat, he leaned forward and said, "The Indian threw himself on the ground at the feet of Canaima and offered his life if only Canaima would spare his family. Canaima held high his great stick and he beat the Indian to death and disappeared in the jungle, leaving the dead man to be mourned by his family." Alejandro sipped the milk of a coconut. Just as he slammed the palm of his hand on the table and said loudly, "He exists," an explosion of thunder tore across the lagoon accompanied by a bolt of lightning that momentarily lit the inside of the tent.

"Oh my God," I cried out.

With fewer dramatics, Alejandro told how Canaima once went to his camp at Mayupa when Indians were sleeping in his house. Alejandro heard a disturbance and went out with a gun. As he shot a bullet into the air, he saw the back of Canaima disappear into darkness.

"Tomorrow," Alejandro said, "we'll make a trip to *Rio de los Buaros* (Buzzard River) to the Pemón Indians and meet the woman whose husband was killed by Canaima."

"Sounds to me like it's just a story. How could Canaima still be roaming after so many years?"

A wry smile crossed his face. "Perhaps there has been more than one Canaima. Perhaps evil Indians, even deranged Indians, use the name of Canaima to get away with murder. Canaima is real. He exists. It is not just a story. This is the mysterious Lost World, you know."

The rain continued to fall. Having had our fill of horror stories, we went back to our shelter, and between massive strikes of lightening, zippered ourselves into our hammocks and tried to sleep.

Blue Skies, Green Hell

"Do you believe there is an evil Indian roaming around?" I asked Jesús.

"No," he answered patiently. "There are no hostile Indians here. The only hostile Indians in Venezuela are far away—in the west—near Columbia. Now go to sleep."

China and I trembled. Before long, we told Jesús that if we lived through the night, we wanted to go back to Ciudad Bolivar. He didn't hear us. He'd fallen asleep.

Despite the raging storm, I fell asleep, but at four in the morning I awakened to strange and unfamiliar sounds. Jingle—jangle; loud. JINGLE—JANGLE. It sounded like people running their hands through buckets of coins or Indians dancing and shaking necklaces of metals and shells that jingled and jangled and clanged around their waists, wrists and ankles. Then I heard twang-twang. The sounds grew louder, faster, closer, and moved from one side of camp to the other. I knew natives were encircling the grounds and getting ready to attack.

China and Jesús had switched from sleeping in the hammocks to sleeping on two cots with mattresses put together. Softly, I called, "Jesús." He didn't answer. I called louder. Still no answer. *How can he sleep with natives dancing all around us?* I quietly unzipped my hammock and poked my head out, but too frightened by the unfamiliar noises and blackness all around, I quickly zipped it closed again. The clanging and twanging and jingling continued to move from one side of our camp to the other. I knew I would be dead by morning.

China finally spoke. She, too, disturbed by the strange noises, suggested natives were surrounding the camp. She awakened Jesús. We told him of our fears, and as the noises moved nearer and nearer to us, I pleaded with Jesús to get his gun and see what was going on. He grumbled something I couldn't hear.

Certain we'd be murdered by a tribe of hostile natives in the Lost World, I quickly unzipped my hammock and fled across the shelter to the big cots lashed together where China and Jesús had been sleeping and got in with them. I broke into a cold sweat. Terrified, China and I listened to the bells, jingles, clangs and twangs that grew louder as they moved to the right, then to the left and back again. Then China heard trumpets and horns and instruments that sounded like flutes made from hollow bamboo shoots. We pleaded with Jesús again, "Will you please take your gun and check the area?"

Slowly and dramatically, he sat up and, speaking first in Spanish then in English, he said, "When you two girls agree on what you hear . . . bells and jingles or horns and flutes . . . then I'll check it out. Until then I'm sleeping and suggest you do the same." Slowly and just as dramatically, he lay down and went back to sleep.

Although strange noises continued, I returned to my hammock and shortly, fell asleep.

We awakened to bright morning sunshine. We were all alive!

Timidly, we asked Alejandro about the noises we'd heard during the night. He gently chuckled and told us we had heard small and harmless animals disturbed by the violent storm. While there are animals that travel in packs and move around the jungle, he believed we'd also heard the croaking of frogs, high pitched shrieks and chatter of monkeys swinging from vine to vine and tree to tree and even nocturnal birds that flit from one branch to another. Many critters, he said, become restless during storms. Wildlife in the jungle come in varying sizes, from small insects to the larger animals like armadillo, tapir, and the cat-like puma. Many make unusual sounds.

The next day, as he'd promised, Alejandro and Vilma led us, by foot and boat, to a settlement of Pemón natives. Again, we carried the boat through the jungle and chopped our way with machetes as we traveled a path overgrown with roots and vines. By now, we were experienced explorers and comfortable working our way through the growth of huge trees and low, thorny underbrush. Vilma, of course, carried the outboard engine. After riding for an hour on the Carrao, we veered away and traveled on the tributary, *Rio de los Abuaros* (Buzzard River). Like the Carrao, the water was black and so still that when I looked ahead, I couldn't see where the jungle brush stopped and the shoreline began. The reflections, clear and undisturbed, were mirror-like images. Occasionally we passed a small Pemón settlement and finally we came upon a curiara tied to a tree.

After a short walk on a path under a cover of branches and leaves, we reached our destination, a village comprised of several palm-thatched round houses where we were greeted by native women and children. The women were short and slender in stature. Their skin was the color of suntanned Caucasians. Some wore their straight shoulder length black hair parted in the center; others parted their hair on the side. Most wore bangs. They wore dresses provided by visiting Capuchin Monks, but were bare foot. One of the women admired my alpargatas and asked if she could have them. I wanted so much to give them to her, but they were the only "shoes" I'd brought with me to Canaima. She also liked my jeans and straw sun hat.

Their broad smiles welcomed us to their compound. They reached out and touched our clothing, skin, and hair. Other than Alejandro and Vilma, few Caucasians had ever seen this part of the world; we appeared strange to them.

A mere generation before, they had lived a Stone Age existence, until the Capuchin Missionaries visited them and introduced them to some of the ways of our civilization. They learned how to farm, grow vegetables, enrich the soil, and were introduced to Western-style clothing. Many Pemóns remained in their villages, while others, having learned about the Western world, traveled to Ciudad Bolivar and even Caracas. Often, some of those who left the commune, returned to it, preferring their peaceful life in the bush to our noisy and fast-paced life in civilization. While our culture had its influence on them, many favored their own traditions and languages.

Friendly and hospitable people, they poured a beverage from a large gourd into a shallow bowl fashioned from a small gourd and passed it around the group for everyone to take a sip. They gave me a gourd they'd used to carry water from the river. I still have it.

Heavy smoke billowed from a hole in the top of the cone-shaped roof of each round house and hung on the trees, blotting out the small amount of blue sky and sunshine that tried to peak through the foliage. The smoke barely disguised the malodorous dampness and mildew. The smell of unidentifiable food cooking permeated the air.

They invited us inside their round house, and showed us a pot of stew placed over a wood-burning fire in a hole dug in the middle of the dirt floor, the source of the smoke that escaped through the hole in the roof. The fires are never allowed to die out.

Members of several families slept in individual chinchorros that hung between the wall of the house and the center pole. They cooked and ate and did everything in their round houses. No air moved and I felt weak from the heat. After a few minutes, I excused myself and left the house. Everyone in our party followed.

Alejandro conveyed our request to take their pictures and they happily agreed. The women and their children stood still and smiled again and again until we finally told them we'd run out of film.

We saw no men. Their absence was explained by the sound of wood being chopped and trees falling in an area beyond the village. The men had their work to do; they cut the wood, fished the rivers and hunted for meat. They never came to the settlement to greet us.

No one mentioned the evil God, Canaima. However, Alejandro subtly identified the woman whose husband, it was said, died at the hands of the evil one.

We left the settlement and returned to our aluminum boat tied to a tree at the water's edge. Quietly, we selected our seats in the boat and headed back to the main river. While our boat silently glided down the dark and narrow tributary to the Carrao and on to Canaima, I reflected on the ancient culture I'd been privileged to witness. The indigenous people had inner peace and qualities sometimes lost in our society. I understood Alejandro's fondness for these people and his faithful love for the world he adopted as his own.

We three remained silent for the rest of the trip back to Canaima, contemplating the Lost World we had found.

Outracing the rain, we arrived back at camp in the early afternoon where the sun continued to shine brightly on the pink sand and golden-colored falls. While Rudy prepared dinner, Jesús went to the airstrip to inspect it. The two laborers had cut down new growth that might have impeded a safe landing for Julio the next day.

China and I went swimming. "I think I'll stay a few days longer if Julio tells me Frank's not back from Caracas."

China said she'd also like to stay and hoped Jesús would agree. The thought of leaving paradise was unacceptable. Told of our desires to stay, Jesús said he'd also stay, providing Charlie Baughan didn't have other guests scheduled to use our shelter. "Both of you have gone native," he said smiling. "I might as well join you."

On schedule and flying the Beechcraft, Julio arrived the next morning. His four passengers were greeted by Alejandro and Vilma and after breakfast, they left on an expedition to the foot of Angel Falls.

Advised of our plans, Julio told me Frank had not returned but would be back on Monday. He also said if we wanted to stay a few more days there would be transportation for us to return to Ciudad Bolivar. Charlie planned to fly to Canaima within a day or two; we could return with him.

We needed food to get us through a few more days so we compiled a shopping list and gave it to Julio. He said Martha would shop and Charlie would bring everything to us.

Julio asked Eric if he needed anything.

He asked for a ride back to CB.

"*Claro que sí*" (Of course).

We waved goodbye to Julio and Eric. This time we did not feel our connection to civilization had disappeared. Instead, we'd made a connection with the wilderness.

That night, Rudy had another surprise for us. He'd packed a barbeque dinner and we went in the boat across the lagoon to an island where the two workers had built a roaring fire. The seven powerful waterfalls, lighted by a full moon, dazzled us as we feasted on hamburgers and salad.

Following the barbeque, we returned to camp and I played some of my favorite seventy-eight RPM records. How incongruous! With the jungle behind us, and in the bright glow of the moonlight, I listened to thunderous waterfalls accompany an instrumental rendition of "Beyond the Sea" and Jo Stafford's vocal arrangement of "You Belong to Me," two popular hits of the day, each with its own special memories and now with new ones being made.

It didn't rain that night but instead it was balmy and delightfully warm. This day, like the others since we arrived at Canaima, had been a glorious one of adventure. Tired and contented, I fell asleep.

Captain Charlie Baughan, intrepid pilot, adventurer, discoverer, founder of Canaima and our good friend. Photo provided by Gaby Truffino—2004

Eric, the photographer on assignment from Germany. Photo by Jesús

I stand atop a waterfall near Canaima. Photo by Jesús

This was our first view of the
waterfalls, tepuis and lagoon
as we walked a sandy trail from
the grassy airstrip to Canaima.
Photo by Marilyn—1952

Ready to go! On expedition,
I wait under a palm tree with
companions, China and Jesús.
Photo by Eric

Vilma and Alejandro Laime ready to lead us on second expedition.
Photo by Jesus

On expedition, Jungle Rudy Truffino prepares a hot lunch. Left to right, Rudy, Jesús, China, and I.
Photo by Eric

It was a difficult climb up a steep and rocky runout.
Photo by Eric

The climb was worth the view of the Gran Sabana.
Photo by Eric.

We visit a Pemón village

Jungle Rudy, Jesus, China and I rest after the climb up the steep runout to the top of one of the waterfalls at Canaima.
Photo by Eric

Pemón women and children showed us their homes.
Photo by Jesús

A photo opportunity with our new friends. Left to right—A Pemón boy, Marilyn, Vilma, a Pemón boy, and China.
Photo by Jesús

Pemóns enjoyed having their pictures taken.
Photo by Jesús

A whispering voice awakened me. "Don't move."

My eyes still shut, I asked, "Who is it?"

No answer.

I opened my eyes, and saw a giant silhouetted against the early light of day standing next to my hammock, a machete raised high over his head.

"Don't move," he whispered again and swung the lethal weapon downward. The wickedly sharp blade glinted in the day's early light. S-S-SH-SH-SHWACH. The machete missed my hammock and sliced the sand. I screamed and saw the giant raise the machete a second time. My stomach churned and bile came to my throat. S-S-SH-SH-SHWACH. It hit the sand again. I pulled the blanket over my head and screamed for help.

Silence followed. I peeked over the edge of the blanket and saw the giant still standing next to my hammock. Then I recognized Charlie Baughan. He held the machete. "Charlie, what are you doing?" I said. "You scared me to death."

"Honey," he drawled, "I didn't mean to frighten you." He knelt so he could talk to me through the net in the hammock. The workers behind him made sweeping motions with their machetes in the sand.

I unzipped the hammock.

"I didn't have time to warn you," he said. "I saw a rattlesnake slither into your shelter and I just had to get it before it got you. It's dead now. We'll all have to be alert and keep our eyes peeled. These snakes usually travel in pairs, so there's likely to be another around here someplace. You're lucky you didn't get out of the hammock." He stood up. "We catch 'em and skin 'em and my wife, Mary, will have a fine new pair of snakeskin shoes."

"I'm still trembling, Charlie, but thank you," I said. "And when did you arrive?"

"I flew in this morning. Just got here. I left CB about six a.m. and made good time. It's eight now. Put on your suit and meet me at the beach, we'll have a swim before breakfast and I'll bring you up to date about what's going on in CB."

What a way to start a day.

It got lots better. Martha had purchased all the items on our list of needed supplies and Charlie had brought them to the camp, so we were all set. And Charlie had news from Frank; he'd be on the late plane from Caracas to Ciudad Bolivar on Monday.

The next four days were delightful. We stayed fairly close to camp, swimming, sun-bathing, playing records and taking pictures. Eric had returned to Ciudad Bolivar with Julio, so we were just seven people in Paradise.

The day of our return to Ciudad Bolivar arrived with the early morning sun.

Sadly, I packed my knapsack, trudged up the path, and over the small hill kicking the sand and hearing it sing as I went along. I couldn't look back. For me, the world would never be the same. Charlie had said he wanted me to enjoy the Canaima experience. Now, I knew what he meant.

Jesús, China and I headed down the path to the airstrip and I couldn't believe my eyes! I saw one plane—an old, old single-engine Piper. Parked. Alone. Charlie's plane.

A high-wing plane, its left wheel landing gear leg/support, partially collapsed, stretched out so far that the left wing pointed downward and the right wing-tip was pointing upward above the horizon.

Charlie read my mind because he couldn't have heard what I'd muttered. He was, after all, a little deaf from having sat a good part of his life behind aircraft engines without high-tech headsets that suppress engine noise. "Now don't you worry, Honey, 'bout that ol' wheel. Watch this." He went to the tip of the left wing, lifted it up high and told Jesús to push the wheel in toward the fuselage to put it in place. "See that? Fixed," he drawled.

Next he opened the door. "You two girls are little, so you won't mind riding back here." He gestured to a small area behind the front seats where two empty five-gallon cans of gasoline sat side-by-side and supported an old wood board placed across the top of them for us to sit on. "I put a towel on the board. You'll be just fine."

I peered in the plane. Whether it had originally been a two-seat plane with a baggage compartment or a four-seat plane, I couldn't tell. Together, China and I didn't weigh much more than the limit for baggage, so I supposed if the plane had been a two-seater and China and I were sitting in the baggage compartment the plane would make it over the trees on takeoff and would climb okay. China and I looked warily at each other and Jesús avoided looking at us entirely. I greatly respected Jesus. *If Jesús will fly in this, I will.*

We climbed aboard. There were no seatbelts for China and me and the knap-sacks were held in place on the floor under our legs. The engine started quickly—which surprised me—and after Charlie ran it up, the plane rolled smoothly over the field of grass, disturbed the locusts, and at lift-off speed, took off like a bird and soared over the line of trees at the end of the strip with room to spare. We climbed to our cruise altitude, circled around our Paradise in Green Hell for one final look, and then had a beautiful and flawless flight over the jungle and savannahs all the way to Ciudad Bolivar. We landed and taxied to the hangar, stopped the plane, and KLUNK, the wheel support collapsed and slipped out under the wing. Taking the wheel with it, the plane fell to the left.

Jesús and Charlie exited first, then China and I wiggled our way off the gas-can-supported-bench, over the knapsacks and through the open door on the right side of the plane. We hopped out and jumped to the ground. We hugged each other. What a great time we'd had!

"Jesús, will you give me a hand here?" Charlie held up the wing-tip while Jesús pushed the wheel in toward the fuselage to put it in place. "See that? Fixed."

Chapter 19

"He's Different"

Dear Mother and Dad   **September 10, 1953**

    When I went to the airport to meet Frank last night, I met the men he'd been flying—Cornell Capa, a LIFE magazine photographer; and Walter Montenegro, LIFE writer. They are here doing an article and pictures for LIFE about U.S. Steel in Venezuela. Wouldn't it be great if we get a little publicity out of it? Maybe just a shot of our plane in the background? Frank asked Mr. Capa about that and he said he only takes the pictures and submits them to the editorial board. Oh well.
    The men invited us back to the hotel for a drink.
    Mr. Capa is a gentle person, soft-spoken. He's very different.
    Montenegro was more talkative. We enjoyed being with both of them very much.
    Yes, I do miss you—you know it.

All my love always. Marilyn

    Frank had another bad night's sleep and at six in the morning the clanging of the two bells perched atop our chrome alarm clock didn't help. He reached out with his hand and whacked the "OFF" button. The clock skidded across the night stand next to his bed and crashed to the terrazzo floor. "Damn clock," he muttered as he donned his dark blue robe with white piping and trudged barefoot to the kitchen where Guillermina greeted him with demitasse. "I hope this wakes me up," he said to her and sluggishly scuffed to the bathroom with coffee in hand. His morning ritual never changed: He'd set the tiny cup of black coffee on the back of the water closet, turn on the shower water, drop his robe, slip off his jockey shorts, step into the enamel-painted yellow shower stall, and stand under the stinging jets of cold water coming from the shower head. He'd put one hand against the shower wall in front of him, rest his head on his arm, and wonder why he had so many morning flights. He'd said many times, he wondered why people didn't like to fly in the afternoon instead of the early morning.

Lacking sleep, flying every day, grabbing an arepa with cheese for lunch, and sweating, Frank's still fragile frame began to show the ravages of stress. In August, he'd flown his regular 65 hours and most flights departed in the morning between six and nine a.m. Despite it being the rainy season, company assets and income increased steadily but at a high personal price.

The cold water beat on his back. The longer the water ran, the colder it became and he needed the frigid water to get going.

After showering, he'd wrap himself in his towel, pick up the coffee cup, and return to the bedroom where he'd sit on the edge of the bed and, still half asleep, sip the strong black coffee.

Half-an-hour later, shaved and dressed in his starched long-sleeved white shirt and grayish-blue pressed trousers—looking for all the world like he'd had a full night's sleep—he joined me at the dining room table.

"Why do I draw so many morning flights?" he grumbled.

I answered his rhetorical question. "That's easy. People want to fly in the morning—the weather is better. They want to get a jump on the day. And they want you to be their pilot." I sipped my juice. "They like you and they like the way you fly." I stirred my *café con leche* (coffee with milk) "Last week, when John Bogart was here, he took me up to demonstrate the new Cessna 180—to show me how slow it can fly before it stalls. While we circled gaining altitude for the demonstration he said he liked the way you fly, 'Like an American.' That's what he said. I think it's a compliment." I started to butter my toast.

As Gillermina placed an omelet and toast in front of him, Frank replied, "Don't believe everything John says. He just wanted to sell an airplane."

We finished breakfast and I picked up a fashion magazine Jack had brought to me from Miami.

"Run me to the airport?"

"Sure. Just have to put on my shoes." I went to the bedroom and slipped on my penny loafers.

"Where're you going today?" I asked when I returned.

"I have to take two guys from LIFE magazine around Puerto Ordaz and then on to Iron Mountain to meet several of the biggies, take their photos and photos of the facilities. Not much flying, lots of waiting." He checked his back pocket to be sure he had his latest paperback novel about the old west by Luke Short.

"You always get to fly the celebrities. That should make the day interesting."

"Meet me at the airport when I get back?"

"I'll be there."

"I'll just want to come home, eat, and get a good night's sleep."

At the airport, just as I started to say goodbye, we saw Frank's two passengers arrive in a taxi. Frank gave me one of his "checklist kisses" and said, "See you later, Button." He turned and greeted his passengers.

I hung back, watched him do the walk-around of the plane, load several impressive-looking camera bags in the cargo compartment behind the back seat, and help the two passengers board. He liked to do those things himself, especially placement of baggage and people. While he was a good judge of weight, it was not uncommon for him to ask how much a person weighed before suggesting where they'd sit. Balance and center of gravity in a light aircraft are important.

After the men buckled their seatbelts, Frank climbed in, secured the cabin by putting all loose things in the plane's pockets and small compartments, and started his pre-flight check.

Just like the star-struck airport junkies who came to the field to watch planes land and take off, I never tired of watching Frank prepare for a flight.

The doors slammed shut and latched. He called through the open window, "Clear. *Libre*," then turned the key, and the engine came to life. He made notes on the tablet attached to the clipboard that rested on his lap. He watched the oil pressure and waited for the oil to reach the desired temperature for a safe takeoff. He tested the brakes, flight instruments and cockpit controls, then the plane slowly rolled away from the hangar and toward the taxiway. The sound of the engine lessened as the plane rolled farther away and sand and stones, kicked up by the prop wash, settled back on the ramp.

Frank's day would be stimulating. And mine? Enjoyable. Today, Madelyn and I had planned to continue refinishing an old piece of furniture, eat lunch at her house or mine, and then bid each other *hasta luego* (until later) as we went to our homes for siesta. After siesta, we did chores; shop, post office, and company business at the bank. We might end the day sitting on a bench under the trees watching the Orinoco.

I'd just arrived home when I heard Frank's plane. I looked out the window in time to catch a glimpse of his plane. He had passengers, so he didn't rock the wings. He'd arrived earlier than expected and I felt sure he'd be relieved to get home. Maybe he'd be asleep even before sundown.

I drove to the airport. We both pulled into our ramp by the hangar at the same time.

He climbed out of the plane, kissed me hello, and at that close range, I smelled the usual scent that followed a long day's work. Not unpleasant, I called it manly. He called it musk.

I thought he'd bid the gentlemen goodbye, but Walter Montenegro, LIFE's writer and the larger of the two passengers, extended an invitation for us to join them at the hotel for a drink. Frank quickly accepted and said we'd all drive to the hotel in our car. With a smile in his voice and a bounce in his step, he chortled, "We really shouldn't go. I'm a little smelly, but Button, I want you to know Cornell Capa and Walter Montenegro. Two of the finest gentlemen I've flown around this part of the Lost World."

Cornell Capa had a neatly trimmed beard, black wavy hair, piercing eyes, and heavy eyebrows. He spoke softly and with a European accent I couldn't identify. He and Walter, he said, could also use a shower, but a drink first.

Capa gestured for me to sit in the front seat. I stepped aside, and the two men wriggled into the back seat of Frank's old car, then I hopped in the front. Cameras and bags of things they'd acquired during their day went in the trunk already filled with two spare tires, automobile parts, old rags and oil cans.

We arrived at the Gran Hotel Bolivar on the Paseo del Orinoco and went directly to Mr. Capa's room located on the second floor in the front of the hotel. A ceiling fan rotated slowly. The room's scarlet red walls shocked me. Capa opened the windows wide and watched between heavily foliated trees the swift downstream movement of the mighty Orinoco River. After he picked up the phone and arranged for ice, water, glasses, and a bottle of Scotch to be delivered, he resumed studying the tea-colored river. Frequently, his glance went to the people scurrying by on the sidewalk below. He looked at everything with scholarly examination and said the faces of people told stories. He talked about how he always looked for the perfect photograph.

In 1946, after serving his time in the Army Air Force, he became a LIFE photographer. His vision was one day to focus on people; common folk, celebrities, indigenous people, and missionaries in South America.

Capa busied himself setting up bottles and glasses on the dresser, and while he made drinks for everyone my eyes fixated on him. I felt drawn to this quiet man with penetrating black eyes.

He sat on a hassock near the window, forearms on thighs, set his drink on a small wooden table, and interlocked his fingers.

"Where do you call home, Mr. Capa?" I asked.

He answered simply, "New York." Then in a faint monotone of short sentences, he explained he'd been born in Budapest, Hungary long before the war. His soft voice, combined with his accent and masked by the street noise, sometimes made it difficult for me to understand him.

"I used to call New York home," I said.

Capa made no comment.

He swished the ice in his glass and glanced around the room, having no idea how his demeanor tormented me; no idea how he haunted me. I regretted coming with Frank and wished I'd stayed home as Capa's silent and masterful mystique troubled me.

What is it about this man? This man who speaks softly but cries out with his eyes. This man who is average in stature but dominates the room. This man who is confident yet private and guarded.

Capa told of his move to Paris in 1936 where he worked as his brother's printer, but near the end of the thirties, when the threat of war towered over all, he moved with his brother to New York. "I've made several long-distance moves,

Blue Skies, Green Hell

so I speak many languages." He paused. "My brother is a photographer. You've heard of him, perhaps? Robert Capa."

Frank innocently asked, "And Al Capa?"

I saw the first hint of a smile as he replied, "No. Al Capp is a cartoonist."

"I'm sorry," Frank said, a little embarrassed, and sipped from his glass.

"The mistake is often made," he replied.

I'd thought about the name Capa all day but only when I heard Cornell say his brother's name, Robert, did I instantly recall the famous photographer of World War II. I told him I had read about his brother and seen his work in magazines, including LIFE.

"Yes. Yes." Poetically is how he talked of his brother whose excellence as a photojournalist was rivaled by few in the entire world. "He photographed the Spanish Civil War, D-Day, many events during WWII, and yes, the Holocaust." He added, "He is in Vietnam now shooting the French Indo-China War. And he's a pacifist at heart."

A decided change came over him. He enjoyed talking about Robert and I saw a hint of a smile crinkle the corners of his dark eyes as he spoke of his brother's dalliances with Hollywood stars and New York society women. "Everyone knows my brother."

"And your work?" Frank pressed.

Unlike his spirited brother, Cornell's bearing suggested a more sensitive and controlled personality. His bent was neither in the direction of war photographs nor in politics, despite his travels with Adlai Stevenson during the Democrat's run for president in 1952. He admired Stevenson greatly and praised the man's dignity and intellect. Capa said Stevenson's ideals reached across the nation, and he was a man for all people, all races, and that he held the torch for peace and justice and the well-being of humanity.

Initially, I'd mistaken Capa's behavior as brooding, even shy. But he was neither. Instead, he was tender and thoughtful. He spoke when the subject interested him.

The traffic in the street worsened, horns blasted, and people shouted. I would have liked to have drawn my chair closer as his voice dropped, and the distractions in the street covered much of what he said. With difficulty, I heard him speak passionately of his vision—not to take a picture but to make a photograph and capture the soul and depth of character. He thought a master behind the lens breathes life and vitality into the subject. And Cornell Capa took loving care of his subjects. His people.

His voice and demeanor suggested a dark spiritual quality that left me uncomfortable—not with him, but with myself.

I wanted to go home. I wanted to stay.

Was he sexual? Maybe. Sensual? Yes.

Handsome? Sort of. Attractive? Yes.

Haunting? Yes.
Memorable? Yes. Very memorable.
I was glad Frank in no way sensed my confusion.

A knock on the door at eight o'clock announced the entrance of a tall gentleman who introduced himself as Admiral Laird. "How do you do," he said and thrust forward his large hand to shake Frank's. His robust voice matched his frame. Capa handed him a drink. "I missed meeting you earlier, Frank. But I've heard about you. They like you at OMC. Let me tell you that." He sipped his drink and loosened his tie. He put down his empty glass, stood up, and said, "Well, folks, it's about that time. Will you join us please for dinner? We can talk more over a good steak or whatever suits your pleasure."

Rear-Admiral Oberlin Laird U.S. Navy, (Ret.) was the Public Relations Director for OMC hired by the U.S. Steel Corporation in 1949. He poured a half drink, raised his glass, and made a toast, "*Buen Provecho*" (good eating).

Frank declined the dinner invitation and said he wasn't dressed properly to grace the hotel's formal dining room. "If you'd not been such nice people, I would have been too embarrassed to even sit here with you. I must go home and shower. When we leave, management might ask us to leave by the back door." Everyone laughed.

We graciously thanked Cornell Capa, Walter Montenegro and Rear-Admiral Oberlin Laird for the drinks and spirited conversation.

On the way home, we stopped at El Triangulito for toasted cheese sandwiches and toddies. "If I'd not been so smelly we could have stayed. Here, they don't mind if I smell."

"I didn't want to stay, Frank."

"That surprises me. But you did get quiet. What happened?"

"Mr. Capa. I liked him very much. Everyone was pleasant. I don't know what happened. Perhaps I was looking to find a supernatural meaning to what might simply be my naiveté." At twenty-three years of age, and only two years out of a cocoon, I was awed by Capa's celebrity. "An award-winning LIFE Magazine photographer. Wow. That's big time. He spoke with such depth. I've never met anyone like him."

"That sounds like pretty serious thinking to me," Frank mused.

I fidgeted with the straw in my paper cup, still half-filled with toddy. "I don't know why, but I'll never forget him."

Frank slowly drove the route home, pulled into the driveway, and turned off the engine.

"What about me, Button? Did I have a mystique . . . when we met?"

I laughed, grateful he'd broken the spell. "Are you kidding? With your sparkling eyes and sex appeal, I fell madly in love the moment I saw you come through the doorway at Olga's apartment." I sipped the last of my toddy, opened the car door, and hopped out. "But Cornell Capa's different. Very different."

Different. Indeed.

I, too young and untested in matters beyond my college campus and two years in the interior of Venezuela, believe now what I only pondered then. I had indeed been in the company of a great artist—as great in his field as Michelangelo in his—and Cornell Capa's flames of genius touched me.

Years have passed, and I have seen this great photographer's work in periodicals and found them in books. And I recall that hot evening in his hotel room when the traffic in Ciudad Bolivar masked many of his words. I'm grateful to have met this giant in our world of arts.

Following his brother's death during the French-Indochina war in 1954, killed in action behind his camera, Cornell Capa's work stood without comparison and gained the respect he so long deserved.

His camera lens was to him as a pen and paper is to an author, a brush and canvas is to an artist; they express impressions and concepts. There is none finer who touches his subjects with such sensitivity yet with strength and vibrancy. One of his photographs of Marilyn Monroe, taken during a break on the set while filming "The Misfits" in 1960, shows a waif, a fragile, vulnerable child, eyes closed and head resting on her arm folded on the back of a chair. He captured this tender moment with the same intensity he captured the strength in an impassioned and intense evangelist Billy Graham, knotted hands raised gripping the air, eyes heavenward beseeching the Lord Almighty to forgive us all. I can hear the Lord—Hallelujah.

And who but Capa could have so compassionately composed the photograph of the funeral procession of Bill "Bojangles" Robinson as it passed a long line of men: The photo shows only their feet in workmens' shoes lined on a curb side-by-side, with rain water flowing in the gutter. You see the same loving care in his photographs of the indigenous people in the Amazon whose cultures have been tragically invaded and destroyed by progress.

His photographs tell stories.

Cornell Capa founded the International Center of Photography in New York and served as its Director for 20 years. The ICP continues as a major force in the field of photography, attracting the best of the best.

*   *   *

Cornell Capa lived in New York City until his death on May 23, 2008 at age 90. He remains one of his industry's most respected photographers.

Chapter 20

Ride Vaquero

Dear Mother and Dad   **September 28, 1953**

I'm so sorry, but this will probably be a short letter.

Tomorrow, Frank rides in a Toros Coleados. You'll remember he started riding in them a little more than a year ago on a horse he borrowed from Horacio called Old Gray. One day last July Frank threw three bulls. Even so he's not a star yet.

At first he said he was startled by the feel of the bull's tail. It was hard, sort of bony with long coarse hair. He said he feared he might even break the tail when he wrapped it around his hand and he didn't like the thought of hurting the bull. You should see his hand the day after he throws a bull. It gets very swollen and black and blue. He enjoys the sport and is an exceptional rider—but me—well I liked it at first, but I don't like it very much anymore. I don't tell him that. I fear for him, his horse and the bulls, too. I think it's cruel. I promise I'll write again tomorrow.

All my love to you both. Love always, Marilyn"

"Ride Vaquero" was the wakeup call I sang to Frank early on a Sunday morning when the "games" called *Toros Coleados* were scheduled. The total event includes many "games" or "runs."

Each game's objective is for one man on a horse, to ride at top speed while chasing a bull, grab the bull's tail, and throw the bull down. Most men participating in the sport are rugged cattlemen who ride the range herding cattle and wrangling bulls for a living. Cattlemen rely on their horses and say that on the range, the horse does most of the work. In this sport, the rider and horse are one.

Unique to Venezuela, Toros Coleados got its start in the mid-1700's when *hatos* (cattle ranches) began to flourish in the llanos and llaneros or *vaqueros* (cowboys) on horseback chased wild bulls that had wandered from the herd.

Blue Skies, Green Hell

They'd grab the bull by the tail, spur their horses to go faster than the bull, and then throw the bull down. From that early beginning, Toros Coleados developed first as a llanero sport. Then it became the national sport.

The glory, the pageantry, the lore-laden history of the Toros Coleados in Ciudad Bolivar stimulates the town folk to wildly celebrate this spectacular event, un *Día de Fiesta* (holiday).

Once a year, a Queen of the Coleados is elected, and dressed in a glamorous gown, rides on a decorated float (flat-bed truck) in a glitzy parade to the fairgrounds. She is accompanied on the float by dark-eyed senoritas decked out in flashy long dresses. The Coleadores (riders in the sport), sharply attired in their white liqui liquis and black peleguama hats, ride tall in their saddles astride their strong and fearless horses in front of the queen's float. The parade proceeds to the grandstand and on to the dirt track where the Toro Coleados will be run. An afternoon at Toros Coleados perfectly suits the Venezuelan's penchant for partying.

Frank began riding in the Toros Coleados in 1952. He rode well and liked a challenge. As far as throwing a bull by its tail, our friend Horacio Cabrera, a champion in the sport, was just the one to show him how to do it. At Horacio's hacienda near Bolivar, Frank practiced until he had finely tuned the techniques of the sport.

So on a Sunday when Toros Coleados were scheduled, Frank exchanged his pilot's uniform for his liqui liqui, and became a Coleador chasing wild bulls in a *manga* (a straight dirt track several hundred feet long and fifty feet wide) where the sporting event takes place.

Not far outside Ciudad Bolivar, a weathered grandstand with a roof and about twelve rows of benches is on one side of the manga. On the other side is a fence with a board attached to it on the outside so people who can't find seats in the grandstand can stand on the board and watch.

Each attempt for riders to throw a bull begins in the manga at the "start" pen or corral, where two or three coleadores straddle horses that nervously snort, rear-up, and pace in circles as they wait for the gate to swing open and their race with a bull begins. Once the gatekeeper opens the gate, a single bull is released and horses and riders begin the chase. One of the riders will take the lead and in a haze of dust, grab the bull's tail to try and throw it to the ground. Everyone screams and stomps their feet until they shout, "*El toro se cayó*" (the bull has fallen). Usually the bull jumps to his feet and is maneuvered by ranch hands into the corral at the end of the manga. That's how it should be played out.

There are many "games" in one afternoon. When a rider and horse have been victorious and the bull is thrown down, the game is over and preparations begin for the next game. Meanwhile, the victorious rider and horse trot to the grandstand and pass the cheering crowd. Pretty ladies who've spent hours sewing colorful rosettes with gaudy streamers will wave one in front of the coleador, inviting him to accept it in recognition of his success. If he stops in front of a lady, she'll pin a rosette on the rider's liqui liqui, and may even plant a kiss on the coleador if she's brazen or if she's his wife. A top rider will end the afternoon with his white suit dirty, but festooned with colorful ribbons, as he accepts his prize. Judges officiate and points are awarded based on where the bull falls and the proficiency of the rider. Prizes may be trophies or even money. Ride Vaquero! I liked the way that rolled off my tongue.

Word spread that the young coleador, the bush pilot from Caracas gentry, might soon be ready for the big time, to ride in coleados in big cities like Caracas. Frank had been impressive in his appearances as a novice and now with a year's experience in the saddle, the fans expected much more from him.

In the world of coleados, nothing equaled the thrill of throwing down a rampaging bull. Every time Frank rode, I relived his first successful ride.

* * *

Coleadores had gathered in the manga in front of the "start" pen where their horses, being restrained, kicked up dirt, pranced in circles, and whinnied, anxious to get on with the race. The corral gate swung wide and a bull roared to a fast start. Three or four riders flew at top speed behind it. With Frank in the lead, the other riders fell back, withdrawing from the competition. Faster and faster Frank rode Old Gray and the thundering hooves of bull and horse ripped past me as I stood in the front row of the grandstand screaming and shouting and coughing as dust swirled in the air clouding my view. The ground shook and I felt the vibration in the rickety grandstand. With Old Gray pouring it on, Frank closed on the speeding bull, leaned way over to his right, grabbed the bull's tail high near the beast's body, slid his leather-gloved hand down the length of the bull's tail, wrapped the hair at the end of the tail around his gloved hand, then spurred his horse to run faster and pass the bull.

Man and horse ran like hell down the manga. Frank pulled on the tail and the bull fell hard on his side and rolled over. Frank had thrown his first bull and the fans screamed and stomped their feet. Frank dropped his bull quickly, the way he'd been taught by the master, Horacio.

While the bull got to its feet and ran to the corral at the end of the manga, Frank and Old Gray turned and trotted past the cheering crowd in the grandstand, stopping in front of the ladies who waved their flashy silk rosettes. The ladies pinned them on his jacket, front and back, even on the long sleeves. In addition, he sported a few lipstick impressions, including mine. He did not receive an official prize, but he won more rosettes than any other rider, and the next day, every inch of his swollen right hand was a beautiful black and blue.

"Were you frightened?" I asked Frank when I caught up with him behind the grandstand where he and Old Gray waited for me.

Blue Skies, Green Hell

"I felt all right. Maybe a little tense." He described how he saw the bull come out of the gate all charged up. "When I saw his mean, fiery eyes, I knew he was mine, and whatever I felt—fear, tension—all went away. At just the right time, I did what I had to do and that damn bull fell like a ton of bricks." He added, "Then I felt great."

Later, our house jumped with the excitement of people coming to celebrate and congratulate Frank. Some riders, still wearing their dirty boots and stained liqui liquis adorned with rosettes, came on their horses and tied them to the fence in front of the house. By carrying buckets of water to the thirsty animals, Guillermina helped the llaneros tend to them.

"In this house, if the men aren't pilots, they're cowboys," I told Guillermina. "Thanks for helping."

Inside, we served drinks to everyone, and thanks to the artistry of Guillermina who had prepared snacks in advance, we served a large assortment of delicious hot and cold *pasapalos* (hors d'oeuvres) some made of cheese others of spicy meat.

Midst all the festivity, Horacio broke away from the crowd and beckoned to Frank. "Frank, Old Gray has been just right for you, but now you need a faster, stronger, more spirited horse." He said he had just such a horse on the savannah at his hato. "He's waiting for you. He's coal black and his name's Trabuco. If you and Trabuco get along, he's yours. Then you go after bigger bulls." A few days later, Horacio invited us to fly to the hato, have lunch and meet Trabuco.

Chemistry sparked between horse and man. Even I, a novice fan of the lowest rank, saw the perfect match. The horse, big and fast, liked to run and Frank let him go as fast as the horse wanted. Trabuco had Coleados experience and I had the feeling he'd teach Frank a lot about a ride down the manga. "Ride him anytime, Frank," said Horacio. "He'll be moved to the hacienda outside Bolivar tomorrow."

Next came the black leather saddle with polished silver tack that Frank ordered from Miami. It arrived on the C-46 and immediately became the center of attention for all visitors to our house. I had a "rig" made to hold it (the rig resembled a saw horse). I put the rig and saddle in a corner of the living room. I polished the rig and the leather saddle adorned with shiny silver disks more often than I did my furniture. I could hear my mother saying, "Whoever heard of keeping a saddle in a living room? Tsk. Tsk."

While it demanded a lot of his time, Frank enjoyed the conviviality of the group and the thrill of the sport. He also joined the Hunt Club, consisting of the same macho men. After a hunt, sometimes they'd ride to our house for drinks and pasapalos. As many as ten horses would be tethered to the front

205

fence, but other times, when there were only four or five horses, they were tied to the fence around our dogs' corral. At first, Loop and Tail Spin went crazy barking and howling, but after a few visits, the dogs got used to their new horsey friends.

One Sunday things didn't go right at the manga. Frank came close to throwing a bull, but it wouldn't fall despite a good hold on the bull's tail and Trabuco's speed. In fact, so focused on his mission, the horse ran too fast, couldn't stop, and ran smack into the fence. CRASH. A section of the fence gave way, and both Frank and the horse went down while the bull slowed, and placidly trotted into the corral at the far end of the manga. Horacio said he thought the horse's ribs were bruised, not broken. Frank, however, couldn't get up under his own power and was helped off the track by fellow coleadores who'd run to his aid within seconds of the calamity. I ran to the area behind the grandstand where the local doctor examined Frank in the medical trailer. Horacio was with him. "Frank, Amigo, Qué pasó?" he asked.

"Damn Bull. It ran so close to the fence, and Trabuco wouldn't give up." Released by the doctor, we walked to our car. "Maybe I didn't react fast enough, Horacio. Can you come back to the house?"

"Not this time. You get some rest and I'll take care of Trabuco. You're lucky, Frank. Lucky this time." They shook hands and Horacio began giving directions to *obreros* (workers) to walk Trabuco up the ramp and into a truck, restore the section of fallen fence, and resume the Toros Coleados.

While driving home, Frank told me the doctor ordered him to bed for a few days to give his sprained ankle and pulled back muscles time to recover. Frank didn't object to stretching out in bed.

After a rub down with a pain-relieving ointment and the heating pad positioned under his back, I asked, "Did you hear what Horacio said as we were leaving? About you being lucky this time?"

"He's right. I have been pretty lucky so far. You know, these llaneros have been riding all their lives. I have too, but not on the range on cattle drives."

"They're tough men. My dear husband, not one of them is a light weight like you. And the weight they carry is muscle and helps them withstand that rough ride. It probably helps them recover, too, when they're injured. It's their living."

Later that evening, Carlos, Julio, Tom, and Irv came by to see Frank. I brought chairs into the bedroom. All talked about how the horses should be ridden and what the riders have to do to throw a bull.

Carlos interrupted the conversation. "We sit here and talk about how it's done. But Frankie's the only one with the guts to do it." I loved Carlos for speaking up and giving Frank the support and praise he'd earned.

Two months after his accident, Frank declared he was ready to ride again—he had another chance to get back in the saddle and in the manga with Trabuco.

Blue Skies, Green Hell

"I'm ready to ride," he said confidently. "I'm ready. I just hope Trabuco isn't skittish from the accident." As he buttoned his liqui liqui he said, "It's my day. I feel it. Do you have plenty of rosettes?" He looked good. He left his peleguama at home; I told him he looked cuter without it.

To the Toros Coleados, I usually wore a white shirt and jeans rolled to mid-shin. Rosettes were pinned all over my shirt where they stayed clean and pressed until I moved them, one by one, from my shirt to that of a rider's.

We drove to the manga. Upon arrival, we saw Horacio waving and he called out, "We've got a bull for you, Frank. We made a special effort this morning at the round up. This one is big and looks mean and mad. Are you ready?"

"I'm ready—and I'll get him."

"I know it's stupid advice, but be careful. I love you." I kissed him, turned and walked toward the grandstand. I'd begun to dislike the sport. So far, I'd not seen a rider, horse, or bull seriously injured. But as I'd become more accustomed to the sport and learned more about it, I saw the possibilities of awful things happening.

On my way to the grandstand, I stopped at Trabuco's side. He stood tall and proud as though he knew he had an important date with Frank and a bull. I petted him, rubbed my face on his neck. "You're a good boy, Trabuco."

Time for the showdown had come.

Like all the other times, I went to the front row of the grandstand. After I watched a couple of runs, Frank mounted Trabuco, and eased him into the manga near the starting corral. Everything looked good. Along with two other riders on horses, they stayed close to the gate, jockeying for position, horses whinnying and snorting. Then the gatekeeper swung open the gate, let loose a wild bull with fiery eyes and the riders were off. Frank sprang to an early lead. The others dropped back. Bending low over Trabuco, Frank raced to the bull. Horse and man were one; strong, fearless, and determined. Trabuco knew the drill and Frank, in the right position, concentrated only on the next objective; grab the tail and pull the bull down. Damn it, he wanted that bull. Although frightened, I, too, wanted the victory for both of them. "Go Frank. Go Frank." I screamed. "Faster, Trabuco! Good boy!"

The dust churned up and everyone choked and coughed, and then all of a sudden the crowd in the grandstand jumped to their feet, screamed in fear as a horse and rider and bull raced from the opposite direction on a collision course toward Trabuco and Frank and Frank's bull. Something had gone horribly wrong. The rider, horse and bull from the prior race were still in the manga. Neither rider saw the other as they hunkered low, leaning out of their saddles on horses galloping swiftly next to their bulls, all unaware of each other's position.

"No . . . No!" I screeched along with hundreds of others who watched the bulls, horses, and men race toward each other. Faster and faster they ran and the crowd rushed from the top of the stands to the first row where I was standing.

Then it happened. Right in front of the grandstand, CRUNCH, THUD, THUD, I heard the thunderous impact of the six colliding head-on. I saw Frank propelled out of his saddle several feet in the air and away from the site of the collision. He landed on his back and shoulder. He didn't get up. The whinnying and groaning of the animals writhing in pain on the ground echoed up and down the manga. The animals tried to get to their feet but fell back in the dirt exhausted and injured. The other rider seemed to be in between the moaning and bellowing animals and wasn't moving. Coleadores, some on horseback and others on foot, rushed to the scene to help. Both bulls, so badly injured, were shot on the spot. Blood from injured animals and dead bulls splattered on the dirt's surface. The crowd made it impossible for me to see anything. I couldn't find Trabuco and I lost sight of Frank.

The once joyous spectators now pushed and shoved everyone. Women cried, people shouted and men flailed their arms and swung their fists wanting to get out of the grandstand and into the manga. Some jumped out, others fell out and all ran toward the chaotic, bloody scene. Pandemonium reigned.

Pinned against the front of the grandstand, I feared for my life, afraid I'd be pushed out of the grandstand, trampled, or crushed in the human stampede. Then, between the hoards of crazed people, I glimpsed Frank being helped by a coleador as he limped away from the scene. I wanted to get to him but I couldn't move.

Horacio's ranch hands raised Trabuco from the turf. The other horse, still on the ground, was in worse condition as ranch hands labored unsuccessfully to get him up. A stretcher brought out to the manga carried the unconscious rider away.

What was left of the frenzied crowd rushed toward the medical trailer in the field behind the grandstand to where much of the action had shifted. At last, I could move. I bulled my way through the crowd and headed for the trailer. People and cars clogged the area. Again, I lost sight of Frank and I didn't know where to go. I wandered for a few minutes. Being short, I couldn't see over the heads of the crowd.

I went to the place where I always met Frank. Not there. I searched for him and called his name, but my voice could not be heard above the din of crazed spectators. Bedlam.

I saw the ambulance leave the grounds. He must be in it. "Frank," I called as I ran after the ambulance, but it was too far ahead for me to catch it or be heard over the chaos. I felt alone and terrified. *Where is he?*

Then I spotted Frank covered with dirt and rubbing his eyes with his blood-smeared hand, looking dazed. He leaned on the shoulder of the coleador who'd assisted him. I screamed for him as I fought through the crowd, but I couldn't get to him, and he couldn't hear me. I panicked. "Let me through. I've got to get through." I pleaded at first and even said *por favor* as I tried to push through the mob. Then I got angry. "Get out of my way," I shouted and pushed and shoved everyone who blocked me. Fighting tears, I shrieked in both English and Spanish telling the people to get moving, pounding them hard with my fists as I went along.

Finally, I reached Frank and resisted the overpowering urge to break down. He was hurt and needed me. "I'm okay," he uttered with some effort. He put his arms around me and held me close.

"I'm okay," he gasped softly.

"Want to see the doctor?" I asked.

"No. I just hurt. I don't think anything's broken. But I hurt all over." He struggled to speak. His eyes, cheekbones, and hands, smeared with dirt and a splattering of animal blood, appeared to be swelling. One sleeve of his liqui-liqui was partially ripped out and the suit was stained with everything from blood to manure; it smelled foul. "Let's find Trabuco. See how he is then we'll go home." I thanked the man who'd come to Frank's aid, and then we slowly walked away from the maddened crowd.

Horacio caught up with us and told Frank that Trabuco might have some broken bones, but he'd call the local vet and ask him to come to his hacienda *prontisimo* (very quickly). "I'll call you right away if the vet thinks Trabuco has to be put down. You go on. I'll take care of the horse." He reached out to hold my arm. "He's got courage, Marilyn."

I drove the short distance home and helped Frank into the house. First he showered off the smeared blood, dirt, sweat, and smells of animals. Then I rubbed him down with Ben Gay and helped him into pajamas. I, too, showered and tossed my outfit—dirtied with blood and other stains—into the laundry basket. We said little until I had put an ice bag on his cheek, the heating pad on his back, and he rested comfortably in bed.

"I never saw it coming, Button." He put his hand over his eyes. He took hold of my hand and squeezed it. "I keep seeing and hearing it over and over." He closed his eyes. "I was riding low and fast, I'd just grabbed the tail. I saw nothing but the dirt passing beneath Trabuco and me and the bull close to us. I heard him breathe and felt the heat and sweat from his body and then the impact. Oh, Lord. The sound of pounding hooves changed to bones crunching and horses whinnying and the horrible sounds of animals falling. I swear, I heard the animals cry."

I went to the medicine cabinet in the bathroom where I had sleeping pills. From a bottle of filtered water we kept in the bathroom, I filled a glass and returned to Frank's bedside. "Here. Take this. It's a sleeping pill. After my appendectomy, I brought back a few for emergencies."

"I guess one won't hurt."

"One," I replied, "will help you get a good night's sleep." He swallowed the pill then slid under the sheet. I sat on the edge of his bed. "I don't know the rules and regulations, Frank, but what I saw was not your fault. Not in any way. Someone opened the gate and the bull ran out. You got the lead and were riding in the right direction. Doing exactly what you should have done. I don't know what the judges or the Board of the Toros Coleados will do about this. I suppose they'll investigate and find out why the signal was given to open the gate and release your bull while another bull, horse, and rider were still running in the manga. That shouldn't have happened. And that rider on the other horse—chasing the bull the wrong way—not looking—how stupid."

The next day, Horacio came by the house with another rider from the Toros Coleados, Rafael Pulgar, also a national champion. They came to see Frank who, feeling somewhat better, sat in a chair in the living room and sipped a cup of coffee. They were shocked to see only a black and blue cheekbone and learn that contusions, swelling, abrasions, and aches and pains were the extent of Frank's injuries. They told Frank the other rider, still in the hospital, suffered a broken arm. Neither knew the fate of his horse.

Horacio said, "You were lucky again, Frank. And it looks like Trabuco was also lucky. No broken bones. Like you, he has to recover from a hell of a bad fall. He's bruised. He's hurting, too. It'll be a while before he'll want to leave his quiet pasture. Now, Frank, you can celebrate." He told us that in their combined years of national competition in Toros Coleados, he and Pulgar had seen only three accidents like it, and in each of the three, one man was killed. "Celebrate now, because," he raised the cuff of his long sleeve to see his watch, "because you're eighteen hours old. You were given the gift of life yesterday—eighteen hours ago."

"It'll be a while before I'll want to leave my pasture, too," Frank said. He stared at the ceiling. In his mind's eye he and Trabuco were back in the manga racing at top speed.

"I think the vaquero won't be riding for a while—any place," I said. *And that's all right with me.*

I feared for Frank, but also for the bulls and horses. I greatly respected the llanero culture, the Venezuelan spirit, the history and tradition of the sport and, yes, the pageantry that went with it. But I never attended another Toros Coleados.

Several weeks later, Frank and Trabuco competed in a Coleados, but they didn't throw one bull. Horacio drove Frank home after the event and Frank quietly told me he and Trabuco had lost the passion to win.

Frank sat in the living room and sipped a Scotch and Coke. There were no visitors. No party. "Once I longed to ride in a really big event. I wanted to ride in Caracas. I never will."

I remained silent, but inwardly breathed a sigh of relief that Frank had hung up his leather glove, retired his saddle, accepted the fact he'd had his fleeting fame as a coleador, and had allowed Trabuco a well-deserved rest in the pasture.

Frank and I—off to the Toros Coleados

I hold rosettes I made to present to Coleadores who successfully throw down a bull.

I look over the bulls in the corral waiting to be let lose in the manga.

Frank astride Old Gray warms up for his ride in the manga.

Frank stands next to his black horse, Trabuco.
Photo by Marilyn

Blue Skies, Green Hell

Flying single-engine planes over the Green Hell? Piece of cake.

Frank retired from the sport and returned to his profession with renewed vigor, though he never regretted the time he'd spent atop Old Gray and Trabuco and riding in the Toros Coleados.

Trabuco was returned to Horacio and to a pleasant savannah near Ciudad Bolivar and Frank was ultimately happier in his plane, smelling raw gasoline and hearing the comforting sound of a smooth running engine.

One day, while at my desk in the office at the airport, Horacio came in to book some round-trips to La Vergareña. A steady client and good friend, we looked forward to his visits.

"Frank's flying," I said, "But he's due back any minute. Why don't you wait? He'd love to see you." I gestured for him to sit then poured a cup of coffee.

Within minutes, Frank landed his white and red Cessna and taxied to the ramp by our hangar. From the office window, we watched him turn the plane, saw the familiar clouds of grit and heard the yellow dirt slam against the building as he jogged his plane this way and that getting it close to the tie-down rings. "That's where he's happiest, Horacio. In his airplane."

We joined Frank as he got out of the plane. "This is pretty nice, my friend. A day's work—no aches, no pains, no bruises."

The usual abrazos (hugs) followed and then the small talk.

Horacio told Frank about Trabuco's great physical condition. "He's still fast, Frank, and he's still yours if you want him." Horacio paused, "and he wants to run." I held my breath and nervously tugged at my necklace. I waited.

"Thanks, Horacio," Frank said pensively. "I enjoy riding. But my place is here." He tapped the pilot's seat in the cockpit. "When I was riding, I lost my focus on this business. These birds need my full attention. To survive here and make money, amigo, this is something I've got to be on top of. Not on top of a horse." He reached across his seat to the passenger's seat, retrieved his clipboard, grabbed his cap, and put it on. "And when it comes down to it, this is what I'm trained to do. It's what I most love to do. Fly." He looked at the glorious blue skies above him. "Just as you have to be riding on the savannahs, I have to be . . . up there." He nodded. As we walked back to the hangar, Frank removed his Ray-Bans, folded them just so and put them in the glasses case attached to his belt. "I don't think I'll ever go back to the manga, grab a tail, and throw down a bull . . ."

Startled, Horacio interrupted. "Oh, Frank. Forgive me. I wasn't thinking about the Coleados. No. No. Though you did well and you had a future in the sport, you and Trabuco had enough. But the horse is fast. I'm thinking about you entering him in the horse races at the *Hippodromo*. I know the perfect jockey . . . ."

And so, Frank, ever in quest of a new challenge and interest, entered Trabuco in the races at the Hippodromo de Angustora (local race track), and the first time out, on December 13, 1953, with a jockey named Negro dressed in yellow and green silks, Trabuco raced like the wind and came in third.

I still have the race program. Because another horse named Trabuco also raced that day, our Trabuco is listed in the program as *Negro Primero* (First Black).

Trabuco earned a proud record for a horse who'd only known the brutal and painful world of Toros Coleados. He seemed to enjoy racing, and we had peace of mind that he would finish the afternoon without injury, return to his pasture, and rest until he had the strength and desire to race again. He deserved his good life.

Neither Trabuco nor Frank ever returned to the manga.

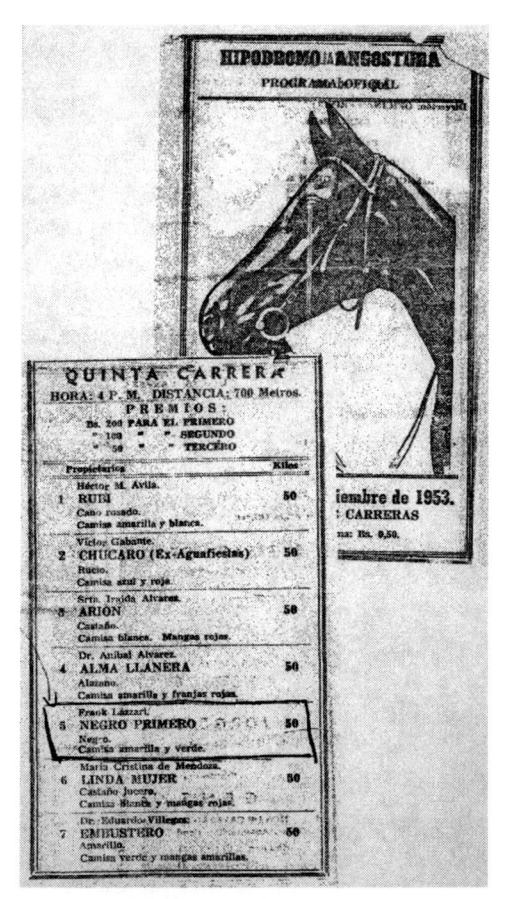

The program from Trabuco's first time out as a race horse.
Hippodromo de Angustora—Dec. 13, 1953

Chapter 21

"Expect the Unexpected"

Dear Mother and Dad   October 9, 1953

    I know you're about to shoot me for not having written in so long. I have a good reason. Frank and I came to Caracas on business. I mean WE . . . both of us on business. This time, I have to attend all the meetings with him then fly back to CB to report to Julio and bring files back to Frank. I've made several such round trips. Frank wants me to sit in on the meetings. The men Frank is dealing with are the same two who Carlos had been involved with when he failed in his attempt to buy the LEBCA license. Now the men may want to work something out with Frank and AEROVEN.
    One man is Charles H. Payne. He was a Navy pilot, invented the jeep, and is a Director at Purdue U. His associate is Col. Benjamin Griffin. He's Director of Washington International Airport. I've got to get going. More—when I can!
    This is such fun. I feel like a secret agent.

Love forever, Mata Hari Marilyn

    I thought I had my day planned. How foolish. Never plan, I used to say. Just always expect the unexpected. It's fun, never knowing where I'll be or what I'll be doing tomorrow.
    I had work to do at my old palace, preparing for the move to our new one. Frank would soon be making the final arrangements with the landlady and I wanted to be ready. Almost everything had to be put in boxes even though my new house was only a mile away. I had a head start in packing so it should have been orderly. It wasn't. The house hadn't looked so bad since the day I moved into it. That time, just like this, Frank was in Caracas.
    Boxes. Boxes. Boxes. They were in every room. Some cardboard and some wood. Large, small, and medium. Some had flaps closed and sealed. Still others had four flaps reaching skyward begging to receive household contents. All had printing on their sides. Some said *Leche Nido*, (a brand of powdered milk),

others had once been packed with cans of oil for the airplanes. I whirled from box to box trying to find just the right cranny for each special item. Good thing I started to pack well in advance of the move. I needed all the time I could get. Boxes stacked in every room of the house suggested we were moving tomorrow.

"I'm not moving soon. I'm not that lucky," I told Guillermina when she offered to help. "I'm packing the things I won't need immediately. I don't know when the move will be." I sat on a box and lit a cigarette. "A couple of days ago, before he went to Caracas, Frank met with the owner of the new house—we call it the house with many angles. She said she didn't know when construction of it would be finished.

"We need to keep out two sets of sheets and a few towels—and anything else you think we might not need for a month or two. The silver bowl, things like that can be packed," I said and gestured toward the dining room table where I'd already placed a few of our precious silver and crystal pieces. "We won't need those things until we're in our new house." I carefully wrapped in newspaper the silver table lighter shaped like Aladdin's lamp and tucked it into a box. "Oh, I wish you were coming with me, Guillermina."

"You'll do fine with someone younger," she sang out and laughed. People from the West Indies, to me, always sounded like they were singing. I delighted in hearing her speak.

Guillermina had told me she would like to move with us, but we already had many people for cocktails, dinner and overnight guests. She feared there'd be more guests and more work in our larger house and it would be too much for her.

Just then the phone rang. With urgency in her voice, Gillermina told me Capitán Julio was calling.

Julio told me Frank had cabled from Caracas. He'd asked Julio to put together some data about our company's performance, costs, and income and to arrange for me to bring the documents to him in Caracas on the noon flight. Frank would be at Maiquetía to meet me. We'd go directly to the meeting. The data he wanted concerned the cargo market and any information that might be useful in negotiations with Americans interested in investing in our company. "He wants you to attend the meetings with him. Frank has a plane, so you'll return to Bolivar with him when he's finished." Julio said he'd get my airline ticket and I could pick it up at the office. He also said I knew the Americans but, in such haste, he did not tell me their names.

I ran to Madelyn's and told her I had to go to Caracas. "I should be gone only a few days. Gillermina will take care of everything. The office will always know where we are. Oh, you know the routine."

Back home, I threw a few things in a bag, showered and selected my most serious-looking outfit to wear; a black and white striped full-skirted halter dress with a long-sleeved black bolero that buttoned at the neckline. Black heels and a black purse completed the outfit. I slipped two gold necklaces over my head, quickly thrust gold earrings into my pierced ears, clipped on several gold bracelets and two rings. I wondered if I'd overdone it with the gold. No. It looked good with the black. Anyway, I was just a homebody from the frontier. What did I know about appropriate dress for a meeting?

I kissed my puppies goodbye and drove to the airport. I parked the car near the hangar and gave the keys to Julio.

He said the meeting had come up quickly. "Frank said he wants you to be very familiar with the paperwork in the attaché bag." He gave me the bag. "You might want to look these over on the plane."

So I left a house full of boxes and headed off on what had all the earmarks of a secret mission. At least I played it that way. "I feel like Mata Hari," I said as I left Julio.

On the plane, I looked over all the material contained in neatly and properly labeled manila file folders. Having developed most of the numbers, looking them over served as a refresher.

A little more than an hour later, the plane landed at Maiquetía. After a hug and a kiss at the foot of the stairway that had been rolled to the door of the DC-3, Frank took both of my hands in front of him, stepped back, twirled me around and said, "I hardly recognize you. You're not wearing jeans and alpargatas." Then he laughed and hugged me again. "Thanks for coming on such short notice. I know you don't like Caracas, but this trip's different. It's all business, and I need you. Anyway, we'll stay at a hotel."

We hurriedly walked to his plane parked on the tarmac.

He opened the doors, loaded my suitcase and attaché bag in the rear seat, and gave me a helping hand into the plane. He closed the door, trotted around to his side, hopped in, and pre-checked the plane. "Clear. *Libre*," he called out the open window on his side, and then started the engine. He talked with the tower, ran up his engine, did his system's check, and we rolled. I noticed his sport jacket and tie were smartly hung on a hangar in the back seat. Flying to Caracas instead of driving? Yes. This was a very serious trip.

We took off, followed the coastline a few miles toward the east, circled to about 8,000 feet, high enough to safely clear the summit of Avila peak. Below, I saw a green valley, fertile farms, and coffee plantations east of Caracas. We took a westward heading and started our descent into La Carlota Field located a little to the east of downtown Caracas. The city sprawled in the valley a few miles straight ahead. The flight took less time than driving up from the airport on the twisty mountain road.

During the flight Frank told me that we'd be meeting with Charles H. "Harry" Payne and Col. Benjamin Griffin. "You know them," he said smiling.

"Who are they?" I didn't have a clue.

Blue Skies, Green Hell

"You met them at Carlos and Madelyn's. Remember the party? You talked to one of the American men about C-46s? And Carlos was going to buy LEBCA? And be my boss?"

"Ouch. *That* Harry! I guess I never heard their full names. But why are we meeting them?"

The men, having remembered meeting both Frank and me at the Freeman's party months ago, were anxious to explore the possibility of a partnership with AEROVEN concerning the operation of C-46 cargo planes and possibly DC-3s. A big scale operation, Frank agreed to hear what they had to say.

"I knew I talked too much that night. I told you."

Frank disregarded my comments and continued talking. "We'll meet them at three o'clock this afternoon." He said he'd also called my father in New York and asked him to obtain Dunn and Bradstreet reports on both of the gentlemen to validate their credentials.

After we landed, Frank opened my attaché bag and leafed through the papers in the folder. He said, "Yes. Yes. Uh—Uh," and closed it. "Exactly what I wanted. Thanks." He said if the Americans request more information than we can provide, he'd phone or cable Julio tonight and have him gather what we need. Then I'd go back on the morning plane, pick up the material from Julio and return to Maiquetia on the noon flight. This meeting had to be really big time.

"Do I have to attend the meeting?" I asked.

"Button, sometimes I get home after a meeting and you have questions. Good questions. You can help me. These are Americans. You understand them better than I."

A taxi drove us from the airfield to a building in downtown Caracas. We passed through the heavy glass doors, and I became more nervous the minute I stepped into the elevator. I felt myself breathing fast and asked Frank to wait a minute until I caught my breath and my rapid heartbeat slowed.

"Nervous?" Frank asked.

"You bet. Like getting ready to take an exam I haven't prepared for. I don't know what I'm doing here." The elevator door opened and I saw a frosted glass door that had the name of a law firm printed in gold. Frank pressed a large button and the door opened automatically. I wished I didn't have to go further. He led me by my elbow.

"You'll be okay."

We entered an office where a receptionist, elegantly attired in a black suit with her black hair pulled tightly back and fashioned into a knot, sat behind an over-sized oval table made of inlaid mahogany. Nothing was on the desk except a pad, pen, telephone, and a vase with a single red rose. She stood up. "Capitán Lazzari," she enunciated syllable by syllable, flashed a smile and lowered her long eyelashes, and by way of acknowledging my presence, she nodded politely.

The rhythmic sound of her high heels click-clack-clicked on the terrazzo floor as she undulated toward polished mahogany double doors with oversized brass doorknobs. Opening one door, she gestured for us to enter. Frank ushered me in ahead of him. I wanted to turn around and run away.

A large, oval conference table with twelve upholstered chairs filled the room. Two chairs had been reserved for Frank and me. Pitchers of water and glasses were placed around the table as were ashtrays. I recognized the two men immediately and warmly greeted them. Harry Payne was the one I'd talked to so openly. They'd contacted Frank through MERCATOR. At the Freeman's party, Frank had given these men his AEROVEN business card with his brother Do's Caracas office phone number scribbled on it.

I was introduced to several lawyers and accountants also in attendance. We shook hands all around and I pretended to be relaxed and comfortable in this very intimidating setting. No one could have guessed I was terrified and wanted to leave.

I would have enjoyed a cigarette, but knew I could not hold a lighter or match without my hands trembling and giving away my nervousness. However, the initial scariness vaporized. I felt more relaxed once the discussions started, and I realized I knew the aviation business and AEROVEN quite well.

Nevertheless, I had determined to simply take notes, listen and not speak until spoken to. That seemed safe. The meeting lacked enthusiasm as deliberate discussions proceeded in an orderly fashion. Frank and I had almost all the answers to questions about AEROVEN activities and operations. The information we lacked was in the file cabinets in our office at the CB airport. I anticipated an early morning round trip to Bolivar.

Frank had a list of things he started to talk about, and the men were very cooperative. They also had questions, so it was a comfortable give-and-take discussion.

The meeting room filled with gray smoke from cigarettes. My eyes burned. I choked and coughed a couple of times. I'd been trying to stop smoking since my doctor told me I had an allergy to nicotine. This meeting didn't help my condition. The building's ventilation system had not been activated or didn't work.

With the spewing of numbers, the heat, and the smell of cigarette smoke, I thought any minute I'd die. I finally gave in and joined the others who were smoking. I reminded myself to ask Frank if this was a typical business meeting. If so, I understood Julio's preference to remain in Bolivar, fly planes, and leave the business to Frank. Thoughts of my quiet morning packing boxes flitted through my mind. That was then. This is now. How incongruous.

Finally, I felt the need to talk about something other than the cruising speed and overall performance of a C-46. I tactfully asked Harry and Ben about their concerns operating a business in Venezuela, given this country's military dictatorship. Overall, their plan would involve investing huge amounts of money in an aggressive scheme for flying cargo throughout Venezuela. I felt confident I'd opened a subject that demanded attention when Frank looked at me and nodded acceptance of my question. I hoped the answer would give us a clue as to Frank's role and future considering the planned growth in the fleet of aircraft and expanded business activities. However, no tipping of their hands gave away their plans for Frank and other AEROVEN personnel. Instead, they made notes.

As the meeting drew to an end, I scribbled a note and slid it to Frank. He read it, then cunningly slipped it into his jacket pocket and looked at his Rolex.

"Gentlemen," he said, "let's call it a night."

At that moment, the secretary click-clacked into the conference room and to the wall-to-wall, ceiling-to-floor oyster-colored draperies that hung from rods on the ceiling. She pressed a button and the drapes, controlled by a motor that made a purring sound, glided open and revealed Caracas, a city of lights sparkling in every color of the rainbow.

"Tomorrow," Frank said in conclusion, "Marilyn will be on the first plane to Bolivar and will return after lunch with the information you've requested. I'll see you in the morning." Many issues presented by both sides had to be studied and checked and rechecked and resolved before either side could make a proposal. A deal of this magnitude would be on the table for a long time.

We shook hands and I breathed a big sigh of relief when we got out of the building. The fresh air was dizzying.

Back at the hotel, the phone lines to Bolivar were operating, so Frank called Julio. He quickly read the list of files he needed and concluded by telling him I'd be on the first plane for Bolivar in the morning.

At dinner, we rehashed everything that had been discussed at the meeting, but what appeared to be eating away at Frank's composure concerned the contents of my last note. He retrieved it from his jacket pocket and read it again: "Does Carlos figure in this arrangement? What's in it for him?"

We sipped our Scotch and Cokes and waited for dinner to be served. Frank lit a cigarette and pensively asked why I thought Carlos might still be in the picture. "You're suspicious?"

"While Griffin and Payne had been in Bolivar, Carlos chartered a DC-3, flew them to see Angel Falls and, in their honor, hosted a Ternera. All the bigwigs in Bolivar attended. Wouldn't their loyalty be with Carlos?" I asked.

I reminded Frank that Payne and Griffin were Dr. Freeman's contacts and Carlos probably made himself indispensable to them. Carlos could do that very well. He'd presented them with an "exhaustive study" of air activities, past, present, and future in Bolivar. Also, Carlos had dual citizenship. He was a Venezuelan and American; a good man on their team. "Have the men used data from Carlos' study in their discussions with you?" I asked.

"They could have. I told them our projections for the future weren't optimistic and I couldn't agree with the figures they'd recited. But our figures reflected light-aircraft activity. C-46s aren't light, and I don't know where they got their numbers."

Initially, Frank had come to Caracas to meet with the owners of AEROTECNICA, a helicopter service based in Maracaibo with their main office in Caracas. He'd not been in touch with the ministry or LEBCA people. "How'd they know you were here?" I pressed on. "Maybe Madelyn told Carlos and he cabled his father." I threw out questions about which I'd made notes all day. "Would they make you Chief of Ministry Communications and Director of the Bolivar operation," and the coup de grace followed. "Then, at pay-back time to Dr. Freeman, would they name Carlos Chief of Operations in Venezuela?"

I reminded Frank that Carlos said he'd be Frank's boss. Whoa.

Frank, a person who liked and trusted people, asked what prompted my suspicions.

"I don't know. They say New Yorkers are skeptical. Maybe I am.

Neither of us slept much that night, tossing and turning and questioning everything we'd discussed and things we'd not discussed. The city streets teemed with traffic through the night with shrill car horns, loud music blaring from car radios and the ubiquitous bang-bang made by drivers' hands hitting the side of their car doors.

At daybreak, as I stepped into the taxi that would take me to Maiquetía in time to catch the first flight to Bolivar, I turned to Frank and said, "I'm afraid. Maybe you'd make a pile of money, but lose your control. AEROVEN is your company. It's your dream."

He told me not to worry and that he'd be at Maiquetía in time to meet me and fly me back to Caracas and the afternoon meeting.

I met Julio at the CB Airport patio lounge where he gave me the papers Frank had requested. Quickly, I ate a toasted cheese sandwich, got back on the plane for my return flight to Maiquetía.

As Frank and I flew in the Cessna over the mountain to La Carlota Field in Caracas, I asked, "If cargo business in Bolivar has such a promising future, why isn't RANSA planning expansion?" RANSA was a cargo carrier based in Ciudad Bolivar; not a large operation, but steady. The RANSA agent in CB was Marcos Castro, Frank's friend, and Frank had not heard anything from Marcos about cargo business growing. I also asked why Jack Perez wasn't planning a big future in Bolivar. With his work drying up in Paraitepui and at the Hato La Vergareña, I'd heard Jack talk about pulling out of Bolivar for lack of work.

"I think there is a positive future in the State of Bolivar. But maybe not in Ciudad Bolivar," Frank countered. "Perhaps in Puerto Ordaz. I don't know about growth in other regions."

"I'm bushed," I said. I'd not slept the night before, had already made a roundtrip to Bolivar, and within minutes, I'd be in a meeting room filled with stress and smoke.

"Today, we'll exchange information and be on our way home. It won't take long. You'll see."

If nothing else, the prospect of the meeting and all its nuances torched my nerve endings and opened my eyes. Frank, though not heavy-handed, felt comfortable wheeling and dealing. But not I. I felt myself getting too excited. Too emotional.

We exited the taxi at the office building. Was it only yesterday I'd not wanted to go to the meeting because I felt unprepared and inadequate? Now I felt prepared and adequate, but I'd have to control the wildfire of inquisitiveness that burned within. Frank tried to calm me. "Much has to be answered before negotiations can proceed toward a conclusion, one way or another."

After everyone exchanged papers with numbers and notes, Frank stood up. "Gentlemen, don't hesitate to contact me any time. We all have a lot to work on and think about."

The meeting ended.

Payne and Griffin stood up, packed their briefcases, cordially shook hands, and left the room. I could read nothing into the demeanor of either one. They'd been pleasant. I liked them. They were fine gentlemen.

Frank slowly gathered his things together.

He'd completed his work with AEROTECHNICA even before he'd met with the two Americans, so his workday was over. However, it was too late to fly back to Bolivar. After a sandwich and a couple of drinks at the hotel bar, we went to our room and collapsed on the bed. I was wiped out. We fell asleep and awakened the next morning.

Our return trip to Bolivar was one of the most perfect flights we'd had in a long time. After stopping for lunch and topping off the fuel tanks at Barcelona, we turned south toward Bolivar. "Fly it, Button. The plane's yours. I'm tired. I'll rest a while." He pushed his seat back and stretched out as best he could in the cramped front seat of a Cessna 170. "Know how to get to Bolivar?" He asked.

"Sure. I've flown it a dozen times. I head south 'til I see the Orinoco. Then I turn left and follow the river to Bolivar." Frank knew I could fly the plane just fine, but he also knew I never took seriously his lessons in navigation and reading charts. "Why use a chart when I know the way? If I see bad weather, I'll wake you up."

I trimmed the plane, kept it at about 3,000 feet and flew south to the Orinoco, turned left and followed the river until I saw Ciudad Bolivar. I started to descend—500 feet a minute. Then I awakened Frank. He rubbed his eyes and yawned. Reaching for the radio, he said, "Button, you didn't leave me much time to talk with the tower."

"You'll be okay. You can do it. The plane's yours."

He landed, taxied to our hangar and shut down the engine. "Stay at the office with me while I talk to Julio."

"Hey, Julio," I called as I walked to our hangar, "You've got the right idea."

"*Cómo dice*" (What's that)? He asked.

"You fly and let Frank take care of the business deals."

We three sat in the office while Frank brought Julio up to date. No doubt about it, Payne and Griffin were sincere in their big plans and we believed they had the backing they claimed to have. Dad had received the Dunn and Bradstreet report for Griffin and sent a cable with a brief message indicating the report rated Griffin highly. While he had not yet received the report on Payne, Dad said he felt certain that Griffin would only be associated with someone equally responsible and that the report on Payne would validate his credentials.

"One thing I question," said Frank, "has to do with their vision for major growth in the interior." The only place where growth seemed inevitable was Puerto Ordaz. He felt the development of one city wouldn't be enough to invest a large amount of money and a number of aircraft. "Frankly, I'm not getting my hopes up," Frank said thoughtfully. He flipped through mail on his desk, then he stood up and concluded, "I feel certain that after they study the real and valid numbers we gave them—and review the problems they may have in the country, Payne and Griffin might say 'Adios' to the whole thing. And I couldn't blame them. They're anticipating tremendous growth in the whole country! No one I know has accumulated stats for all of Venezuela—and that's what interests them. I'd like to believe in their vision, but, in all honesty, I find it difficult."

"You mean, Frank, after all this, nothing may come of it?"

"Button, it wouldn't be the first time. If contracts were signed following all the meetings I've attended, we'd have to buy ten more planes. You know? I, myself, wouldn't buy into this company based on the facts and information we have."

I stared into space thinking about the stress of the last two days; and maybe for nothing. I wondered how Frank could stand the pressure. For the moment, I wouldn't have blamed him if he gave it all up and went back to flying left seat on a regular commercial airline. That was what he'd been trained to do. If I'd spoken of this with him, he would have told me deals fall through, but important contacts are made that might be productive later on. His business acumen—always keen.

Frank stayed at the airport to talk more with Julio.

I drove home, entered the house and looked around at all the boxes.

Boxes. Boxes. Boxes. Some cardboard and some wood. Large, small and medium. Some filled with top flaps closed and sealed, others part-way filled . . . .

Guillermina had done a fine job sorting through things and packing.

I went next door. "Madelyn," I called. "Anybody home?"
"Come on in," she answered.
"What's up?"
"Carlos got a cable this morning and had to make an urgent trip to Caracas. That's about all."
"Oh?"
She brought a cup of coffee to me.
I'd been away three days. Frank and I had suffered two days at a tedious business meeting in Caracas from which nothing was likely to result. Carlos had gone to Caracas on a secret mission. And now Madelyn and I sat drinking coffee at the old wooden table on chairs with cattle hide for seat covers and lighting cigarettes as though nothing at all had happened.

Chapter 22

"Welcome—Bienvenido"

Dear Mother and Dad   **October 20, 1953**

I don't know how Frank stands the stress of meetings. He said sometimes we get a contract, but other times we wind up with nothing. He says, "that's the way the cookie crumbles." Frankly, I don't know how he sleeps with so much on his mind. It's never just one thing. It's everything. And it never lets up.

Well, after the meetings, we flew back to Bolivar and a week later, we moved into our new house—and Frank went back to Caracas. Frank drove the station wagon to Caracas. His brother, Do—who'd been in CB on business—drove back with him.

Instead of moving to a house neighboring the airport in Bolivar, we should have moved to Caracas. Oh, heaven forbid! I look forward to seeing you October 31st.

All my love, Marilyn

Cable from Frank in Caracas—**October 29, 1953**

"FLY TOMORROW FIRST LAV TO MAIQUETÍA—STOP—WILL MEET YOU—STOP—WILL STAY A FEW DAYS IN CARACAS—STOP—FAMILY WANTS TO SEE YOUR PARENTS—STOP—WE WILL DRIVE BACK TO CB—STOP—FRANK."

My parent's plane from New York, scheduled to arrive early in the morning at Maiquetía on October 31, would be the end of the first leg of their trip. For days before the flight, Mother felt insecure about going through customs and immigration and then transferring to the plane to Ciudad Bolivar. Because neither Mother nor Dad spoke Spanish, she'd fretted for weeks about making the transfer.

"Oh, Arvid," she'd say, "suppose we don't know what anyone is saying and we get lost."

Blue Skies, Green Hell

"Now, Dotty," he'd reply, "we'll be okay." That would calm her—Dad was always right.

I flew to Caracas the day before their arrival in Maiquetía and on the morning of the big day, Frank and I drove from Caracas to the airport. I knew they'd be happy to see us and thrilled with the change in plans.

I always enjoyed seeing the white LAV Lockheed Constellation with tri-color stripes land softly on the runway following the eight-hour flight through the night. I'd breathe a sigh of relief and say to Frank, "Oh, those engines must be so tired."

After their plane landed, it taxied to the area in front of the three-foot high cyclone fence with gate where we waited anxiously. It stopped and the portable stairs were rolled to it, locked in place, and the door of the Connie opened. What a great looking plane. So aerodynamic, it looked like it was flying even when it was parked on the tarmac. A few seconds later passengers began to appear in the doorway and start down the stairs.

Mother paused in the plane's doorway. She looked radiant in a chic gray suit and white blouse. Despite hours of restless sleep on the plane, every hair was in place and her makeup perfect. Dad, behind her, also paused to look around and absorb the splendor of the airport on the shore of the Caribbean with the high mountains behind. When they spotted us they waved vigorously. Mother walked with feather-like footsteps as she descended the stairs. I could almost hear her breathe a sigh of relief when she saw Frank and me. Suddenly, the gate near us flew open and a cadre of photographers and other people from the press rushed out toward the plane. "*Bienvenido*," (welcome) they shouted.

They headed straight for my parents. "My God, Frank. What's Dad gotten into? Why this reception?"

"It's not your Dad, Button. It's your Mother they want."

"Stay here," he said. "I've got to see what's going on with the press." Frank pushed open the gate and hurried after the press corps to my parents.

"Hello," Frank called and embraced Mother and Dad. "*Qué pasa*" (What goes)? Smiles and laughter followed as Frank learned the press waited at the plane to greet a fashion editor from New York and they assumed Mother was she. With the question clarified, the photographers waved frantically to the real fashion editor who came down the stairs behind my parents. I understood the photographers' mistake when I saw the bedraggled fashion editor's tangled hair, makeup worn off, and dressed in a wrinkled suit made of mattress ticking.

It took only a few minutes for my parents to be cleared through Customs and Immigration and for me to say, "*Bienvenido*. So now you're the celebrity," I teased Mother, and kissed them both. "I think I've written to you that our plans change frequently. But I knew you'd like this one. We'll drive back to CB after we spend a couple of days in Caracas with Frank's family. How do you like that?"

"Marvelous," answered Mother enthusiastically. "I'd hoped we'd get a chance to see Frank's family," and then she whispered, "I didn't like the thought of transferring to another plane at the airport. Beyond *Buenos Días*, I can't remember anything from my high school Spanish classes."

Arrangements had been made for Mother and Dad to stay with Bully at her home. We, of course, stayed with Frank's mother.

Plans for the remainder of their first day left little time for resting, but Mother and Dad were up to the full schedule of activities and parties.

A great benefit in traveling between Venezuela and New York is the lack of jet lag. There is only a half-hour difference in time.

Everyone in the socially prominent Lazzari family took turns entertaining Mother and Dad at dinner parties at home, a soiree at the Valle Arriba Country Club, a horse show at the Club Hippico, cocktail parties at poolside, an evening of dinner and dancing at the new Hotel Tamanaco, and dinner and a musicale the final evening in Caracas at the home of one of Frank's sisters.

Frank's mother played piano. Frank, Armando and Maria (Frank's sister) played guitars. They played all kinds of music, but mostly Venezuelan joropos and waltzes, and played them very well. One of the guitarists would sing and anyone who knew the words would sing along in either English or Spanish. Even I had to perform my vocal solos, "Vaya Con Dios" and two old-time American songs, "My Blue Heaven" and "I'm Forever Blowing Bubbles." I hated that bubble song, but I sang "scat" and the family loved it. I couldn't avoid performing. Venezuelans are fun-loving party people and Frank's family, bright conversationalists and musically talented, knew how to host a party.

Mother and Dad got a kick when the ensemble would be playing and singing, and Mrs. Lazzari would suddenly stop. That cued everyone to stop. She'd turn to one of her offspring and stoically say, "You played an F sharp instead of a G." Then she'd slowly turn back to the piano and the music would resume. Mrs. Lazzari, an octogenarian and an accomplished pianist, often said she tired of playing poker and mah jong and would like to get a job playing piano in a supper club or a cocktail lounge. The children appeased her, "Sure. That's a good idea." She could have. She played that well.

All the family tried to bring my family up to date on all the clan's news. Mother and Dad fit right in with these gregarious party-lovers. But now the time had come for us to start back to CB.

Because of the late hour, and everyone's need for sleep, we arranged to pick up Mother and Dad at Bully's house at 4:00 a.m. instead of the customary midnight time of departure. Even if we had trouble on the road, allowing time for repairs, we'd still make it to Soledad, on the north bank of the Orinoco, before 6:00 p.m.

Blue Skies, Green Hell

Before dawn, my parents and Bully waited at the curb in front of her historic house which, in colonial days, had been a customs house. Bully and her husband, noted American architect Don Hatch, made extensive renovations to the charming building, but it retained its colonial flavor.

No moon, but a few lights on Bully's front porch and one street light illuminated the area. The foliage from old trees formed a canopy over the sidewalk. Bully wore a red robe and her black hair hung long and loose. She held her tiny son, Donny, in her arms while, Jennifer, her toddler, stood close and held her hand. Shadows of leaves gently blowing in the breeze played over Bully and the babies. Mother and Dad, excited and nervous, kissed their hosts goodbye and got in the car. Frank loaded luggage into the back of the station wagon.

We all waved and whispered our goodbyes. Tears welled in Mother's eyes—an unusual departure from her usual stoic demeanor outside the family. Later, she would reminisce wistfully about that morning and how she felt part of a dream in a romantic Spanish setting, far from home—and she loved it.

At that early hour, while Caracas slept, Frank made fine time through the city and up the mountain on the south side of the valley. The air grew cold and crisp and we closed windows. Mother and Dad fought sleep for fear they'd miss seeing something as we left Caracas and drove to the llanos. The sun rose and we stopped at a small restaurant to have an omelet and stretch our legs. Then we were off again and the scent of the fresh morning dew filled our senses.

Frank rested, Mother and Dad slept, and I drove until the peace and quiet ended abruptly and rocks started flying, banging on the hood and smacking its under-carriage. Everyone awakened. Mother and Dad had been forewarned about the noisy part of the road filled with dirt and flying rocks. Our dear passengers got a kick out of tying triangle-folded handkerchiefs across their faces. They agreed the bandit-type masks did provide some protection against inhaling dust.

Mile after mile, we rode through the llanos and, at last, on to a paved roadway, through the oil fields. About twelve hours after leaving Caracas, we arrived at Soledad on the north side of the river. Dad questioned why we had to walk through the box laced with chemicals to disinfect our shoes and why the guardsmen sprayed our tires. Frank explained about the "hoof and mouth" problem and added that boxes of chemicals are also at the CB airport for arriving passengers to walk through. We drove on board the ferry and crossed the Orinoco.

"Well, Dot," Dad said, "Did you ever think you'd be crossing the Orinoco?"

As Mother watched the swirling eddies and whirlpools, I pointed to the large rock in the middle of the river with marks showing the varying water-levels.

"I still don't believe it." She looked toward the back of the boat and beyond to the road we'd just traversed. "Caracas seems so far away. Was it only this morning we said goodbye to Bully and her beautiful babies?"

"We can't tell you what a thrill this trip has been, Frank. In all our travels, we have nothing to compare it to," Dad said.

"And your vacation has just begun," Frank asserted. "You'll like every minute in this new world. Your daughter does." He smiled and squeezed my hand.

We drove through Ciudad Bolivar, the same route Frank had driven me when I first arrived. We eased up and down the narrow streets with old colonial Spanish buildings, passed El Triangulito, "You'll like that place. Good arepas and toddy," Frank said.

"Sounds good to me," Dad replied enthusiastically. He was always ready to try something new.

Finally, we came to Avenida Táchira with the flower-covered wire fences, beautiful colonial houses, and the Catholic school called Nuestra Señora de los Nieves (Our Lady of the Snows).

"It's all so beautiful," Mother gasped.

"I had the same reaction, Mother."

Dad started to open his camera bag. "Don't worry about taking photos," I said. "You'll have plenty of time for that. And you'll have sun every day. Look, here we are."

Frank turned onto our unpaved road and dust rose high in the air. As it settled, they saw our large white house with red tile roof surrounded by its impressive black wrought iron fence. Two barking dogs ran up and down the length of the fence and jumped high in the air. Josefa ran to the gate, shooed back the dogs, swung open the gates and Frank drove into the carport.

"Hello. Hello," she called. "*Bienvenido.*"

"How about this. Do you like the welcoming committee?" I called as I hopped out of the car.

"Dogs and Josefa, they're well-trained in greeting people," Mother answered.

"In this household, they have to be. You'll see. It's every pilot's favorite hangout.

At this watering hole, you'll meet commercial pilots, bush pilots and legends. We love it that way. And you will, too. We moved in about three weeks ago. We still have finishing touches to take care of."

Frank and I thanked Mother and Dad for bringing us good luck; we'd never had such a fast and flawless drive between Caracas and CB.

It took only a good dinner, shower, and one night's sleep for everyone to feel fit and up for whatever came along—and everyday something different did come long.

Dad, a man who loved flying as much as a pilot, went flying with Frank, Irv, and Julio every chance he could. He'd come home in the late afternoon and sing out, "I flew to Caicara del Orinoco." I chuckled at his pronunciation.

Blue Skies, Green Hell

In a matter of days he'd been up the Orinoco and downstream to the Delta at the Atlantic. He'd met executives from the Orinoco Mining Company and enjoyed talking with them about doing business in a foreign land.

Friends dropped by most every night for cocktails and dinner. We served at home or went to dinner at the Rojas's and the Banta's. Sometimes we ate at the Grand Hotel in the city, sometimes at El Triangulito, or an Italian restaurant called La Florida on Avenida Táchera. We took them to our famous open-air movie and behaved sedately at the Black Horse Café. We all enjoyed dancing and swimming at the country club. Mother and Dad loved to dance as much as we did.

It didn't take long before they had the routine nailed. At first they found this lifestyle a little unsettling. "How can you plan or get anything done?" Mother asked.

"I don't. I have to be flexible."

They quickly adjusted and actually liked it. Mother said, "Dad and I wake up every morning and wonder what the day will bring. One thing we know, it will end with friends and a party. I don't know how you keep up with the demands of entertaining. So many dinner and overnight guests would get to me."

"I couldn't do it without help," I assured her. "However there have been times when a maid has walked out during a dinner because so many uninvited guests attended she couldn't deal with it. But that doesn't happen often. Anyway, before I hire anyone, I warn them."

On days when Frank had no business trips, he'd take us all for a flight and Mother learned the delight of sightseeing from a light aircraft. Especially, she thrilled at landing on a grassy strip instead of a paved one. A little nervous at first, she quickly learned to enjoy every minute aloft in the small aircraft. I usually sat in the back seat with Mother, but once in a while Frank would ask me to sit in the front; he wanted Mother and Dad to see me fly. Mother was a little scared at first, but Frank leaned back and said, "She does okay. She loves flying and does the maneuvers; she just doesn't like to navigate."

We four flew over the powerful Caroni Falls, soon to be tamed by construction of the Guri Dam, and we flew to Horacio Cabrera's Hato La Vergareña where we enjoyed a *ternera* (barbecue).

"Hey, Mother. Want to try horseback riding?" I joshed.

"I'll pass on that."

They raved about our house, but commented on the lack of window screens. "We moved in just before you arrived and haven't had time to have them made," I explained.

Dad declared, "I'll build them for you." And build them he did. Frank rounded up tools and accompanied Dad to the lumber yard where he purchased wood, screening, and nails and whatever else was needed. Voila! Within three weeks, with time out for day trips, Dad had built screens for all the windows. He even constructed screens that he bolted to the fancy black iron doors at the back of my living room.

At the breakfast table we talked about everything; I talked about the gorgeous clothes they'd brought me, and they talked about the latest excitement on television. "Can you imagine Arthur Godfrey fired Julius La Rosa right on television for everyone to see?" Mother asked.

"Julius who?" I replied.

"And what do you think of Joe McCarthy and the hearings in Washington?" Dad asked.

"Joe who?" I replied. "I guess I've been away too long. I have no idea what or who you're talking about."

Oh my God. I did it! I'd led with my chin. I opened the door to trouble and wished I could have vaporized.

"Oh yes, sweetheart," Dad jumped in. "You've been away so long. We miss you so much. We were just talking about that while we were flying to Maiquetía. When are you and Frank coming home? You simply must take a break."

He kept it up until I stood and interrupted. "Dad, Ciudad Bolivar is my home. My home is not in Garden City, or even in the U.S. And I need no break. You see how we live. We have friends, fun, and whenever I want to, I go with Frank to places few people have seen or even heard of. My experiences defy description. Just as you've gone along with Frank on trips to places you've never heard of, Dad, I do the same thing. Every day is an adventure." I went to the server where Josefa had placed the coffee pot. "Would either of you want more coffee?" They shook their heads no. "I have a very good life. I wouldn't swap it for anything."

While I poured my coffee I thought of things to say, but they'd be hurtful and I didn't want to do that. I loved these people even if they repeated too many times their need for me to visit with them at their home in New York—and to bring Frank.

I carried my coffee back to the table.

"Frank keeps busy and his responsibilities never stop. We've been in business two years. We're making money, but we have big expenses. We operate three Cessnas and a Beechcraft. We're buying office equipment. And, Dad, can you imagine the cost of the inventory we have to keep? Have you seen our parts department? We have thousands of spare parts. It's a huge investment. And our tools? Also, we pay salaries to six employees. Three are well-paid full-time pilots. No one's going to fly this part of the world if they're not well paid. And insurance? All our employees receive benefits including insurance and we have an enormous bill for insurance on our aircraft. Frank has established a bona fide air service. It's a small airline and he wants to add planes. He's the only bush pilot who is trying to fly the bush on a large scale. I help out at the office

Blue Skies, Green Hell

often. Maybe someday we'll have an office manager and I'll be able to visit you, but please understand, it's not that we don't want to, we just can't get away now. And I can't predict when . . . ."

"We know you'll come home when you can," Dad said and the conversation ended. "I'm going to walk over to the airport. Frank said he thought Charlie Baughan would land this morning. I'm looking forward to meeting him." Dad put on his cap, said he'd see us later, and left.

"I'm glad Dad has the airport across the street—it's like his playground. I confess, it's my playground, too."

We sat quietly for a moment, then Mother broke the silence. "I have something to trouble you with and I'm so sorry." She had a hemorrhoid problem. "I don't know what to do," she said. "What a time to have this happen. I'm so embarrassed."

"Don't worry, Mom, I'll go to the pharmacy and see what the druggist has. I'm sure Venezuelans have that problem, too"

I understood her embarrassment and hoped the suppositories the druggist sold me would help. She promised if they didn't, she'd tell me and we'd go to a doctor.

When Dad came home from the airport with Frank, his exuberance told me something good had taken the sting out of the morning's conversation and the world settled back on its axis. He'd met Charlie Baughan, bush pilot, extraordinaire. "Oh, we had a nice talk. Come to think of it, I guess Charlie did most of the talking. He's quite a guy! A very kind gentleman. I like him"

"Everyone does. He's a legend. He's one of my favorite people."

Early the next morning while we ate our breakfast, Frank came home from the airport and proudly stated to my parents, "Today, you will have the thrill of your life." He smiled and waited for someone to egg him on.

I obliged. "What have you planned?"

"It's being firmed up now with Julio."

The phone rang. "Ah, that'll be him." He picked up the receiver. ". . . That's great. What time? What can we bring? Maybe Marilyn should talk with Martha. Okay. Whatever you say."

He hung up the phone and announced to Mother and Dad, "At 11:00—that's in three hours—Julio will fly you three and his family—Martha, her mother Mrs. M, and the three kids in the Beechcraft to Angel Falls and Canaima where you'll stay overnight and come home tomorrow afternoon."

The greatest adventure Mother and Dad would ever experience in their lives had been planned the day before by Frank, Julio, and Charlie. Martha and her maid purchased and prepared all the food needed for the outing. Julio

233

juggled his calendar in order to fly us. Because he had business in the city, Frank couldn't make the trip.

"How about it, Mom? Are you game for this?" I asked.

"Oh, dear. I still feel—you know."

"It's just overnight—a once-in-a-lifetime opportunity. You'll be okay. You bring suppositories and I'll bring something for pain." With Mother's health issue settled we packed towels, toilet paper, toothbrushes, shorts, slacks, and bathing suits in tote bags. We were ready to go.

The plane, loaded with all the baggage and food, including a cake Martha had baked for the occasion, was set to roll.

"Swanny, sit up front with me," invited Julio as Dad strode toward the airplane. "You'll get great pictures of Devils' Canyon in Auyántepui, Angel Falls, and Jimmie Angel's plane—if the weather's clear."

Frank held my hand and said, "I'm sorry I can't be with you, Button. But what I have to do is important. You'll see when you return. I promise. Have a great time." We embraced and kissed and said another "goodbye." I turned and headed to the plane that would take me to my favorite part of the world.

Julio did the pre-flight and thrilled Dad when he ran up the engines and started to taxi. Dad had never before ridden in the cockpit of a twin-engine plane. SNAP-SNAP went his camera.

We taxied and turned on to the runway. Julio pushed the throttles forward, held the plane with the brake, and then eased back on the throttle. He released the brakes, advanced the throttle, and the plane rolled fast, the tail came up and we began our Canaima adventure. SNAP-SNAP.

About an hour after the takeoff, flying in clear skies and light wind, we were near Angel Falls. Good luck stayed with us as the usual cloud-cover over Auyántepui had not developed and we approached Angel Falls head on. SNAP-SNAP. Julio banked and we circled in front of Angel Falls a few times then circled the other direction so that everyone on board took pictures of this most unusual occasion—Angel Falls without clouds! We hooted and hollered and punched the air like everyone does at the sight of Angel Falls. We flew over Auyántepui and circled the remains of Jimmie Angel's crashed Flamingo, Spirit of the Caroní. SNAP-SNAP. Even Mother forgot her problem and bounced around in her seat to see Angel Falls and Jimmie's plane.

As if that wasn't enough, Julio flew the few minutes from Angel Falls to Canaima and made several turns around the pink beach, the lagoon, the jungle, and the seven golden waterfalls. SNAP-SNAP.

Dad, overwhelmed and thrilled, had just settled back when Julio banked the plane for landing in the grassy strip cut by the Pemóns at Canaima. SNAP-SNAP went the shutter as Dad caught the action through the windshield.

"Hey, Swanny. How's that?" Julio was always up to the challenge of a grassy-field landing.

"Thrilling! I'm speechless!"

I walked with Dad and Mother through the tall weeds, up and over a small hill of sand, and before them lay Canaima. Eden. Paradise. A breathtaking sight. This small band of noisy adventurers fell silent.

We selected our lean-to and I offered my parents their choice of sleeping in cots or hammocks. Mother and I selected the hammocks and Dad said he'd go with a cot. SNAP-SNAP.

I also explained the toilets were anyplace up in the hill behind the camp. "Just pick any private place and dig a hole for your toilet. Fill the hole with sand when you're finished." They didn't seem shocked or dismayed, but I sensed from their blank looks this would be a test of their mettle. "Take a flashlight with you at night. During the daytime, use the john in the plane. That's what Mrs. M. does. Oh, by the way, the lagoon is your bathtub," I said. "You'll be swimming in the water from Angel Falls." Having seen Angel Falls, Canaima, and the wonders of the Lost World, I felt sure they'd deal with the primitive arrangements and lack of conveniences. Not a bad trade.

After lunch, all but Dad, Martha, and Mrs. M went swimming. Dad never swam, Martha thought she might be pregnant, and Mrs. M didn't want to get her hair wet. Mother said the water felt good on her you-know-what and she stayed in the lagoon longer than most. SNAP-SNAP.

Rudy Truffino, aka Jungle Rudy, the general manager, took the group for a ride in the aluminum boat with outboard motor around the lagoon and close enough to the falls to ride the turbulent water and feel the spray. SNAP-SNAP.

The evening barbecue and music from the record player enhanced the halcyon setting. It had been a wonderful excursion.

We sat up until quite late listening to the sounds of the jungle, the pounding roar of the waterfalls, and just talking. Canaima is magical.

Tired from the day's exhilarating activities, Dad went to asleep right away. After falling out a few times, Mother finally found comfort in the hammock. Sleep came quickly to both. I walked the beach for a while and renewed my obsession for this part of the world.

Following breakfast, we lolled around the camp, went swimming and when Julio said he thought we should think about leaving, we packed up and took one last look at Canaima. No one really wanted to leave.

"I'll never forget this trip, Marilyn," Mother said.

"I can't think of a place in this world I'd rather be," I replied.

"I can understand that. This trip has been a thrill."

Dolefully we walked to the plane, boarded, and headed back. We landed in CB before the six o'clock deadline. Frank met us and drove us home.

Forever, Mother and Dad spoke of their trip to Canaima as a thrill of a lifetime.

I opened the front door of my house. "Frank," I screamed, "A piano. You bought a piano for me." I hugged him. "Mother, Dad, look. A piano. Where did you get it? I can't believe my eyes." A beautiful Baldwin console piano was appropriately placed in a corner with a bouquet of flowers on top and a loving note from Frank. What a guy!

"Button, I bought the piano in Caracas, and only learned two days ago that it would be delivered by RANSA C-46 yesterday. It arrived while you lolled around Canaima." He also had purchased sheet music, a book of popular music, and a book of classical music, too.

Though out of practice, I played familiar tunes on piano, Frank played guitar and we all sang. The impromptu musicale made our transition from paradise to home so easy.

Mother and Dad's five-week vacation had flown by. We loved having them with us as did our friends who attended their farewell party. In addition to our AEROVEN family, Charlie Baughan and Frank's brother, Do, attended. Do and Frank played guitars, I played piano and everyone sang; another Lazzari family musicale.

Mother stands on "two-rut road" in front of our new home.
The road is now a four-lane highway with traffic lights.
Photo by Swanny

I stand with Frank and
Mother ready to go
flight-seeing.
Photo by Swanny

Mother, Frank, Marilyn and Magda Banta with her dog, Katy. Frank's days off meant hanging out at the airport or flying!

Mother and I in front of our shelter.
Photo by Swanny

That's Dad dressed in casual wear!
Always the businessman, he enjoyed
his sojourn to Canaima.

Two restful scenes of the beach at Canaima.
Photos by Eric—1953

Upon arrival home I found a gift from Frank. A new piano.

In one of our small planes, we flew Mother and Dad to Maiquetia where they departed in the huge LAV Constellation for New York. We shared hugs and shed tears.

We were champs at saying goodbye.

Chapter 23

King of the Jungle

Dear Mother and Dad   **January 11, 1954**

As you know we went to Caracas for Christmas and because Frank had to get some permits for I don't know what—we stayed until two days ago. Now we are back in CB.

The good news is that business is booming. Today we had 5 trips.

Our new Cessna 180 is a favorite. Everyone's crazy about it and it's been working since it arrived. Of course, this is the dry season when we fly a lot. Frank says the company should be putting money away for rainy days—but I don't see that happening.

Carlos and Madelyn with baby Lilly went to the US. It's lonesome without them.

I send you all my love, Marilyn

"What's new?" Frank asked as he came through the front door and dropped on the sofa. He didn't wait for my answer. "What a day with the accountant. He always has bad news. You have any news?"

"You had a visitor, Charlie Baughan."

"More bad news? Did he hit us for a fill-up?" He poured a glass of iced tea, took a few sips then leaned his head back. "He's already into AEROVEN for several tanks of fuel for his plane. The accountant asked about it. Maybe we should put Charlie on the roster and let him fly off his debt."

Following a cocktail and dinner, Frank retired early and put Charlie Baughan out of his mind.

A few days later, while working at the office, I heard the voice of Mary Baughan, Charlie's wife, cut through the silence. The piercing shrill ripped through the air like a dart. It bounced off my eardrums and sent shivers through me. "Time is of the essence." She always announced herself like that. "Time is of the essence."

241

Mary sprinted like a contender for a gold medal as she ran toward our hangar. Blown by her own swift motion, her auburn hair flew in all directions. Charlie's twin Cessna was parked on the tarmac—not in our parking area.

When she spoke, she sounded haughty, but I knew Mary and the front she put on. It didn't bluff me, but it served Charlie well. He'd sent her to AEROVEN instead of coming himself. A tough mission that required guts required Mary. Charlie's southern way came across far too mild-mannered for him to square off for a tank of gas he couldn't pay for.

I greeted Mary at the office door.

"We need gas, Marilyn. Quickly." She was out of breath. "Charlie's in the airport manager's office now. We must depart the minute he returns to the plane." She continued in her falsetto voice. "Marilyn. We have very important guests on board. VERY important real estate developers from New York." As she said VERY, she pinched the fingertips of her right hand together pretending to hold a pen and swished her arm from left to right as though underlining the word VERY. I believe they'll work out an agreement with Charlie to provide funding to develop Canaima."

What she meant was maybe they'd soon have money to pay off their debt to us. Frank had told me in clear and certain terms not to give the Baughans anything until they showed some sign of paying their current debt for gasoline. A plane full of potential investors wasn't the sign Frank looked for.

I should have told her I understood her problem, that I couldn't authorize gasoline unless they paid for it. But I didn't.

"Come in the office, Mary," I said. "Let's talk in there."

I knew what I wanted to say, but didn't know how to say it. I had in mind that giving Charlie gas might be the answer to one of our company's problems and start something good for him.

"You know I'm an officer of AEROVEN." That was true—even if only on paper.

"Yes," she answered, somewhat impatiently.

"And I have authority to make agreements." That wasn't true. I had no authority whatsoever to do anything in the name of the company. "Sit down, Mary." I gestured to a chair, poured two glasses of iced Kool-Aid, and gave one to her. I sat in the chair next to her rather than behind the large imposing desk.

"I like you, Mary, and I like Charlie. I want to see you both succeed with your Canaima resort, not only because of our friendship, but we're *paisanos* (countrymen) and we help each other." I had her attention. "Mary, you know Charlie owes the company money for gasoline he's pumped from our tanker on several occasions."

"I know," she sighed softly, losing her bravado.

I pressed forward, nodding to a file cabinet in the corner. "We have the exact amount noted in there. But that's not important right now. "I took a deep breath. "I want to offer you a deal. If we agree on it, we'll shake hands and hold our husbands to it. If they want a written contract, they can work it out."

"And the deal?"

"Sometimes we have to refuse trips because we have planes available but no pilots to fly them." I looked out the window and gestured toward the twin Beechcraft. "If someone wanted to charter the Beechcraft for a flight this week, we wouldn't be able to book the business. None of our pilots certified to fly multi-engines are available." Mary understood. "When we can't accept a reservation, it's the same as making a financial contribution to our competitor's general fund—if they have one. Charlie comes to CB at least once a week. My deal is this. We'll contact Charlie when we have a trip but no pilot to fly it. We usually have a few days lead time. Charlie works it into his schedule and flies our trip. He can work off his fuel bill at the going hourly rate for pilots of his experience. The men can work out that detail, too. Every time he flies for us, he'll fly down his debt. After that is paid, if he wants to, he can continue to fly for AEROVEN as needed."

She nodded and we shook hands.

"It's fair, Marilyn. I know your company has a payroll to meet and other expenses and can't be giving away the store." The register of her voice dropped another octave.

I saw her reach into her bag for a tissue. I turned my back and walked to the chalkboard on the wall. I added Charlie's name to the roster of pilots available for assignment. I sipped my Kool-Aid to moisten my dry mouth and wiped my sweaty palms on my jeans.

"We're having rough times," she said. "This is Charlie's last trip in the twin Cessna. We can't afford the payments anymore. It will be impounded when we return to CB."

"Let's go fill your tanks. You'll be out of here and in Canaima in time for your New Yorkers to behold the world's most glorious sunset. That ought to get them to open their wallets."

The gas flowed and minutes later, the Baughans took off. As I watched them head south I imagined Mary in the co-pilot's seat telling Charlie about the deal. He'd like it. He'd fly anywhere in any plane and I'd given him a way to pay off one of his debts—and make some money, too.

Now, I had to tell Frank. He'd be back from his flight any minute and I still hadn't formalized the script. Then I saw him on final, watched him land, taxi to our ramp, shut-down and secure the plane.

"Hi, Button," he called as he opened his door, jumped out of the plane, and strode toward the office, clipboard in hand.

"Hi. *Cómo le fue*" (How'd it go)? I called. Frank's spirits were high. I hoped they would stay that way after I made my still-unscripted presentation.

He did his paper work, never noticing the addition of Charlie's name on the chalkboard. "Let's go for a drink before we go home. See who's at the patio lounge," he invited.

I have to tell him before we get over there. "Ok, but first—can we talk?"

"Sure, Button. What's up?"

I still had no game plan. Here goes! "Mary and Charlie flew in today."

"With rich people?"

"Do they know any other kind?"

"I wish he'd get something going with Canaima. The poor old guy needs some luck."

"He had some today. And so did we." The words flew out of my mouth, and now I didn't have to figure how to get started.

He looked puzzled. "What have you done?" Then he joshed, "Sometimes I'm afraid to leave you in the office alone."

"Look at the chalkboard."

"Button," he said, his voice rang with astonishment. "He's on the roster! You hired the most famous bush pilot in all Venezuela—the King of the Jungle—to fly for AEROVEN?"

"I did! But I have more to say." I put my index finger to my lips. "After your last meeting with the accountant, you mentioned the possibility that Charlie might be able to fly off his debt. And another time, you and Julio mulled over the pros and cons of accepting a contract offered by some Italian royalty—explorers—heading to the Brazilian border to look for diamonds. Again, you mentioned Charlie." No one on our roster wanted to fly that route; the flight was long and hardly any radio contact with anyone between CB and Brazil. The charts are not good and road maps, which most bush pilots use, only show rivers, mountains, waterfalls, air strips, and some small villages. In the interior, there's no network of roads, highways, railroad tracks, or other landmarks pilots often use to visually check their routes. "Well, putting Charlie on the roster is really your idea." I had to make that point. "Charlie is more familiar with the Lost World than anyone we know." I paused and told Frank the whole story.

When I finished, he stood up, walked to me, and hugged me. "You're right, I had forgotten Charlie. The idea is a good one. I like it. Julio will, too. Thanks for remembering." He smiled. "Did you make a contract?"

"Verbally. With Mary." He didn't respond. "No details. He'll fly for us—as needed—to pay off his debt. You establish the pay and benefits. Incidentally, she said he'll fly the explorers."

Charlie Baughan's discovery, the exotic beach he named, Canaima.
Photo by Swanny

These three palm trees were growing in the lagoon at Canaima as early as 1953.
Photo by Marilyn

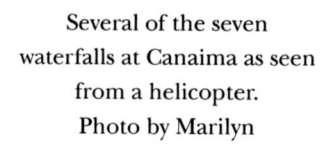

Several of the seven waterfalls at Canaima as seen from a helicopter.
Photo by Marilyn

He laughed. "I'm sure Charlie feels good about being able to work off his debt. It's good for his self-esteem. It's good for us, too. We might even get new business when people know they'd be flying with the legend, Charlie Baughan, King of the Jungle."

Two days later, four explorers with a lady writer / photographer destined for diamond hunting on the Brazilian border landed in CB and we signed the contract to fly them and supplies to their border camp in the Amazona region with additional flights as scheduled and as needed.

The explorers had a short-wave radio at their camp as did Charlie at Canaima. They agreed to contact Charlie by radio and he'd get their messages to us, one way or another. Thus, a communications system between the explorers and AEROVEN was established.

That was how we learned the explorers were closing down their exploration camp and returning to Bolivar well in advance of their scheduled date to withdraw.

It was in March while at Canaima with tourists, when Julio called the explorers' camp and learned that two of their group had left the camp and were hiking to Canaima; the other two would follow once arrangements had been made to fly the lady back to Ciudad Bolivar.

Back at CB, Julio related the revised plan. "The men are concerned about the girl. They say she's gone native—especially when the moon's full. Then she shouts. She runs around the camp. Sometimes she's nearly naked." To complete the picture, Julio said he'd learned she had a pet snake.

"This is a job for the King of the Jungle," Frank said.

"Sure is," Julio quickly agreed. "Let's see what we can arrange."

By now, Charlie had worked off his debt but continued to fly trips for regular flight pay. Nonetheless, his twin Cessna remained impounded and parked on our lot. Mary, employed in a business office in Caracas provided the steady income they needed to pay bills.

Given all the details of the mission, Charlie said, "I've seen the lady. I call her Eve. She's very beautiful." He lit his long signature cigar. His forehead furrowed as he considered the trip. "I've seen her with the snake." He shook his head from side to side. "I'll fly her back even if she's naked, but the pet snake? I'd prefer if it stays in the jungle."

"You haven't told us about her acting strangely," Frank said.

"Frank, I'll make the arrangements and keep you posted. I've seen my share of people who act confused out there in the jungle. Hell, I get confused myself, sometimes." He puffed on his cigar. "But I'm a gentleman from Georgia. I wouldn't share any of the little lady's secrets."

Chapter 24

"ASA. It's a Rough Place"

Dear Mother and Dad   **April 10, 1954**

Frank obtained a permit for us to fly into La Paragua and two other diamond mines. We expect to earn a lot of money this year, but a diamond or gold strike isn't something we can count on every rainy season. To help out with AEROVEN finances during the rainy season, Frank, Shorty and Julio incorporated a construction company they call ECUAVEN. You'll recall Julio is an engineer. He'll head up ECUAVEN.

Frank's brother, Do, has been here since February as his company, MERCATOR, has a contract to survey land near Puerto Ordaz and San Felix. Julio, for ECUAVEN, will sub-contract some of that work. It is ECUAVEN'S first job.

Frank says they might get a job from OMC to paint the houses at the Port.

To answer your questions . . . (1) No, I haven't seen Madelyn in a long time. Our paths don't cross. I miss her so much. However, I've become quite close to Magda. She's Irv's wife. You met her when you visited. I like her very much. We pal around. (2) I don't know when I can get home. I'll work on that.

Much love as always. Marilyn

"Hey Frankie," Carlos called as he exited his car parked in front of our gate. "Have I got news for you!" He swung open the gate and walked up the driveway just as Frank opened the kitchen door that led to the carport.

"*Qué pasa?*" said Frank. "Come on in. I'm just finishing breakfast."

"I hope you've got planes ready to go to Asa and two other mines. My buyer just got back. He says the diamond strikes are big. You'll be able to retire if you get your planes down there." He lit a cigarette. "SAN's there. Where've you been?"

"You haven't heard? We're about to lose our contract with OMC. I've been away—trying to save the contract, but it's not working out. Their big shots in the U.S. decided it was better to buy their own plane. We'll operate it for them but there's not much money in that."

"Then you really need to get moving on Asa. The three mines are on contiguous rivers—Asa, Paragua and Chiguao. They're maybe fifteen minutes apart by plane or a day on foot through nasty jungle. Frankie, it's risky flying. Bad weather and you'll fly low. There's no time to get altitude. But, you'll have visibility—even though it's poor. Frankie, it's a rough place, but seems to me you don't have a choice. You've got to get there."

"Thanks, Junior. I'll go see the governor today, I'll need permits to fly in there and I know SAN will do all they can just to keep AEROVEN out."

Within a week, the permits were in Frank's pocket.

"Button, if Carlos is right, this will save us." He started tossing work clothes, shaver, toothbrush and paste in a bag. He'd wear no fancy shirt and cap with braid on the visor flying mud-covered miners and buyers from one mine to another. "It seems I'm still on the go. I thought I'd have more time at home once the AEROVEN license was issued, but it's not in the cards. Don't get me wrong. I'm not complaining."

"I'm glad Irv's going with you. I wish I knew more about where'll you'll be. All Carlos says is, 'it's a rough place'"

"We'll take two planes. We'll have to see what goes on down there. When I come home, I'll have a lot more to tell you."

"With Julio in Puerto Ordaz, and you and Irv at the mines, who'll run the show here?" I asked.

"Tom will be available to fly, and our new girl has a good handle on things in the office. I'll be back to write checks and take care of correspondence. Eventually, I hope she'll be able to be the office manager."

"Am I going to be fired?" I asked coyly.

"Maybe so, Button."

The new girl recently graduated from a school of accounting and had been referred to us by the owner of the school. Despite her youth, she was a major improvement over other office workers we'd had.

The only problem with the new girl was her inability to speak English. Many of our clients were Americans who spoke no Spanish. However, Julio insisted they could work around that. My Spanish was good and Martha's was excellent. We'd help the new girl.

I was delighted with the arrangements. At last, I could stay home and enjoy things like tennis and tea with my friends.

Frank continued. "Martha has trained her, but while I'm away, will you stop by . . ."

". . . and keep my eyes peeled? Of course. I'll do what I can. If I run into a snag, I'll try to get hold of Julio."

Magda and Irv arrived at the office. The men readied their planes, kissed us goodbye, and rolled on to the taxiway, leaving two sad, lonely wives behind.

"Frank says living conditions are awful." We watched them take off, one after another. "The money better be awfully good."

"Where are the mines?" Magda asked as they flew out of our visual range.

"Asa, Paragua and Chiguao."

"Where's that? Them? They?"

I shrugged my shoulders. "They're names of rivers. Diamond mines are at each. I've been to the Paragua River, but not the other two. Let's look at a map."

It didn't take long for Irv and Frank to develop a routine. If someone in the mine wanted a trip to CB, Frank flew it and took the opportunity to do some office work before he returned to the mines. Irv came home on weekends unless business between the mines was brisk. Irv and Frank each flew about 100 hours a month and money was flowing in. Tom flew the charter trips out of CB. With everyone pitching in, we stayed on top of the business.

ECUAVEN business was brisk, so we didn't see much of Julio. He was never available. When I asked the new girl if she'd heard from him, she'd casually say he was in the field and couldn't be reached.

When Frank came home for even one overnight stay, he was deluged with phone calls and business meetings. The meetings were always in the evening at our house and most often occurred after dinner. But I was happy to at least see him and be with him—even if I only hung out on the sidelines and watched and listened. We had very little time together. Sometimes, when talks went into the late hours, I went to bed and put a note on his pillow. What hurt me was when I awakened in the morning and found he'd showered, eaten breakfast and gone to the office without having read my note. I loved him so and felt very upset over his exhausting work at the mines along with his un-shared responsibilities in CB.

He'd return home from the mines coughing and sneezing and his chest hurting. Brown discolorations developed on his teeth and he scratched mosquito bites until they bled. His time at home was busy and left no chance for him to sleep long enough to regain his strength and recover. Carlos had said it would be rough. Carlos was right.

Flying between the mines was difficult. The weather was usually bad. Landings on grassy fields were challenging; ruts developed after storms, grass was slippery and never the same length—and that made a big difference. Mud was a problem, too. Lots of takeoffs and landings in foul conditions rendered the flights uncomfortable for passengers and grueling for Irv and Frank—if not downright dangerous. They flew practically non-stop from morning 'til sundown. Diamond buyers and merchants with businesses set up at each mine flew between them daily—as did hopeful independent miners. Frank and Irv also flew food, all kinds of miscellaneous freight, and parts for broken machinery. Frequently, miners became ill and had to be airlifted to the closest town for medical help. Seriously ill or injured miners were flown to CB.

Living conditions were uncomfortable. For Bs50, (fifteen dollars at the currency exchange rate in 1954) AEROVEN bought a shack made of wood and thatch. It had a dirt floor, no electricity and no plumbing. Frank and Irv bought hammocks. Because of continuous rain and dampness, their clothes and shoes were always wet. Frank said he couldn't light a match in the morning because of the dampness. The two longed for sunshine, dry air, dry clothes and dry hammocks.

I wanted to visit the mines and asked Frank to take me.

"That's no place for you. I'll take pictures to show you."

Pictures, taken from the air, showed two rivers in the jungle converging and a town along one of the banks of one of the rivers. The pictures told me nothing.

Frank said good food was unavailable at Asa, and even bread was scarce. So, one weekend when Frank and Irv were both in CB, Tom invited Magda and Irv, and Frank and me to his kitchen to learn the art of making bread in the bush. He arranged his kitchen with a workstation for himself and four chairs for us, the audience. Shirley was visiting in the States.

"I use only flour, water, a little oleo and a little sugar." With his hands, he moved the mass around on a board. "Then I knead the mass." He put the mass in a skillet on top of the stove and turned it several times while it cooked. He did not use yeast. Then he said, "You wouldn't have this touch of luxury in the bush, but for you, I'll add icing." He prepared a batch of vanilla icing and poured it on the hot bread. "You could add raisins if you want to make a coffee-cake."

The bread surpassed my expectations.

"If you bake bread like this, dear," I said to Frank, "I can visit you in Asa. You won't have to take me to a restaurant. We can eat at your house. This bread, heated and with cheese, would be a great lunch."

"You haven't been there?" Tom asked.

"Would you take Shirley?" questioned Frank.

"Sure. If she wanted to go."

Frank looked surprised, then said, "Okay, Button. If you want to go, the trip is yours." He added that in view of the poor sleeping conditions, I could visit when he had a Bolivar—Asa round trip the same day.

One morning, unexpectedly, Frank returned from Asa and called me from the office. "Your dream comes true today. I have to go back to Asa to take a replacement part for someone's equipment and then I'm coming back to CB. Come to the airport right away—and wear your boots," he said. "Today, you will see Asa."

Frank, already in the plane with the prop turning, saw me at the hangar door and beckoned for me to hurry to the plane. Ramon helped me board, slammed the door, and slapped the outside of the plane indicating it was safe to move out.

We taxied fast and were airborne in jig time. In a climbing turn, the plane soared up to about 600 feet before Frank welcomed me aboard. "It won't be as exciting as your first trip to Angel Falls, but seeing a mine is memorable."

We headed southeast, flying over peaceful savannah and stretches of rivers that looked like ribbons shining through the foliage. He flew around nasty looking clouds and started his descent about an hour and a half after we'd left CB. As he made his turn to the left, I saw the small airstrip carved in the jungle. He made a low and slow pass over it, looking at its condition. "It's no worse than this morning. With so much rain, planes going in and out chew up the airstrip and it really can be bad." He advanced the throttle and pulled back on the yoke. "We can make it." The nose of the plane pointed up and I fell back in the seat. Up and around we went for the final approach. We landed, and the plane slowed. We taxied through puddles. Finally, we rolled to an area near four drums of airplane fuel. Each clearly marked AEROVEN.

Not seeing our second plane, Frank said, "Looks like Irv's out. You may not get a chance to see him."

"Wow! What a place!"

We hopped out of the plane and he gave a box containing the replacement part to a worker waiting at the airstrip.

A narrow clearing in the jungle had been made for the strip and the squalid shanty town it neighbored. Branches of trees hung low over a muddy path that led to the makeshift town, blocking out much of what little daylight there might have been.

As we walked to the main part of the town, the smell of burning damp wood filled the air, and I choked on the white smoke that hung low over everything. It also reeked so strongly of spoiled grease I could taste the rancid fat the food cooked in.

We stopped. "Want to live here?" Frank queried.

"We must be in the poor part of town," I said.

"This is the town. The mining goes on over there." He pointed in the direction of the river I'd seen from the air.

Navigating ruts, we crossed the path to a walkway made of slats of wood. Scattered thatched houses and decrepit tents of all sizes littered the clearings made to accommodate a temporary town. "Here today. Gone tomorrow. This place will be here until there are no more diamonds. Then everyone will pack up their tents and equipment and move on to the next place where they hear there's been a strike, and the jungle will reclaim this town." He wiped a splash of mud from his face with the back of his hand. "A few years from now, probably, you won't be able to find a sign of this mine. Maybe in a hundred years archeologists will."

I walked ahead of Frank on the walkway we shared with sorry-looking bedraggled bearded miners wearing torn and stained ponchos, and ladies of the night, equally sorry-looking and bedraggled. Lined up side-by-side at the edge of the road were shacks where industrious women tended wood fires as they fried *empanadas* (meat-filled patties) in grease-covered skillets. Men stood in line waiting to pay an exorbitant amount of money for their lunches. At other stands ladies sold fried *plátanos* (plantains), rice and black beans.

"Those are the restaurants, Button. Do I recall you said we could eat at restaurants?"

Then we stopped. "Here's my house," said Frank and swung open a wooden door. "This is where I live. *Adelante* (Enter)."

"Oh, my God!" Daylight came through the sieve-like slats in the door of the one room structure. I saw no window. Two hammocks, hanging on hooks attached to the walls and an upright pole in the center, swung over the dirt floor. Flattened cardboard boxes covered the ground under and at each side of the hammocks.

"The cardboard is supposed to prevent dampness in the ground from getting into the hammocks." He coughed. "It's also where we stand our boots at night—if they are wet. If they're dry, we sleep with our boots on."

A wooden box served as a table for a Coleman lantern and personal items that included a Luke Short paperback novel about the old west in the U.S. The pole in the center held a mirror they used for shaving. Nails in a board affixed to the wall supported hangers, shirts, and khaki trousers. A sterno stove, a couple of ceramic cups and paper plates rested on another wooden box. I wondered if they cooked anything other than coffee. I saw no cans of food.

"I had no idea it was like this." I put my arms around him, hugged him tightly and our eyes met. I wanted to cry. "I don't see a bathroom. Where is it?" I asked.

"You don't want to know."

"What do you eat?" I asked

"I buy empanadas from the lady on the street—at one of those restaurants," he replied, sheepishly and then smiled. He shook his head. "We're doing okay. I shouldn't have brought you here." He pushed back hair that had fallen on my forehead. "I miss you so much, Button. These separations are hard for both of us. And they never stop, do they?"

Blue Skies, Green Hell

"I miss you, too. But I have a clean house and clean sheets and good food." I looked around at his hovel. "When I see this mess, I miss you more."

"This is what bush pilots do. I'm flying for money, yes, but I'm also bringing in medical supplies. There's a doctor here. He gives me a list of his needs. I give it to the *farmacia* in CB. I pick up the supplies before I return. It works out okay. We don't charge him anything. The return flights usually don't have passengers and the supplies don't take up much room."

"How's Irv making out here?"

"Doing fine for a *gringo*. He's sick, too. You know, he doesn't speak much Spanish and only a few here speak English. But he makes out okay. You know that smile of his. That cuts across all language barriers." I understood the need to speak Spanish; to negotiate prices whether for flights or for empanadas, and to speak Spanish with in-coming pilots and passengers to learn about weather conditions beyond Asa. "He actually seems happy."

"I like Magda. With Madelyn gone so much, Magda and I are buddies. We get along fine. She's fun."

He picked up the Luke Short book, put it in his back pocket and suggested we leave.

"We're lucky we have this." He opened the door and we stepped out onto the wood walkway. He looked around. "Not the house. I mean lucky to have the permit to fly here."

He helped me around a hole in the walkway. "Without the mines we'd be in deep financial trouble. Because of this place, we're making big money—more money than we ever made before."

"There's the movie theater," he said and pointed to a wooden building on cement blocks. It looked like the best building in town. "It has its own generator." Further down the street I saw more shacks and bodegas and another place he simply called the Chief's office. Frank explained, "He's not a mayor, but he keeps law and order. I call him *Jefe* (Chief). We have to keep him on our side."

"I don't know how you do it."

"It's hard here. But in three days we grossed Bs 9,000 (about $3,000 in the currency exchange at the time). Irv and I? We'll make it."

"I know you're not allowed to fly in alcohol, but is there any drinking here?"

"Oh, yes. Plenty. It's not openly for sale, but people bring their own. There are fights in the late evening. Sometimes I hear gunshots not too far off."

"Shots?" I gasped.

He back-pedaled. "It's not dangerous for us here. Button. They all need us. We provide the only way out—unless they want to walk! You've seen enough and I need a shower. Let's go home."

"Coming home for a few days?"

"I have to come back tomorrow after I work at the office."

And so, while he flew between the three mines, I waited at home. I watched the sky. I listened for his plane. That's what bush pilots' wives do.

Days and weeks passed. Nothing changed. The company made money. We missed each other and time together was short.

"Rain. Rain. In all my years here, I've never seen it rain like this." I stood on my porch looking across the dirt road to the rain-swept airfield and talked to my dog, Loop. Since Tail Spin's death, Loop was my constant companion. She missed Frank, too. "Rain. Good for farming. I don't know what else." I glanced at the sky, and then at my watch. Almost six o'clock. Time had run out. "I've got the willies, Loop. He was supposed to come home today, but I guess he flew until it was too late." I patted her little brown head.

From my rocking chair, I watched the airfield.

The rain eased.

I was still sitting there thinking about Asa and Frank when Carlos' car came splashing up the muddy road. He blasted his horn and stopped the car. I opened the gate and went to the car. As Madelyn stepped out, Carlos said, "How's Frankie?"

"Welcome back, nice people. I've missed you. Frank's in Asa," I replied. "So's Irv. We base two planes there. They work all the time."

"Making lots of money?"

"You bet."

Carlos repeated his oft made comment, "It's a rough place."

"I know. He took me with him one day." I pulled a cigarette from my pocket and lit it. "He was supposed to come home today, but I guess he flew trips too late to get back. Or maybe the weather's too bad."

"A few minutes ago, I saw my buyer, Oscar. He just got back. He came on SAN—the last flight out. The airstrip was shut down."

"Asa shut down? Why?"

"He didn't know."

"Did he see Frank? Irv?"

"He didn't say. I don't know what's going on down there."

Madelyn said, "If you're going to be here for a while, I'll come in and visit."

"Oh, great. I've missed you. You spend so much time in Caracas you're practically a *Caraqueña*" (a female native to Caracas).

We three chatted a few minutes about dogs and maids and friends, then Carlos said, "I'll be back in a little while." He waved and drove off. A pregnant Madelyn and I walked to the gate.

Blue Skies, Green Hell

We hugged. "Welcome back," I said as we went in the house. "Rafaela, please bring coffee," I called. "Like old times, Madelyn. The coffee pot's always on. I learned that from you."

"How I've missed you." She sat at the dining room table. "I wanted to talk with you, but our paths never crossed." Softly and stoically she said, "I'm pregnant."

"I noticed. Should I say congratulations?"

"Carlos is happy. I'm going to the States to have the baby. The last time we were in New York, we left Lilly with Carlos' mother. I miss her so. I'll be happy if I can bring both my babies back with me. I won't return without them." She sipped her coffee. "Marilyn, I don't know if we'll ever come back to CB."

"Oh, no. Madelyn." I gasped." Life here without you? It can't be."

"Carlos will be back and forth between Caracas and here, but I think we'll probably live in Caracas. His dreams for big things here seem to be on hold. I don't know when we'll move, but that's what I think will happen."

The news shocked me. "It won't be the same without you and Carlos. I can't believe it."

"I know. Once you and Frank came to CB we had good times." She paused. Her voice dropped. "Now? I don't know what we'll be doing, or where we'll wind up."

"Even though you've been away so much, I always knew you'd be back and we'd have good times again at the movies or playing games. Oh, Madelyn. Is this goodbye?"

"I didn't plan it that way. But I had to tell you. I'm sad, too."

We sipped coffee and just looked at each other. We'd come a long way together. We'd shared so much—the two of us. The four of us.

"I couldn't have made it here without you. I've told you before." I swallowed the lump in my throat and changed the subject. "Did you know Martha is pregnant?"

"I heard," was all Madelyn had to say about that. They'd never been close friends.

Madelyn and I enjoyed the time we had together, but it flew by too fast.

Carlos returned, honked the car's horn, and we hugged again.

"Stay in touch and when you come to Caracas, you can find us by calling Carlos' father." As the mud splattered behind his car, I watched them leave. No one, outside my family, had ever meant so much to me as Madelyn.

Just then, Magda, came walking down the muddy road carrying her folded umbrella and a small bag containing her pajamas and toothbrush. She planned to stay overnight if Irv did not return to CB.

"Why didn't you call me? I'd have picked you up."

"I'm fine. The walk is good. Anyway, it's not raining now. Just a little muddy."

"No dogs?" Magda and I often brought our dogs with us when we stayed overnight at each other's house. She had three friendly Dobermans.

"They're muddy and wet. Oh, brothers, we don't need them."

Magda often said, "Oh, brothers," making the noun plural. I thought it a charming mannerism. I told her about my visit with the Freemans and Madelyn's pregnancy. That brought on another, "Oh, brothers."

"Carlos said the Rojas, Van Hyning and Freeman families have babies while the Lazzaris and Bantas have dogs. I told him we're just wiser."

I gestured to a rocking chair and she sat down.

"Carlos told me the Asa strip is closed."

"Why's it closed?" she asked.

"He didn't know."

Rafaela came to the dining-room window that overlooked the porch and asked if we'd like a glass of wine. She held up a bottle of Málaga from Spain, a gift to me from Governor Sanchez Lanz. Then she said dinner would be ready in half an hour.

"*Bueno*," I answered. "Magda. It's awful there. Frank's so skinny, and he's living on greasy empanadas and cheese. I worry about him. He's got a cough and his teeth have brown stains. He says Irv's doing okay."

Rafaela brought two glasses of wine on a tray and left them on the table between the rockers. "*Salud*" (Health), I said and we touched our glasses. I added, "*y mucha suerte*" (and much luck). We sipped the Malaga. I lit a cigarette. "Magda, SAN only has one plane at the mines. It's here tonight. I can't imagine why the field is closed."

"Maybe conditions became unsafe? Mud? Ruts? Irv's talked about those things."

"Frank was due back today."

"Irv thought he might come home tonight, but I never know when he's coming. If there's business, he flies." She sipped her wine. "He wants to buy out Julio or buy a plane and put it in AEROVEN in exchange for shares. He's so determined he doesn't realize he's suffering. He's got this goal."

"Frank has to come back—even for a couple of hours—to do paper work. Julio's never here to do it."

I heard the tinkle of the small dinner bell. We went inside, ate dinner in silence and returned to the porch where we sat, rocked and looked across the airfield at the tiny lights in houses and bodegas. And I worried. I picked the cuticles on my fingernails and smoked too much. Even when it was raining, Magda got up every once in a while, walked to the fence and back to the rocker.

"I'm glad we're together," I said.

We spoke very little, but dozed off and on until about six o'clock when the light of day broke the horizon. We watched the morning flights line up for takeoff. I poured coffee Rafaela had left with us before she started breakfast. "Someone ought to be home by seven-thirty or eight if he got an early start," I mused.

We'd been watching planes take off and land when Rafaela called us for breakfast. She said it would be a good day, not too hot. Sensing my anxiety, she tried to lift my spirits with small talk.

Magda stayed and we busied ourselves with chores. I fixed breakfast for Loop and Chucho, my yellow and black bird from Canaima. Then I showered and put on a clean dress. Magda sprayed a fine mist on the orchids that grew on logs attached to the black decorative iron doors at the far end of the living-room. We just killed time.

At ten o'clock, I drove Magda to her home. "Thanks so much for staying and helping with the orchids. I'll come by later to bring you back to my house. Have dinner with us and stay over. For now, I'll hang out at the airport. If Frank gets home, I doubt we'll go to the movies. He'll be tired and want to go to bed early." In despair, I added, "Or maybe he'll have a meeting. Or maybe he won't even get home."

"Oh, brothers."

"I'll be back for you later."

I drove to our hangar. In the office, I greeted the new girl.

"Have you heard from Julio?"

"*Nada. Él esta todavía in Puerto Ordaz*" (Nothing, He's still in Puerto Ordaz.).

"*Yo no se porque mi esposo esta tan tarde.*" (I don't know why my husband is so late).

I sat down on the sofa. *Where is he? What's going on at that air strip?* Then I said I was concerned, he should have been home yesterday. "*Volando en Asa, no es fácil*" (Flying in Asa isn't easy), I said and lit a cigarette.

"*Señora? Tiene un momento para hablar*" (Do you have a moment for us to talk?)

"*Sí, cómo no,*" I answered.

"*Señora,*" she spoke hesitatingly, her eyes fixed on the pencil she twirled between her fingers when she wasn't sketching small interlocking boxes on her tablet. "*Yo tengo una amiga . . .*" (I have a friend . . .) Softly, she told me of her great concern for her friend who had fallen in love. "*El hombre está casado . . . y tiene niños*" (The man is married . . . and has children.). She asked me for advice; what could she tell her friend.

"*Esperaté un momentico!*" (Wait a minute!). I struggled a little with my Spanish, but she got my message that anytime a woman gets involved with a married man—especially with kids—it's very bad. No one wins. I suggested she tell her friend to see her priest for advice.

Just then I heard a Cessna overhead and ran out of the office and watched our 180 FLD on final approach.

I was glad that conversation was over. I forgot it.

My heart raced. The plane landed and taxied to our gravel ramp, kicking up dust and stones as it pivoted on one wheel until it was properly aligned with the other planes. The engine shut down.

Then I saw him at the controls and shouted, "Frank!" I shouted louder. "Frank!"

I ran to the plane and we embraced—for only a second. Frank looked preoccupied; a man on a mission. He reached into the plane and grabbed his clipboard.

"What happened?" I asked. "We heard Asa was closed. Is Irv okay?"

"He's fine. We're both fine. It's that damned SAN again." He looked at his watch and made a note on the clipboard. "First, they did everything to keep us from flying between the mines. Now—yesterday afternoon—an officer in the *Guardia Nacional*, stationed at the strip, declared the airfield closed. He all but accosted me as I walked to my plane to leave and come home. The guard said someone reported we were hauling liquor into the mines and the matter would have to be investigated before our planes could move. He let the SAN plane take off last night. But not me. He wouldn't listen to me." Frank said he unleashed his fury on the guard in a loud voice and used a few unkind words. "Finally," he continued, "the chief came out to the airstrip to investigate the raucous face-off. Thank God. He pleaded on my behalf. He told the guard that AEROVEN is the only air service used by the governor of the State of Bolivar and that I was the only pilot the governor would fly with. Only then did *el gusano* (the worm) back down and say we could fly. It was too late for me to leave. I'm furious. I couldn't leave earlier this morning. The weather was bad."

He strode fast to the office. "I suppose Julio's not here? He's never here, damn it." He burst through the door, flung the clipboard on the desk, and grabbed the phone.

Frank rang the governor and spoke to him directly. "I've been in Asa over a week. I am dirty and wet and I smell. I need a shave and a shower. I've got a heavy cold and a cough and I'm tired. But, *con su permiso* (with your permission), I want to come to your office to talk with you. It's urgent . . . Yes . . . I just landed. Thank you, sir." He coughed and hung up.

"Where's Irv?"

"Flying. He's okay."

"Can you stay home for the weekend and rest?" I asked.

"I hope so. And Irv will be in tomorrow. He needs rest, too."

"What about your house? Aren't you afraid to leave it alone for a weekend? Won't someone move in?"

Our new Cessna 180 parked at the muddy
Asa airstrip near 4 -55 gallon drums of avgas—our fuel depot.

At the end of the day, Magda and Marilyn wait at the airport for
their husbands to come home—or to hear news about them.

"The chief watches it for me," Frank rubbed his finger tips together, "for a little grease." He turned, started to walk away then stopped and said, "I'm going to the governor's right now. I'll demand he put a policeman at the airfield in Asa to inspect every plane that lands there. This great indignity to me is inexcusable, and I'll demand an apology for that officer's untoward behavior."

He whipped out his car keys from his pocket, left the office, got in the car I'd driven to the airport, and rolled out of the parking lot at top speed.

In Spanish, I commented to the new girl that it was good the governor's his friend. "*Él nunca está tan furioso. Creo que es muy serio.* (He's never so angry. I believe it is very serious.)."

I called Magda, asked her to come over, then I walked home. We three ate dinner quietly. Exhausted, Frank went to bed. Magda and I read, then called it a day and retired early.

Irv flew home the next afternoon. He reported that an inspector had been stationed at the airport to be sure no planes carried alcohol.

A few days had gone by after Frank and Irv returned to the mines, when the SAN plane, a Cessna 170, taxied from its berth at Asa to the head of the strip. It turned and started its roll on takeoff when a beautiful wild chestnut-colored stallion dashed out of the forest and onto the dirt strip in front of the on-coming plane. The pilot tried to avoid the horse, but instead plowed into the frightened animal. The pilot and his passengers walked away from the crash.

As fate would have it, SAN's only plane that had been operational was totaled.

The horse was killed on impact.

I felt very sorry for the horse.

Chapter 25

"I Call Her Eve"

Dear Mother and Dad   **April 14, 1954**

    A while back, we flew explorers—four men and a woman, to a place in the jungle near the Brazilian border so they could search for diamonds. The men were Italian Counts and the girl an American.

    A week or so ago, two of the men walked from their camp to Canaima. It took them twenty one days. Charlie brought their message to us. They asked us to fly to their camp and to fly the girl back to CB as she had gone "native"—especially when the moon is full. Seems she runs in the jungle, almost naked and shouting.

    Well, dear Charlie Baughan said he'd fly her back. Today he left at six a.m. It seems the girl doesn't want to leave so we don't know how successful Charlie will be in bringing her back. It's noon time. He isn't back yet.

    I'm at the airport and will stay until they get back.

    My love and devotion, Marilyn

    A beautiful woman in the jungle who enjoyed the sensuality of a snake wrapped around her naked body was much talked about in our flying community. Charlie Baughan had been told by one of her Italian diamond-hunting associates that she'd "gone native" and didn't want to return to civilization even though their expedition was declared over. So when Charlie departed for the explorers' airstrip to fetch the young lady, at their request, those of us who'd heard the story wondered how it would play out.

    According to her associates, Jean was a free-lance writer, photographer, and a Manhattan socialite. Those credentials didn't fit the image of a jungle nymph.

    Frank, always fair-minded, put forth his thoughts. "Let's wait. See for ourselves. None of the pilots who've flown to their base camp have said anything about her behavior being unusual. Even Charlie. And he's been there more often than the others. So, hold back your judgment."

That Charlie was overdue caused concern and speculation. Some thought he might have stopped at Canaima. He liked to show off the place. Frank thought he might have been delayed by bad weather as it was the beginning of the rainy season. Others in the hangar thought perhaps Charlie refused to bring the girl because she would not give up the snake. Visibly annoyed by the guessing game, Frank thought the bizarre assessment of the situation was totally out of order. He walked away from the small group of gossipers whose eyes were scanning the skies for the sight of AEROVEN's FLD that Charlie was flying.

The assemblage breathed a unified sigh of relief when FLD came into view and finally touched down. Charlie taxied to our fuel tanker. After he shut down the engine, Jean stepped out of the plane. Wearing blue jeans, a white shirt, and carrying an oversized pocketbook, she stood tall and slim; she had all the right things in the right places. With Charlie at her side, they walked leisurely toward the hangar. A light breeze blew her lustrous blonde hair and she swished it from side to side. Cascading this way and that, sometimes covering one eye, she'd brush it back with one hand and shake her head imperiously.

Charlie drew me aside and said she had no snake and that she appeared to be happy, in control of herself and quite healthy. He said they'd talked all the way back and Jean was not only attractive, as he'd said after meeting her at the explorers' camp, but also smart and well-traveled. She spoke several languages. He'd been around this old world of ours and used one word to characterize her: "Class."

The sage old bush pilot, Charlie, always referred to the young lady as "Eve." In the beginning, when he started to make flights to the jungle camp, he had met her but did not recall hearing her name, so he made one up. He said, "The jungle is a paradise. I call her Eve."

When I met the young lady, I understood his choice. She was Eve.

Pleasant and mannerly, she said the polite things: "How do you do?" "My pleasure." "It's a beautiful day." I didn't believe for a minute she was "out of touch" with reality, as we'd heard, so I gave my nod of approval to Frank and he invited Charlie and Jean back to the house for coffee and arepas with cheese.

As was our custom for all meals, we sat at the dining-room table. Our maid, Josefa, wearing a light blue uniform with starched white collar and cuffs appeared with a pot of strong Venezuelan coffee and a pot of tea, as well. About to ask our guest which she'd like, Jean told Josefa she'd prefer juice.

Our dining room furniture—with red seats—still smelled new. I was proud of its contemporary (1954) design with inlaid wood forming subtle patterns. My few objets d'art were artistically displayed in the two servers, each with sliding glass doors. Unlike Jean, we weren't rich people with friends in high places who probably wouldn't have been overwhelmed by a new suite of dining-room furniture. But we'd come a long way from the second-hand furniture—partially eaten by termites—that we'd used only the year before. We were proud of our

Blue Skies, Green Hell

achievements. Although Jean professed her fondness for roughing it in the untamed jungle, I was happy she did not have to rough it at our house: She'd been invited to share the home and hospitality of one of Bolivar's respected gentry.

Right off the bat, Jean told us she had no plans, no money, didn't want to go back to the States, she loved the jungle, and smiling coyly at Charlie, said she would quickly accept an invitation from Charlie to go to Canaima with him if he offered one. His open invitation to her was genuine. Before Frank and Charlie left the house to return to the airport, Frank invited her to stay with us until she went to Canaima. Looking at me he said, "See you at the patio lounge about five o'clock," and to Jean, he said, "*mi casa es su casa*" (My house is your house).

I asked Jean if she'd like to shower and change her clothes and offered to have Josefa launder anything of hers that was soiled. "Josefa will hang them in the sun. They'll dry quickly."

Jean followed me to her bedroom and bath off the hallway. She said some of the clothes she'd brought with her were clean, but she'd put those that were soiled in the paper bag I gave her and leave it in her room for Josefa.

Later, after I heard the shower running, I went to her bedroom to pick up the bag. Probably in her haste to wash off the jungle, she had forgotten to close the bathroom door—or maybe the afternoon breeze blew it open. Because the floor was terrazzo with a drain in it, we needed no shower curtain. She stood under the shower, massaging her body with special soft and delicately scented soap brought to me by Jack Perez months ago. Her eyes closed and face tilted upward, foamy shampoo dribbled from her hair down her body as she luxuriated under the magical spell of the soap and running water.

In our house, showering with the bathroom door open was a "no-no" as we never knew when to expect an overnight visitor. Because of over-crowded conditions at the hotels and their frequent lack of electricity, we hosted numerous guests, mostly pilots, and Frank's brothers. While we delighted in having our visitors stay over, it became second nature for me to live with my privacy guarded.

I tucked away in the reservoir of my mind a mental note to tell Jean about our "no—no" house rules and our frequent house guests.

I took my terry cloth robe to the bathroom and, unseen by Jean, who continued to derive great pleasure from her long and luxurious shower, hung it on a bathroom hook, returned to the kitchen, and gave Josefa the bag of soiled clothes. Josefa had already prepared lunch and placed it on the buffet server in the dining room.

"That was wonderful," sang Jean, as she floated light-heartedly into the dining room wearing a towel, wrapped sarong style around her body. Apparently, she had not seen the robe. "I found your shampoo and washed my hair and I saw your manicure set," she said waving an emery board.

"That's fine," I said. "I should have offered them to you. *Mi casa es su casa*," I felt badly for not having provided her the feminine things she'd probably been living without during the time she'd spent in the jungle.

"Lunch?" I asked.

"I'll just snack a little," she said, serving herself a small bowl of fruit and a heated soft roll. "I'm not acquainted with Ciudad Bolivar. Is it really the last outpost, as I've heard?"

"Well, there's not much south of here. And CB lacks a few things. I can't get my hair or nails done, if that's what you mean. But I get them done when I'm in Caracas." What a peculiar question, I thought. "It's quite civilized. I play tennis at the tennis club and swim at the country club. They're not full service tennis and country clubs like we have in New York. Far from it. They're, well, sort of limited. I'll show you tomorrow. Perhaps we'll go there for a swim and lunch."

Jean spoke softly. "You're from New York and you like it here in Bolivar." I wasn't sure whether it was a statement or a question. Later, I realized, she would look to me for answers to her own bewilderment or confusion. And she had a lot of questions.

Asking me about missing the good things in life like the opera, gourmet restaurants, and Fifth Avenue shopping, she gasped when I told her I look forward to the arrival of Jack Perez in the C-46. "He brings me special things from Miami like Wonder bread, peanut butter, Campbell's tomato soup and Hershey's chocolate syrup."

"My God! How exciting is a loaf of bread?" She laughed and pointed her finger at me. "You tell Frank you must live in Miami and he can commute." Her manner of speech was decidedly haughty, and I laughed over her preposterous solution. I had not gone native and still enjoyed soft white bread.

"We live here because this is where Frank is based." I served myself a small portion of *carne frita*, *arroz* (fried meat, rice), and a soft roll. I passed the basket of rolls to her and continued chatting. "I like things just the way they are." *Why am I defending my life here?*

"Do you miss New York?"

"Not now. I enjoy being with our pilots and their wives. One thing for sure, they're different. Jean, I love my life here.

"And watching Frank ride his horse at the Toros Coleados, winning prizes of silk ribbons was more fun than going to dinner at the Russian Tea Room before a concert at Carnegie Hall. I've done all that. Besides, we do a lot here that we can't do in a more structured society. I'd tell you some, but you'd think we were crazy."

She nodded in agreement. "You're free-spirited. I am, too. I wasn't brought up to be free-spirited. It just happened. My mother, well . . . ."

"Do you miss New York?" I asked, breaking the silence that followed her unfinished sentence.

"No," she replied sharply.

I decided not to pursue that further. She was a complex young lady.

Josefa interrupted our discussion to announce that she'd pressed and folded Jean's clothes and they were on the ironing board in the laundry room.

"I'd like to see the Coleados. You say Frank rides in them?" She asked.

"He used to."

I tried to explain the sport, but doubted she understood.

"Is it dangerous?"

"Uh-huh. Frank was in an accident awhile back."

"Was he hurt?"

I nodded, "But lucky, too."

"What happened?"

I told her about the massive collision with two bulls, two horses and two riders.

"Oh, my. Frank still rides?"

"Not so much. That was then. Now is now. He's like that."

She was mesmerized. "He's quite a man," she said.

I nodded, thinking she seemed a tad over-interested in Frank's *machismo* (manliness). I continued, "Let's get your clothes."

The laundry room, located in the rear of the house off the kitchen, was pleasant and sunny. A screened wall that faced a small orchard of lemon, avocado, and mango trees provided a tranquil setting with shade and privacy. The air was heavily scented by the blossoms on the lemon tree.

Jean's clothes were folded in a small stack on the ironing board. "I have a maid who lives in. And look—I have an iron, an ironing board, washing machine, and drying lines are strung outside in the sunshine. We're not quite as primitive as some would like to believe." I gestured to Loop, stretched out and sound asleep in the shade under the mango trees. "Loop thinks it's pretty nice here, too. And we've installed a perch in one of the avocado trees for a large black, blue and red Toucan who thinks this is home. Sometimes he stays with me in here while I iron."

"It's very pretty here. But—the jungle is magical. Everything about it. I hated to leave." She paused and closed her eyes. "And to answer your question about missing New York—I don't want to go back."

As we stood admiring the trees and enjoying the freshness of the air, I wanted to ask questions but I didn't. She'd put me on the defensive in almost every subject.

She ambled slowly to the screen wall. "I think I'd like this room better without the screen wall." She paused. "Yes. The wall should go."

I was about to contradict her, but given her love for the jungle, she surely wouldn't be bothered by pesky wildlife and I simply would be on the defense again.

"The scent of the lemon tree is delightful," she cooed, inhaling the sweet aroma of the fruit. Perhaps the scent reminded her of something in the jungle.

She inhaled the scent deeply as her cover towel dropped to the floor.

One time, after Charlie had walked into the jungle camp near the airstrip and saw her sleeping in a chinchorro naked except for a beaded "thing-a-ma-jig" worn by young Indian girls, Charlie had described her as a work of art. Because he had a penchant for exaggeration, I doubted his evaluation. This time, I believed he'd told it straight.

She stood tall, confident, comfortable and naked—admiring a lemon tree. Eve.

Jean was in no hurry to dress, but I reminded her we'd be going to the airport at five o'clock to have a few drinks with friends.

She selected a pair of navy blue slacks from the small pile of clothes.

"I worked as a writer on a fashion magazine. Modeled. Traveled. Went to England, France and Italy. In Paris, I was offered a job to be a Dior model. I've done a lot of things."

She stepped gracefully into the tight slacks and slowly pulled them up over her hips'

"Jean, we're going to have to hurry a little."

She continued to talk. "I met my associates in Italy. They were coming here to search for diamonds. After I told them I was a writer and photographer they invited me to join them to record the trip. I leapt at the opportunity."

She put on a white blouse, closed some of the buttons, and tucked the blouse in her slacks. Gently, she pulled up the zipper. "I must write to my agent," she said and swished her hair. Her erotic moves, sensual and suggestive, were in no way offensive, and with no makeup, no jewelry, and her freshly shampooed blonde straight hair hanging below her shoulders, she was radiant.

"My turn to shower," I said. "We'll talk more later, and meet Frank at the airport at five."

I showered with the bathroom door closed, dried off and slipped into a white halter dress with large blue flowers and an easy swing skirt. My friends and I wore slacks or jeans with flat shoes or alpargatas during the day, but dresses and high heels in the evening. None of us wore makeup other than lipstick except for grandiose occasions when we applied eye makeup.

Jean and I met Frank at the unusually quiet patio lounge, so after one drink we drove through the woods to the small French hotel and restaurant in the woods, Le Normandie, for a gourmet dinner on the front porch—al fresco. The quaint candlelit restaurant and the delicious French cuisine combined to make a pleasant evening. Gregarious, as usual, Frank told lively stories about flying and Jean animatedly told stories about her days in Europe. They shared tales about photography. I seemed to be left out of the conversation and thought Frank was overdoing his attention to Jean.

Frank had a flight the next day so we left the restaurant shortly after dinner and drove home. As we made our way home through the darkness, slivers of the moon peeked between tree leaves and cast geometric patterns on the dirt road that weaved through the forest. The sound of the car's engine was drowned by music made by nocturnal critters, insects, and rodents each awakening and rejoicing in the blessed coolness of the darkened forest.

At home, I asked Jean if she wanted something to help her sleep. Having traveled from the jungle to civilization, enjoyed a gourmet dinner, and lively conversation, I thought she might feel over-stimulated, perhaps disoriented.

Declining my offer, she assured me this first night in a real bed would be so delightful that she'd luxuriate between clean sheets and sleep soundly.

In the privacy of our bedroom and the comfort of Frank's arms, I softly asserted, "I think you overdid the 'mi casa' thing with Eve."

"You're too sensitive, Button. I'm just being polite and trying to entertain her." He turned off the light. "But, I get the message. Let's go to sleep."

The light of day and Frank's alarm clock worked together to awaken me. I had a house guest and would have to think of things for us to do. As I said, our house guests were usually men, and just so long as there was food, drink, and Frank, I had little to do with their entertainment.

"You could go swimming. I'm sure you'll find something to do," Frank said as he stepped out of bed and into the shower, a few steps away. He dressed quickly. The pilots had new uniforms—blue pants, caps with a slim gold braid on the visor and white shirts. He looked sharp.

"I'll walk to the airport," he said as he dabbed his lips with a linen napkin after taking the last sip of his breakfast coffee. "I'll be back late afternoon. Enjoy your day—and visitor."

Jean, up and fully dressed in blue jeans and a blouse, joined me at the breakfast table. "Do you have orange juice, please?" She asked Josefa.

After breakfast, I asked Jean if she wanted to see Frank's horse. No. Did she want to go to the club for a swim and lunch? No. Tennis? I could get two more for doubles. No.

She was lethargic. "What is it, Jean? Is something troubling you?"

"It's kind of you to invite me to stay with you, but . . . I . . . I . . . miss the jungle," she murmured softly. Much of the bravado from yesterday had been replaced by listlessness. Or malaise. "I'm uneasy here. It just seemed right out there. It was me. I enjoyed my freedom." Her eyes scanned my house. "This . . . it's not freedom. But you're happy on this . . . this frontier?"

Here we go again. "Yes. I have as much as I need here. There's not much, but everything. It may be a paradox, but it's so. Can you understand?"

267

I recounted my conversation of long ago with Capt. Mendoza who explained how fortunate I was to be comfortable living in two worlds, each so different.

A drive around Ciudad Bolivar seemed to be an idea worth pursuing. Most of my out-of-town guests liked to see this outpost on the Orinoco. Maybe she would, too.

"Want to come with me downtown? I need a few things. I'll show you around." Within ten minutes we were navigating the narrow streets and steep hills of colonial Ciudad Bolivar. "We're having a little party tonight for Frank's brother, Do, and one of his engineers. They're arriving from Caracas on the six o'clock plane. I slowed and shifted into second as I drove down a steep hill, swung around the Free Market on the river bank and looked for a place to park.

"Bolivar is an old Spanish town—houses with balconies, red tile roofs. Spanish explorers looking for El Dorado settled here. Some of the original houses still stand." I didn't want to sound too much like a Chamber of Commerce so I said no more. If she wanted to know more, I was sure she'd ask.

I parked the car and we walked to the river's steep embankment of rocks and cement. The river was many feet below the road. Atop the embankment, a low cement wall supported high cement columns, located about fifteen or twenty feet apart for the length of the paseo. "See the long slots on the sides of the columns that face each other?" I asked. She nodded. "The river rises a lot during the rainy season. When it is perilously close to the top of the embankment, large boards are slipped down in the slots, one on top of another, to build a high wall. It helps moderate the amount of flooding in this area."

We climbed a few steps to the paseo resplendent with tropical flowers in a garden with free-form reflecting pools weaving around huge *Uva de Playa* (Grape) trees. A two-lane road on the river side of the paseo handled the westbound traffic while a two-lane road on the side of the paseo where stores lined the sidewalk carried traffic eastbound.

"This is *El Paseo del Orinoco*. Of it, someone wrote, 'It's tranquility and enchantment of a time long ago that won't return.' "

Pensively, she repeated, "Tranquility and enchantment . . . it won't return."

"Let's walk the paseo. It's pretty and we'll get a breeze from the river. There are benches under the trees." River traffic was light in 1954. Only small fishing boats plied its waters. And of course, the ferry.

"Are there Indians here? Primitives?" she asked.

"They're far from here. They're nearer the Brazilian border, in the region southwest of here called Estado Amazona (Amazon State). I think that's where you were. They're friendly and visit Bolivar for medical reasons, but prefer to stay in their own villages. Monks are teaching them modern ways. Charlie Baughan can tell you a lot about the native population. That man's been all over Venezuela," I lit a cigarette. "Before he was a bush pilot and found Canaima, he was a Captain on TACA. That's where Frank and Charlie met. They know each other from way back. He probably told you about settling Icabaru." She nodded. "Did he tell you why he became persona non-grata and the government threw him out of there?"

"No. What happened?"

"I don't know. It will probably remain another mystery of the Green Hell."

Jean thought for a few moments then laughingly said, "He's a dreamer."

"Yes," I agreed. "But there's a place for the likes of Charlie Baughan in our world. He's a dreamer. But call him a futurist. Call him a visionary. There'd be no progress without people like Charlie. And he's so kind, I love him. And admire him."

"Yes. You're right," she said. "We need people like Charlie. People who see tomorrow—and move us into it."

We stared into the waters in silence. Finally Jean broke the spell. "Is Frank coming home for lunch?"

"No, he has an all-day trip."

"He's away a lot, isn't he?"

She couldn't have missed my sigh, "Yes, but I don't mind his day trips, or once in a while, an overnighter. It's his job."

"When he's in Ciudad Bolivar, does he ever come home for lunch?"

"Sometimes." The questions about Frank bothered me. "He'll be back for the party tonight. He'll grill the steaks. Let's go. I've got to shop."

We arrived home just as Josefa was ready to serve lunch of *arroz con pollo* (chicken with rice).

At the table, I asked Jean, "Is there someone in the States you'd like to write? Your mother? I write to my mother two or three times a week."

"No. Not my mother," she said quickly, and after a few silent moments added, "Well, I should write to my agent. *LOOK* magazine paid me an advance of $1,000 for my story about this trip."

"I'll put the typewriter and paper on the table. Someone should know you're back in civilization. Our guests will arrive about six. They'll stay over. By the way, Charlie'll be staying over, too. We'll have a full house, as usual."

I expected about fifteen people for dinner. Josefa would prepare food for more and when the time was right, Frank would barbeque the steaks while I played hostess.

Charlie was the first to arrive. "I saw Frank at the airport doing his paperwork. He'll be right along."

Then Frank arrived with Do and Alejandro Popoff, an engineer on Do's staff. Alejandro had been a witness to our not-so-secret marriage two years ago. They were followed by a host of other people including a few uninvited guests. It was ever thus.

Alejandro and Do were working in Puerto Ordaz and San Felix. The work, a prelude to the construction of the Guri hydroelectric dam near Puerto Ordaz, would last many months. We were pleased Do had chosen our home for his company's weekend headquarters rather than a hotel. Do was my favorite of all Frank's siblings.

Learned and wise, Do had a special way of keeping his values in order. He called me *Catira* the first time we met and his nickname stuck. It means a fair-haired or fair-skinned person. In the 1950's, light-haired, fair-skinned people were not common in the Venezuelan interior where the majority of the population was Spanish, Indian, African or *mestizo* (a mixture usually of Spanish, Indian or African). Because I'd often felt conspicuous, I'd darkened the color of my hair a tad—sometimes it turned out too dark. From week to week, my hair was never the same color and became a subject for conversation!

The evening's festivities took place outdoors on the patio. The green wicker sofa, chairs, tables with candles were arranged to accommodate small conversational groups. Around the perimeter of the patio were a few live potted trees and plants. Tall torches made of bamboo and stuck in the ground, would be lit after nightfall. Although a wicker bar and bar stools attracted most people, the door from the patio to the kitchen opened and closed all evening allowing guests the option of another place to drink at a make-shift bar set up on a kitchen peninsula.

A stereo phonograph player on a rolling table piled high with 33 1/3 LP records started playing Glenn Miller's American pop, and before long, it played our pre-distribution copy of Aldemaro Romero's latest LP, "Dinner in Caracas."

Jean made a quiet entrance, and though dressed in white shirt and blue slacks, she dominated the patio with her poise and classic presence. Her speech, lofty and eloquent, attracted most everyone's attention. After I introduced her all around, she confidently sashayed from one group to another. The guests, made up mostly of Ciudad Bolivar's flying community, were enjoying everything and it looked like Jean was enjoying them. Everyone wanted to know about her experiences in the jungle. Reticent to say much about them, she said she loved the freedom there. That it all seemed "right." I heard her say, "Here, we're so controlled by traditions, habits and preconceived notions we have no freedom."

Someone asked about her plans for the future. I wanted to hear the answer, but all she said was, "I have no plans."

Josefa had prepared a fine meal and the buffet table in the dining room overflowed with good food. Colorful candles and brilliant bougainvillea freshly cut from our garden decorated the table.

Frank's steaks were grilled to perfection and, of course, anything anyone wanted to drink was flowing at the bars. Following dinner, the torches and table candles were lit and to the delight of everyone, Frank brought two guitars to the patio where he and Do played and sang Trinidadian calypsos, and Venezuelan joropos. As usual, I sang "Vaya Con Dios" in Spanish plus a Venezuelan classic I'd just learned, "*Alma Llanera*" (Soul of the Plains). Everyone joined me in singing "My Blue Heaven." I didn't do that "bubble" song.

I was feeling no pain until I noticed Jean slowly sidle toward the wicker chair in which Frank sat. That's when my head cleared. She stopped, nonchalantly lounged on the right arm of the chair and gently put her left arm around his shoulder. She continued to chat with guests. Then she leaned close to him. Perhaps a little too close. She whispered something to him. They both laughed. Her long hair cascaded softly between her breasts. While she chatted with him, he glanced at her partly open blouse. I watched her stand up, flirtatiously toss her long hair then amble toward a group of people to engage them in conversation.

I stared with sullen anger at Frank. A crooked smile and lock of dark wavy hair that drooped on his forehead gave away his condition; he'd had way too much to drink. I turned aside. He obviously liked her attention and I couldn't look at the stranger he'd become. That was not my husband.

Charlie stood at the open kitchen door, and when he caught Frank's attention, he called Frank, asking for his help in finding a corkscrew. On the patio, someone put on the Mantovani recording of "Beyond the Sea." Wistfully, I recalled Canaima and China and Jesus. What a good time we'd had.

Slowly, I moved toward the kitchen door and chatted with others who I assumed also watched the playfulness of two grown adults. I opened the door and slipped into the kitchen. The whole time, fire blazed in my eyes.

"Frank! How dare you? How dare you flirt with that woman? What's going on?"

He didn't answer. He sat silently on one of the stools at the makeshift bar.

"You've had too much to drink," I said.

Charlie ran his fingers through his hair and poured a double from a Jack Daniels bottle. He, too, sat on a kitchen stool—way too small for his girth.

I prattled on. "I can't understand her. I don't know what she values. I don't think she knows. She's confused. Yes, that must be it. Charlie. You saw the whole thing out there. Disgraceful"

"Out there? On the patio? Honey," he drawled, "I saw nothing disgraceful."

"What do you mean? They were openly flirting."

"You misread Eve. I know her. I promise you, little lady, she's being friendly. That's the way she is." Circling the rim of his glass with his index finger he said, "I saw nothing wrong." Then looking toward Frank he added, "As for Frank, well, I suggest we put him to bed."

While I'd angrily spoken my piece, Frank had folded his arms on the peninsula, put his head down and had gone to sleep. Charlie half led and half dragged him to the bedroom, dropped him on the bed and closed the door.

"Earlier this evening," Charlie said after he returned to the kitchen, "Eve told me she wants to go back to the jungle. Now, does that sound like someone who has lascivious designs on Frank? I'm going back to Canaima tomorrow. She's going with me."

"Does Frank know?" I asked.

"He does, if he remembers."

Do came into the kitchen. "You're missing a great party."

"I saw all I want. Did you see Frank flirting with Jean?"

"Catira," he put his arms around me. "Frank's a red-blooded normal guy who had too many drinks. Forget it." He looked around. "Where is he?"

"Charlie put him to bed. He's sleeping it off," I said. "Do, are her values different from mine."

"Are you saying yours are all right and hers are all wrong?"

Feeling abandoned, I sighed. Neither of my two closest friends agreed with me.

"Everyone likes Jean." Do said as he lit a cigarette. "She's charmed them all and there isn't a man out there who hasn't given her the eye. Old Julio, hell, I saw his eyes light up the minute she came in. He never misses a beautiful body. He even asked her to dance. And she made Alejandro feel young and virile. Ginny [his wife] would be steaming if she were here. Irv laughed at her stories and he's another one who might have danced with her, but he's having enough trouble holding together his own marriage to Magda, that spitfire of his. But he was looking." Do sipped from his drink, lit a cigarette, and watched the smoke drift upward. "And me? Well, I never miss a good looking *gringa*. And Frank is solidly into flying, his business, and a little lady he calls Button. Now, go back out there. Enjoy the party."

Do put ice cubes in a short glass, poured a healthy shot from the Dewar's bottle, and then added a splash of water and a twist of lemon. Handing the drink to me he added, "She told me she's free-spirited and open-minded and that life in the jungle with the Indians felt right."

I couldn't comment.

Knowing he had me cornered, he continued. "What's normal to her shouldn't be threatening to you. What's liberal today will be conservative tomorrow. What's avant guard today is passé tomorrow. That's the way life is." He took a drag on his cigarette. "Her societal group in New York may be a step ahead of ours, and what's right for her, you view as far out. Right now, as you say, she may be confused. But that may not be the word. Struggling. That's it. Perhaps she's struggling with issues; struggling with cultures. Is she a sophisticate from New York and the world—or—having been introduced to a primitive society, would she prefer to be with the natives?" He sipped his drink. "Does she prefer being in stylish Rome and Paris or with the primitive Yékuana tribe where she can wear what she wants and may be needed as their doctor or dentist? She did that, you know. Earlier she told me. She helped them. Even pulled some teeth. Maybe she found she has a better meaning for her life—more charitable, less self-centered—and she feels good. Could the Yékuana ways have so shattered her preconceptions that her life will be changed forever?"

"And what now, Dr. Lazzari?" I asked. Do always made sense, but especially when he'd had a few drinks and got on his soap box.

"Ah, come on, Catira. Forget it. It's all over."

It wasn't easy, but I rejoined the party.

The next morning, I got up, put on a robe, and met Charlie and Jean at the door as they were leaving. I thanked them for coming and bade them goodbye as they left for Canaima.

I heard later that Irv, who never drank very much other than a beer or two, flew Alejandro to Puerto Ordaz. Julio called and said he'd take the day off, something about Martha not feeling well. Frank slept until noontime.

Do awakened and dressed early as he had business in Bolivar, but before he left, we chatted over breakfast and a cigarette. Jean, of course, was the subject of conversation.

Impressed by Jean, Do resumed the previous evening's conversation about her as though there had been no interruption for sleep. "She'll find herself," Do said. "Give her time and distance. She'll sort this out. But I am more disturbed by her companions, the Italian associates. They did her a disservice by talking about her," he said, referring to their comments about Jean having gone native. He reminded me that her associates were away all day mining and Jean, most probably, was lonesome. "Who else could she make friends with if not the Indians—or a pet snake, if, indeed, she had one. A pet snake? Who cares? You have pet dogs and birds." He added that if she liked to be naked—well, so what? If it was hot and steamy, maybe being naked just felt good. Maybe she was on her way to the river for a swim to cool off. The Indians wouldn't care—half the time they run around naked themselves. Hell, diamond miners, men and women, are often naked when they work in the rivers." He looked at his watch, "Hey, I'd better get going." He stood up and put on his sunglasses. "You and Frank were great last night. You reintroduced her to civilization, to conversation, to music, friendship, laughter. Hell, to a party. Catira, she'd been deprived of so much for so long." Do thought she'd handled it well and added, "Now she has the experience to learn and compare life's undertakings—primitive and civilized—if you can call us civilized. May I borrow your car for a while?"

I regretted I'd not asked Jean about some of the stories we'd heard. But when I thought further, I'd hear Do's voice in my head saying, "Why did you want to know? What difference would it make? She told us she enjoys freedom in the jungle. She admires the Indians and their ways. How much more does she have to say? Drop it." Then I could hear him follow-up saying something like; "Boredom and the snake were her companions; the jungle her sanctuary and refuge."

Jean and Do, unknowingly, helped me through another stage of growing up.

Some years later, I read about Jean Liedloff in Vogue Magazine. A short item reported that the New York socialite and writer had returned from her fourth visit to the Orinoco.

One of her visits had been to the Tauripan Tribe near Auyántepui. She made three expeditions to the Yekuana and Sanema tribes on the Ventuari River in the Amazon Region near Brazil, spending many months each time studying their behavioral characteristics and culture.

During the 1970's, she was back in the news as the acclaimed author of the best-selling book, *The Continuum Concept: In Search Of Happiness Lost*, in which she reveals that living with the indigenous people caused her to radically change her own view of human nature. She has devoted her life's work to this study, offering a new understanding of how we've lost our well-being and showing practical ways to regain it for our children and ourselves.

She writes in The *Continuum Concept,* "I had a wildly romantic love and awe of the great, uncaring forest, and while preparing to leave, was already thinking of ways and means to come back."

On the back cover of the book is a quotation from *The New York Times Book Review:* "Deserves to be read by Western parents, child psychologists, and other social engineers concerned with restoring self-reliance and well-being. There are remarkable insights here." The book has had twenty-six printings.

Also on the back cover of Jean Liedloff's book, is a quotation from Gloria Steinem: "A book we all should read . . . to help us become nurturing parents and advocates for our own child within, to understand what we missed, and to restore it."

Jean authored several articles for magazines including *Mothering Magazine* and *Saturday Evening Post. Mothering Magazine* has called her a "living treasure."

People with whom she appeared on television include Barbara Walters, Hugh Downs and Johnny Carson. She would have liked to appear with Oprah Winfrey.

Several years ago, while researching this book, my editor insisted I call Jean Liedloff. I did not want to, but, as I said, he insisted. He said something like, "Open every door to the past." Jean was delightful and we chatted for an hour. She was a psychotherapist, never married and, when we spoke, she shared a houseboat in Sausalito, California, with her little cat, Tulip. She put Tulip near the phone so that I could hear her purring. She did not remember a snake being a pet, but did recall returning from one trip with a monkey.

Jean said she remembers very little about her first expedition and did not remember me nor recall the visit at my home, the party or Frank. She did remember Charlie Baughan and Julio Rojas. Of Charlie, she said, "Charlie? He was crazy," and we again agreed there is a place for visionaries and dreamers like Charlie in our world. Of Julio, she said seductively, "Oh, yes. I remember him."

Of the indigenous people, she said she learned about them by "observing human nature." The natives, she recounted, wore no clothes except for a loin cloth, usually red, and "strings." She recalled they took vines and other things they grow, rolled it in bark and put it in their mouths under their lower lip. "It may give them a high." From her comment, I presumed she had not tried the custom.

She said, *LOOK* Magazine lost her photos of that first expedition and her article was not published.

As we said goodbye, she commented it was good to talk with someone "from old times." I was happy I called her.

Jean died on March 15, 2011, a month before I sent this book to the publisher.

Chapter 26

Search and Rescue Operation

Dear Mother and Dad   April 20, 1954

In this business, we get into everything! Now, it's a search and rescue operation. It was all put together tonight.

Six days ago a small private plane, a Navion, flown by a private pilot, left Caracas but did not reach its destination. Today, 30 planes arrived from Maiquetía.

They are part of a search and rescue operation. Other local planes, like ours, have been asked to join the search. The pilot of the missing plane filed a flight plan for Caicara, up the Orinoco about an hour and a half from CB. Frank was called by Governor Manuel Eudoro Sanchez Lanz who asked Frank to volunteer some aircraft to join in the search. What a life!

More later. All my love. Marilyn

There's a reason why our community of airmen refers to them as "Sunday Pilots;" from Monday to Friday they're professionals—doctors, lawyers, and business executives. Textbooks and flying magazines refer to these people as private and recreation pilots; they fly for the sheer love of flying. Some may be over-confident in their skills. While their planes have the basic instruments, instruments don't provide all the answers a pilot needs.

In the interior of Venezuela in 1954, meteorological information was unavailable. When you wanted to know weather conditions between you and your destination, you talked to pilots who had just come from there, or when you were in the air you turned on your air-to-air radio frequency and talked with other pilots flying within the range of your radio. A good option was to keep your eyes on the sky, watch weather conditions, and read cloud movements and formations.

High-tech navigational aids were non-existent. You had charts (maps) and a clear plastic odd-shaped ruler called a plotter to help you plan a route.

Paved airfields in the interior were few. Most airstrips were swaths cut in the savannahs or rainforests. The jungle was dense. A Green Hell, indeed.[13]

Sunday pilots, unknowingly, flirted with trouble. They often learned their avocation at flight schools at airports where they acquired the basic knowledge and skills to earn a pilot certificate.

Professional pilots usually learn to fly at four-year colleges and universities with aviation majors or in the military, and become commercial pilots—career pilots. They are top notch pilots who keep on learning and training. Flight experience is invaluable.

Venezuela's interior was fly-for-pay country, not fly-for-fun. But despite newspaper articles about private pilots lost and never found, they kept on coming and getting lost and professional pilots kept being called to search for them. In Venezuela, there was no rescue helicopter service, no Civil Air Patrol, but you could count on professional bush pilots to volunteer to help.

And that's just what they did one starry night.

Frank had returned from an early flight and, for a change, came directly home without an entourage of pilots and other friends. We dined early, near 8:00 p.m., and then we carried our coffee to the patio to enjoy peace and quiet under a starry sky. Our conversation was mundane. It had only been a short time since we'd entertained Jean Liedloff and so part of it concerned her. We wondered to where she had wandered.

Changing the subject, I said, "I'd like to fly to the moon. Think it will ever happen?"

The sound of the ringing telephone shattered the evening's stillness.

"Damn," he said. "It never fails."

The second ring was followed by the voice of Josefa who'd been washing dishes in the kitchen. "Capitán Frank. *Teléfono, por favor*" (Telephone, please).

"¿Quién?" he asked.

"El Gobernador Sanchez Lanz."

He got up from the lounge and stamped out his cigarette. His voice trailed off as he went in the house.

A few minutes later, he returned to the patio and sat on the foot of my lounge. "I'm sorry, Button. The Governor's called a meeting, eight-thirty in our hangar. Remember we watched a couple of military planes land just before six?"

"Yes." I sighed. "Are we about to have a party?"

"No. Nothing like that. The Air Ministry asked the Governor to organize a search and rescue effort to find a small airplane missing with four people aboard; those military planes are in the search and rescue." He stood up. "Come on inside. I'll tell you what it's about while I wash up. I've got to get going. Come to think of it," he set his demitasse cup on the cocktail table, "I think you can help me with this one. It's a job for both of us."

While he stripped off his work shirt, washed up, and changed to a long-sleeved guayabera sport shirt, he explained the Air Ministry and Military had been searching for a plane that had been reported overdue. The search was already six days old. The flight plan, filed in Caracas, identified the route it would fly to Caicara and the airfields along the way where it would land if it had an emergency. Caicara is a rural village 225 miles up the Orinoco from Ciudad Bolivar. Routinely, a search covered between five and ten miles each side of the route identified on the flight plan. Now the search would be expanded to include the 225 miles between Ciudad Bolivar and Caicara and about 100 miles north and south of the Orinoco; a highly unusual departure from the norm.

"Can you come with me tonight?" He splashed after-shave on his face.

"I'll meet you there. I have to wash up, too."

He stood in the doorway of the bedroom, anxious to get going but compelled to tell me more. "The two men missing are prominent medical doctors from Caracas, Ramela Vegas and Rafael Ernesto Lopez."

"And they are?"

"Lopez is one of the founders of Centro Medico. In 1947, they called him a great visionary. He was vice president of the group that founded the hospital." Centro Medico was the largest and most advanced medical center in Caracas. "Vegas," he continued, "is Dr. Big in medicine, investments and society. Both are well-heeled and generous philanthropists. They were flying in Vegas' plane; a Navion."

"Pillars of the community, so to speak," I said.

"Yes." He hesitated then said, "Their two passengers were ladies. I'll see you."

When I arrived at the hangar, Frank had already determined we could put one plane into the search and rescue operation each day for the duration of the search, and he was calling other air service owners asking them to join the search. Each pilot who agreed to fly was asked to recruit one or two people to go along as observers. Departure from CB, destination Caicara, would be at 6:00 a.m.

As word of the missing plane and the search operation spread rapidly through Ciudad Bolivar, town's people called to volunteer their help. Frank told me to invite to the briefing everyone who wanted to participate in the search; pilots and observers. Between calls, Frank asked if I'd fly with him as an observer.

"Sure." I loved to go flying anytime, anyplace. The S&R would be a new experience.

"And call Pulgar," he said. "See if he can join us. Ask him to meet us at the airport at five-thirty tomorrow morning. Oh yes, he should bring a gun and machete."

Blue Skies, Green Hell

"Pulgar. Good choice."

Rafael Pulgar was a friend of Frank's from the Hunt Club and a fellow Coleador. He worked at Western Union and I knew him as Pulgar, the man who sent my telegrams to my family in the U.S.

Months before the S&R, while hunting with Frank and Pulgar, he taught me how to shoot at moving targets with my rifle by having me stand on a narrow wooden bridge and shoot mango pods floating down a fast-moving stream.

Still on the phone, Frank gave a thumbs up when I advised him Pulgar would fly with us. He hung up. "Pulgar is a man of the land. He knows how to survive in the wilderness."

By 8:30 p.m., the work area in the hangar had filled with people. They sat on benches, 55-gallon drums, and rungs of stepladders. Usually, no one worked in the hangar after dark, so one bulb with a green metal shade that hung over a massive workbench provided the only light. A Captain in the Air Ministry opened the meeting by thanking everyone for volunteering and related the efforts already made to find Dr. Vegas and his passengers. So far, the search had been concentrated along the route south from Caracas to Caicara.

On the workbench, the Captain spread a map showing the land between Ciudad Bolivar and the base of operations in Caicara and north and south of the river. A grid was drawn on the map and pilots of military, air ministry, private, and commercial planes were assigned sectors on the grid, each to be searched by two planes. One plane would fly north and south while the other would fly east and west. The Captain advised the group that 55-gallon drums of fuel for the S&R planes had already been flown to Caicara in C-47 cargo planes. Fuel would be available until the search was concluded.

Frank received his assignments. We'd fly one sector during the morning, return to Caicara, gas up, eat lunch, and fly another sector in the afternoon. We'd return to Caicara, refuel, and fly home.

The Captain read from a list of instructions; land in a suitable and safe clearing near any sign of a small group of houses or even a lone person. He told us to ask if anyone, within the last few days, had seen a plane, heard an airplane engine missing, heard an explosion, or seen columns of smoke.

Further, because planes would be landing and taking off in rough, uncut, and untested fields they had to be light, no excess baggage. He strongly suggested only the most essential items be taken; machetes, first aid kits, guns, spare parts, and water.

Then the captain made the final announcement. "The doctor's plane is a single-engine Navion." He paused. "It's green."

Gasps echoed throughout the hangar.

"It's crazy," Frank muttered. Forests swallow a plane as soon as it hits the trees. Sometimes the tail assembly pokes up through the leaves. But the likelihood of seeing a green plane in green trees or on green savannahs and meadows

279

was slim; not much chance of surviving a plane crash in Green Hell. "Naïve. A Sunday pilot," he muttered softly.

The preferred colors for planes flying in Venezuela were silver and white. White planes are easiest to spot in an emergency and also help keep the interior of the plane several degrees cooler than outside temperature.

The meeting ended and the crowd dispersed. I caught up with Frank engaged in conversation with Governor Sanchez Lenz and two men I'd never seen before. The Governor had been quiet and I assumed he had nothing more to say having carried out the Air Ministry's request to assemble the right people for the mission. The Governor gave me an *abrazo* (hug) and Frank introduced me to the two men, Dr. Lopez's two brothers. Frank said he'd invited them to stay overnight at our home.

Walking to our car, I asked Frank if he had learned any details about Dr. Lopez's excursion with Dr. Vegas and their wives. Frank's answer was brief and he dismissed my question as though it hadn't been asked. "We have a job to do. We don't ask questions." He brushed something from his eye. "The women are not their wives."

That was the end of our peaceful night under a starry sky.

By 5:30 a.m., the airport buildings and the control tower were ablaze with lights. It was hard to speak above the din of airplane engines being run up and their systems checked.

In the baggage compartment behind the rear seat in Frank's plane, I saw a toolbox, a box with a few small spare parts, and a first aid kit. I added my Savage 22 rifle to Frank's guns, ammunition, the Very pistol, extra flares, and several bottles of water.

Pulgar arrived early. He wore his pistol in a holster on his belt and the sharpened edge of the machete he carried glinted in the light outside our hangar. His gear was added to the cache behind the back seat. A thermos of coffee had just been set in the plane when Frank returned from the terminal and said he'd filed the flight plan. We boarded the plane. I sat in the right front seat. Pulgar sat in the back. It was 6:00 a.m. and we were ready to roll.

The sky, cloudless in the early dawn, looked inviting. Had it not been such a tragic mission, it would have been a beautiful day to go flying; CAVU—clear air and visibility unlimited. Four single-engine planes and two twins moved slowly on the taxi strip in front of us. One by one, they turned on to the runway, increased their speed and took off. They headed west up-river to Caicara. Then it was our turn.

Single-engine planes were preferred for the search as they could land and take off in savannahs where information might be received from *vaqueros* or *campesinos* (cowboys or field workers). Twin-engine planes could seldom land in small clearings. When pilots flying twins saw something that triggered their interest, they'd try to contact small planes in the area or return to Caicara where a small plane would follow their lead. The twins, of course, had greater fuel capacity, could stay up longer, and cover more distance in less time.

We were airborne when the CB tower operator's voice crackled through the radio. He wished us good luck and a safe journey. A nice touch.

We left the good earth, turned left 180 degrees and flew up and away from the sunrise and civilization on the south bank of the Orinoco. We flew at about 1,500 feet for one and one half hours to Caicara. Along the way, we looked for signs of wreckage or survivors. Frank said, "Planes just don't fall out of the sky and disappear. They leave telltales like skid marks or a trail of broken tree limbs. Maybe you'll see only the tail assembly peeping from tree tops." The region was flat. Miles of desolate wilderness. I also saw a mix of large tropical forests with savannahs and meadows carved out within them. From our altitude, the land below looked like a tapestry in shades of green.

"Why do you suppose," I spoke loudly to be heard over the sound of the engine, "reports of the missing plane were never in the newspaper and yet the search has been going on for days? Who authorized this massive effort?"

Frank didn't answer.

"This is costing the government plenty of money."

"I don't know the answers to your questions," he said stoically and detached as he adjusted his trim.

After awhile I mused, "I wonder who the female passengers were."

"Maybe the ladies on the flight are medical professionals on a medical mission to the interior." Changing the subject he said, "That's Caicara ahead."

Flying low over the small village in the middle of nowhere whose population numbered about 1,800, I saw houses made of mud compound with metal or green plastic corrugated roofs and roads that looked like slashes in the earth's surface. Bronze-colored children ran in the roads and waved to the incoming planes.

On the outskirts of Caicara, I saw the airfield and a small shed that served as a shelter for waiting passengers. I quickly counted about twenty aircraft. Some were parked. Others, flown by pilots from Ciudad Bolivar in the east, San Fernando de Apure to the west and Calabozo, northwest, jockeyed for parking places next to the airstrip. In addition to military planes, other planes joining the operation were owned by oil companies normally used for pipeline inspections, and planes from steel companies and large construction companies whose aircraft usually carried personnel and spare parts to and from their field operations. They came from all points of the compass. I thought it unusual for the Governor, Air Ministry, and military to participate in a search for civilians. I also thought better than to query Frank.

A windsock told Frank the direction in which to land and, once on the ground, military personnel marshaled us to our parking space. Accustomed only to a single-engine plane making a few visits each week, the little town's houses and the ground they stood on shook with the thunder of the heavy C-47s.

At the airstrip command post, a large map spread on the ground was marked with the same grid lines we'd seen at the meeting in our hangar. Each pilot checked the map to confirm his sectors. Frank received confirmation and a few last minute instructions. We stretched our legs and chatted with others involved in the search while local workers topped off the planes' gas tanks.

With refueling completed, we boarded our plane and took off.

Caicara is on the south side of the Orinoco. Both of our designated sectors were north of the Orinoco which pleased me immensely. Most of the terrain north of the river is savannah land with morichales (heavily forested areas) bordering rivers and tributaries. They are not as foreboding as the dense rainforests south of the river where you fly over rainforests and finally jungle. The difference between rainforests and jungle is the amount of annual rainfall. Frank planned to fly about three hours, return to Caicara, refuel, eat lunch and fly to our second sector. Our plane, a Cessna 170, could fly about four hours on a full tank of fuel.

"Is there a place for lunch?" I asked.

"There's an arepa stand near the airfield," Frank said. "They also sell *ChiCha* (a drink made of rice)."

"You can have arepas if you want, but I brought along cheese sandwiches, water, crackers, fruit and napkins. The water won't be cold, but it won't have amoebas, either. I brought enough for us three and a little more in case of an emergency."

I flew the plane while Frank studied the chart. "You disobeyed the Captain by bringing along a bag of lunch," he said. "I disobeyed him, too. I brought an extra chart."

"I also brought binoculars—and my camera."

I flew the plane due north until Frank said we were entering our sector. "Start to descend," he said. "Go to 1,000 feet. Then we'll see what we can see."

Although the plane was cruising slowly, everything below seemed to be whizzing by swiftly.

"I can't see, Frank. If a plane's down there I'll miss it!"

"You'll get used to it." Frank took the controls. "We'll descend to 800 feet when we're over morichales, you know—the heavy foliage by waterways? And we'll go lower if we see something to confirm. You'll be okay."

We crossed our sector, first in one direction, then the other and saw nothing suspicious.

"How come there are clearings in the middle of the forests?" I asked.

"Sometimes they're caused by fire. Maybe a lightning strike," Frank replied. "And sometimes local people burn the land or cut down the trees to clear the land for farming. They may need the wood for building their houses. Even mud houses with thatch roofs use wood."

We'd been flying two hours when Frank spotted a group of men on horseback near a large clearing. He circled and landed. We got out of the plane, met the men and explained our mission. They gestured wildly and spoke excitedly. Yes, they'd seen a plane, a green plane. No, they couldn't remember when. Yes, its engine was missing. Yes, it fell in flames. No, they heard no explosion. No, they couldn't remember where. According to their reports, whatever could have happened to the doctor's plane did happen. Pulgar questioned them all.

While most told their stories, others took more interest in our plane and approached it hesitantly.

Frank asked me to stand guard. "Don't let them get on the plane. They can look inside, but keep them out." Then he added, "Button. They're gentle people. They're curious. They've probably never seen a plane up close before. They don't understand."

He was right. They didn't understand—neither my Spanish nor my intentions as I tried to keep them off the plane in a kindly manner. Later, Frank told me the men on horseback had spoken a dialect very difficult even for him to understand. Pulgar fared much better.

Frank found it impossible to separate their facts from fiction. We took off, followed all leads, but drew blanks.

Landing near another small group of men on horses, we asked the same questions and got the same answers. Sometimes, while we were talking to riders, other aircraft on the search would join us and the pilots would share updates. And so the time passed.

Back in Caicara, we noticed most of the pilots had also brought lunches in paper bags. Many sat on the ground under their planes to eat or stood in the shade of the plane's wings. Others simply stretched out on the ground to sleep. A gentle breeze wafted across the savannah and despite the large number of planes and men, it was quiet. Eerily quiet.

It felt good to step out of the plane and stretch my legs. Oh, how they ached and we still had a few more hours to fly. Slowly, I stretched my arms over my head, bent down. Even my back felt stiff.

By 1:00 p.m., we'd finished eating and the local gasolineros had refueled our plane. We were ready to board and head out again. The terrain in our new sector was much the same as that which we'd flown over during the morning with a few more square miles of rainforest. Frank flew at about 1,000 feet; at that low altitude, the turbulent ride came as no surprise.

My eyes felt dry and my limbs continued to ache from being confined in the small plane. Pulgar and I shared the binoculars. No one spoke. We watched the forest pass under us. We saw nothing.

From one second to the next, the engine kicked and missed and the nose of the single-engine Cessna dipped. We didn't lose all our power, but we started losing altitude, and our bodies tugged and strained at the seat belts. The plane vibrated.

Because of his training and experience, Frank was in the habit of scanning the sky around him for other aircraft as well as the ground below for open spaces. He said we'd flown over a clearing in the forest and he'd head back to it. Fortunately, we had enough airspeed for him to make a 180 degree turn. "If we're lucky, we'll get there. If we're luckier, it'll be long enough for us to land in."

Frank called to Pulgar in Spanish to tighten his belt and hang on.

"Tighten your belt, Button. Slide your seat back so I can see out your window."

I scrunched to my right to give him the room he needed to work.

He fought the controls—pulling and pushing knobs, flipping switches, and making adjustments. Because we'd been flying low we had no excess altitude and our glide path was short. He did whatever it took to maintain altitude. As we descended, I peeked ahead and had an unobstructed view of the clearing with scrub brush and small trees scattered here and there.

I felt the plane start to fly a little sideways as we flew over the trees; Frank was side-slipping the plane for a short landing. The vibrations worsened as the engine's performance deteriorated. It was missing badly. He had neither airspeed nor altitude to fly over the untested field to look for obstructions before landing; it was make it on the first try—or else.

The Stall Warning blared; there wasn't enough air going over the wings to keep the plane aloft. We floated over the tree line and were so close to the trees' top branches I instinctively pulled my knees up to my chin. I saw bachacos (ant hills) in tall grasses and narrow paths that crisscrossed the field. The diameter of young trees that had looked like mere twigs from 1,000 feet, were sturdy saplings and the bushes were thick, large enough to snag a wing or the tail assembly or tear up a landing gear. He straightened the plane. We were a few feet off the ground when he pulled the yoke fully back and the plane flared. It dropped into the clearing and rolled and bounced on the rough terrain. He applied pressure to one brake then the other to avoid ground obstacles and to slow the plane as it whizzed toward the trees at the far end of the clearing. The scrub brush banging the belly of the fuselage never let up and I felt we were going too fast. "Oh, my God," I said softly and closed my eyes.

And then it was over. The plane stopped a few feet in front of the tall trees at the far end of the clearing. Frank turned off the ignition. It was quiet.

I exhaled the breath I'd been holding.

Blue Skies, Green Hell

"Everyone okay?" Frank's voice was soft, but strong and steady.

"I'm fine," I said.

"*Estoy bien*," Pulgar replied. "*Gracias a Diós, Y a tu también*" (I'm okay. Thank God and you, too).

"Mayday. Mayday," Frank called on the radio. Aircraft should have been in the area, but no one replied to his transmission. "Well, let's see what the hell happened . . . although I think I know."

I slid my seat forward and hopped out then Pulgar exited from the back seat.

We three walked around the plane, looking at it from low and high and after a quick examination of the plane's exterior, Frank said he saw only superficial damage to the fuselage; a few minor dents and scratches. The exterior damage might affect the plane's optimum performance, but nothing we couldn't fly with. We'd have more drag caused by the small dents on the leading edge of the tail assembly. But the propeller had been roughed up with dings and chips. Much worse, one of the blades was slightly bent.

Frank slapped it as he walked past. "This could be serious. Even if I can fix the problem with the engine, it might be tough getting out of here with this prop." He didn't elaborate. "Pulgar, let's get the tools." They unloaded everything from the compartment behind the rear seat.

"See the rock over there?" he said to me gesturing to a spot near the edge of the clearing. "Take these extra flares and the ammo for our guns over there. And the thermos of water. Take your rifle, too. Can you handle all that?"

"I can." I slung my rifle in its case over my shoulder. With two hands free, I picked up the other items.

He handed me the Very pistol. It looked like an ordinary pistol with a snub-nose barrel. "This is a Very pistol—a flare gun. It's not too effective in daylight, Button." I watched as he loaded it. "But if a plane goes over, shoot a flare, anyway."

I nodded. "Okay."

He placed the cardboard box containing parts and the toolbox 50 feet into the clearing. Then he trotted to the rock where I stood and drank from the thermos.

"Keep your eyes and ears open and load your rifle." He lit a cigarette. "If people come, don't be afraid. They'll be like the people in the savannah we met this morning." He sipped more water, stamped out his cigarette, broke apart the butt and scattered the tobacco to avoid starting a grass fire. He pulled a handkerchief from his back pocket and wiped the sweat from his forehead.

"Animals? Wildlife?" I asked timidly.

"Just butterflies, Button. The ones in your tummy." Then he added, "I don't really know. Maybe jaguars or tapirs, you know, the kind that roam outside CB?" He sipped more water. "They're probably out there, but unless the plane disturbed them, they won't come out of the woods 'til after dark when it's cooler. I've got to go look at that engine, damn it."

"Indians?"

"If there are any, they'll be friendly. Just smile and be nice. Then gently call me."

"And snakes, Frank?"

"Possibly. You know, they're not all deadly."

"I don't like any of them."

"Give yourself distance if you can. If a snake seems to be coming toward you, shoot it." He walked to the plane. He knew what had to be done and our chances of flying out depended on him.

"Pulgar," Frank called to his friend who'd already started hacking the bushes, tall grass, and weeds from the field. In landing, our plane's wheels had flattened the grass and Pulgar had a clear path to follow. "Can you help me roll the plane into the clearing? Over there where I've put the boxes." He looked at his watch. It was 3:10 p.m. "If a plane flies over, we want them to see us, but we have to leave enough room for someone to land."

At the aviation academy, Frank's studies included classes in aircraft engine maintenance and repair. If he determined the cause of the malfunction, he'd probably know how to fix it. The plane's cowling was held in place by Phillips Head screws, and a quick inventory of the tools in the toolbox revealed the Phillips Head screwdriver was worn and barely serviceable. He dug further into the tool box and removed a file. Using the file and a rock, Frank shaped the screwdriver and finally removed the screws that held the cowling secure. He pulled the plane's spark plugs and realized his worst fear. They all needed to be replaced, but the box of spare parts contained only two new plugs. The others in the box had been used and should have been pitched out long ago. Surely, back at the hangar in Ciudad Bolivar, he'd learn why our toolbox contained worn out tools and used spare parts, and why this plane was overdue for routine maintenance. I read his thoughts; he'd get to the bottom of this and heads would roll.

Frank looked into the sun. It would set soon and a lot of time had already been lost. The trip back to Caicara had to be made in daylight with our arrival no later than 6:00 p.m.

If we were to get out of this field before twilight, he had to move with haste.

Only Frank's filing and hammering and Pulgar's whacking of the machete broke the silence in the hot steamy savannah. I sat and scanned the sky and then the brush.

He installed the two new plugs, then using the same file and rock he'd used on the screwdriver, he cleaned the carbon residue from the remaining plugs, regapped their electrodes and reinstalled them.

Blue Skies, Green Hell

With the cowling back in place, Frank paced off the length of the field and looked over the topography. Pulgar had done a fine job eliminating obstructions.

We three gathered by the plane. "Let me tell you where we stand," Frank said. "If we can get up and out, we'll make it back to Caicara." He gestured southwest. "The field is long enough, under normal conditions. But these aren't normal conditions." With his handkerchief, he again wiped sweat from his forehead. "We have two new spark plugs plus four with regapped electrodes. If we can get up enough power and speed to get this plane in the air, and if the wind doesn't shift, and if the damaged prop doesn't add too much drag, I believe we have a chance." He unscrewed the top of a thermos bottle and took a swig of water.

He lit a cigarette, held it high and watched the smoke drift.

"How's it look?" I asked.

"The wind's light. It's okay. It's coming from the east." He hated to play the "what if" game, but he laid it straight out for us. "We'll fly out from west to east, same as we landed." Then looking at the field ahead, he muttered, "I think it was the spark plugs that brought us down. I just hope it wasn't a load of bum gas. We're using fuel from those drums brought to Caicara." Then he took his fuel tester and drained a fuel sample from the tank in each wing, held each test up to the sky and studied it. "Looks okay," he muttered. He stared at the trees at the end of the field. "We've got to get over those trees. Okay. We've done all we can, but we have options. We can try to fly out, walk out, or wait for a plane to fly over, come down and help us. What do you think?"

"You have to call the shot, Frank," I said.

"Pulgar?" he asked.

"*Tu tienes que hacer la decisión*" (You have to make the decision), he answered.

"We have to lighten the plane," Frank said. "Strip it bare."

He pitched out the toolbox containing the useless tools, although Frank's retooled Phillips Head screwdriver was spared. Evidence, I thought.

Odds and ends that had collected in the baggage compartment over time were dumped. I put my lipstick, cigarettes, matches and *cédula* (Photo Identification required of everyone by the Federal Government) in my shirt pockets and pitched my heavy pocketbook. Reluctantly, I tossed the leftover lunch. I felt like a bandit when I hid my Kodak Hawkeye camera under the front seat.

It was almost 5:00 p.m. "At five it's light and at five-thirty it's dark," Frank reminded me. "There is no dusk, no dawn in the tropics. Time's running out, Button."

He turned to Pulgar. "Thanks, *amigo*," and speaking in Spanish he said. "You've cleared this place so nicely, we'll name it Pulgar Field. And we won't forget it." He smiled and gave his friend an *abrazo*. "First, I'll fly out alone, circle luck and land. Then I'll know more." He spread his extra map on the ground. "We're about here," he said pointing to a spot north-east of Caicara. "Take this," he said, and gently folded his pocket compass into my hand. "The river is south. Maybe fifty miles. There's always activity on the Orinoco. Caicara is west."

Pulgar and I received Frank's unspoken message. We simply nodded.

Frank kissed me. "I'll get you out—we'll all get out. We'll all get home." He started to walk away, but he turned back. "Button, Pulgar's a good man, he knows his way in the wilderness. He'll get you out—if it comes to that." As he walked toward the plane he called over his shoulder, "*Ayúdame, por favor, Pulgar*" (Help me, please). They pushed the plane to the back of the clearing.

I fought that choked-up feeling you sometimes get when you want to cry—or throw up.

Earlier, my heart had pounded with fear when the engine missed and Frank prepared to make the forced landing. For just a wee moment my mind leapt back to the C-46 when both engines quit over the Caribbean. I tried to block out that heart-stopping episode.

Now he had to test the plane. I'd seen him go through this routine many times; install a new engine, test the plane; replace the magnetos, test the plane.

He climbed into the plane, closed the door, buckled up, and turned on the ignition. The engine whined and kicked over. It sounded rough as he ran it up and went through an abbreviated pre-flight check. I knew the plane would start, but Frank's comments about getting enough power and speed, possibly having contaminated fuel in the tanks, and having a damaged prop ripped through my head. I prayed he'd get off the ground safely. The trees looked near and tall.

Then he let the plane roll and gain speed. I saw his flaps set for a short-field takeoff. The tail came up early in his roll and the plane lifted off the ground. I saw its nose point skyward. He skimmed over the trees. He was airborne. The engine gave all it could, but 145 horses were not pulling.

He circled the strip and started to sideslip for a short landing when I heard another aircraft overhead.

I looked in the direction from where the sound came and saw Pogo in his shiny new plane. I got off a flare from the Very pistol just as Frank's wheels touched the ground. He'd made it down safely and Pogo, one of the pilots from Ciudad Bolivar, had seen the flare. Rocking his wings as he passed overhead, Pogo circled, made his approach, side-slipped the plane and landed.

Frank taxied his plane to the side of the clearing, shut down the engine, hopped out of the plane and trotted to me. He said he'd seen the flare and had seen Pogo.

"Good job, Button. Now, if Pogo's got a couple of plugs, we're in business. If not, we'll rethink our situation. This ship won't make it with two people aboard."

Pogo, with two observers, taxied to our plane. He was a cute kid with blonde hair and a bright smile. I imagined he was twenty-two and probably came from a rich American family who gave him a new plane, an allowance, and here he was. He'd make a trip if an air service needed a pilot, but he never seemed to need money. Pogo, a carefree kid, just hung out at the airport in Ciudad Bolivar. We called him "Pogo" because he usually had a Pogo comic book rolled up in his back pocket and that's all we ever saw him read.

Frank explained our situation.

"I've got some plugs," Pogo volunteered. His observers jumped out of the plane and Pogo opened the baggage compartment. Like everything about Pogo's plane, his toolbox and the spare parts were shiny new. "I've got two plugs. You can have them."

"That'll help. Now, I have four new plugs plus two I fixed. I hope that does it. By the way, you got a spare prop in there some place?" Frank joked.

Using Pogo's new, shiny Phillips Head screwdriver, they removed the cowling, changed two plugs, and replaced the cowling. Pogo said he had room for one person in his plane.

"Pulgar, *vayas tu con Pogo. Yo me voy con Frank*" (Go with Pogo. I'll go with Frank). I said. I wanted to be with Frank, no matter what. I also weighed less than Pulgar.

"Pogo, you go out first," Frank suggested. "If I go first and have trouble, I might block the strip and you'd never get out."

"I'll stay 'til you get it started," Pogo replied.

"It'll start, all right. The question is power. And the damaged prop. And I'm not sure about the gas. It looks clean, but I don't know. I got off when I was alone. But I didn't have full RPMs. We've already thrown out a lot of stuff, and now with your two new plugs, we've got a better chance." Frank was concerned, and I saw a serious, subdued Pogo. "It's the damn prop."

"Looks like I've got plenty of room for takeoff," Pogo said reassuringly.

"I paced it off. It'll be enough for you, even with three passengers. That's for sure."

"I guess I'll go. See you in Caicara. Hey, amigo, vaya con Diós" (Go with God). Pogo's passengers had already boarded.

"Thanks. He'll be with all of us," I said. "*Hasta luego*, Pulgar" (Until later). I waved.

Pogo walked to his plane and called back to Frank, "I'll circle 'til you take off, then I'll hang on your tail 'til we see Caicara. I'll land first."

"Thanks, Pogo. I owe you one."

"Okay. But you owe me two—two plugs."

In his baggage compartment, Pogo found room for our equipment, useless tools, used plugs, my heavy pocketbook and some of the other things we'd reluctantly tossed out of our plane. My camera was still under my front seat. He started his engine, roared down Pulgar Field and flew over the trees with plenty of room to spare. He was up in seconds.

"Our turn, Frank said." We boarded our plane. I slid my seat back, buckled my belt tightly, and moved as far to the right as possible. I sat low and the nose of the ship pointed upward so I saw only the instrument panel and blue sky above.

The engine whined then it caught and roared. Frank pressed hard on the brakes as he increased the power. The plane's vibration exceeded the usual. He eased back on the throttle and moved the plane to where the cleared field began.

The engine was rough and the tachometer's needle was not quite where it should have been. I said nothing as Frank pushed the throttle forward. The plane rolled and the tail wheel lifted. Then I saw the tree line. The plane gained speed. *Too slow.* I looked at the tachometer. *Not enough RPMs.* I peeked out the side window and saw the flaps were down. Straight ahead, I saw the line of trees. They were coming at us fast. Under the best conditions, the most crucial part of flying an aircraft is takeoff. Frank put back pressure on the yoke and we lifted off. He kept his right hand on the throttle. I squinted through my eye lashes as we struggled over the tree tops. He retracted the flaps. The plane vibrated, but we were on our way to Caicara. Pogo pulled up next to us, saluted and then circled back to tail us. It was about 5:45 p.m.

"Now, we just have to keep her going for a while."

We flew south and through the side window I watched the sun dip behind clouds and then below the horizon. We didn't say much. I don't know what Frank was thinking. But me? I listened sharply for I didn't know what and felt every vibration. Once in a while Frank said, "We're doing okay, Button."

At the Orinoco River, we changed our heading to south-west. We kept the river in sight. The flight seemed long, although it wasn't, and we congratulated each other when we saw Caicara in the distance. Just a few street lamps lit the main street and Plaza Bolivar.

Pogo pulled ahead of us and increased his speed. We lagged behind, still at a slow but safe speed knowing Pogo would buzz the town and circle until vehicles came to the airstrip, lined up side by side on both sides of the field with their headlights lighting the strip. This was the usual method of lighting a field when there were no lights at the field's edge and a plane needed to land after dark. One by one, the cars and jeeps came from the town and lined up on the sides of the airfield. The airstrip's illumination was good. Pogo landed and rolled quickly off the field. We were on final. Then we landed and rolled to a parking place next to Pogo's plane, stopped and shut down the engine.

Almost shocked by the sudden quietness, I felt an emotional let-down rather than jubilation. Frank pushed his seat back and stared through the windshield.

After a few moments, Frank said, "When I started to have engine trouble, my first concern was for you." He patted my thigh. "If you had become—ah—hysterical, I couldn't have made it." He paused then turned his head and looked at me. "I'm thinking about your last trip on the C-46. Now you've got this to add to your memory book!"

"Back there—when I heard the engine miss—I thought about that trip in the C-46, too. But you weren't with me. This time, I wasn't as frightened. I was with you."

"The old plane came through," he said unbuckling his seat belt and beginning his after-landing and securing checklists.

"You came through, Frank."

Pogo and his passengers had already been taken to town.

It was 6:30 p.m. "Do we sleep in the plane?" I asked.

Just then a jeep came to our plane and picked us up. The driver of the jeep introduced Frank to his passenger, the Mayor of Caicara.

"Button," Frank said, "This is the Mayor of Caicara. We've been invited to his house."

Having been up since 5:00 a.m. and flown seven hours and forty minutes, we were exhausted. As I left the plane, I grabbed my camera. I shook the Mayor's hand. The invitation sounded fine. "*Gracias y mucho gusto a conocerle, Señor Alcalde*" (Thank you, I'm pleased to meet you, Mr. Mayor).

As we drove off the airfield, I noticed a group of pilots standing around a plane that had landed earlier. The Mayor's driver stopped the jeep. "*Qué va*" (What goes)? Several men left the group and jogged to our jeep. Frank didn't hear the conversation as he was writing on the clipboard he'd brought from the plane. But I listened.

The Mayor looked perplexed as he talked with one of the pilots in the group.

"Frank," I said.

He raised his head. "Yes?"

"I think they're talking about a plane down somewhere northeast of here. Not the Navion. I think they may be talking about us. Maybe someone saw us."

A pilot in the group had indeed reported having seen a plane down. The group, now including the Mayor, had begun to arrange a search and rescue for the downed plane, until Frank interrupted and said we were the ones in that downed plane. The Mayor had not realized he'd picked up survivors of a crippled plane that had made an emergency landing, and then limped back to Caicara. He extended an invitation for everyone to have drinks and dinner at his house to celebrate our safe return.

The streets in Caicara were dirt and the houses, including the Mayor's, were made of a mud compound and only a narrow curb separated the house from the street. We felt good. We were safe. But we still had that 225 mile trip home tomorrow in a crippled aircraft.

The walls of the Mayor's house were about two feet thick and the front door was made of heavy wood planks, joined and held together by four cross pieces nailed on the inside. I saw no lock. Each of the three windows, without glass, faced the street. Curtains hung from strings tied to upright bars over the windows. The interior of the house was typically Spanish, having rooms on the perimeter and an open courtyard in the center with trees and plants. The metal corrugated roof of the house extended over a walkway that passed in front of the doorways of the rooms and around the courtyard. The floors were cement.

Members of the search and rescue operation who had accepted the invitation to stay overnight at the Mayor's had hung their chinchoros in the courtyard between trees and posts used to hold up the roof of the house. Candles burned everywhere and provided the only light. Electricity in Caicara was available only intermittently.

Until now, the stress of the emergency landing, the rough flight back to Caicara and the thought of the flight home tomorrow had occupied my mind, but the appetizing aroma of food cooking filled the courtyard and suddenly I realized I was hungry. The household staff had prepared dinner for everyone; casave, fried plantains, black beans and chicken with rice. It was superb as was the demitasse of strong black Venezuelan coffee served at the end of the meal.

Shortly after dinner the men settled in their chinchorros.

The Mayor walked toward us and gestured to a chinchorro for Frank.

"*Y para la Señora,*" said the Mayor, "*Es mi placer a ofrecerte mi cuarto y mi cama. Yo dormiré con los hombres en el patio. Hasta mañana, Señora*" (And for the señora, it is my pleasure to offer you my room and my bed. I will sleep with the men in the patio. Until tomorrow). He nodded his head, shook my hand and left Frank and me standing in the bedroom.

"I'd rather be in a chinchorro near you," I whispered to Frank.

"You'll sleep okay. It's been a long day." We sat on the edge of the bed. "Pretty nice," he said bouncing lightly on the mattress. "I'm sorry you can't be with me outside, too, but you're the only woman in the search party and the Mayor has offered you his room and bed."

"Frank. Have you thought about Mrs. Vegas and Mrs. Lopez?"

"No, Button, I haven't." He reminded me, "I've said it before. We don't get involved. We don't ask questions. We're bush pilots. We do a job. And when it's over—we go home." He reminded me that the doctors are important in Caracas. "They've each done fine work and if they're found alive, they'll continue to do good work. If we don't find them, well, the good work is what will be remembered." He kissed me. "I love you, Button." He left.

I never brought up the subject again.

Blue Skies, Green Hell

There was no bedroom door, only a colorful drape covered the opening. The interior walls were the same as the exterior ones, but inside the Mayor's bedroom, the walls were painted white and the hand-hewn woodwork was dark brown. I saw one window with a half curtain tied to the iron bars; shutters mounted on the interior wall were open. The large mahogany dresser, rocking chair, and bed were polished and the sheets and pillow cases were sparkling white and inviting. I kicked off my shoes and collapsed on the bed. I blew out the lone candle on a mahogany night stand next to the bed. The bed was comfortable and I was very tired.

Despite the heat and strong coffee I went to sleep. I don't know how long I slept, but I awakened when my jeans and checked cotton shirt stuck to my sweaty body. I rolled over and fell asleep again. However, I awakened several times—my sleep interrupted by visions of shiny machetes swinging at jungle trees and vines, and by scenes of men riding on huge horses that flailed the air with their front legs high. I pulled the pillow over my head when I heard boisterous children cavorting on the wreckage of a burned airplane with bodies still strapped in it. I saw a Stone Age Indian standing close by my bed. Terror wouldn't leave me. Without opening my eyes I prayed to God for the dawn to break quickly.

I drifted off again, but the vision of the Indian tormented me. "Go away," I said aloud.

I stretched, rubbed my eyes, and opened them slowly. The dim daylight of dawn peeked through the window and lighted the room and, indeed, I saw an Indian standing next to my bed. My mouth was dry with fear, intimidated by the vision of this barefooted Indian wearing only a red loin cloth. He had a broad nose. His black hair was cut off all around just over his ears. He had bangs. I'd seen pictures of Stone Age Indians and knew this Indian came from another civilization. He carried a stick in one hand and a puppy in the other. I reminded myself no hostile tribes inhabited this region of Venezuela. I blinked my eyes. We continued to stare at each other. The room was lighter now. I saw his large black eyes fixed on me and his face wore no expression. Finally, I closed my eyes and remained very still, barely breathing.

I opened my eyes slowly. The Indian had vanished.

I heard stirring in the courtyard and had just put on my shoes when three darling little girls, wearing white dresses, came in the room carrying a basin of water and a towel. They removed the candle, placed the bowl and towel on the night stand. I thanked them and they stayed on, giggling as they watched me splash the water in my face and on the back of my neck. The cool water refreshed me and helped me recover from the tormented sleep.

Just as they left, Frank came in. "Good morning, Button. I see you had early morning company."

"You saw him?" I whispered slowly.

"I saw three little girls. Looked like they didn't want to leave. They probably never saw fair skin and blue eyes before." Frank smiled.

"I don't mean the little girls. Early this morning. At daybreak," Speaking a little louder, I said, "I woke up, opened my eyes and I saw an Indian standing by my bed staring at me. I was scared." I put my hand on my chest. "He wore only a red loin cloth. He had a stick in one hand and a puppy in the other."

Frank waited a few long seconds then said, "How about some coffee, Button."

"I wasn't dreaming," I insisted and repeated my story. This time I spoke with a sense of urgency. "Didn't you see him?"

"Did he touch you or speak?"

"No. We just stared at each other."

"I'll look into it," he said. "Now, let's get something to eat. Another pilot said he had new spark plugs in his plane and he'd give me two. As soon as we've eaten, we can go to the airport, get the new plugs and be on our way home. Adiós, Caicara." He added, "We'll check the gas. The tanks were probably filled last night."

"What time is it?"

"About seven o'clock."

"May I borrow your comb? Pogo has my pocketbook in his plane."

Although breakfast was a delicious omelet, pastry and coffee I felt unsettled about the incident with the Indian and didn't eat much. "I want to say goodbye and thank the Mayor and ask him . . ."

Frank interrupted me. "He's already at the airport. We'll meet him there."

We learned Pulgar, with Pogo and the two observers, had taken off shortly after 6:00 a.m. Destination CB.

The fellow who'd driven us from the airfield to the Mayor's house the night before came to our breakfast table and said he'd drive us to the airport when we were ready.

We followed the driver to the jeep.

We'd driven about five minutes, when I shouted excitedly to the driver and Frank, "*Pare. Pare.* Stop the car! Stop the Car! Where's my camera? There he is, Frank. My Indian."

The jeep stopped and I hopped out, my Kodak Hawkeye Brownie in hand. The Indian was standing at the side of the road just behind the fence made of barbed wire strands that encircled the airfield. He was barefoot and still carried the stick and the puppy. I approached him, and from a fairly close range, I took his picture, then we stared at each other, just as we had in the early morning hours. I wanted to take his hand and Frank saw me begin to reach out.

"Button," he said calmly. "Don't. Get back in the jeep. Please."

"He frightened me and I feel foolish. He's a gentle person—just like you said."

"The car, Button," he softly urged.

I looked the Indian in the eye, nodded and smiled. I turned and got back in the jeep. As it started to move toward the airfield, I looked back toward the barefoot Indian once more. Again, our eyes met. With the stick in one hand and a little puppy in the other, he watched us drive away.

At the airfield, the Mayor greeted us and thanked us for staying at his home. He walked with us to our plane and while Frank accepted the new plugs and went to work installing them, I told the Mayor about my early morning encounter.

"*Sí. Sí.*" he replied. "*Él me dijo. Yo sé lo que pasó*" (Yes. Yes. He told me. I know what happened). The Mayor explained that twice a year, the Indian, well-known to him, walks to Caicara from his tribal village on the Ventuari River, more than one hundred miles south. Usually he brings things to sell or trade. Customarily, he arrives early in the morning, enters the unlocked house and goes directly to the Mayor's bedroom to awaken his friend. This time, instead of seeing the Mayor, the Indian saw me. He told the Mayor he was terrified when he saw the woman with light eyes and light skin. The Mayor laughed robustly as he told the story. "He was as afraid of you as you were of him." The Mayor told Frank that he himself had only seen people with my coloring in the movies, never in person.

It was about 8:00 a.m. when we saw one of our planes on final approach.

"Do we have a plane in the search today?" I asked.

"We should have one every day until the doctors are found, or the operation is called off. That's Irv. He's come early because we didn't make it home last night and there was no way to tell CB about our delay."

We told Irv about our forced landing and rescue, and then we were ready to head back to Ciudad Bolivar. Irv stayed on to receive instructions and join the morning search.

Because of the damaged prop, we limped back to CB with the plane vibrating and not operating at peak performance. The engine purred unwaveringly.

As we flew toward home, my mind wasn't on the forced landing, the propeller, the rough trip or the restless night I'd had. It wasn't on Dr. Vegas or Dr. Lopez. My mind was on the Indian. Obsessed by my memory of him, I couldn't erase his vision from my mind's eye. I remember him to this day.

All photos by Marilyn

Two Cessnas receive fuel near the small service building at Caicara airstrip

We landed several times in savannahs to ask cowboys if they had information about the missing plane.

A few minutes after we landed in a savannah to talk with cowboys, we were joined by another S&R aircraft.

Frank valiantly made an emergency landing when our plane's engine malfunctioned. He made temporary repairs.

Plaza Bolivar in Caicara.

The building with windows on the right is the home of the Mayor of Caicara. Our crippled plane limped to the Caicara airstrip where the Mayor met us and invited us to have dinner and stay overnight at his house.

I shall forever remember my encounters with the Indian who carried a stick and a puppy.

Although the search continued at least until mid-May, there was no sign of Dr Ramela Vegas, Dr.Rafael Ernesto Lopez, their companions or their green plane.

They were never found.

Chapter 27

The Phenomenon of The Catatumbos

Dear Mother and Dad   **August 12, 1954**

This letter is just a few lines to let you know that I am well. I know how you worry about me.

Frank and I are in Lagunillas, near Maracaibo. He has business here. He's looking over the ATSA helicopter operation with the thought of doing chopper work in Bolivar.

Love you very much. Marilyn

When Frank invited me to go with him to Lagunillas on the eastern shore of Lake Maracaibo, I didn't know it was his last ditch effort to save AEROVEN. He thought a helicopter to provide pipeline inspections to oil companies north of the Orinoco might just be the infusion of new business AEROVEN needed. Frank's LAV pilot friend, Manuel Mendoza, an owner of ATSA, a helicopter company headquartered in Caracas with a base at the Shell Oil camp at Lagunillas, agreed to Frank's visit.

"If we buy a helicopter, I've got to know what it's all about. If we don't buy a helicopter, perhaps ATSA would be interested in basing one of theirs at our hangar in Ciudad Bolivar and we could operate it for them." But before any financial plans could be discussed, he wanted to observe the ATSA operation and learn more about it. "Want to join me?"

"I can be ready in ten minutes," I said.

The next day, we flew on LAV to Maracaibo and arrived at 4:00 p.m. The city is on the western shore of the lake.

Frank had made arrangements to borrow a car for a couple of days from an ATSA representative. "I think we'll be here no more than three days," Frank told the young rep who met us at the airport.

"That'll work," the rep replied. "I have business here. Just let me know in advance when you'll be back." He gave Frank his business card with a Maracaibo phone number. He told us a room had been reserved for us at a Shell Oil guest house in Lagunillas near the ATSA office and helicopter pad and gave us a map and directions. Lagunillas is on the eastern shore of the lake, and further south than Maracaibo.

We stayed overnight in Maracaibo and before leaving the next day for the oil camp we went sightseeing. Known for its trees, exquisite gardens, and flowers, Maracaibo is in western Venezuela. It sprawls on the west side of the narrow channel connecting the Gulf of Maracaibo to Lake Maracaibo. Before moving on to the oil camp, I wanted to meet the local indigenous people, the Guajiros, who live outside the city. I'd seen an article with photos in a magazine and they'd been described as being musically-talented pastoral nomads who roam near the Venezuela-Columbia border. The article recommended a trip to their Maracaibo community.

We were not disappointed. The traditional clothes worn by the ladies were long, bright full-skirted dresses that flared over thong-sandals with large pom-poms of wool. Small fires for cooking seemed to be everywhere as the Guajira women cooked food for sightseers to sample and buy. The smoky air produced a sharp, pungent aroma. I bought no food, but did buy a pair of blue and red sandals with big red wool pom-poms.

I would have enjoyed staying longer, but Frank said, "Let's get going, Button. I'm anxious to get to the camp and I'm not sure how long the drive is."

We crossed the channel by ferry to the eastern shore of the lake then drove south to Lagunillas, the center of oil activities. On the way, I saw more oil pumps and derricks than I thought existed in the whole world. The ubiquitous off-shore drilling rigs with tall derricks dotted the lake as far as I could see.

We registered at the guest house and dropped off our luggage. We located the ATSA office nearby and met the office staff. I met Captain Nava who invited me to fly with him to oil rigs on the lake while Frank conducted business. Nava introduced me to a helicopter adventure.

The young pilot from Argentina helped me aboard, checked a few things, started the engine and off we flew. The Bell chopper looked like a clear plexi-glass bubble with a boom in the back made from an erector set and a rotor overhead. It had room for a pilot and one passenger and there were no doors. I tightened the seat belt and hung on for dear life. We flew from the ATSA helicopter base in Lagunillas and over the camp operated by Shell Oil. Nava pointed out club houses, private homes and commissaries. He hovered over the Shell Lagunillas Clubhouse and said we'd be dining at that club later. After a while, the chopper set down and we walked to a nearby site for lunch and a cold drink. Capt. Nava asked if the heat bothered me.

I giggled and shook my head. "I live in Ciudad Bolivar."

"I've heard about CB." Nava nodded and gave me an all-knowing smile.

Back in the chopper, with belt secured tightly, Capt. Nava ascended and after he'd reached his desired altitude, he flew level, and even then it felt like the chopper's nose pointed slightly downward. This and the lack of doors caused me a little concern, at first.

"*Estás bien?*" (Are you okay?) Nava asked, above the din.

"*Sí. Muy bien.*"

We flew about an hour over the lake to an offshore drilling rig. We approached it slowly, hovered, and then gently set down on the oil platform.

"*Vámanos,*" he said "*Te ensenyo lo que tenemos aquí*" (Let's go, I'll show you what we have here).

Nava spoke Spanish loudly so I'd be able to hear over the noise from the rig. He introduced me to the rig manager and rig hands, and I listened as the manager, who spoke English, told me about drilling for oil. He talked about the derrick, its height and drilling depths. I learned about mud pumps, shale shakers, concrete piles, drilling and construction platforms in Lake Maracaibo. A huge operation, it boggled my mind.

We flew back to the base after sundown. I'd gotten used to the noise and the strange sensation of flying in a helicopter without doors and fixed wings. The breathtaking view of derricks all with colored lights ablaze looked like candles on a birthday cake.

ATSA flies personnel and parts 24/7. Nothing stops the oil flow, so nothing stops the choppers. I learned a lot about drilling oil, the helicopter operation, and the service it provides.

"I'd like to make a night flight to a rig," I said. "I can't imagine how you locate a destination platform out of the hundreds there in the black lake."

He replied that he was going off duty, but the pilot who had the evening tour would be coming on and suggested I might go with him if he had a flight after dinner.

"I'll never be the same, Frank," I said as I bounded into the office where he was working. "What a thrill. And Capt. Nava is so kind. He spent the whole day with me."

"And he'll be with us tonight. We're going to the Shell Lagunillas Club for dinner with some of the pilots. Tomorrow night, we'll go to the other Shell Club. I heard they show movies."

After dinner, we bade our pilot friends a good evening and strolled to the guest house. Frank didn't want to go back to the ATSA office. He just wanted to talk about the ATSA operation. "The paperwork," he said, "is so disorganized." He wrinkled his brow. "I don't know how they can run an operation like this?" He said he'd have to stay another day to better understand it. "Do you mind staying? It'll take me that much time to see it all."

"Mind? I love it here. It reminds me of a carnival. You should see it from the air after sundown."

"It's a clear night and there's something wondrous I heard about today. I want us both to see. Everyone here talks about 'the phenomenon of the Catatumbo.'"

As we drove to a dike by the lake, he spoke softly, almost reverently about the atmospheric phenomenon. "Catatumbo looks like lightning bursts in the sky, every few seconds. Every night."

We reached the gravel-covered dike, walked up its gentle slope, stood motionless at the top, mesmerized by the flashes of lightning.

"It's silent," I whispered. "There's no thunder. It's silent lightning. Yet, it lights the whole sky. How long has this been going on?"

"No one knows. No one knows where it originates or what causes it. Its history is also unknown. I've heard it said that the lightning was first recorded in a poem written in 1597 and it has been seen hundreds of miles away. It's like a beacon for ships navigating in the gulf."

We lit cigarettes and watched in silence. I counted three or four strikes each minute. Fascinated, we sat on the gravel for almost an hour and observed the display.

Geologists, at the time, thought the Catatumbo lightning came from south and west of the lake, but a hostile native tribe, the Motilones, inhabited the area. Geologists had tried to find the place of origin, but none had succeeded. Some had even lost their lives in their attempt.

We drove back to the camp in silence.

When we arrived at the office the next morning, we told the staff about our evening's entertainment. They confessed it remained a bewilderment to them.

I spent the day with the ATSA secretary and learned her responsibilities. "There's not much order," I told Frank. "I couldn't figure out how she kept track of everything." I saw you with the office manager. How do things look?

"Understanding the phenomenon of the Catatumbo is easier than sorting out that operation."

In the evening, we forewent the opportunity to go to the movies at the Shell Club, instead, we drove to the dike, sat on the gravel, and watched the phenomenon of the Catatumbo. It was a better show than the one playing at the camp theater.

On the morning of the third day, we said goodbye to our new friends, drove to Maracaibo and flew back to Bolivar. We were both so deep in thought, we spoke very little during the flight to Maiquetia. But between Maiquetia and Bolivar Frank said, "I'm not as hopeful about creating a helicopter service or working with ATSA in a combined effort. The inventory of parts for one chopper would be costly. We'd need to have several people licensed to fly and right now there are none. We'd have to have a hell of a contract written in concrete with oil companies before we start—before we can assume such financial responsibilities."

"I like the thought of a new operation, new opportunities," I said then paused. "Without choppers, what do you think we'll do to increase income here?"

"I'm tired of thinking about it, Button. I don't know anymore. We fly almost every day, but we don't have money. I have to see the accountant. That may be the place to start."

* * *

Scientists now know the Catatumbo originates over the mouth of the Catatumbo River where its water flows into the largest body of fresh water in all South America, Lake Maracaibo. The Catatumbo lightning is a unique weather phenomenon. It is the world's most powerful generator of the upper tropospheric ozone. Ozone protects the earth's atmosphere from the sun's ultraviolet rays. In Maracaibo and Lagunillas the "silent lightning" and darting electric arcs are mysterious, but near its source the lightning loudly crackles and booms. Studies are on-going and still there is little data to explain the phenomenon. There are theories about why the lighting strikes occur, but still, nothing is definite.

In 2010, the Catatumbos inexplicably vanished. For the first time since 1597, the greatest night show on earth disappeared without a sign, and four months later, also without a sign, it reappeared. The riddle continues, defying man's attempt to decipher its meaning.

The area is now in a Venezuelan national park and the Catatumbo lightning can be seen by tourists who care to venture to that mystical part of the world. Small tour groups operate for those who are highly adventurous.

The nearby Motilones, no longer hostile, are mostly Roman Catholic.

* * *

In May 1956, Captain Nava was killed when his helicopter crashed in the lake. Debris was widely scattered. The cause of the accident was never determined.

Chapter 28

The Meeting

Dear Mother and Dad   September 10, 1954

It's about 10:30 a.m. and all AEROVEN has been here since 9:30. Even Shorty and Tom are here and you should hear the noise. There's a big meeting going on.

Arguments. Much yelling. They switch back and forth between Spanish and English. I'm in the kitchen. I stay close by. Sometimes Frank calls me in to take notes.

I know I'm just rambling. Just hearing Julio makes me mad and I can't think straight. I used to like him. But that's changed. He's got some kind of a problem!

Poor Frank—like he doesn't have enough problems—now he's got that jerk.

Frank has to go to Miami on business. I don't know when—but I'll let you know. Maybe we can meet.

More later. All my love. Marilyn

The three AEROVEN partners established a small construction company they called ECUAVEN. Julio, a college-educated engineer, was named President. The company was borne out of the need to generate income all year that would provide a reserve fund to support AEROVEN during the rainy season when flying decreased, but most expenses remained the same. Historically, during this low-income-producing season, income earned by AEROVEN was sufficient to pay most of its expenses, but seldom were there sufficient funds to pay Frank and Julio their full salaries. Both men always took pay cuts.

According to the new arrangement, a sufficient amount of money earned by ECUAVEN would be paid to Frank and Julio to offset the historic pay cuts. The reserve would grow. AEROVEN would break even.

Conditions changed; AEROVEN hit pay dirt flying two planes between the mines, and ECUAVEN wasted no time nailing down two lucrative contracts. Both companies were sitting pretty—or so they should have been.

Blue Skies, Green Hell

Because Julio spent most of his time in Puerto Ordaz, Frank left the mines one day a week to work at the AEROVEN office. He took a day off for R&R whenever he could.

A new girl in the office, employed in March, deposited checks, handled record-keeping, and basic accounting.

Tom came back on board. Although he remained a "standby" pilot and received an hourly wage for flying and waiting time, he agreed to give AEROVEN priority over other companies that might want his services. He flew AEROVEN business out of Bolivar, and between the three mines as needed.

One Saturday when Frank was in CB, he came home for lunch and said, "The accountant came by the office. When I'm in town, seems like everyone knows it and they practically stand in line to see me. Anyway, he wants me to call a meeting." Frank asked the maid to prepare a light lunch; a sandwich would be fine. He had to return to the office as soon as possible.

"One for me, too. Please. We'll be on the patio."

"He wants to discuss the financial matters of both companies. Wait 'til you hear this." We sat on the sofa and cleared the cocktail table of dogs' toys to make room for our sandwiches. I didn't expect to hear Frank tell me that Julio had withdrawn almost all the money from the ECUAVEN reserve fund, *and*, apparently, tapped the AEROVEN account, too, just before he went to Ecuador after his father passed away. That was in June. "He told me he needed to *borrow some* money for his trip. It seems he took practically the whole kit and caboodle." Frank lit a cigarette. "God almighty." He raised his eyes and looked into the sky. "I've been flying my ass off in Asa to build up the AEROVEN account, and this guy filches who knows how much from *that* account. Sure, he said he'd repay it upon his return. But what is he doing with all the money?"

I put my feet on the cocktail table made from a sliced tree trunk. "Wow. He's been back from Ecuador since July. Does he still owe the money?"

"He does. The accountant said there are other serious matters. He contacted Shorty and asked him to arrange to attend the meeting."

We enjoyed a brief breeze that blew through the patio.

"Where'd that come from?" Frank asked.

"That was Julio making a quick visit to CB to help you in the office."

"I called Do at the Port," Frank said and leaned forward. "I told him the accountant had requested this meeting." He paused and sipped his tea. "Wait 'til you hear this."

"What happened?"

"Do said I should buy out Julio or fire him. I should take whatever steps are necessary to get rid of him. That's exactly what Do said." He repeated, "I should get rid of Julio."

"I'm shocked. Oh, my God. Why did he say that? What does it mean?"

305

"Do said he'll tell me details when we see each other. He thought Julio might try to shakeup the operation in the mines when he works there while we're in Miami. And I don't know what he'd shake up. He hasn't even been there"

The meeting was called for September 10th. Shorty arrived the day before. He worked with Frank and me as we put the final touches on data that would be useful at the meeting in Frank's discussion of the Asa operation.

"I'm optimistic about the future of ECUAVEN," Shorty said as we shuffled our papers.

"We'll have to see what the accountant reports." Frank replied. "The whole team will be here. I didn't want to pull Irv out of the mines, but Tom's coming. You know, he's been flying between the mines for us. He's smart and observes a lot. He and Julio are still thick as thieves. But I believe he can be objective."

Shorty usually defended his friend, but now he appeared to be a mite suspicious of Julio's untoward behavior. "Frank, Marilyn—for your ears only—I'm thinking of taking a leave from MERCATOR and coming here to work with Julio. He can't manage the ECUAVEN operation. I want to help—I also want to see what's going on."

"Off hand, I think it's a good move for ECUAVEN, but you'd be risking an awful lot." Frank understood Shorty's value to MERCATOR.

"*Vamos a ver*" (Let's see), Shorty answered. "I can't plan on doing it as quickly as I'd like. I am committed to several jobs for Do. I'll keep you posted."

The meeting convened in our dining-room. All major company meetings were held at our house. The office was small and far too busy and public. Usually, only board members were invited. Others attended if Frank knew they could contribute information on an agenda item.

At the start of the meeting, I served coffee and Danish pastry and stayed around to offer second servings. I had to hear this meeting. Frank greeted Julio, Shorty, Tom, and then turned over the meeting to the accountant whose financial analysis of the company started on a bittersweet note.

The accountant said AEROVEN had made more money during the last three months than during any other three month period in the company's history. "You fellows flying between the mines made more than Bs 45,000 in August alone. That's excluding most weekends (about $13,600 in 1955 or $117,000 in 2012). In one two-day period, you grossed Bs 3,700 (almost $10,000 in 2012). That's a company record!" He smiled. "I know it's been at a great personal sacrifice. I've heard about the conditions. But, after paying salaries, bills due, bills overdue, and paying off the bank's overdraft AEROVEN's surplus is very low. It's damn near zero." The accountant scribbled marginal notes next to his handwritten agenda.

Blue Skies, Green Hell

The accountant pushed his chair back from the table and stood up. He placed his hands on the table top, leaned forward, and slowly looked at each man. "Gentlemen. I ask you, what's going on? I don't know where the AEROVEN money's going and I cannot balance the ledger. A few withdrawals are noted as 'reimbursement.' They are not explained!" He sat down. "ECUAVEN was established to create a reserve. A stopgap. An emergency fund. Now we learn AEROVEN not only has little surplus, but the ECUAVEN fund is damn near empty. What does this mean?"

Julio started to explain that income from ECUAVEN was needed to purchase equipment to build a competitive construction company. He said he could get a pipeline contract—with the right equipment. And he could get a sub-contract to work on the planned Guri Dam. "We've got to plow back earnings, Frank, to purchase equipment."

Frank replied, "I understand about plowing back, but I didn't know we were establishing a construction company to rival Morrison-Knudsen. I thought you were developing a small company to create a reserve fund to safeguard the future of AEROVEN. Remember, the mines might stop producing and AEROVEN might lose a contract."

"You worry too much," Julio said casually.

The meeting heated up and that's when all hell broke loose. The modulated voices of the team players slipped back and forth between English and Spanish. They stood up and paced around the room, waving their arms and the shouting began. Some team! Tom and the accountant remained quiet. The accountant asked Julio about withdrawals.

"I have already stated I will make full restitution as soon as my father's estate is settled. *"No hay problema, amigo"* (There's no problem, friend). Casually, he brushed it off with a wave of his hand. I wondered how Frank could stand this arrogance. I saw him work effectively in Caracas with Payne and Griffin and I'd seen him put Carlos in his place so nicely they remained good friends. I'd seen him get in and get out of LEBCA, and he'd remained good friends with that company's owner, but this nasty situation involved his partner who I believed was no match for any player in the aforementioned business discussions. I suspected something underhanded here. And, obviously, so did Shorty. He'd already said Julio couldn't go it alone with ECUAVEN. The team quieted down and settled back in their chairs at the table.

I went to the kitchen and poured a cup of coffee for myself. I was setting down the coffee pot when I heard the accountant announce two additional problems. He said ECUAVEN was overspending. The ratio of income to expenses was way out of balance.

"As I looked over the ledgers," continued the accountant, "I saw an apparent co-mingling of ECUAVEN reserve funds and AEROVEN funds. The accounts are to be separate. *Qué pasó* (What happened)? Frankly, gentlemen, I thought pilots were good mathematicians. I see things that baffle me. What are you doing?" No one answered. "It's something when the accountant doesn't understand what's going on. These practices must be stopped. Avoided." He waved papers. "These records are next to impossible to understand. And you fellows give me no help."

Julio looked at the ceiling. "I've told you. I borrowed money and will pay it back. What more can I say? I've been working in the field and did not have time to manage the books. Perhaps . . . ah . . . I should account for my time? Want me to do that, Frank?""

"Perhaps you should—if your time is so short you can't handle the administration of ECUAVEN," Frank replied. He nodded, raised his eyebrows and looked at Shorty. "Maybe we need a time-and-motion study. Isn't that what they call it? We may need to be more efficient. We can't afford to hire more help. We'll have to fix it, Julio. Won't we?"

Julio sighed audibly but said nothing.

I almost dropped the coffee pot on the kitchen floor when I heard the accountant talk about the lack of ECUAVEN receipts for business expenditures. Calmly, the accountant continued. "With such large unexplained withdrawals, there may be insufficient funds to meet ECUAVEN'S short-term liabilities. I'll hope some money has been deposited recently and that I have simply not received the bank statement."

Julio defended his position. "I'll get the deposit slips to you. And I'll send receipts. They're all in Puerto Ordaz." A third time, he repeated his pledge to return the money he'd borrowed. "*No hay problema.*"

Julio didn't have a problem, but seeing his brand new shiny Chevy Malibu parked in front of the house gave me one.

The accountant had one final request. "When it becomes necessary to change figures in the books, please date and initial the change and annotate the change—state the reason—at the bottom of the page. This shouldn't happen often. Also, be legible." He slammed the book shut and said, "Some of the writing is clear, but some I can't read." Finished with his part of the discussion, he asked if there was additional business to discuss.

Julio grabbed that invitation. He said he'd been asked by Frank to work the Asa operation for an indefinite period of time, "While Frank and Marilyn are in Miami Beach." He made it sound like we intended to have a fun-filled vacation romping on the silver sand in Miami's playground.

For the benefit of the accountant and all others at the meeting, Frank said, "Hold it right there, my partner." He stood up and looked at Julio. "When I can get away from here, I'm going up to Miami to buy Jack Perez's Noorduyn Norseman and check out in it, so we can carry freight and supplies all year to La Paragua and other towns scattered throughout the deep interior—to make money all year—even when it's raining. Do you remember, Julio? Making money is one of AEROVEN 's goals." He sat down.

The accountant looked perplexed. "Buy a plane? How do you pay for it?" He riffled through the papers he'd just reviewed. "*Qué va*" (what goes?) His voice hit a high pitch.

Frank explained, "Never forget, my friend, we're bush pilots. We fly the bush—to towns in the deep interior where supplies of all kinds are needed all year long—building materials, medical supplies, food, grain. Name it, we fly it. He sipped his coffee. "We can't carry much cargo in a Cessna and certainly not in bad weather." He explained he'd already lined up work for the heavy, single-engine utility plane that can fly eight hours non-stop with a payload of 2,720 pounds of cargo and has a higher altitude limit. "Jack Perez owns the ship and has made the payments reasonable. The plane will pay for itself beginning the day after it lands at Bolivar." He sat down. "I'll arrange for cargo to be delivered to our hangar and I'll be flying the first day the Norseman is here and every day until every pilot here checks out in that aircraft." Quietly, he set his pen on the yellow tablet on which he'd doodled and leaned back in his chair. "I may take a couple of days in Miami to rest. Maybe I'll see a doctor. I've been flying between the mines since April. I'm tired. I'm sick. I've got to get rid of my cough. Even my teeth are stained." He put the top on his fountain pen and put his pen in his shirt pocket. "The matter of the Asa operation is internal company business and not an accounting issue." He smiled as he looked at the accountant and nodded. "Thank you for coming. You've been helpful. I'll be in touch with you shortly." The accountant filed his papers in his leather attaché bag and left.

Frank leaned forward and his eyes penetrated Julio; no sparkle, no easy-going smile. "I believe, Julio, you were going to talk about the Asa operation. Do you want to continue?"

"Yes. Thanks, Frank." He said in the course of working the Asa operation, he'd change some systems—reorganize. Wow! That's when everything hit the fan again. They shouted at one time—in both languages!

"What would you change, Julio?" Frank asked.

"Perhaps, ah, ah, the rate structure." Julio's voice was soft.

"You've been to Asa? You're familiar with the rate structure, are you?"

"I haven't been there." He paused, "but I've looked over the books, Frank. I just want to help," he said obsequiously.

"Here," Frank said, "you might want to look over these papers before you start to improve anything in the mines. Take them home with you and study them. We can meet again to answer your questions. And feel free to talk with Tom about flying between the mines. He's been flying there." He pushed to Julio the papers with statistics and maps we'd gathered in preparation for this meeting. Then he slid photos of the muddy airstrip and our new mud-splattered Cessna

180 parked in the muck at Asa next to four mud-covered 55-gallon drums of fuel. The last photo showed the squalid shack he'd call home.

"Before I adjourn the meeting, I'll tell you about the pilot I just hired."

Julio interrupted. "You hired someone without discussing it with me?"

"Damn it, Julio. I'm flying the bush and you're in Puerto Ordaz or some other place—wherever the hell ECUAVEN is working. I can't communicate with you. I exercised my presidential authority, Julio. While I am in Florida, Tom and Irv can't carry the entire AEROVEN work load by themselves. Charlie Baughan's not always available. I've hired Rafael Romero. He'll handle the flights out of CB, and work the mines, as needed. Right now, he's also qualified to fly the Noorduyn Norseman the minute it arrives."

"And what about ECUAVEN? Who'll be there to back me up?"

"If that becomes a problem, perhaps Shorty will fill in for you at the Port. I won't be gone long."

Shorty nodded. "I can arrange that. I just have to give Do a heads up."

Julio was set to speak, but Frank didn't recognize him. Instead, he stood up and adjourned the meeting. "Thank you all for coming today."

Shorty remained at the table and shuffled papers while Tom and Julio left.

"I'm sorry I blind-sided you, Shorty, telling him you'd fill in at ECUAVEN if necessary. You and I really hadn't gotten that far in our discussions, I know."

"That's okay. But, I remind you, I can't start until I finish some work with Mercator. I also think we should arrange for an independent auditor to review all the books before I get involved. I don't know how long that will take. But our accountant seemed very upset. Frankly, so am I."

"Right you are. I won't go to Florida until you're ready to come down here. Jack will understand."

"Yes. I have a CPA in mind. Actually, I like the idea of working ECUAVEN. I'll learn about his construction operation." They shook hands. "Frank, I'll be in touch."

"Take whatever time you need."

I had a headache and retreated to the bedroom to lie down. A few minutes later, Frank came into the room and sat on the edge of the bed. "I wanted to tell everyone about Rafael Romero, but I didn't have the energy. Button, we're lucky to have gotten him to fly for us. He's been flying the bush for years." Frank continued to speak as he walked to the bathroom and splashed water on his face and neck. "You should see his log book. Thousands of hours. He's a quiet family man. He plays guitar. Aldemaro Romero is his brother; he's an orchestra conductor in Caracas. That record we have, "Dinner in Caracas," that's his latest release. I understand Rafael could have played in his brother's orchestra, he plays guitar that well."

Frank stretched out on the bed. "I'm exhausted. I really need a few days vacation. Yet, I feel guilty as hell about it." He lay there staring at the ceiling. Mercifully, exhaustion over took him and he slept for an hour.

That evening, after dinner, Frank and I sat quietly outdoors and talked about the morning's row. He said everything would be okay. Tom would be a great help—he had already advised Julio about Frank's meetings with Governor Sanchez Lanz and the Chief in Asa and he cautioned Julio that business-as-usual would best be the order of the day in Asa, Paragua and Chiguao. "Button, this is a helluva business. There's always someone making things difficult. Double-crossing. Now it's my partner. At least, at the meeting, he acknowledged he'd borrowed the money and would pay it back. Everyone heard that."

"It should all be better after we get the Norseman working."

Chapter 29

The Vacation

Dear Mother and Dad　　　　　　　　　　January 13, 1955

　　Our trip to Miami was so short—and all work.
　　We flew back to Caracas on KLM. What luxury!
　　Then we drove back to CB in Frank's old car. That old car just won't die. But we are home. The Norseman arrived in Maiquetia the day after we did. That's where our good news ended. The other news was all bad. First, while we were away, our dear German Shepherd, Baron, died while playing at Magda's with her dogs. He was only 13 months old. He died of a broken heart. Julio had the Vet do an autopsy. The report said he'd been born with a small heart that burst while he was playing.
　　Magda buried him at the airport and put flowers on his grave.
　　Since we're back, we've had nothing but trouble. I've never seen Frank so depressed. It worries me. I'll keep you posted.

All my love and devotion. Marilyn

Our work with Jack Perez in Miami concluded in two weeks. He had the Noorduyn Norseman ready to fly and we closed an affordable deal in November 1954. Jack checked out Frank on the Norseman and then we stole a day for shopping and another for sun-bathing on the crowded sands of Miami Beach. Frank enjoyed his long—awaited vacation. However there had been no time for him to see a doctor or dentist.
　　We located Mother and Dad, who had been visiting friends in Ft. Lauderdale, and joined them for dinner at a fine restaurant and a colorful Cuban club for dancing. Our Miami sojourn ended when we received notice that the Norseman's paperwork was almost completed and it would be ready to fly to Venezuela shortly.
　　I met the young pilot, Ned, who'd fly the Norseman to Maiquetia. He showed me the interior of this aircraft manufactured in Canada. "This plane was designed for flying the bush."

Blue Skies, Green Hell

Loaded with our assorted purchases that included chairs for our living room and tires for the Norseman, I commented that the plane was like a flying truck. "What a plane. I've never seen such huge tires and wheels on a single-engine plane. And speaking of huge—that's some engine!"

"Your Cessna wing span is about thirty-six feet. The span on this baby is over fifty feet. And the wheels? They're big all right. The landing gear doesn't retract. If this plane loses its engine over the ocean, we're finished! We'd just hit the water and flip over. And with this load of cargo," he raised his eyebrows, looked in the fuselage, and whistled. "We'd sink. We'd go right down to Dave Jones' locker. Want to fly back with me?"

"Not on your life—or mine."

Ned laughed. "My bag's in the plane and I'm ready to go flying."

I was ready to go flying, too, on a KLM luxury airliner to Venezuela. As we approached Maiquetía, a change came over Frank. The animated man, whose eyes sparkled after he'd visited the KLM cockpit and chatted with the pilots, suddenly became dispirited. He stared out the window and closed his eyes. "I'm wondering what's happened since we left Bolivar."

We picked up our old car at Maiquetía, drove over the mountain to Caracas and stayed long enough to celebrate Christmas with Frank's family. Shocked when Do told us that during our absence, Baron, our young German Shepherd had died, we bid everyone a quick farewell and departed for Ciudad Bolivar. The long drive was without incident.

Before going to our house, we stopped at the airport. Julio greeted us. "You want to be brought up to date before you go home?"

"Should I?" Frank said tentatively.

"First, I want to tell you how sorry I am that Baron died. He died at Magda's. She buried him over here." He gestured to the back of the ramp. She puts flowers on his grave every day. He was such a good dog. So proud. Not like our hound, Blunder!"

"I heard you arranged for an autopsy. Thanks. That was thoughtful. We'd never have known the cause."

"And now for the rest of the news." Julio shuffled his feet and sat on the corner of the desk. "When you left, we thought Irv was still in Florida buying an airplane. He wasn't. He must have returned to Caracas long before we knew because a day or two after you departed here, he returned to Bolivar. He never cabled us. He just showed up. He'd bought a used twin Cessna and it had been licensed under AEROVEN. You and I had agreed on that arrangement. But what we didn't know was his plan to come to the airport every day—hours before the new girl arrived—and take all the early incoming calls to book flights for his plane. None for ours."

"How'd you stop that?"

"I fired him."

"What the hell gets into you two. You and I talked about that potential problem. You should have worked out something with him. Given him direction."

"Frank, I haven't got the savvy you have dealing with people. That's why you do the business and I fly the planes." Julio thought the discussion closed.

"Julio, you re-hire him. We need him. I'll get to the bottom of this. And until we sign a contract with him, he'll stay off the phone. He'll fly for us, as usual, and we'll pay him for the use of his plane when we need a twin. We'll work it out. What about Shorty? Is he working with you at ECUAVEN?"

"He drops in often enough to learn about the operation and to keep up with things. I think it'll work out."

"We haven't been home yet, but I'll swing by Irv's and make an appointment to speak to him tomorrow. The Norseman's in Maiquetía and will be coming here as soon as the paperwork with immigration, customs, and the air ministry are finished. You know that always takes time. I want it here and working as soon as possible."

Frank and I left the office. As we drove to Irv's, Frank said, "Baron died and I've got to deal with this crap again."

At the Bantas, we talked about Baron's death, and Magda and I cried and hugged. "Magda, thanks for all you did for him. He lived a short life, but was so loved."

Then Frank spoke to Irv and appealed to his sense of good judgment.

"I know what you're saying, Frank. But Julio fired me. I can re-license my plane with LEBCA. I can fly my plane with passengers anytime I want and for any company that charters me and my plane. I can be independent. Frank, I won't fly for AEROVEN if I'm putting money into that guy's pocket."

"Let's meet tomorrow afternoon, Irv, after Julio re-hires you. He must do that. Then you tell me what it is you want. We'll work it out."

But the next day, while Irv flew a morning trip in one of our Cessnas, Rafael Romero had an afternoon flight in Irv's twin. Upon his return, the main gear collapsed while landing at Ciudad Bolivar. The plane spun around on the runway and into the grassy field next to it; the plane was totaled. Arguing over use of Irv's plane ended.

"Frank. I like you, but after I collect the insurance, I'll go back to Florida and I'll buy another plane." Then mild-mannered Irv affirmed, "Frank, I mean it. I won't fly with AEROVEN. Not as long as Julio's around. I'll come back to CB and fly the plane with a LEBCA license."

"I'm disappointed, Irv. Let's cool down. Talk it over."

"It may be temporary." He smiled. "Frank, I want to come back, fly my plane all over Venezuela and make enough money to buy Julio's shares. I want to fly AEROVEN with you. That's my goal, if you'll have me."

"Irv, you know you've got a home here. We'll work things out. Stay in touch. And don't forget, when you're in Florida, you have responsibilities here. Magda is number one. You were gone a long time when you bought the twin. I understand buying a plane takes time. But leave her some money and cable her once in a while. I don't mean to intrude."

Chapter 30

The Norseman, Our Cash Cow

Dear Mother and Dad   **February 16, 1955**

The Norseman is flying. At last! Frank has flown it more than the others. It is painted white and blue. It looks nice, even though it's such a truck! They call it, "The Cow."

It's big and clumsy. They painted nose art on the plane—a cow with wings trying to fly—tears are coming from its eyes. When it's flying, the plane looks like it's going so slow you wonder how it stays up. Since the Norseman's been working, business has been very good. It takes much more cargo than the Cessnas and stays aloft 8 hours, so we can haul more freight for longer distances.

The cow was down with a busted jug (engine cylinder).

We had to go to Maracay to get a new one—and other parts for inventory. The place there has everything. It's far—but nearer than going to Miami or even Caracas for parts. Our hangar is always full of cargo for the Norseman. As you can imagine, we're pretty happy. Frank feels better.

Love always, Marilyn

The Norseman arrived in CB with a great thunderous roar that shook the whole city.

"That's our cash cow," Frank said, watching it on final. "I feel like I'm King Midas. We're back in business, Button."

Until Frank had time to check out Julio on the Norseman, he and Rafael flew heavy schedules. They alternated flying the plane and out-flew all the other single-engine planes in Bolivar. Irv had checked out in it, but he was in Florida. Once again, we made enough money to put AEROVEN into the profit column. We received notes from the accountant, "Looking good" and "great job." The few words said a lot.

Julio found time to stay in Bolivar a few days. He said he was anxious to check out and join the ranks of those pilots—Frank, Rafael, and Irv—qualified to fly the Cow.

Blue Skies, Green Hell

Frank and I worked in the office one Sunday while Julio practiced landings. We heard the plane come roaring in and then a BOOM as the Cow smacked down on the runway followed by the sound of the wooden plane spinning on the ground—cracking, snapping, splitting. The moaning sound of the Cow's engine dying was pathetic. In a great cloud of grass clods and dirt, it collapsed on its shattered right wing. The noises made by the Cow breaking up would have made an earthquake sound sweet. Julio had ground-looped the plane.

"What the hell was that?" shouted Frank as he hot-footed to the window and looked out in time to see the Cow conclude its spin on the grass and fall dead next to the runway. When the dirt settled, Frank saw the Cow facing backwards and the right wing in pieces—scattered over the ground.

We jumped in the car and sped to the plane. Julio was unhurt. Only his ego was blemished. "Julio, why don't you take off a day or two? Shooting landings and takeoffs requires full concentration. Maybe you're tired and were distracted." Frank cabled the bad news to Jack who replied with worse news. He could not locate a new wing.

"We get out of one problem and go right into another," Frank said, as he looked around the cavernous hangar full of cargo for La Paragua. "1955! It's been a helluva year so far, Irv's twin collapses and Julio cracks up the Norseman! We'll have to move the fresh food by Cessna. The rest of the freight can wait."

"What can you do now?" I asked.

"We fix it. Isn't that what Charlie Baughan would say?" He laughed and rolled up his pressed, white long-sleeves. "We fix it," he repeated.

On Monday, Julio returned to Puerto Ordaz and ECUAVEN, while Frank with Bud Small, our mechanic, brought the pieces of the wrecked wing to the hangar, examined them, and worked on sketches of the parts they'd have to make.

"Hey, lots of ribs can be salvaged." Bud smiled. "Don't worry, Frank. I'll make a list of wood that we need to buy. When I'm finished with it, the wing will be good as new." Frank advised Jack of the plans and told him they'd have the Norseman flying in ten days.

I looked at the damaged wing and pieces of it spread out on sawhorses and workbenches in the hangar, and thought the date was ambitious.

Every day, from early morn until well beyond closing time, the hangar filled with the ZIP-ZIPping of saws and whrrring of drills as Bud cut new ribs for the wing and repaired or replaced the long pieces of wood that were the wing's leading and trailing edges. Next, they applied special fabric to cover the wing. That's when I smelled something that reminded me of when, as a kid, I made model airplanes. I smelled "dope." WOW. It brought tears to my eyes. I brought the pedestal fans from home and set them up in the hangar.

The wing was painted with several coats of "dope" that caused the fabric to tighten. Then it was painted white with blue trim. When I tapped it with my fingers, it sounded like a drum. I knew Frank would work out the logistics of the final step which would be to attach the wing to the fuselage. His main worry concerned the probability of the repaired right wing not weighing the same as the left wing. "After a test flight, that can be fixed, if necessary," he said.

Work on the Norseman continued steadily and on the ninth day after the accident, Frank took it up for its test flight. It handled perfectly and the Norseman, with Frank or Rafael at the controls, was back in action.

So Julio practiced on Sundays, while Frank and Rafael continued to alternate weekdays flying the Cow, loaded with supplies, to La Paragua and other villages all the way to the Brazilian border. Again, we beat out all competition. By now, VETA had three light aircraft, SAN had two and RANSA was putting its first on the flight line.

One evening, after Frank had completed a CB-Caicara round trip in a Cessna, about four hours of hard flying in unexpected, unseasonal turbulent weather, he said he'd rest a bit before we'd decide where to go for dinner.

While he slept and I did a little mending, I heard an airplane in the distance coming toward Ciudad Bolivar. The clock read a few minutes after 6:00 p.m. and the dark of night had fallen. Someone had raced the clock and lost. The bad weather Frank had flown in all day had arrived over CB and now the unknown pilot had ceiling zero, wind, and fierce rain. I put my sewing down and went to the living room window. I said aloud, "Where'd this rain come from? Hmm. And someone's in trouble . . ." I couldn't see a thing. Then it hit me. "Yikes," I yelled. "It's the Norseman." I ran to the bedroom. "Frank. Wake up," I shouted and shook his shoulders. "The Cow's overhead. It's raining and it's after six." I shook him again.

Frank bolted upright. "A squall—Hey, it's Rafael. Let's go."

We ran to our car parked in front of the house, made a fast U-turn and sped to the airport entrance across the street a short half block away. The airstrip was black. "We've got to get headlights on the runway," he said as he drove through the airport entrance. There were no runway lights at the CB airport even for emergencies. "Other cars will come. God help him. He probably can't see the runway."

"I've got the keys to the company car. Let me out. I'll get it," I yelled over the sound of rain beating on the car. I hopped out and ran for the car parked by our hangar.

He called, "Park near the end of the runway. Put on your bright lights and park with your lights shining on the runway. Stay off the runway." He sped away.

Within minutes, someone magically appeared and began to direct the fourteen cars that streamed into the airport. They lined up on each side of the runway at right-angles with their headlights shining on the wet paved strip. The Norseman had been circling, and then it started to descend in the blinding

Blue Skies, Green Hell

rain and certainly on instruments. From its sound it would land in the usual direction, south-west to north-east. Sheets of blinding rain swept across the airfield. No one was in the tower and I couldn't see the windsock. I couldn't imagine what it would be like to land blind—and that's what Rafael would probably have to do.

He'd just turned on to final approach, when he switched on the Cow's landing lights. They shone brightly and we hoped he could see the runway. Next, he had to land safely. Not a time to skid. Not a time to ground-loop. The wind and rain played games and the cars were parked perilously close to the edge of the strip on both sides.

I held my breath.

Slowly, slowly, the Cow plodded on, lower, slower. Through blinding rain, I barely saw the plane. To see better, I hopped out of the car. Would he have to make a crosswind landing? I couldn't see the windsock, but I saw rain sweeping across the field. Oh, my God. I heard him throttle up and then reduce throttle a couple of times. *How can he see?* He crabbed the plane and then flew straight. He was flying just above stall speed. Ok. Ok. Rafael. Now. "NOW" I shouted as I heard him throttle all the way down, saw his plane flare and wheels touch the runway. It plowed through puddles on the runway, spraying water as high as the plane's wings to both left and right over the parked cars. The Cow rolled past and a wave sloshed over me and my car. As it slowed, the spray lessened and the big plane rolled to a stop. I imagined Rafael collapsing on his seat back—exhausted—maybe saying a prayer of thanksgiving.

The rain eased off. Some cars left the airport, others drove nearer the plane, and when Rafael opened the passenger door to exit the plane, many people applauded. He smiled shyly and acknowledged the crowd with a modest wave of his hand.

Although the crisis had ended, a dozen more cars driven by curious people from the town arrived and parked every which way near the Cow to see the plane and the pilot. Rafael left the Cow parked on the runway where it had stopped.

While Frank parked his car near the Cow, I drove the company car back to our hangar, then trotted to the Cow. Frank and Rafael stood talking in the glow of a few headlights still shining on the plane. A small group had gathered.

Rafael explained he'd been flying on instruments and knew he was nearing CB, but could see nothing except blackness. When he saw two rows of lights emerge, he knew we'd lit the runway with auto headlights and he'd made it. He also added, he'd crabbed the plane on final in order to see through his open side window. He had no visibility at all through his front windshield.

After the crowd dispersed and cars' headlights disappeared, total darkness fell on the airfield. Frank and I drove our car back to the AEROVEN ramp. Rafael followed us in the Cow.

The Norseman, affectionately called, The Cow.

After a long day of flying, Frank rests at home
in his *Chinchorro*.

Blue Skies, Green Hell

We secured the plane and Frank invited him back to the house for a drink. He said he felt tired and needed to sit quietly a while with his wife, who surely had heard his plane and would be anxious for him to come home. Rafael Romero: A quiet, loving husband.

We were soaked through and our nerves were shot. Frank said he'd rather be flying the plane than sitting it out on the ground wondering what was happening up there.

*   *   *

Five months later, on September 29, 1955, Rafael Romero, the quiet man who lived a quiet life, crashed on takeoff at the Ciudad Bolivar Airport flying the Norseman with six passengers on board. The plane was totaled and all souls were killed on impact. The cause of the crash was never determined. News of the crash reached the pages of the New York Daily News.

Rafael Romero, killed flying the Norseman in 1955.
Photo clipped from newspaper.

Chapter 31

"Oh, Brothers!"

Dear Mother and Dad   April 22, 1955

Irv is not back. He's buying a plane in Florida, but no one has heard from him in weeks. Frank hears about him from Jack and friends in the ministry. He heard that Irv's still mad at Julio and has made arrangements to fly his new plane under the LEBCA license unless he can buy out Julio. Everything is a big, dark secret. Since Irv's troubles with AEROVEN, Magda is acting strangely. I feel badly. She's my friend.

All my love and devotion forever, Marilyn.

Irv cashed the insurance check he'd collected from the loss of his twin Cessna, fanned the bills and stuffed them in his wallet. He kissed Magda adios. "I'm coming back with another plane and we'll fly the pants off Julio. He'll be out. We'll be in." That's what he told Magda and Magda told me.

In Miami, with the help of Jack Perez, Irv bought a Seabee, built by Republic Aircraft. "Here's a photo of it," Frank said taking an aviation magazine from his desk drawer and opening it to an article about the plane. An odd looking aircraft, the six-cylinder Seabee featured an egg-shaped cabin, high wing, a long, slender boom with tail assembly and a single engine secured on top of the middle of the cabin with its prop facing toward the rear of the plane. "It's called a 'pusher.' With the propeller facing the tail, it looks like the aircraft is being pushed through the air, like a ship or submarine is pushed through the water by its propeller in the aft section."

I looked at the photo of a plane with the egg-shaped cabin. "Look. It's got tiny wheels and small pontoons on each wing! Wow! It's a funny looking plane, Frank. It says 'The Bee is an amphibian. There's room in it for a pilot and three passengers.'"

"Yes. Jack wrote that Irv fell in love with this plane and thinks it'll be just right for both rivers and savannahs in the interior."

Blue Skies, Green Hell

"If llaneros are leery about flying in single-engine Cessnas, I can't see them standing in line to reserve a seat on this bird." I handed the magazine back to Frank.

That problem never arose.

Frank heard from Jack that Irv took off from Miami and headed for Venezuela. He never made it. "I guess the Bee isn't as efficient on fuel as we thought," Frank said and snickered. "The plane ran out of gas fifty miles from Aruba and he crashed at sea. Wouldn't you know—he had no raft or life vest on board and floated on a wing for twenty-one hours until an Italian freighter rescued him. He left the freighter in Caracas and returned to Florida. When he collects the insurance, I presume he'll buy another plane. That's our Irv," concluded Frank.

In the meantime, Magda suffered. She led me to believe he'd not contacted her and she was without money.

I was at the office when Magda came by for a short visit. "I don't know what to do," she said to me. "I owe the rent, the utilities. I owe everybody." She started to cry. "I sold my dogs."

"Frank will help you out with money until Irv comes back. He likes you both. Stay with us—at our home—and something good will happen. Why does Irv do this? When he gets to Miami, it's . . ."

". . . like he doesn't think of me anymore. I know. I'm lonesome without him . . . and now with the babies [her dogs] gone . . ."

"Your dogs have good homes. Your friends will take care of them."

"Frank hasn't heard from Irv?"

"No, Magda. Irv doesn't contact Frank any more than he contacts you."

Magda sighed. "I guess I'll go home."

"Come to dinner at our house. Then stay over."

"I'll go home now. Thanks."

"To what? You can't stay alone. Stay with us." I urged.

"Please don't, Marilyn. I'll be okay." She leaned on the door frame and sighed. "Marilyn, I have to get away and think. I've asked Charlie if I can go to Canaima for a while. I've got to do something, but I don't know what."

When Frank returned from a flight and sat at the desk to complete his paperwork, I told him about Magda's visit. "She's not heard from Irv and won't stay with us. She's sold just about everything to make ends meet. She's worried. She's lonesome, too."

"He'll be back." Frank shuffled his papers and put a binder clip on them.

"She says he won't be back."

323

Frank threw down the pencil he'd started to twirl and said, "Damn it. I spoke to Irv about that when he was getting ready to leave for Miami. I asked him to leave money for her and stay in touch." He looked up at the chalkboard. "He's needed here, too." He picked up his pencil and resumed twirling it. "I expect him to come back. He's such a big kid."

"A big kid? He's way older than you are."

"Let me know how you think we can help her. If she needs anything, I can help her out until . . . until he comes back. You know him. He'll just show up one day with a big smile and another airplane."

I'd been shopping and stopped at Magda's house on my way home. People in the stores told me she had moved. I couldn't believe it. She hadn't told me and we'd been close friends! I walked to her front door, but as I approached, I looked through the dining room window and saw the house was empty. "Oh my God. It must be true."

I sped to the airport where I caught up with Frank. "Magda's moved. I've just come from her house. It's empty. I went to town this morning, did some shopping, chatted with some of the town's people. Some think she's living in the apartment above a store on the paseo operated by her two German friends. They're both men. She may clean house for them. Cook. That's the rumor." I sighed.

"I'm disappointed in Irv. Do you know the guys Magda's staying with?"

"She's spoken of them. She'll be safe. They'll help her." I looked out the office window. "But she never told me anything other than she wanted to go to Canaima—to think. She never told me about moving in with those boys . . ."

"Irv won't like that."

"Frank. He hasn't got a right to like it or not. Magda knows more than she's saying."

"Irv left me with a problem, too," Frank grumbled. Irv had bought a Mercedes-Benz and Frank co-signed the loan papers. "I'm not going to make his loan payments. I'll see if I can sell the car or return it to the dealer in Caracas." He spun a silver ash tray on the desk. Magda had given it to me for my birthday. "I expected Irv to return—work a deal to fly again for us." He repeated, "What got into him?"

A few days later, Charlie Baughan landed, taxied to our ramp and parked his old Piper. He came in the office and without greeting us, put his straw hat on the desk, nodded to me, and sat in a chair in front of the desk. "What's that boy of yours doing, Frank?"

"My boy?"

"Irv Banta. Magda's at Canaima. I flew her down a week or so ago. That poor little lady," he drawled.

"Ah," I interrupted. "The rumors can't be true."

Blue Skies, Green Hell

As Charlie carefully unwrapped a large cigar, he said, "That young lady is alone." He lit the cigar, took a few puffs. "She is alone in this world! How could Irv leave her stranded here. She says she's got to think. She can stay at Canaima as long as she wants. I'll pay her to do some work. But that's no life for that young girl. Have you heard from Irv?"

Frank pushed the silver ashtray toward Charlie. "No. Nothing. He's got a job here if he wants it." He threw his hands in the air. "I don't know where the hell he is."

"I'm going back to Canaima after I shop and stop at the post office. I'll check her mailbox. I hope there's a letter from Irv." Charlie started to leave.

"Hey, Charlie," Frank said. "Thanks for looking after Magda. If she needs money, let me know. "As he left, Charlie tipped his straw hat.

"He's so kind. What a gentleman." I picked up my pocketbook and slung it over my shoulder. "Charlie's so good-hearted. He hasn't got two nickels to rub together, and he's taking care of her. I'll see you at home. I'll walk."

I threw the ball to Loop and she raced for it just as Frank drove up and parked in front of the gate. Loop yapped and jumped and spun in the air. She didn't know whether to fetch the ball or greet Frank. Her affection for Frank won.

"You rate in Loop's heart," I said as he opened the gate and knelt to pet her.

We sat on the front porch rockers. "Charlie stopped at the office before heading back to Canaima. He picked up Magda's mail. He had a letter from Irv. I hope she'll receive good news."

"Oh, I pray she comes back to see me. She's hurting."

"I hope so, too . . . Irv left her and he stiffed me with his damn car. I've got to get rid of that."

I didn't see anything of Charlie or Magda for a week. Then from out of the blue, I saw Charlie's plane land and within minutes he pulled in front of my house driving our company car. Magda was with him. "I'll be back in a while, Magda," I heard him call to her as she hopped out of the car and he headed to town.

"Marilyn," she called through the dining room window. As I went to the door, I saw her tenderly touch the rockers we'd sat in one night—about a year ago—while we waited for someone to come from Asa with news about Irv and Frank.

"Come in, Magda," I said. "We'll have coffee. I'm so glad you came. I've worried so about you." We hugged.

"Oh, brothers! Thank you, Marilyn." We sat at the dining room table and she told me she'd decided to go back to Maiquetia with Charlie. She'd stay with a German girl friend who lived in Caracas until she left for the US next week. "I've heard from Irv." She said stoically, "It's over. He sent money to me." He'd given her a rough time and probably the hurt of his leaving was less painful than not knowing where she stood with him.

325

"Did you hear about what happened? On his way back from Miami in the Seabee?" I asked.

"Yes. Charlie told me. Oh, brothers! Twenty-one hours floating on a wing." She grew quiet and at that moment, I felt maybe she didn't want it to be over. "I used to worry about him when he didn't make it home when I expected him—or when he was overdue. I always felt I was alone—far from my family in Germany. I only had you, Marilyn. Now I really have something to worry about. What am I going to do?"

"He'll be back. Frank's counting on him. He'll come with another plane. When he does . . ."

"He won't be back." She said firmly.

"Magda. You are young. Very young. You have your whole life ahead." At the time she was 24.

Again, she acted strangely secretive and I felt she withheld information she preferred not to share. I wished she had remembered how we bush pilot wives support each other in difficult times.

We sipped our coffee.

"What can I do to help you, Magda? We've always helped each other."

She said she had all she needed to get to the States. "I'm going by ship to the US. I'll visit with my sister there. After a while, I'll probably go home—to Frankfurt. To Germany."

"Going by ship? Wonderful. You need the time for the transition." We hugged. "Do you have dresses to wear on the ship?"

"Oh—I'll be all right."

"Of course, you will. And I know how I can help." I went to my closet and selected several dresses I'd never worn. "I should never have bought these on my last trip to New York. They're way too sophisticated for me to ever wear in CB—but they're perfect for you on a cruise. Try them on."

She did, one by one, and looked stunning in each.

"Oh, I love this copper-colored satin. It's gorgeous. I can't pay you."

"My gift. Take them all."

"And this off-the-shoulder black. Wow." She twirled and the skirt flew out. She looked radiant and so beautiful.

"They're yours," I said. "You'll be the belle of the cruise. Have a marvelous trip. Have fun."

I put the dresses in a shopping bag.

She hung back. For the moment, I didn't think she really wanted to leave. She seemed so confused.

Out front, Charlie tooted the horn and Magda and I said goodbye to each other. We hugged. Tears from her face blended with those on mine. "Please. Keep in touch with me, Magda. And when you see Irv, tell him Frank says he'll welcome him back, anytime."

Blue Skies, Green Hell

She hesitated then nodded and left.

I waved to Charlie as he picked her up and they drove away. A few minutes later, I watched Charlie's Piper take off with Magda. They turned north to Maiquetía. I knew they could not see me, but I waved a kiss to both and watched until they'd flown beyond my vision.

*   *   *

The love story starring Irv, the handsome U.S. bomber pilot, and Magda, the beautiful German bride, ended abruptly.

Not long after Magda left, I was in town shopping and Frank was on a flight when Irv quietly arrived back in CB, unannounced, on the noon flight from Maiquetía. He walked to the hangar and asked Ramón if Frank was around. After Ramón explained Frank's absence, Irv hailed a taxi and drove off. Ramon told me the taxi went in the direction of Irv's home, but returned in minutes and Irv boarded the 1:00 p.m. flight back to Maiquetía. I wanted to believe he had come to talk with Magda about reconciliation, but Magda had already left for the States: He missed her by days. She left no forwarding address.

By coincidence, sometime later, I met a couple in Caracas who told me about a beautiful young lady named Magda who had lived in CB. She'd been the queen of a north-bound cruise ship they'd been on—and the ship's captain's favorite cruise companion.

I learned Magda and Irv divorced. Magda never contacted me. I missed my dear friend and will always fondly remember Magda.

*   *   *

When Magda and Charlie flew off to Maiquetía, it was also the last time I saw my dear friend, Charlie Baughan.

On December 8, 1956, Charlie Baughan, King of the Jungle, was killed when the twin Beechcraft he was flying crashed into a coastal mountain. He was 52 years old. He'd departed Canaima; destination Maiquetía. Mary, Charlie's wife, was in the plane with him and six passengers. The weather at Maiquetía had been inclement and Charlie advised the tower he would let down over the Caribbean and visually fly the route to Maturín, a small city inland and to the east, where he'd intended to land. That was his last communication. A search team found the wreckage of his plane 190 feet from the summit of the coastal mountain. All souls were dead. Jesús Indriago had been among those in the search and rescue operation. Indriago had been Frank's and my friend. I'd shared eight glorious days of expeditions at Canaima in 1953 with Jesús and his wife. Ironically, the Beechcraft was the same one AEROVEN had previously owned.

Capt. Irv and Magda Banta.

Marilyn and Magda—Good friends to the end.

Madelyn and I were in Caracas at the time of Charlie's memorial service in The American Church. The officiating pastor at the Memorial Service said Mary and Charlie would be buried at Canaima. Frank and I had been married in that church on October 1951, and Tom and Shirley Van Hyning had been married there seven months later in May 1952. That church is now The United Christian Church.

The two most intrepid and most famous pilots of those early days of bush flying in Venezuela—if not in all South America—Charlie Baughan and Jimmie Angel, had been killed in crashes during the same year. Jimmie Angel's ashes were scattered over Angel Falls. Nearby, Charlie and Mary Baughan rest in peace, buried close to the pink beach and the original airfield at Canaima.

For more about Charlie Baughan and my search for his grave in 2004 and 2007, see the Epilogue.

Chapter 32

Gods with Gold Braid

Dear Mother and Dad,   May 4, 1955

    This will be a short letter as only one item is news.
    Tom Van Hyning was killed Tuesday, May 3, in a plane crash while landing at the Hato La Vergareña. He was not flying an AEROVEN trip. We're in shock. You can't imagine how it has affected us. Frank is very upset. He stares at the airport across the street, but doesn't talk. I still rather expect that any minute, Tom will come walking down the dirt road—his arms swinging and his cowboy hat perched jauntily on his head.
    The plane burned. One wonders why such a tragedy should strike such a happy family. Shirley's 30, Patty's 2, and Tom was 35. They would have been married 3 years on May 21. They were so in love.
    Forgive this short letter, but I can't write more now.

Love, Marilyn.

    Dr. Manuel Eudoro Sanchez Lanz, Governor of Bolivar State, always telephoned Frank at home when he wanted to book a flight, so one evening in April 1955 when he called the house, only the nature of the flight startled Frank. Sanchez Lanz said his wife and her friends wanted to go up in a plane and do aerobatics. "*Se puede hacerlo*" (Can you do it)?
    Because the Governor had been responsible for AEROVEN's presence and subsequent success in Asa, Frank felt a sense of indebtedness to him and an obligation to grant the request, but in doing so, he said, "Our single-engine Cessnas aren't constructed to do aerobatics. We can do a few maneuvers that will resemble aerobatics, but they'll be limited for safety's sake."
    The Governor laughed. "Okay, just take the girls up and give them a few thrills."
    "We can do that," Frank replied. Arrangements for the flight were made for the next evening at 5:00 p.m. "The airport will be busy at that hour, but we'll fly high and south of the field. We'll be beyond and higher than the air traffic

pattern." Frank thanked him for calling, returned to the patio, and told me about the upcoming air show.

"Will you fly it? I asked.

"I don't think so. I'm not sure my ears could take the pressure of aerobatics anymore. I think Julio will be around to do it. If he can't make it, I'll call Tom. He likes to stunt."

Julio, available to make the flight, told Frank that first he'd review the plane's Information Manual to confirm the maneuvers approved for that aircraft.

At the appointed hour the next day, three ladies and their husbands, including the Governor, arrived at the airport. Julio taxied the Cessna from AEROVEN's hangar to the tarmac in front of the terminal and patio lounge where he greeted the ladies and helped them board the plane. The evening crowd of revelers enjoyed cool drinks and waited for the "air show" to begin. Socializing at the airport's patio lounge had long ago become a nightly ritual routinely attended by pilots, including Tom Van Hyning, and a few folks who simply liked to hang out with pilots.

Julio taxied the Cessna to the head of the runway and ran up the engine. In my mind's eye, I saw him check the RPMs, the ailerons, elevators, flaps, and brakes; not much to check in a single-engine Cessna, but he'd give the ladies the full treatment. I envisioned them holding their breath, perhaps tee-heeing a little. Maybe they felt a tad nervous and wondered why they'd been so foolhardy as to get themselves into this situation.

Satisfied with the instrument readings, Julio advanced the throttle and began to roll down the runway, gaining speed rapidly as he went. The tail wheel lifted, the plane went airborne, and the onlookers cheered. Julio circled the field climbing higher and higher over the flat and uninhabited land south of the airport.

The pilots agreed, aerobatics should never be done lower than 1500 feet altitude; Julio was way higher than that. We could hardly see his plane when he reached the altitude he deemed necessary to safely perform a "few thrills" to entertain the ladies. In the clear sky overhead, the white plane glinted and reflected the rays of the setting sun as Julio performed chandelles, lazy eights, steep turns, and a corkscrew spin. Although it probably scared the dickens out of the ladies, he even did a stall and recover.

The show attracted attention and a number of on-lookers curiously speculated about who might be the plane's passengers. Others wanted to meet the intrepid pilot. The show over, Julio descended, landed the plane, and taxied to a place in front of the patio lounge. After he shut down the engine, the ladies stepped out of the plane screaming and shouting with delight and waving to the sizeable and noisy crowd that had gathered to cheer and applaud. The Governor kissed his wife and when everyone saw that the Governor's wife had been one of the daring passengers, they cheered all the louder.

Julio taxied the plane back to the ramp outside the hangar, closed and secured the plane and the office, and then joined the group to take his share of the dew from Irish Mist. His cap pushed up off his forehead, his crinkled eyes and impish smile revealed his delight in the accolades thrown his way by the joyous bystanders who got a thrill just rubbing shoulders with the courageous pilot. The Governor bought a round of drinks for everyone and the ladies, exuberant and animated, continued to talk about their flight even as they departed.

"That's a trip they won't forget," Frank said jovially. "How'd they do? Anyone get sick?"

"Nary a one," replied Julio. "Good thing. I forgot to stow those small paper bags . . ."

After the crowd had dispersed, and only a few people lingered, Tom said, "Hey, Julio. What were you doing up there? Loops?"

Julio lit a cigarette.

"Got an extra cigarette?" Tom asked. He bummed cigarettes more often than he purchased them. "What you flew was no loop."

In defense of his flying skills, Julio replied, "Hey, pal. I flew the aerobatics approved in the book. This plane's not rated to do loops. There'd be too much load imposed on the plane—stress on the wings. The structure won't take it. It's not listed in the book. I just did a few stunts that would make the ladies happy."

"I can fly a perfect loop in that plane," Tom said, his head held high, his chin jutted out and his eyes tightly shut, the usual pose he struck when he made a point. "You'll see, Julio. One day, you'll see."

"It can't be done. Want to bet?" Julio answered.

"I'll bet my life on it," he called over his shoulder as he left the group and started to head for his car.

"Hey. What have I been hearing about a loop or no loop?" Frank had been talking with a bystander, but now wanted to join the discussion.

Tom halted in his tracks, spun around, and headed back to the table where Julio and Frank sat along with a few of the other stalwarts. He repeated what he'd told Julio.

"I fly by the book," Frank said. "And you do, too, Tom. If the manual doesn't state that the plane is approved to do a loop, I wouldn't do one. You wouldn't either. Julio knows what the plane can do." He lit a cigarette and thoughtfully drew on it. "I didn't see a loop. I saw a couple of chandelles." He drew again on his cigarette. "But, hell, loops aren't our business. None of us would do them in a Cessna. But why are we discussing the aerodynamics of flight. We all passed that course years ago. See you later, gentlemen. Come on, Button. I'm beat."

A week or so later while flying one of our competitor's Cessnas on a beautiful May day with blue skies and wispy clouds, Tom was scheduled to carry one passenger to Urimán south of Auyántepui. Then he'd fly back northwest, over the Green Hell, and stop at Horacio Cabrera's Hato La Vergareña to pick up a passenger. The final leg of the trip would be a short run home to Bolivar. After a full day of flying, he'd be tired. No doubt about that.

At La Vergareña, workers in a field near the grassy airstrip said they seldom looked up when a plane flew over. Usually, the pilot of an incoming plane buzzed the field, circled the ranch house, did a climbing turn, circled the field, landed, and waited for the hato driver to show up with the passenger or a package—whatever the mission called for.

The field workers had often seen and heard aircraft come and go. This time, they said, the plane sounded different and that caught their attention. They looked up in horror as they watched the small white plane with navy stripes make a low pass over the grassy airstrip at an unusually high rate of speed, pull up in a high and wide looping arc, and then plummet downward, slamming into the ground. With a great explosion, the plane burst into flames.

The workers rushed to the crash scene and pulled Tom's body from the wreckage. Crushed beyond recognition, Tom had died instantly.

Next day, the headlines in the Ciudad Bolivar daily newspaper screamed the news; *Al Hacer Un Viraje y Fallarle El Motor Se Precipito a Tierra una Avioneta—El Piloto Habia Combatido en la Ultima Guerra* (On Making a Turn and Attempting to Land, The Motor Quit and The Light Plane Crashed—The Pilot Had Been in the Last War).

The news story included a photo, and reported Tom was age thirty-five. The workers' story about the loop, received considerable attention.

Something horrific happened that beautiful day, Tuesday, May 3, 1955. Tom Van Hyning was killed in a fiery plane crash.

Tom grew up on a farm in Ohio and at age sixteen fulfilled his childhood dream of learning to fly. He dominated his world—the sky—and his style of flying came straight from the textbook.

He served in World War II as a Captain with the U.S. Intelligence Mission in Paraguay, South America. Including his military service and three years in the Venezuelan bush, Tom had been flying nineteen years. He had more than 6,000 flying hours. "No better way to start the day," Tom would say with a broad smile, "than by hearing the steady roar of a healthy engine and smelling raw gasoline." Everyone called Tom a top-notch pilot. They also called him complicated. He played many roles.

Standing over six feet tall and ruggedly handsome with strong, chiseled facial features, he strode with a theatrical flair across the tarmac at the airport to his single-engine aircraft. He even dressed dramatically, often wearing a narrow black ribbon tied in a loose bow under the collar of his authentic cowboy shirt, an extra-wide leather Indian belt with ornate silver and turquoise buckle, and a western cowboy hat worn at a rakish angle. Bystanders at the airport would talk about "that man" and try to guess his name or the name of the movie they'd most recently seen him in. Tom never missed a cue, strutting here and there flashing a Hollywood smile. A showman.

Capt. Thomas Clark Van Hyning: 1920-1955.

At home with his wife Shirley and baby Patty, he played another role; family man, quiet and devoted. I heard that Tom and Shirley, with Patty on her daddy's lap, frequently sat around a lamp whose colors shimmered, and they prayed together.

Tom's greatest joy was Patty and he'd hoped Patty would have a sister or brother as soon as possible. Shirley did her best to fulfill that desire, but miscarried two times, maybe three, during the years we shared our lives. His first reason for living was being with his family and his second was flying.

And there was the quiet Tom. Frank and I often played Canasta with Tom and Shirley—men versus ladies. Usually, Shirley and I won and in my mind's eye, I still see Tom throwing his head back, laughing and smiling broadly when it became obvious Shirley and I would win again. Neither Tom nor Frank ever became upset when they lost. They laughed it off. We four also went to the movies. Our times together were enjoyable, and lots more sedate than when we gallivanted and played hard with the Freemans.

Blue Skies, Green Hell

We reminisced many times about our excursion to the savannah to meet the aliens from the UFO when Tom played the role of light-hearted adventurer.

Early on in our friendship, and with our continued lack of business coming from the trips up and down the river, Frank felt compelled to re-evaluate and reverse his assessment made in 1952 of Tom's untoward behavior. When Frank realized few people from the river towns were frequent flyers, he knew he'd made a great error in his judgment of the man. Frank and Tom were mature, got beyond that incident, and we felt good about our friendship. Shirley and I were good friends. Both of the men were so fair.

Free-spirited and happy, whether over the jungle, or anyplace else, with or without passengers, Tom often would sing, banking the plane from one side to the other in rhythm to the song, "He Flies Through the Air With the Greatest of Ease," one of the songs he most liked to sing. It broke the boredom and passengers loved it.

And somewhere within this extraordinary persona, lived an eccentric. Tom often had a musty, macho smell about him. On someone else, it would have been called a touch of body odor. "Bathe every day?" he'd ask. "Why? It's going to be hot tomorrow and I'll just sweat again."

Before I'd interact with Tom, I'd first determine to which Tom I'd be speaking; the wannabe theatrical matinee idol, the conservative family man, the socially fun friend, the light-hearted adventurer, or the free-as-a-bird eccentric.

"Green Hell is to the south, and living hell is Ciudad Bolivar on the Orinoco," some said. Tom didn't believe that for a minute.

"It's true, when you cross the Orinoco you cross into another world," he said. But Tom liked that other world, simple and free of modern trappings. Tom thought Bolivar defined peace.

On the day of the accident, I'd been with Shirley and little Patty. We had lunch together, did some shopping and went back to Shirley's house for afternoon tea. Both Frank and Tom were flying. Frank thought he'd be back early in the afternoon; Tom didn't know when he'd return. He told Shirley it probably would be close to the 6:00 p.m. deadline.

I left Shirley's, drove to my home a few blocks away, and had just put the car in the carport when Frank, driving the company station wagon, pulled up in front of the house. Martha sat next to him in the front seat. He beckoned for me to get in the wagon. I hopped in the back seat. No one said hello.

"Hey, what's up?" I sensed something wrong. I could not have anticipated Frank's answer.

"It's Tom," he said stoically.

I hesitated. "What?"

Frank waited a long pause.

Martha stared out the windshield of the car and then closed her eyes.

"He's dead," Frank said. "He crashed . . . landing at La Vergareña. We have no details. The hato radioed the Ciudad Bolivar Tower. They advised VETA. Then VETA told us. Tom was flying one of VETA's planes." Frank's voice was barely audible.

Flying the Noorduyn Norseman, Julio had already departed CB for La Vergareña. At the hato, workmen constructed a coffin in which Julio would fly Tom's lifeless body home. Frank took my hand. "You and Martha, go tell Shirley and stay with her. Whatever you think has to be done, please do it."

Martha, Shirley, Magda and I, wives of the bush pilots in CB, were close friends. We had good times together, understood each others' complex lives, and, most importantly, we understood our complex men. An exclusive support group, we were like sisters. In crises, we were never alone.

The townspeople admired our men, held them in awe, and looked upon them as a different breed on this last frontier. Like Tom said, townspeople thought pilots were Gods with gold braid.

"I'll call Dr. Batisttini. We may need him," I said.

"That's good," Frank replied.

"And then I'll contact Mr. Williams."

"Who's he?"

"He's the new Protestant missionary. I'll drive out to his house. He lives on the far side of the airport."

"Maybe he can help with the final arrangements," Frank said thoughtfully. "Be careful, Button. It's lonesome out there."

"I'll ask him to come to Shirley's tonight and you two can talk."

"That's fine," he answered. "I'll see you at Shirley's later." Martha and I got out of the station wagon and Frank drove back to the airport.

We passed through the ornate iron gate at the entrance to my driveway and went in the house. I advised my maid that neither the Captain nor I would be dining at home, and asked her if she would prepare something for us to eat later and put it in the fridge. Then I told her Captain Tom had been killed in a crash. She wilted and dropped into a dining room chair. Clutching the top of her uniform, she wept, "*Ay, la señora y la nena tan bella*" (Oh, the señora and the beautiful baby girl).

I called Dr. Batisttini. "Dr. B? Have you heard about Tom?"

News traveled fast in Bolivar. "I'm still in shock," he said. "Tom and I had a tennis game planned for tonight. Do you have details?"

"Not yet, but Julio's at La Vergareña where it happened. Martha and I are going to Shirley's now. Frank asked us to tell her. Will you join us?"

"I'll go there right away."

It was after 6:00 when Martha and I, in my car, pulled up in front of Shirley's house. She stood on the lawn under the mango trees in front of her house, a place from which she could look up through the trees and see Tom's plane coming home. Upon seeing us, she walked to the curb. Little Patty toddled behind, hanging on to Shirley's skirt.

"Hello," someone said. Silence followed.

"It's Tom," Shirley said, making a statement, not a question. "He's late."

"Yes." I whispered.

Dr. Batisttini parked his car behind mine at the curb and, still wearing his white shirt and tennis shorts, joined us under the trees in the front yard.

Shirley picked up Patty. They walked up the path to the front screened door of the house, opened it, touched it tenderly, briefly, and went inside. Tom had just installed the door. He had no desire to kill an animal, but he wanted to keep his family safe and free from harmful critters. "Bugs and critters can live," he'd say, "so long as they stay outside."

Carrying Patty to her room, Shirley held her baby close, kissed her, then put her in her crib. She came back to the living-room where we three stood, uncomfortable and inadequate. She looked from one of us to the other. Finally, Dr. Batisttini told her Tom had crashed at the Hato La Vergareña.

"And?" she said.

"He died."

"Are they sure he's . . . ?" she asked, desperate to hear something else, something hopeful she could hold on to.

"Yes. He died on impact." Dr. Batisttini replied.

"Oh," she said in a very thin voice. Her eyes clouded with grief.

"We have few details," I added. "He crashed on landing."

"Landing," she said in disbelief. "Landing? He's landed there so many times. Any cattle on the strip?" she asked.

Cattle often grazed on the strips in the savannahs, and when that happened, the pilot would fly low over the field to scare off the cattle, make a climbing turn, go around the field again and land safely.

"No," I replied. "Nothing like that."

Shirley left the room and walked outside. She stopped under the mango trees, looked up through their leaves. The late afternoon shadows were long and the fading light in the sky filtered down through the trees in long slim shafts making lacey designs on the cement walkway.

Martha went outside and put her arms around Shirley. They stood, gently rocking from side to side. They wept.

In the baby's room, shaded by old fruit trees, I stood at the foot of Patty's crib. The sweet scent of baby powder filled the room. Wearing a pink pinafore with a ruffle at the bottom, the toddler, almost two years old, waited for her daddy to come home, pick her up, kiss her, and call her Princess. And she was that; a happy and beautiful baby.

Her arms reached up to me and I gently lifted her out of the crib. I held her close.

337

I tried to imagine what it might have been like in this room before dawn. Tom had an early takeoff, so he would have left the house before daybreak. Wearing his cowboy hat at the usual rakish angle, he would have quietly walked into Patty's room, raised the top of her screened-in crib and lowered its side so he could lean close to her and kiss her goodbye as she slept. He would have promised his Princess he'd be back later. Darling Patty, I thought. You have so much life ahead . . . without your dear daddy. "How can something like this happen?" I laid Patty down in her crib. We'd had such a pleasant day together.

Shirley and Martha returned inside the house. Dr. B. spilled pills into a small white envelope and said, "Take these, Shirley, tonight or whenever you need them. They'll help. You might need them to get some sleep."

"Oh, Dr. B. I don't understand." She dabbed her eyes with her handkerchief.

"No one can, Shirley. It's God's will. Tom's safely home." He shook his head, slowly. "Only this morning, Tom called me from the airport and said he'd be home by six, in time for tennis. This, after a long day flying. Quite a guy!"

She looked at Dr. B and almost smiled as she asked in a hushed voice, "Do you think he was singing?"

"Could be. We know he was happy. He loved to fly . . . and loved to sing." He closed his black medical bag. "Mostly, he loved you and Patty. I'll be home tonight. Call if you want." He looked at Martha and me, nodded "I'll see you tomorrow." He left.

"Whatever happened? Landing!" Again, with a small hanky, she dabbed at tears of disbelief and stared out the door and at the playful shadows made by the light breeze blowing through the leaves. "Sometimes there's a cross-wind there. But Tom's landed there in a cross-wind dozens of times."

The setting sun signaled the day's end.

She turned and said to Martha and me, "We never talk about—anything like this." Shaking her head slowly, she turned and went into the pink and white tiled bathroom to Patty's combination tub and dressing table and ran water in the little tub. The water was warm having been heated all day by the burning sun beating on the rooftop water tank.

I went back to Patty's bedroom, removed her pinafore and carried her to the bathroom for her nightly bath. Shirley held her, and then turned to Martha and said, "Do you think about—about this?"

Martha slowly nodded her head. "I think about it. But Julio'd rather fly than do anything else." She sort of giggled.

"And you, Marilyn?"

"I know something can happen. I'm uneasy when Frank's overdue or doesn't get home when I expect him. But you can't take a pilot out of his element. I live with it." I thought for a moment then added, "We wives, have long, lonely hours and share the same unspoken worries. There's a bond between us. We know we're here for each other. We don't have to talk about it."

Blue Skies, Green Hell

Shirley nodded.

With Patty's bath and dinner finished we put her in bed and greeted friends, neighbors, and other people who visited to pay their respects and bring gifts of food. I slipped out and drove ten miles on unpaved roads without street lights to carry the sad news to Mr. Williams. There were no telephones and I was glad I found him at home.

"Do you know Tom's religion?" asked Mr. Williams.

"Not really. The family prayed. Their faith had something to do with—'I AM.'"

"Probably Christian Science," he said.

Mr. Williams followed me in his car to Shirley's where he comforted her. Later, he and Frank planned Tom's graveside memorial service to be held the next day.

Martha and I stayed with Shirley through the night. We didn't sleep very much. We didn't talk very much, either. Frank left just before midnight. He expected government inspectors to arrive from Caracas on the first flight and he'd fly them to La Vergareña in the morning. I wanted so much to be with him—to help him through this night, but he insisted he'd be okay and that Shirley needed me.

It was after sunrise when I left Shirley's and went to the airport. I met Frank. We said nothing, but clung to each other. "Are you okay to fly?"

He shook his head. "I've got a job to do."

By 9:00 a.m., Frank, with the officials on board, idled his plane and waited for tower clearance to fly south to the hato.

After he departed, the maintenance crew cleaned the AEROVEN hangar. Tools and spare parts were locked in the storage room. They tidied the office, set out cookies and had iced Kool-Aid in thermos jugs. By noon, the main part of the hangar was ready to receive the coffin. Early in the day, Julio had radioed the tower from the hato and reported that the coffin, made of heavy metal with welded seams, took longer to build than planned. His return to CB would be delayed.

At about 1:00 p.m., Frank and his passengers in the Cessna, and Julio with Tom's coffin in the Norseman, returned to Ciudad Bolivar. The two pilots, memorializing their friend and fellow flyer, flew their planes in formation to Ciudad Bolivar.

Julio landed the Norseman, taxied and parked one hundred feet or more from the hangar. While flying toward Bolivar and within radio distance of the office, Julio had called Bud Small, our mechanic, and advised him the coffin's welded seams were not completely sealed and body fluids were leaking. When the large, cumbersome-looking plane landed, Bud was standing by and made the necessary weld repairs then taxied the plane closer to the building.

Airport workers struggled as they carried the heavy metal coffin into the hangar and placed it on two large, heavy-duty sawhorses in the middle of the cavernous space. A black funeral pall covered the coffin and over that was a large floral arrangement of bougainvillea from Shirley and Patty. A stanchion was placed near each corner of the coffin. On each was placed an empty quart-size can of airplane oil with a tall candle affixed to it. Other candles on empty oil cans were placed on workbenches, stepladders and on the floor in front of the floral pieces. Flowers delivered throughout the day were placed against the inside wall and long workbench in the old hangar. It looked bizarre; the hangar, its decrepit overhead work light turned off, flowers and blazing candles on oil cans all around.

Townspeople converged on the hangar to pay their respects. Shopkeepers and service people who knew Tom and Shirley were the first to arrive at the airport to offer condolences to the young widow. Demonstrating enormous community sensitivity and solidarity, they mourned the loss of one of these courageous airmen who they knew provided help and comfort to so many people living in the deep, lonesome interior.

Hundreds of townspeople, on foot, assembled in lines in the airport parking lots and when the lines started to move, the people walked slowly into the hangar and past the funeral bier. Some thought I was Shirley. We hardly resembled one another, but we were young, had light hair, fair skin, and we looked foreign.

Later, when Martha arrived with Shirley and Patty, the line halted temporarily as Shirley looked around and saw the unique and appropriate arrangements. She smiled. "This is nice. Tom would like it," she said.

I took her hand, "Yes, Shirley, he does. I'm sure he sees it all."

She stood near one end of the coffin and, speaking softly in Spanish, graciously acknowledged each person who came in the hangar to express sympathy until the last person had filed past.

At 3:30, the cortege began to form and we were asked to leave the hangar and proceed to our cars. As I exited the building into the bright sunlight, I stopped short. Stunned. I gasped and put my hand on my forehead and closed my eyes. Then I opened them. Wide.

I'd been thrown back in time—like seeing an old movie about old Spain. The throng of mourners crowding the hearse and milling around were assembling in the large parking lot behind the last car in line. Everyone wore black; women wore black veils over their faces. Because it was May fourth, the beginning of the intensely hot summer, some held black umbrellas over their heads to provide shade and protect themselves from harsh rays of the burning sun. People mopped perspiration from their faces and necks with handkerchiefs.

In this sea of black, we American women were the only ones dressed in bright colors.

I saw a black and gold horse-drawn hearse. It looked like a huge open-sided black box on a platform with large black wooden wheels easily three feet in diameter. The hearse was ornate with gold filigree painted on a border near its black roof and also on the four corner supports. The lone black horse had brightly polished brass tack.

The first car behind the hearse was the company station wagon driven by Julio. Shirley, Patty and Martha rode in it. Frank and I, in Irv's Mercedes were next. A couple of other cars carried close friends.

True to Venezuelan tradition, the crowd walked behind the cars toward the cemetery. I heard women sobbing loudly and talking about la nena, the little baby. That some had not known Tom or Shirley or the baby, was of no consequence. They cried, overcome with grief, just as they would have had Tom been a member of their own family. A tragedy in their town had befallen one of them.

The cortege, moving only as fast as the people could walk, began the painfully slow trip of a few miles to the cemetery. As we progressed along Avenida Táchira, women dropped out of the procession to walk to their homes. Customarily, only men walked the full distance to the cemetery. Groups of people on the sidewalks watching were respectful and quiet; the silence was broken only by the clip clopping of the horse's hoofs and creaking of the carriage's wooden wheels rolling on the macadam road. We arrived at the city's walled cemetery on a hillside by the Orinoco.

Frank and I walked to the top of the red dirt hill where few plants and no grass grew and then to the gravesite under a large shade tree. We joined other mourners there. Tom's coffin, carried up the hill by cemetery workers, was still covered with Shirley and Patty's blanket of bougainvillea. Other floral pieces, brought to the cemetery in the hearse, were placed around the site.

Frank and I held hands as we looked southward and saw the lightly foliated savannahs. I sighed, and Frank squeezed my hand as we looked northward, across the mighty Orinoco River to the flat and barren oil fields beyond. The river shimmered in the sunlight.

Mr. Williams, the missionary, his head bowed, had begun preaching the memorial service when he was interrupted by the sound of a small plane flying overhead. Patty, embraced lovingly in her mother's arms, pointed her tiny index finger skyward. "Ai'-mane," she said for "airplane" and then murmured softly, "Daddy," With great difficulty, Mr. Williams regained his composure and concluded the service.

The cemetery workers lowered the huge metal box into a concrete vault, shoveled in dirt and then covered it with flowers.

The propeller from Tom's Cessna, twisted and bent, was placed on top of the flowers.

The crowd dispersed.

Shirley, Martha and Patty walked down the hill to their vehicle where they waited for Julio. Everyone else walked to their cars or to their homes. Julio,

Frank and I remained at graveside a few minutes. Frank and I said our last silent prayers and then, holding hands, we headed down the hill to Irv's Mercedes.

Julio stayed behind, but I'd taken only a few steps when I turned and saw Julio remove a cigarette from his pocket and place it gently on the ground near one of the floral pieces. It would not be the last cigarette Julio would place at the gravesite of his good friend.

At the car, I asked Frank, "Did you learn any more today from the inspectors?"

"Not really," he replied. "The article in the paper reports the workers in the field saw Tom buzz the field, going very fast, then pull up and they described a loop." He looked up in the sky. "Maybe they saw a loop and maybe they didn't. Maybe they saw him buzz and then do a climbing turn. But in their excitement, maybe they didn't see what they said they saw." He wiped his brow with his handkerchief. "God, it was awful." With difficulty, he whispered, "It looked like his plane dove into the ground and then fell back on its underbelly. The engine smashed into pieces. The wings were flat and the tail assembly withstood the impact. The fuselage disappeared—consumed by fire. Because there was nothing to inspect, even the examiners didn't have the answer."

Frank felt strongly that Tom would not have tried a loop at such low altitude. Even recalling Tom's challenge to Julio, he was certain Tom wouldn't have called the shot at that time.

"Was it pilot error? Or equipment malfunction? The speculation at the airport favors pilot error. The newspapers play that up, too, possibly because so many people heard Tom challenge Julio about the loop. Me? I can't buy pilot error," Frank concluded. "In fairness to Tom and his training and experience let's give him the benefit of the doubt. Gods with gold braid don't make pilot errors."

Martha invited friends back to her house for refreshments and to visit with Shirley and Patty who had planned to stay there overnight. I had thanked Martha at the cemetery but gave my regrets. I was emotionally exhausted. Frank told me he'd stay with Julio a while before coming home. He had to. He and Julio had lost their complicated friend and, at this time, they were brothers.

Frank parked the car in front of Julio's house. I hopped out. "You keep the car, Frank. I'll walk. I need to."

The quiet walk helped me think back over the past twenty-four sorrow-filled hours; my life would go on, but I'd be stronger. At age twenty-five, I'd grown up a lot.

My maid met me at the door. Dressed in black, she told me she'd been to the hangar and walked part of the way to the cemetery with the cortege.

"If I'd known, you could have been in the car with us," I said in Spanish. "I'm so sorry."

"I shall miss Captain Tom," she said. "And you, Señora. Are you all right?"

"I will be."

"Señora," she said. "Last night, Captain Frank came home a few minutes before midnight. He poured a glass of milk and stood at the living room window looking out at the black airfield. Later, he sat in a chair and stayed there all night."

"It brings it close to home, doesn't it?" I sighed. "I'm going to rest a while."

I dropped onto the bed, stretched, and stared at the ceiling. I remembered an article I'd clipped from a magazine and put in the drawer of my night table next to the bed. I opened the drawer, took out the article. It included a passage from the MGM movie, "A Guy Named Joe," and I read it again. The words could have been Tom's. Or Frank's, Julio's, or Irv's.

> "When you're up there.... everything's kind of still, and you've got a feeling you're half-way to heaven. You don't even seem to hear your own motors—just a kind of buzz far off... like the sky was calling you ... like the sky was singing you a song.... And somehow it's never eight o'clock up there ... it's always now. The earth's so far below you don't care about it anymore. It's the sky that's important. The sky is your pal. You feel like nudging the sky and saying, 'Hello sky—how are you today, sky—and how was the moon last time you saw him?' The wind-draft comes straight off the morning star, and the clouds float toward you like old friends you never want to say goodbye to ... and you say to yourself, 'Boy, oh boy—this is the only time a man's alive—it's the only time he's free!' And the old sky, he smiles back and says, 'You're right, brother—you're right.'"

Crash Scene—Hato La Vergarena

Capt. Frank Lazzari and an inspector
study the crash scene.

YV-C-JAG tail and wings

73 JAG's tail assembly

Aircraft's tail assembly

JAG's Venturi and a shoe

JAG's engine

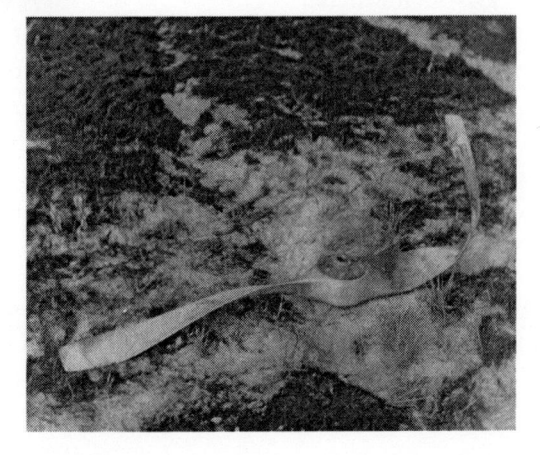

The aircraft's propeller was placed on Tom's grave.

Chapter 33

"There's No More Bolivar"

(Continued from Chapter 1—**May 24, 1955**)

"Hey, Button. Wake up, sleepy-head." I'd slept so soundly in the front seat of FLA, Frank's voice startled me. I looked up and saw the small crystal cross still swaying slowly in the gentle breeze. Frank opened the Cessna's door. I heard him say, "I must be overworking you."

"Oh. How could I have slept through that storm? Ramón and I checked the tie-down lines then the wind and rain returned. He suggested I wait in the plane until the weather cleared. And your trip? Are you okay? And the ailing diamond buyer?" I rubbed my eyes and shivered.

"Hey. Slow down." Frank climbed into the seat next to me and put his arm around me. "What is it, Button?"

"I'm okay. I guess I was tired."

"I made it fine. It was a local storm. I started out at almost 1,500. Got some buffeting—but—after a few minutes, it cleared and I had good weather all the way. Before I left, we talked about those unreliable weather forecasts!"

"How is the buyer you picked up at La Paragua? I didn't get a message to tell me to get a doctor."

"I didn't give one. I think the buyer had too much aqua caliente the night before—or the doctor did. Anyway, we landed here and the two went off in a taxi—somewhere."

"I know. 'We don't get involved. We got them here—and that's our job.' I learned that lesson a long time ago." I raised my hand and pointed to the crystal cross pinned to the ceiling, in the center near the windshield.

"Frank, who put the cross up there?"

"It's been there so long, I don't know."

"I saw it and began to recall all the men who have flown this plane. And tried to think who might have pinned the cross there. I thought of Tom. Oh, Frank. What a waste."

"Let's go to the office and see what's up. I just landed. I haven't been there yet."

Ramón greeted us with news. "Mr. Shorty called. Please call him? He's in Puerto Ordaz. He wants to see you. Your brother, Do, is with him."

"Button, want to come with me? We can have a sandwich at the airport and then fly out to see Shorty and Do. It's a short trip."

"Thanks, but I know what you'll be talking about; ECUAVEN and AEROVEN and money and accountants! I don't feel like being there." I handed him my car keys.

After lunch, Frank filed his flight plan and came back to the hangar.

"Sure you don't want to go flying? The weather's clear. It's a beautiful day." As he spoke he removed the keys for FLA from the hook near the chalkboard. He loved that old plane.

"Next time." I walked with him to the plane. We kissed.

I watched him do all the routine things and take off. In my mind's eye, I saw the pictures of Tom's plane; crashed and burned. *I've got to get over this!*

"Wow, what a day. I don't know how he does it," I said to Ramón.

On his return trip to CB, he buzzed the house and a few minutes later, bounded through the front door. "Button! Button!" he called joyously.

I came from the kitchen. "Hey." We stood in the living-room.

"Button," he said exuberantly, "I sold the company—my shares."

I gasped, wiped my hands on my apron, and pushed back my hair. "You sold your shares in the company? Just like that?" From out of the blue, in seconds, my world crashed and burned. I could hardly breathe.

"I don't understand, Button. This is not a new idea. We've talked about this."

"No! No! We've not talked! You have. And only when you were in despair. I thought we were a team. You and I. We talk over everything. Ever since we came here and you made a trip with Julio and left me to answer the phone at the office, we've been a team. You were flying and I was in the office. Remember? You held meetings in our house and I attended—even took notes. You included me in the Griffin—Payne business meetings in Caracas." The words poured out unbidden. "You've often taken my advice. But now, you don't ask for my opinion about something that directly concerns me as much as it does you?"

He listened attentively, then he said "Button, you've known, one way or another, we'd return to Caracas."

"I didn't think it would happen this way nor so soon. Selling your dream wasn't ever mentioned." I barely whispered. "And that's another thing." My voice rose. "You've already decided we will go to Caracas. What happened to Maracaibo? I don't like Caracas, but that's not important to you—you and your . . . ."

My remarks went unanswered. "And I sold our furniture, too," he blurted.

"*Ay Díos mío*" (Oh, my God!)! I shouted. "How could you do that? My beautiful new dining-room and living-room?" I walked in circles. "How unthoughtful! That, we never discussed!" He put his arms around me. "Go away!" I said and pushed him.

"I love you, Button. It's a good deal for us—all around—both of us," he said. "You know there are no moving vans that travel between CB and Caracas. The furniture can't be moved in just any truck—not on that road. And flying everything—crating it all? Not really an option."

I felt defeated. "I suppose so."

"We'll buy everything new."

"I've always trusted you. I've been so proud of you."

"Trust me again. Let's talk. We'll discuss everything. It'll be a good move for the dogs. They're always sick here and their vet is in Caracas. They'll be better off there. They'll be more comfortable. So will you. It's never hot there."

"I've never complained about the heat! Just leave me alone!"

I walked to the large double wooden front doors, opened one and went to the yard. I walked around the outside of the house and looked at the tree where Loop caught and killed two large green iguanas, the black iron fence across the front of the house where Loop raced up and down when Frank took off and landed. I saw the little garden of marigolds I grew from seeds Mother sent me. I touched one of the screens my Father made for the windows. As I passed the patio I recalled the parties, the dancing, the laughter, the fun, the games, the piñata I made and hung from the ceiling of the patio for Frank's last birthday party when he turned thirty-one. I bent over and straightened out a stone in the barbeque pit my Father built for us, and I reached up to fondle a leaf of the avocado tree where Rochford, the toucan, used to perch. Tenderly, my hand touched the wicker furniture I had just repainted and had new covers made for its cushions. It would seat no more parties. I saw Teddy's overturned water dish where earlier he had spilled the water on the terrazzo floor so he could lie in it and cool off. And I cried and cried.

Loop joined me and together we walked toward the laundry room. Passing the small grove of lemon trees, I filled my lungs with the sweet scent of the blossoms. I admired the screened wall in the laundry room, built and installed by members of the Project Club; Madelyn, Magda, Shirley, Martha and I. Together, we five ladies moved mountains. We met every two weeks at one of our houses for an all-day work session. We did projects we couldn't do alone and which our husbands never had time to do.

We screened in my laundry room and sewed slip covers for Shirley's living room furniture. After we painted a room in Martha's house, we made screens there, too. When Magda's Doberman had puppies, we read how to cut their tails and that was our project at her house.

The Mending Club met each week—same five ladies. We repaired our own things, helped each other and then served lunch and tea. What a good life. A happy life.

Whenever we wanted to play tennis or swim we went to the country club. Our days were full and fun. In two cars, we often drove an hour north of the

Blue Skies, Green Hell

Orinoco to San Tome, an oil company's camp, where we shopped in the food commissary. If Frank or Julio had to fly there on business, we'd go in the plane and shop while he worked. Our daytime social life, filled with activities and camaraderie, rivaled the evening's activities when we just had good times with our friends at the airport patio lounge or at our house.

Loop and I passed the clotheslines Frank had just installed for me. He'd buried the "T" shaped metal uprights in cement in the ground and strung plastic-covered wire from one to the other. He did a beautiful job. He told me they'd last a lifetime. Whose lifetime? Loop and I continued our walk into the carport. In my mind's eye, I saw Mother standing there with Chucho, my moriche bird from Canaima, perched on her head. Mother had never been so close to wildlife.

The porch in the front of the house held a special thought. I lost my breath and tears filled my eyes as I recalled when Magda and I sat there all night, wondering what caused the airstrip in Asa to close and waiting for word about our husbands who suffered there.

I looked across the street. My airport. My runway. The first hangar we used. My mind filled with glorious memories of my marvelous life in Bolivar; the best years of my life when living had been a game, filled to the brim with love and happiness—and with tragedy and death, too. But mostly, my life had overflowed with adventure. All that. Over. Dashed.

I walked back inside the house. In the kitchen, Frank had made coffee in the new demitasse machine Do had given us. He handed a cup to me.

"You sold your shares to Shorty?"

"Yes."

"Did you know about this when you went to see him?"

"No. It just came about."

"I should have gone with you." I dropped my head.

He gave me his handkerchief and I wiped my tears with it. "Can we talk, Button? I want you to understand." He took my hand and we sat on the sofa.

"Shorty wanted to talk about taking over ECUAVEN. He's about ready to do that. He knows I'm tired of hustling work for AEROVEN—one airplane can't keep the whole company going."

"Frank, you've always found a way to keep the company alive. Always. I don't want to leave. "

"Shorty asked if I wanted to sell AEROVEN. He knew shares of AEROVEN would include ECUAVEN and that's what he really wants to own. Now, Shorty will be the major shareholder and president of both AEROVEN and ECUAVEN."

I didn't understand. "Why couldn't you have bought out Julio, taken the Norseman and put it to work in Puerto Ordaz. You have great contacts there. You've always said Puerto Ordaz would be the important city in the future—not CB. Maybe Irv would come back if it's just the two of you. We could stay here.

We could start again." Words flew from my mouth and most didn't make much sense. I knew that.

"Button, your Bolivar isn't here anymore."

He shocked me. "What do you mean?"

"Tom is dead and Shirley and Patty have gone back to the States. Madelyn and Carlos won't be back. Magda and Irv have gone their separate ways. Who knows where Martha and Julio are headed? And Charlie Baughan—so much a part of your life in CB." I took the hand he held out to me and he drew me close. I rested my forehead on his chest. With his hand under my chin, he tilted my head upward. "Button. There is no more Ciudad Bolivar."

We'd said our last goodbye to friends at the Cerro Bolivar base camp and walked to the plane. I opened my door. Frank walked to the center of the airstrip and stopped. The wind was strong. I wondered what he was thinking. Was it his first landing at Cerro Bolivar? Or his last takeoff—about to happen? I didn't intrude into his last moment as a Captain and President of AEROVEN.

Chapter 34

"Can We Make A New Dream?"

Dear Mother and Dad   **June 3, 1955**

    I love CB and can't think of leaving and moving to Caracas. I've had the best years of my life here. I've had good friends and adventures . . . and blue skies every day. How I love to fly. Maybe I'll never fly again! Most of all, I enjoyed being a pioneer—an adventurer.

All my love. Marilyn

    I'd shed tears of joy departing our first home; the little white palace next to the Freeman's. Now I wept tears of sorrow as I prepared to leave my radiant home filled with remembrances of good times, laughter, and love. Only Loop and our recently acquired German Shepherd puppy, Teddy, enjoyed the whole experience as they bounded through and played in piles of tiny wood chips used to pack precious and breakable objects we'd take with us.
    In 1952, as a young girl, I'd brought nothing with me to CB, so every possession, even the tiniest and most insignificant item, had a special place in my memory. Now as I packed boxes with glasses, dishes, linens, lamps, books, and precious personal belongings, I gently held each item and reflected on its short history.
    I cradled each one of six small, yellow plastic refrigerator storage bowls that Frank had purchased for me when we moved into our beautiful home. I caressed my face with the stuffed panda he'd won at the local carnival for having flown upside down in an airplane on wires.
    Frank packed his log books and a weighty pile of reference books about aerodynamics and aeronautical information. In all the years we lived in CB, they'd been prominent on a shelf in a book case that Frank had built as a boy. They'd settled a few discussions with pilots who visited, and I read them to be better informed about the skills demanded of professional pilots. Frank and I'd sit up late while he explained subjects I'd not fully understood from reading his books; like density altitude as related to aircraft performance.

When we "oh'd and ah'd "over the new yellow plastic refrigerator containers, we never thought our dream would end this way.

He packed two large framed diplomas from the school of aviation in Maracay that had hung on the bedroom wall. Finally, he packed a large portrait of himself in his TACA uniform. He looked so young. Such a boy. The years in CB had taken their toll. Most were very good years, but lately a pall hung over our universe.

I didn't understand how Frank could leave Bolivar and his dream without hurting. But, once the issue of selling the shares and the household furnishings had been settled, he was ready to move on. He walked with lighter footsteps and while his eyes found some of their lost sparkle, my eyes were red and wet.

I dawdled over every chore, every aspect of the move, trying desperately to steal a few more days in my beloved home. Forlornly, I sat on the floor among the packed boxes and smoked.

After a little time and a lot of love, we'd made Bolivar our own, and I couldn't give it up without a lot of pain.

The afternoon before we left, we went to the airport to say goodbye to friends.

We parked at the low cyclone fence, the car facing the airfield and the savannah beyond. I remembered the morning, not long ago, when Frank flew into a black sky to rescue an ailing diamond buyer in La Paragua. "I'm a bush pilot. This is what I do," he'd said. And I remembered Rafael Romero's night landing in the rainstorm. I gazed across the field, stared at the taxiway and the runway to etch them in memory. I remembered all the routes to Paraitepui, Auyántepui, Angel Falls and my obsession, Canaima. I turned and looked at the terminal and its outdoor stairway to the control tower that I climbed during another storm. The airport had been my playground. There'd be no playground in Caracas. I looked up into the sky. I thought I saw the speck that was Frank's plane. No. I'd never see that speck again.

A warm breeze blew softly across the airfield. For CB, it was the beginning of a balmy afternoon at the airport patio lounge. For me, it was the last one I'd ever experience but always remember.

By chance, Martha and Julio sat at a table at the patio lounge. They were alone. "Frank," called Julio. "Join us. Have a drink for old-time's sake."

How incongruous. The person who'd recently given Frank a check that bounced, the man who "borrowed" company funds and, as yet, had not paid them back, now asks us to spend a social drink together for old-times' sake. And dear sweet Martha smiled and giggled.

We sipped one last drink with them. Then while Martha and I embraced and promised to keep in touch, Julio stood up and Frank accepted Julio's extended hand. Frank was such a good person.

"I keep a messy checkbook, Frank," he said and added, "I'll send another check to you at the MERCATOR address. Okay? Bs 4,000 was it?"

"Yeah," Frank replied, indifferently.

As Frank turned and walked toward the car, I heard Julio say, "I didn't think it would come to this, Frank."

Frank continued walking. He didn't look back.

At home, I asked Frank what he thought of Julio's last comment.

"I can guess."

We sat in the living room. Frank closed his eyes and rested his head back. My records had been packed and the house was strangely quiet. Where once we had no time together for sharing our joys and problems, and were forced to leave notes to each other, where there was no time without family and friends intruding into our private lives—now—we had quiet time together in an empty house and we had nothing to say.

I cast my eyes around the room and visually embraced every piece of furniture. I recollected when each had been purchased and I suffered the haunting memory of when Frank gave me the piano. Even lacking knick knacks on tables and decorative accessories on the wall, the room still looked like a picture in a home magazine. In a last desperate effort, I asked Frank to help me comprehend why we had to leave and how we could look forward to good times in Caracas. "I can't sit by and allow you to destroy your dream. To watch our dream fade without trying one more time." He stared at the ceiling. "Frank. Why are you giving up—letting Julio beat you?"

Sorrowfully, he said, "There's nothing else we can do. I've met with many people in the government and can't get a subsidy. I've written so many proposals, my fingers have calluses. You know I've tried to get a contract to carry mail. That fizzled, too. We've got the best fleet of aircraft and facility. Yet no one wants to merge. They'll buy, but not merge."

"You've done everything you can except go it alone. That's what you could do."

"No. That wouldn't do." He stood up, put his hands in his pockets and walked to the front windows that overlooked the runway. "I don't want any part of this anymore."

Shocked, I asked, "Frank? Is it Tom's death that . . . ?"

"Button. No." He paused. "No, but when I saw Shirley and the baby at graveside and wondered how those two would make it without Tom, I thought of you. I thought of how much I have taken for granted." He sighed. "You've been at my side—through good times and bad. And I was away a lot; weeks in Caracas, months in Asa with, at best, one night a week at home, overnight trips up the Orinoco, and south to the Brazilian border—all beyond radio contact. It's my country and I felt at home everywhere. I didn't think of how difficult it might have been for you. You handled it all so well. Even your experience in the C-46 and our own forced landing—you handled them with maturity. You never let me down now."

"I had good friends—bush pilots' wives. With Madelyn's help, I made the transition, and after that I felt no hardships. I love it here. Yes, I missed you when you were away and I worried about you when you were overdue, but I shall fondly remember Ciudad Bolivar forever. And these years? I shall remember them as the best years of my life."

"Button. I spend more time on the ground trying to get work than flying. I love to fly. But I'm tired. Just tired of it all." He watched the last DC-3 from Caracas land. Then he turned and faced me. "I'm as saddened and disappointed as you and I won't ask you to bear with me. I did that years ago. But I will ask you to have confidence in me. We both want a family, and I have agreed with you; having such instability in our lives here didn't make raising a child a real possibility. Maybe in Caracas we'll have stability. And maybe we'll like that. Button. Can we make a new dream?"

Two carpenters came to the house and assembled a crate for the piano and at that moment my life ended. When they hammered the last nail into the large box, I felt they hammered the last nail into my coffin. Teddy sat by my side. "Next time I play piano, we'll be together in Caracas." I kissed his head.

Caracas, back to the congested city, back to an unalterably dull and routine existence, back to conformity, back to . . .

Blue Skies, Green Hell

On the morning of our departure, we put Teddy and other precious possessions in Irv's Mercedes which I'd drive. Teddy and I were assured a comfortable ride.

Frank borrowed an old pickup truck with a green canvas cover from MERCATOR and loaded it with boxes containing things we'd chosen to keep. Loop rode with Frank. Theirs would not be a comfortable ride.

The fridge, the gas stove and the crated piano had been taken to the airport. They'd be flown on a cargo plane to Caracas.

The time to take the long, the last drive northward on the hot, dusty road to Caracas had come.

All bases had been touched. I made a final walk through the house. I heard the nightly gathering of friends and the laughter. Guitars from days not so long ago played again. In the kitchen, the aroma of home-made cake filled the air, and I smelled steaks cooking on the outdoor grill. I heard the sizzle of beef fat dripping into the fire and the clinking of ice cubes in happy drinks. Ghosts flew planes on final approach, and I heard the dogs running and panting and spilling their water. I thought of Tail Spin, who died when he was only two years old, and 13-month old Baron who died while I was away and was buried at the airport—he'd be forgotten and his grave overgrown with weeds. The green grass glistened with dew and I breathed the scent of roses on the vines. Where did the years ago?

It was time to leave.

I went to the truck, kissed Loop through the open window and gave it one last shot. "We can't start over? Here? Puerto Ordaz?"

"I needed you when we came to CB. I need you now as we start a new life in Caracas."

"I have no friends in Caracas." I glanced around the airport grounds and heaved a sigh. I dropped my head, and closed my eyes. *I have no friends here.*

Teddy paced impatiently from one side to the other on the back seat of the Mercedes. As I approached the car, I said, "It's okay, Teddy." But it wasn't okay. In two days he'd be in a kennel for I didn't know how long.

So, on that glorious, typical Ciudad Bolivar morning of July 15, 1955, I drove up Avenida Táchira with trees and fences festooned with bougainvillea, then up and down the narrow hilly streets through the colorful old colonial city. I passed the Triangulito. Finally I drove down the slippery cobblestone ramp that led to the old ferryboat and drove aboard it for the last time. I'd completed a round trip that started in September 1951 when Frank proposed marriage and we'd enthusiastically talked about moving to Ciudad Bolivar—the last frontier—pioneers building an air service.

355

Marilyn Lazzari-Wing

On that last morning, the front yard looked lonesome, even the airfield across the street was devoid of everything we'd held precious . . . not even an airplane.
Photo by Marilyn—July 1955

Ours were the only two vehicles on the ferry.

"Let's stand at the stern," Frank said as he approached my car.

I opened the door. Frank and I, and with Teddy on his leash, walked to the back of the boat and watched in silence as the ferry drifted away from Ciudad Bolivar. I looked up into Frank's suntanned face. He showed no emotion.

I looked back at Ciudad Bolivar on the promontory as it began to fade in the morning fog.

When we drove southward from Caracas a lifetime ago, I'd begun the transition from youth to maturity. Now, without ceremony, I'd completed that passage. As I stood on the deck of that ferry, I realized that in those halcyon days living and loving in Ciudad Bolivar, I'd never even seen this scenario coming. I was reminded of that old quote I could not quite pin down: "The years teach us much that the days never knew."

"Are you looking back?" Frank asked.

"Yes. One last look."

He put his arms around me and we watched Ciudad Bolivar disappear.

"For me, CB was a game," I said, "and you gave me the confidence and encouragement to play and to win. I loved that game."

"You played it well, Button."

Blue Skies, Green Hell

"'You can do it.' That's what you said to me time and time again. I've grown up a lot. And I never could have done it without you. I trusted you." I turned to him. "I trust you now."

"Let's go to the bow," he said. "Let's see where we're going." Frank reached out and took my hand.

Postscript

Shorty Ramirez, the silent partner was in complete control of both companies. As President and major shareholder of AEROVEN and ECUAVEN, he dominated everything. Shorty took a leave of absence from MERCATOR, and his boss and good friend, Do, assured Shorty he'd be welcomed back at MERCATOR anytime. Shorty appreciated the assurance and said his only mission was to pay off the ECUAVEN debts. "My dynasty will end when that has been accomplished." He chuckled. "Some dynasty!"

Since Julio admitted he owed Frank money, had "borrowed" funds from both companies that he could not repay, and personally was in debt, Shorty neither trusted nor defended his old friend, Julio. He told us, "If Julio doesn't like the new arrangement, he'll just have to live with it. He has no choice."

Based entirely on my letter to my parents dated March 14, 1956, Caracas, Venezuela

Nine months after we left Ciudad Bolivar, Shorty called us at our home in Caracas and said he had news. He invited us to join him for dinner at pricey Tarzilandia Restaurant in a suburb of Caracas. The restaurant, a rustic group of small private dining areas with thatch roofs, was our favorite.

"Did he win the lottery?" I asked.

"He's setting us up," Frank said and laughed. "I think he must have bad news."

Frank was right.

After we were seated, and wine and dinner had been ordered, Shorty said, "Frank, you are out of AEROVEN and ECUAVEN, and I know you two have had more than your share of sorrow since coming to Caracas, but you both gave so much of your lives to AEROVEN, I feel obligated to bring you up to date about the business. I wish I could give you good news. I can't.

"When I could finally take a leave of absence from MERCATOR, much time had passed. But this transition had to be done correctly. I conferred at length with my lawyer, and took my personal accountant with me to CB and Puerto Ordaz. I wanted him to audit the books for both companies. He went back years. I've spent considerable time studying the records, the final audit report, and the accountant's recommendations." He started slowly and just a tad louder than a whisper. His lips hardly moved when he spoke and his eyes squinted from behind strong eye glasses. "But, *amigos*, if you think things were bad when we last met—well—they are worse than we could have imagined." He raised his glass and made a toast. "To my *paisano* (countryman), *mi gran amigo,* Julio. He stole our company. Right from under us."

"What?" Frank said.

"He stole our company, Frank. I so regret he swindled you. I am the one who brought him into this business. And he swindled me, too. Or should I say, embezzled?"

"Up until now, he admitted he borrowed money—from me and both companies, but he promised to repay it. He has not repaid me. What happened to the companies?" Frank asked.

"I think you'll know when I'm finished with my report." He patted his lips with the white linen napkin and sipped water. Shorty withdrew a bundle of papers from his attaché bag and put them on the table. He didn't refer to them. He knew the reports by heart. "A thorough search of all records and a complete audit of all the books revealed thousands of *Bolivares* (the currency) are unaccounted for from both companies. AEROVEN? Bad. But not so bad. It's ECUAVEN that took the beating. The debts for that company total Bs260,000." He breathed deeply and waited until his news sank into our souls. "That company is in the hole for Bs260,000. He has milked ECUAVEN dry." (Bs260,000 was about $90,000 in 1955, or about $780,000 in 2012).

"He says he was going to get a contract to build a part of the Guri Dam. He ordered materials. That's what he says, but has yet to produce the receipts, and I don't see a great inventory."

"I spoke to him about that a long time ago. I cautioned him," Frank said. "I made it clear we're not competing for work with Morrison-Knudson."

"Frank, AEROVEN survives. You alone kept that company flying. True, we should have seen profits in that company, but we don't. You made it big in Asa, at a great personal sacrifice, and the Norseman was a gold mine in the sky. You and Romero, God rest his soul, are to be commended for that. I don't know where all the money went. The accountant doesn't know. Worse yet, Julio says he doesn't know! It's just missing! And, if you had hopes of recovering the money Julio owes you personally, I'd say forget it."

"I thought of putting an embargo on all his things," Frank said, "but I didn't want to hurt his family. They had so little. "*Es patético*" (It's pathetic.) Am I disappointed? Yes. Am I mad? Damn right! As you know, before I left CB last July, he gave me a check for Bs 4,000 and it bounced." (DOL reports the amount was worth $1,333 in 1955 or $11,433 in 2012). He cast his eyes downward. "When we said goodbye the night before we left CB, Julio said he'd send a check for me to MERCATOR. I'm still waiting."

Shorty continued. "The man has no scruples! He bought a new 1956 Olds 98."

I gasped.

Blue Skies, Green Hell

"I will sell the Olds and if there is money after the car is paid off, the money will be put back into ECUAVEN to help pay off debts." He paused, took off his glasses, wiped them on his napkin and slipped them on. "I have relieved Julio of all his power—all his authority—all his responsibilities. He cannot collect money or sign checks. He is prohibited from making a mark in the books. He is out—finished with ECUAVEN. I will manage everything concerning ECUAVEN. I will work night and day and pay off the debts, Bs 260,000. As for Julio, he is just a salaried pilot. He is no longer manager and has none of the fancy titles he had given himself after I bought your shares and you left. His only income will be his salary of Bs 2,500 per month. It's not what he earned before, but until he learns how to hustle up some business, that'll be it. If he gets work, fine. If he doesn't, I don't care. I can always sell a plane if we can't earn enough to pay expenses. My mission is ECUAVEN. I have left MERCATOR, as Do expected I would. I need to be present everyday to control and manage both companies."

"So you and I—we wind up behind the eight ball while he just flies away," Frank said.

"We have our self-respect, self-esteem, and good reputations intact. He cannot make that claim. I considered putting Julio in El Dorado (a Venezuelan prison). I have all the proof necessary to do so. But if I did that, I'd have to support Martha and the kids and so Julio making Bs 2,500 is better than that."

"I'm speechless," I said. "How could a man throw away so much—a lovely wife and four kids?"

"To top off all this, Julio has a beautiful apartment—with lovely modern furniture—for his mistress." He looked up at the thatched roof above us.

Frank raised his eyebrows in disbelief. "Mistress?"

"Yes. The one we simply called 'the new girl'! Until now—for me—she had no name. She had no face. And Julio had the cojones to take me to see the apartment." Shorty, a gentleman I'd never known to use a profane word, took a hefty swallow of wine and his face flushed. Although embarrassed, he continued. "*Todo eso* (All that), while Martha lives on boxes and with barely enough money to pay the bills. I do not believe Julio has told Martha about his financial problems—nor about his—ah—relationship with the new girl." Shorty told us he'd already fired the new girl and would shortly hire someone to manage AEROVEN. "I have someone in mind. Julio can't do it. He can fly. That's all I allow him to do. And he can hustle work—if he can!"

"I've left you with a terrible burden," Frank said.

Shorty ordered demitasse and when we'd finished sipping it, he tried to suppress a chuckle, and crinkled his eyes behind his thick lenses. "This may be my last meal in this fine restaurant."

"I should have seen it coming." Frank poured a glass of wine for me. "He double-crossed me. I busted my chops and the rotter defeated me. AEROVEN never was a loser."

"*Correcto.* Right, Frank. AEROVEN was no loser."

I hadn't said much as the two talked about Shorty's plans and Julio's fall from grace, but with the revelation of Julio's dalliance, my mind flashed back to the day Frank came home from Asa with such serious problems the governor's intervention was required. That was the day the new girl asked if she could speak with me and then told her story that started with, 'I have a friend . . .'

"Maybe I could have prevented some of what happened, Frank." I shook my head from side to side. "I was so naive, I couldn't see then what I see now. The new girl told me her friend was in love with a married man with children. She asked me for advice. I'm not much older than the new girl—and she asked me for advice! What did she think? *Imagínate* (Just imagine)! She was talking about herself. What a mess! I am so sorry I didn't tell you at the time. So much might have been avoided."

Frank smashed a cigarette out in a large ashtray. "I might not have recognized it any quicker than you. I trusted him."

"My friends," Shorty sighed. "I've had a long day. We've talked a lot and there's more to the story. Much more. But not for now. For another time."

* * *

Shorty, true to his word, paid off all the debts owed by ECUAVEN. In doing my research for this book, I contacted Do's son, Pancho. He was a young boy when he visited Frank and me in Ciudad Bolivar. Pancho told me Shorty did return to MERCATOR and trained him in MERCATOR'S field work. After Armando (Do) retired, Pancho assumed control of the company. Shorty married on September 24, 1955. Amadeo Ramirez, a most honorable and respected man, died during the nineteen-nineties.

Epilogue

Research is what prompted me to return to Venezuela in May 2004. More than fifty years had passed since I'd been there. To write **Blue Skies, Green Hell**, I needed to verify conditions in Ciudad Bolivar, its airport, my house and the AEROVEN hangar. Were they still there? I needed to walk on the pink sand and swim in the burgundy-colored water at Canaima. Had progress destroyed its natural beauty? I needed to watch Angel Falls with volumes of water drilling into Devil's Canyon and the jungle below. I needed to see the airfield on top of the high ground called Paraitepui. Was it still there? I needed to pray at the gravesites of Tom Van Hyning and Charlie Baughan. I needed to find them. Could I find Baron's grave?

With our friend, Bob Sonderman, piloting his twin engine Piper Aztec, my husband Jerry and I flew from Charallave, a private airport south of Caracas, over the llanos to the mighty Orinoco River and landed at the airport in Ciudad Bolivar.

The AEROVEN hangar stood abandoned. The painted words on our hangar, "*Vuele Por AEROVEN*" (Fly AEROVEN) were still visible through faded paint. I peered through a broken window pane and saw the empty work place filled with junk where Bud Small, our mechanic, had re-built the wing of the Norseman and where Tom Van Hyning's lifeless body in a steel coffin had lain in repose on sawhorses. I could not find a trace of Baron's grave.

The airport terminal had been totally renovated. Gone is the famous and popular outdoor patio lounge where all the pilots and their wives gathered at the end of each day. The patio lounge is now glass enclosed. It smells of cigarette smoke and I doubt fresh air has entered it since it was walled in. The Control Tower is now on the opposite side of the field. Its stairway is probably indoors. My heart broke a little.

I showed Jerry and Bob the house where I'd lived across the street from the airport. Its ornate black iron fence has been painted white. The house is still the prettiest in town. The one-lane dirt road that passed in front of the house is now a heavily trafficked four-lane highway with traffic lights. So many hangars and buildings have been erected at the airfield across the street, the house no longer has a clear view of the runway.

From the Paseo Orinoco, I saw a bridge that spans the river at Ciudad Bolivar. No longer does a ferry cross the mighty Orinoco. The Gran Hotel Bolivar did not resemble the splendid hotel of yesteryear where we talked and had drinks with Cornell Capa, Walter Montenegro and Rear Admiral Oberlin Laird. The lobby has been reduced in size. There could no longer be elegant balls at the hotel like the one I attended in honor of the nation's First Lady, Mrs.Perez Jimenez. So much had changed.

We passed the cemetery, but it was closed and locked, so I didn't learn whether Tom's grave with propeller atop is still there.

"Bob," I said, "Let's go. I don't want to see anymore. Frank was right. 'There is no more Bolivar.'"

During our brief stay in CB, we stopped in front of the airport terminal where a plaque posted in front of an old airplane says the plane is a replica of the one that Jimmie Angel and his wife had crash-landed on the top of Auyántepui. I learned from Karen Angel, Jimmie Angel's niece, some of the original parts were used in building the replica. Other parts are still at the School of Aviation in Maracay—the same flight school from which Frank had graduated so long ago.

We departed Ciudad Bolivar for Canaima the beautiful beach discovered in the jungle by Charlie Baughan. We wanted to find the graves of Mary and Charlie Baughan.

On January 28, 1956, Charlie Baughan, King of the Jungle, was killed when the Beechcraft he was flying crashed into a coastal mountain. All souls, including his wife, Mary, died in the horrendous crash.

Madelyn Freeman and I were in Caracas at the time and attended the memorial service in the American Church. Five caskets were lined up side-by-side near the altar; Mary and Charlie Baughans' and three passengers in the aircraft.

I read in the newspaper, a neighbor of Charlie and Mary's, Mr. Mulherin, was at the Baughan apartment making all the final arrangements for the disposition of the Baughan household. I called him and volunteered to help write letters to friends and to their daughter, Bonnie, and to help pack some of their personal belongings. Charlie's little white dog played in and around the boxes. I don't know what happened to the dog.

It was so unseemly . . . the two most intrepid bush pilots, Charlie Baughan and Jimmie Angel, both Americans, had been killed in crashes during the same year. Another coincidence—Angel's ashes were scattered over Angel Falls and the remains of Baughan were buried at Canaima. Both locations are in the Canaima National Park established in 1962. It is one of the world's last remote wild lands.

I recall that when I attended the Baughans' memorial service, I learned they were to have been buried at Canaima. I assumed they would be buried near the airstrip. So, in May 2004, after we landed at Canaima, Bob, Jerry and I, under a blazing sun on a hot and humid afternoon, trekked both sides of the 6,800 foot paved airstrip examining everything that suggested something might be buried. We stopped at every sizeable collection of rocks and mounds of dirt received our attention. We found nothing. An empty, never used control tower and a DC-3 without engines guard the runway. We needed no approval to walk the edge of the runway. The area remains a vast wilderness in the Gran Sabana.

Blue Skies, Green Hell

We rested for a few minutes in the shade of the small wooden airport terminal that resembles a picnic shelter. The field, equipped neither for passenger nor aircraft services, is used by small planes that carry tourists on one-day trips, and ancient bi-planes that deliver supplies. Canaima is accessible only by plane.

From the moment we started trekking the sidelines of the airstrip, I felt uneasy. Finally, I said to Jerry and Bob, "We're looking in the wrong place. I'm sure this is not where the original airstrip was cut by machetes in the jungle—the strip we landed on."

No one at the airfield recollected the strip being located elsewhere. We asked a friendly National Guardsman stationed at the airport about the graves. He knew nothing about them, but joined us as we walked through jungle growth to a thatched hut overgrown with tropical foliage where a wizened old man, George LeRoy, lived. George said he had been living at Canaima a long time. He wore long gray hair in a pony tail, a scruffy beard and was dressed in tattered shorts and shin-high boots. He told us about prospecting for gold and, in self-defense, having killed seven people with his knife. He also said he knew the location of the graves. He was our only hope.

Led by George and accompanied by the Guardsman, we walked under a canopy of jungle on a narrow overgrown trail and came upon the vine-covered graves of Baughan, his wife, and Alejandro Laime. Without George, we'd never have located the site.

Bob cut down the vines that covered the headstone and read the inscription:

> *"Here in the land of tomorrow lie the mortal remains of Captain Charles Cornelius Baughan intrepid pilot and adventurer discoverer and founder of Canaima, born in Harolsen, Georgia, 6 September 1902 and his faithful wife and companion Mary McKinney Ware de Baughan born in Sheldonville, Kentucky 24 February 1903. They died 28 January 1956 in Capaya, Miranda, Venezuela. Patriots and friends of Venezuela."*

Alejandro Laime's grave is near Baughan's. It bears only his name and the dates, 1911-1994. His grave is marked by a cement platform topped by a large rust-colored iron cross, about four feet tall. A free-form piece of metal is attached where the vertical and horizontal bars intersect. Directional signs to the graves of Laime and Baughan are non-existent. I'm sure the graves are near the original airstrip. They are a short distance behind the never-used control tower.

We went to the headquarters of the park and met the Park Manager, Eduardo Gomez, and commented about the overgrown grave site of the founder and discoverer of Canaima. His reply was simple; the park is on a small budget.

He said he'd try to have the small cemetery landscaped and a directional sign posted. We visited Canaima three years later in December 2007. Again, we had a difficult time locating the graves. We ultimately found the grave yard, overgrown with weeds and vines. At the base of Laime's grave was a container that held a burned candle. No directional signs pointed the way. Once again, Bob cut down the vines and other scrub brush.

While I had photos of Laime, I had none of Baughan. I wanted one to include in this book. Bob Sonderman led us to the nearby rustic *Campo Ucaima*. It had been established by Jungle Rudy Truffino, and is now operated by Rudy's daughter, Gabrielle. I gave Gabrielle copies of fifty-year old photographs of her father and she gave me the photograph of Charlie Baughan that appears elsewhere in this book. I have a video of Gaby talking about her father and Charlie, and she is heard saying, "Yes, Charlie was the first one here." That should settle any dispute about the founder of Canaima.

Gaby took me to the nearby grave of her father. Under a canopy of heavily foliated trees, on the side of a foot path to his airstrip, Jungle Rudy lies beneath a grave marked only by a concrete cover and a wooden cross. He was about 70 years old when he died.

Overall, Canaima has changed little. One old hotel with cottages, designed to blend in with the landscape, looks abandoned and the jungle foliage is making a great effort to reclaim it. Two small hotels—called camps—are superb. They have successfully blended the accommodations with the scenery. The grounds are beautifully maintained and views of several waterfalls and tepuís are stunning. Charlie Baughn would have liked them. We do.

Now we could move on to another mission. To validate what I had written about the geology, geography and unique weather conditions around Angel Falls, Canaima, Auyántepui, and Paraitepui, and the imposing jungle that surrounds those places, we flew with Bob in his Aztec south from Canaima to Santa Elena de Uairén on the Brazilian border. We visited with Raul Arias, owner of the Raul Helicopter service, and he shared with me info about some of the early pilots named in this book. We chartered one of his helicopters with chopper pilot, Captain Rafael León at the controls. Leon flew us back north to Canaima, setting down to explore, wherever necessary, to get answers to our questions. We flew over Paraitepui. No longer an airfield, indigenous locals live there on what they call, *un altiplano* (the high ground). The land is barren, flat and suitable for their small village. It is also the staging ground for hikers who plan to climb the tallest tepuí called Roraima.

On the way to Canaima, we landed on top of Roraima and Kukenon, tepuis that surely resemble the landscapes of other planets with strange and scary rock formations. Capt. Leon worked the chopper inside the canyons and gorges of Auyántepui. We flew so close to Angel Falls, we put our arms out the chopper window and felt the spray. What a ride!

Robert Sonderman's Piper Aztec was our chariot during three visits to Venezuela in search of the past. Here it is parked at the Ciudad Bolivar Airport in 2007.
Photo by Marilyn

2007—The AEROVEN Hangar at CB is painted and looks good. But it is a derelict and abandoned building filled with "stuff." I could not find Baron's grave.
Photo by Marilyn

The words, "Vuele por AEROVEN" (Fly AEROVEN) have faded but are still visible after years of basking in Ciudad Bolivar's glorious sunlight.
Photo by Marilyn

A replica of Jimmie Angel's plane—made from parts of his original plane as well as parts from other planes—on display in front of the CB Terminal.
Photo by Marilyn

The author chats with George Leroy who led us to the lost gravesites of Charlie Baughan and Alejandro Laime.

The graveyard, overgrown by vines and weeds, is home to the remains of Charlie Baughan, discover and founder of Canaima.

Charlie and Mary Baughan's gravesite has been very badly overgrown each of the three times we have visited it.

Alejandro Laime's grave is identified by a very large cross with his name and dates of his birth and death years recorded on a palette affixed to the cross. We've not seen it overgrown and, often, we see a candle at its base that has recently burned. We've been unable to learn who cares for Laime's grave.
Photo by Marilyn

"Jungle Rudy" Truffino, Camp Manager for Charlie Baughan's Canaima, is buried near Ucaima, the camp he established for tourists and is managed by his daughter, Gabrielle. The grave is located on a foot path between the camp and his private airstrip.
Photo by Marilyn

2007—Marilyn and Jerry Wing, adventure travelers, stand at the base of Angel Falls during one of their visits to one of their favorite Venezuelan sites.
Photo by Robert Sonderman

Blue Skies, Green Hell

Of the jungle between Venezuela and Brazil, much was destroyed during the sixties by a huge fire that raged out of control for five years. Now, vast savannahs grow where the jungle had flourished. All that remains of Green Hell, in some of that region, is a forest of tall burned trees. The two-lane Pan American Highway goes through it.

Years later, as I continued my quest to locate my old friends, I was thrilled when I successfully found Jesus Indriago in Caracas. Actually, it was Bob Sonderman who obtained Jesus' phone number. Late in 2011, I called the number from my home in Tennessee and Jesus answered the phone, I cried with joy. He did, too. He was pleased I'd "found" him. So, we are the two known survivors of those "good old days." He is one of the main characters in Chapter 18, Paradise in Green Hell. I cherish his friendship.

During the ten years I worked on BSGH, I tried many times to reach everyone with whom I interacted in Venezuela. Unfortunately, most have passed away or their whereabouts are unknown.

Our trips to Venezuela, the land of my fondest memories, have been perfect. The people we met have been hospitable, helpful, kind, and interested. Food good. Hotels wonderful.

Like Charlie Baughan, I think of myself as a patriot and friend of Venezuela.

Beyond The Dream

August 1955: Frank was employed as Office Manager by ATSA in Caracas. We rented a house with a fenced garden for Loop and Teddy. I became pregnant.

August 1955: We located Carlos and Madelyn in Caracas. They lived in an apartment three blocks from our house. Good times returned.

November 1955: I miscarried twins.

June 1956: Carlos and Madelyn returned to the states, permanently. I was devastated.

October 1956: Frank's mother died in October. He was devastated.

October 1956: Two weeks after his mother's death, Frank resigned from ATSA.

January 1957: Frank wilted under the loss of our twins, the death of his mother, the deaths of good friends Bill Murphy, Tom Van Hyning, Charlie Baughan and Rafael Romero, and luckless employment. His spirit was broken. He experienced depression. A little-known malady at the time, no professional counseling was available. Our worlds fell apart. We agreed to separate. It was amicable.

March 1957: As we parted, he said, "I'll write you. Okay?" I returned to the states. At twenty-seven years old, I had lived a rich, full life that overflowed with adventure. After one year's separation, I visited Frank in Caracas. We were still in love, but not ready to reconcile. The divorce was final in 1958. For many years, he sent me gifts, cards, and Christmas cards. Through Olga Towne, we maintained contact with each other.

July 1960: I married Ed Waldeck. Our good life together was snuffed out after 36 years in 1996 when he died.

1982: Frank phoned and shouted into the phone, "Button! We made a terrible mistake." I told him I knew that. "Please come back," he begged. I wanted to return. I didn't, and regretted that decision. He was the manager of a bank in Caracas.

Marilyn Lazzari-Wing

Mid-1990s: Frank died of cancer. I heard that shortly before he died, he married the woman who had taken care of him during his illness. He never stopped smoking. After he left Ciudad Bolivar, he never piloted a plane again. Aviation lost one of its great pioneers. What a waste!

1997: I married Jerry Wing. We traveled the world and enjoyed adventures in the Antarctic twice, the Arctic once, two safaris in Africa, scuba-diving in the South Pacific, kayaking in oceans all over the world, and many more exciting episodes. We returned to Venezuela three times. We are retired and live a quiet life in Tennessee.

2004: At age 74, I re-learned to fly at Sporty's Flight School, Clermont Airport, Batavia, Ohio. Then I began to write *Blue Skies, Green Hell.*

Where are they now?

Alive and enjoying life
Jesus Indriago
Marilyn Lazzari-Wing

Where abouts unknown
Irv Banta
Magda Banta
Carlos Freeman
Madelyn Freeman
Col. Benjamin Griffin
H.R. (Jack) Perez
Malvina Rosales
Shirley Van Hyning Stahlmann

Those who have died
Mary and Charlie Baughan
Cornell Capa
Horacio Cabrera de Sifontes
Alejandro Laime
Armando (Do) Lazzari
Frank Lazzari
Jean Liedloff
Bill Murphy
C. Harry Payne
Amadeo (Shorty) Ramirez
Martha and Julio Rojas
Rafael Romero
Olga and Bob Towne
Jungle Rudy Trujillo

What happened to the families
Magda and Irv Banta—Divorced
Mary and Charlie Baughan—Both killed in plane crash
Madelyn and Carlos Freeman—Divorced
Marilyn and Frank Lazzari—Divorced
Bill Murphy—Killed in plane crash
Martha and Julio Rojas—Divorced
Rafael Romero—Killed in a plane crash
Tom Van Hyning—killed in plane crash

Acknowledgments

Blue Skies, Green Hell, a true story about bygone years of bush flying adventures in wild Venezuela, was a work in progress for ten years. It required research and, most of all, assistance from many people. I apologize to contributors of information whose names have been omitted.

BSGH takes place in Venezuela; Caracas, Ciudad Bolivar, and other places in the interior. Jerry Wing, my husband, suggested I write the book after he found the box of letters I had written to my parents during the years I'd lived in Venezuela. Their discovery is described in the Introduction to *BSGH*.

To connect with someone in Venezuela who could help me locate people and records of events held long ago, I telephoned The American Church in Caracas and left a message for the pastor of the church. To my delight, the next day, Pastor Charlie Pridmore returned my call, and, upon hearing my request said he knew just the right people who could help. He led me to Bob and Linda Sonderman, Americans and members of his congregation. He told me Bob was a bush pilot who probably knew some old-time pilots in the flying community and Linda owned Alpi-Group, a travel agency in Caracas. Before we hung up, Pastor Charlie also told me the name of the church is now The United Christian Church. What a blessed way to start my search into the past. I am indebted to Pastor Charlie and the Sondermans. I met Pastor Charlie and his wife at dinner parties at the Sonderman residence in Caracas during our trips there. My husband, Jerry, and I went to Venezuela for research purposes and one Sunday, we attended Pastor Pridmore's church service. It was a joyous and memorable occasion. Thank you Pastor Charlie Pridmore and your daughter, too, who located old newspaper articles about the deaths of several old bush pilot friends.

Before I started writing, I contacted Knoxville, Tennessee's Don Williams, an award-winning author, publisher, teacher of creative writing, and member of the East Tennessee Writers' Hall of Fame. I took his course in writing and later he agreed to edit my manuscript. After Don's masterful review, I tweaked the manuscript from time to time. Thus, mistakes that crept in are mine, not his. For your encouragement, boundless patience, and your time and talent, thank you, Don.

Jerry wondered how I could write about the sensations, emotions, smells, sounds and techniques of flying single-engine aircraft after the passage of more than 50 years. So, at age 74, I was accepted as a student pilot at Sporty's Flight Academy at Clermont Airport in Batavia, Ohio. Twice a day for two weeks in 2004, from the left-seat of a single-engine Cessna 150 trainer, I learned to fly again. I performed maneuvers and experienced all the sensations I'd need to write a convincing story about bush flying in light aircraft. Thank you, Sporty's, and my flight instructor, Tom Randall, MD and CFI.

The planes flown by my bush-pilot husband, Frank, included single-engine Cessnas, a Twin Beechcraft, and a single-engine Canadian-made Noordyne Norseman. We were also involved with an historic Curtiss-Wright C-46 Commander troop transport from WWII. I had to learn about these vintage aircraft.

I thank Dick Ward, author of *Beechcraft Twin Bonanza, Craft of the Masters* for information about our Beechcraft, and Rebecca Looney, Assistant Curator at the Cradle of Aviation Museum in Garden City, NY, for information about the C-46 and the Norseman. I thank Steve Assaly in Ontario, Canada for providing technical information about the Norseman. Thanks to Dick, Rebecca and Steve.

I'm fortunate to have in my log book of celebrity pilots the names of four who helped me when I needed validation and answers to many questions about aircraft and flying them. The first was Col. Jim Rushing, Southeast Region Commander of the Civil Air Patrol. I called for his help on and off through the years. He always had the answers. Thank you, Jim.

Through conversations with Knoxville resident, Buddy L. Brown, Colonel, USAF Ret. who flew the U-2 and SR-71, I sought a variety of information about atmospheric hazards that create problems for pilots and aircraft. Thank you, Buddy.

Stan Brock, Knoxville resident, famous co-host of TV's *Mutual of Omaha's Wild Kingdom* helped me with technical data about the C-46. Today, Stan pilots his C-47 on Remote Area Medical (RAM) expeditions. Staffed by all volunteers, RAM is an organization he founded that holds temporary clinics across the U.S. and overseas to provide free health care. His C-47 saw military service on D-Day. Thank you, Stan.

Re-learning to fly prepared me for co-piloting Bob Sonderman's twin Aztec during our three research trips to Venezuela. What joy that was! For accuracy, Bob reviewed sections of my book that referred to flying single-engine aircraft in Venezuela. Bob and Linda arranged our trips within Venezuela and helped locate people from days long ago. They hosted several parties to which they invited pilots who were early birdmen in Venezuela. Some of them had known Frank. Thanks, Bob and Linda.

Herb Scher, Director of Public Relations, the New York Public Library on Fifth Avenue in New York City, provided the information about the two huge stone lions perched on the front steps of the building. Thank you, Herb.

I still speak Spanish, but writing it is something else. Help came from my very special niece, Vickie Bedo, Arline and Bill's daughter. She taught Spanish and is retired from her position as principal of a junior high school in Texas. Thank you, Vickie.

Doug Franklin is my very special nephew who is humble about his string of achievements, and asks only to be acknowledged as being a "helpful nephew." Doug answered my questions about how to do almost everything on the computer. His emails with instructions fill a notebook, three inches thick. Thanks, Doug.

I met Olga Towne in 1951 when I first arrived in Caracas. It was at her home in Caracas where I met Frank. Much later, we were neighbors in Tennessee and she translated letters from English to Spanish I wrote to former acquaintances in Venezuela. Olga also gave me several books from her personal library about the flora, fauna, climate, culture, and history of Venezuela. Olga passed away in the fall of 2010.

Olga referred me to her niece Maria (Ginny) Izquierdo and two nephews, Rafael Izquierdo, and Armando (Pancho) Lazzari. Ginny helped with translations, but most importantly fulfilled my difficult quest for current information about specific people in Venezuela with whom I had interacted long ago. Rafael shared with me his vast knowledge about living in the Venezuelan jungle and about the snakes that slither there. Pancho Lazzari (son of Do Lazzari), filled in missing information about people who had been employed at his father's business in Caracas and are named in BSGH. Thank you, Ginny, Rafael and Pancho.

In order to make complete the story of my encounter with Cornell Capa, I located him in New York City. He filled in missing information about the people who were with us when we met in Ciudad Bolivar. Capa died in 2009.

I reached Jean Leidloff by phone at her house-boat, in Sausalito, California. We talked for an hour. She said it had been good talking with me about the "good old days." Jean died in 2011.

Several times, I found myself in serious trouble working in the high-tech world of cyberspace. My computer crashed—often. More than once, I "lost" the entire manuscript. Thanks to Stephen Hoyt and Robert Malcolm, owners and operators of The Computer Guys in Knoxville, TN, I finished *BSGH*. Thanks Steve and Rob.

Sincere appreciation to Thompson Photography in Knoxville. The staff at Thompson enhanced most of the old photos that appear in this book and helped transfer them to the publisher. Thank you to staff members; Charlotte, Anne, Gene and especially, Mark Barnes.

Thanks to Tom and Assistant Manager Phil in Office Max, Powell, TN for their assistance in rapid reproduction services.

The final proof read of *BSGH* was masterfully done by my good friend and neighbor, Doris Keeling. A voracious reader of mostly fiction pieces, I was ecstatic when she said she could hardly put down this true adventure about old time airplanes. Thanks, Doris.

Marilyn Lazzari-Wing

In a letter to my Mother, dated May 28, 1952, I wrote, "If it were not for my sister, Arline, and her husband, Bill, moving to Caracas, I would not have traveled to Venezuela." I would have missed the greatest adventure in my life. Thank you, Arline. Bill passed away in 2010.

I thank Jerry Wing, my husband, for suggesting I write the book, for encouraging me to never give up, and most importantly for being able to see that individual events that happened in Venezuela, when viewed in their totality, revealed dimensions I had not seen. It took the passage of fifty years before I saw the whole picture. He said, "The years teach us much that the days never knew." Those words of wisdom provided insight and direction. Author of the quote is unknown.

I also thank Jerry for having survived sharing our home with the ghost of a handsome and talented young bush pilot. Jerry, supportive of my work, continues to understand the hours I spend in my office are vital to the completion of *BSGH*. Thank you, Jerry It will end soon. I promise. I love you for all your help and understanding.

Footnotes

1. Preface: Information from Birth of Flight, produced by Mill Creek Entertainment.
2. Chapter 1: The standard pattern is to the left. CTO said right was okay. There would be no traffic and it would save time.
3. Chapter 1: In 1974, Venezuela switched to a numerical scheme with alpha suffixes for registering aircraft.
4. Chapter 2: Idlewild Airport was rededicated and named John F. Kennedy International Airport in Queens, New York on December 24, 1963, in memory of the nation's 35th president.
5. Chapter 2: In the nineteen fifties, it was routine for pilots to stroll the aisle and chat with passengers.
6. Chapter 2: On December 24, we were married in a quiet wedding at The American Church in Caracas, the church I had attended since arriving in Venezuela. Arline and Frank's brother, Armando (Do) were witnesses. My mother and father, visiting us for the Christmas holidays, also attended.
7. Chapter 9: A "sideslip" is a maneuver that allows the plane to lose altitude quickly, without gaining speed, thus not rolling far after landing. The descending aircraft will move forward in a direct line toward the runway although the plane is turned a little sideways to the landing strip. Shortly before the wheels touch the ground, the pilot straightens the plane for a safe landing.
8. Chapter 11: For fifty years, I asked every doctor I met, if they'd heard about calcium as an antidote for an allergy to penicillin or to counteract the effect of taking many medications. None had. In January 2004, while researching the matter for this book, I read the following on the internet: "*Bienvenidos a Baxter Venezuela*. (Welcome to Baxter of Venezuela). "If alkalosis is severe, administer calcium gluconate IV as contraindicated in previous severe allergic reaction to drugs..." Alkalosis is a chemical imbalance in the blood. For weeks, I'd been taking a variety of medicines prescribed by a variety of doctors. The chance I had alkalosis is very possible. Founded in the U.S., Baxter Laboratories was established in Venezuela in 1956. It was 1952 when my doctor in Caracas administered the calcium intravenous, the antidote for my allergy.
9. Chapter 13: Halazone is a disinfectant for drinking water.
10. Chapter 14: Flight Attendants.
11. Chapter 18: Jungle Rudy Truffino and Alejandro Laime are now legends. Both died in the 1990s and are buried in Canaima National Park not for from the pink beach. See the Epilogue.
12. Chapter 18: Many of Eric's photographs are included in this book.

[13] Chapter 26: For five years, in the nineteen sixties, a forest fire burned thousands of square miles of jungle in Bolivar State and everything in its path almost to Brazil. The jungle was reduced to burned tree trunks that now stand tall and eerie in lush savannah land. Much of the fierce jungle never grew back. The Pan American Highway goes through the area.

CPSIA information can be obtained at www.ICGtesting.com
Printed in the USA
LVOW100407201112

307984LV00004B/5/P